BLAZE:

Operation Persian Trinity

Andrew Thorp King

21 Gun Publishing
Po Box 2057
Media, PA 19063
www.21gunpublishing.com

For information about wholesale and special discounts for bulk purchases, please contact 21 Gun publishing at info@21gunpublishing.com

Manufactured in the United States of America

Cover design by Pete Macphee http://www.swampyankee.org/

ISBN-10: 1-50103-624-6
ISBN-13: 978-1-50103-624-8

Author Contact:

Andrew Thorp King
info@andrewthorpking.com

Electronic adaptation by www.StunningBooks.com

ACKNOWLEDGMENTS

This novel is dedicated to all that know me and yet, still love me. To all of my family, close friends and business partners.

To my son Griffin and my daughters, Chloe and Violet. Thank you for allowing me to lock my office door on so many Saturday afternoons to transport my mind into the world of Blaze McIntyre. Thank you for being the source of so much joy in my life.

Although there are too many great friends to mention, I'd like to thank Rami Dakko, Richard 'Tricky Dick' Downes, and Barry Eitel specifically for their encouragement in the writing of this story and for all their solid support as friends. I'd also like to thank all of the fellas at the Old Havana Cigar club in West Chester, PA. The camaraderie and friendships that exist there are one of a kind.

Special thanks to Tom Wallace for all of his keen input and wise suggestions in the shaping and editing process. The manuscript benefited greatly from his ideas. Thanks to Pete 'Swamp Yankee' Macphee for doing a tremendous job on the cover artwork. He nailed it on the first take. Thanks to Gina Settembrino for taking the author photo. And a big thanks to Keith Reed of Extreme Ink Tattoo in West Chester, PA for sketching the header images above each chapter.

"Writing a book is an adventure. To begin with, it is a toy and an amusement; then it becomes a mistress, and then it becomes a master, and then a tyrant. The last phase is that just as you are about to be reconciled to your servitude, you kill the monster, and fling him out to the public."

- *Winston Churchill*

"Being Irish, he had an abiding sense of tragedy, which sustained him through temporary periods of joy."

- *William Butler Yeats*

"If I had to define courage myself, I wouldn't say it's about shooting people. I'd say it's the quality that stimulates people, that enables them to move ahead and look beyond themselves."

- *Clint Eastwood*

"Our revolution's main mission is to pave the way for the reappearance of the 12th Imam, the Mahdi. Therefore, Iran should become a powerful, developed and model Islamic society. Today, we should define our economic, cultural and political policies based on the policy of Imam Mahdi's return. We should avoid copying the West's policies and systems."

- *Former Iranian President Mahmoud Ahmadinejad*

"And in that day will I make Jerusalem a burdensome stone for all people: all that burden themselves with it shall be cut in pieces, though all the people of the earth be gathered together against it"

- *Zechariah 12:3*

CHAPTER ONE

Wardak Province, west of Kabul, Afghanistan

Blaze McIntyre could see it out of the corner of his eye. An abnormal wind blew behind him. It was a welcomed relief even with the sand it kicked up in his face. The tent behind him quivered from the wind's effects. Blaze focused on the men that had caught his attention. He continued cleaning his gun without looking down. Something didn't look right. He held tight to his weapon feeling a premonition that he might very soon need to use it. It was not a typical day in the desert and he sensed that what he saw was not a typical conversation between blue and green. Just beside the checkpoint area something was brewing. Blue looked calm, but increasingly nervous. Green looked abrasive and increasingly angry.

Blue was the term used to identify those serving with the ISAF (International Security Assistance Force) sent by NATO. Green was the term used to describe those serving in the ANA, the Afghan National Army. All based on uniform color.

The checkpoint had been quiet and uneventful for days. When Blaze arrived at the camp he aroused suspicion and curiosity. His guarded mannerisms fueled the curiosity. Blaze was busy holding secret meetings with several equally mysterious MI6 members. He barely interacted with anyone else there on the NATO side. No one on either the ANA side or the ISAF side was really sure why the hell the clandestine service guys were even there. Blaze sensed this and was glad that his designs had fleshed out. He liked keeping everyone guessing.

His gaze was securely affixed on the arguing soldiers. He could hear the voice of the Afghan soldier in green getting louder and he could see, even with his distant view, the contortions of the Afghan soldier's angry face flinching with agitation. The ISAF soldier's temperament had not changed—despite being yelled at—but it was clear the nature of the conversation was heading in a tense direction. Although Blaze was in Afghanistan on specific CIA business, he knew that he couldn't ignore what he was witnessing. He knew he would have to get involved.

The shot crackled with terror from the gun of the angry ANA soldier. Brain matter flung with an arched trajectory from the head of an unlucky ISAF soldier. Two other NATO-sent ISAF blues tumbled to the ground and howled in agony. Medics scrambled to rescue the wounded blues that surrounded the scene.

His position twisted sharply and he saw the aftermath of the shot. The Afghan soldier had fired quickly and the shot had not been visible to Blaze. But the seriousness of the situation was indeed clear to the American spy. It was time for him to get into the mix.

His legs took on a trajectory of their own as he charged towards the scene of this stupefying growing "incident". His reaction was instant, but not well thought out. This was, after all, not the typical premeditated spy op he was accustomed to. This was normal warfare with all its spontaneity and unpredictability. The circumstances called upon the instincts that Blaze had honed back in his days in the Marines.

He saw his three newfound MI6 friends responding in kind close by, as they drew their weapons and ran towards the firefight. Blaze took out his Walther P99 as he ran to fight along side his British pals.

Several more Afghan soldiers emerged from behind the checkpoint area ahead. They ran with anger and were screaming and shooting their weapons. Sand swirled in the hot air mirroring the chaos of the moment. Other Afghan greens were fleeing, clearly trying to separate themselves from the rogue Afghans that had turned on the blue ISAF NATO soldiers that they were supposed to be working side by side with.

By the time Blaze got close enough to the checkpoint scene gone wrong, the bullets were flying everywhere. Several whizzed passed his head as he tucked and dodged his way forward. He simultaneously attributed divine protection and Irish luck to the fact that his head was still in one piece. A contradiction in belief that somehow worked well for him.

He said a quick prayer internally that the Almighty would follow him and swarm him with a "pillar of cloud," as He did for the Israelites fleeing hordes of Egyptian marauders in ancient times.

He heard a scream to his left, and saw one of his new MI6 buddies go down with a thump. Blaze kept moving, it appeared not to be a fatal hit.

Blaze raised his Walther P99 and began firing while running. All the good Afghans had already fled the scene, and all that remained were rogue Afghans shooting brave ISAF soldiers. Blaze killed three rogue Afghans quickly and effortlessly. Two others almost escaped the path of his bullets, but ultimately found death from the flying lead.

His foot trampled the fingers of a dead Afghan turncoat as he continued to spring forward. An excruciating pain surged abruptly in the side of his right calf. Blaze tried to continue running, but fell forward to the ground after only a few steps. He had been hit. He was down.

Blaze had been shot before, and knew the pain of a bullet, but this one hit a particularly sensitive and vulnerable spot. He reached down and clutched his ankle in an attempt to calm the unbelievable pain caused by the flaring nerves that spazzed inside his leg. His eyes flinched and closed as he braced the unrelenting agony. He held in his screams as to not draw attention to himself. He had always disciplined himself to not yell and scream like others in battle. He knew the value of holding in expressions of pain. He opened one eye as he held tight his leg. The Afghan was only a few feet away, and his gun was closer.

Blaze shifted his fallen body with precision. He positioned himself to shoot the oncoming Afghan maggot before he got turned into a bleeding dead pile of red.

Blaze's head tilted back and he escaped any feeling of prolonged pain as he felt a dizzying transition out of his body, while the oncoming bullet transitioned its way through his forehead. Death had come.

CHAPTER TWO

The McIntyre residence, Romeo, Michigan

Blaze hated hearing the acronym PTSD uttered by anyone. He despised all the extraneous and insulting new implications it had recently come to carry. He knew *Post Traumatic Stress Disorder* was real, but he refused to have it applied to him. Ever. The nightmares, the mental terrors that plagued him during waking hours, and the images of horror that constantly shrouded his psyche, were all part of the job. Blaze did not welcome any diagnosis or treatment for his condition. He instead pursued assimilation.

His chest was pounding as his heart beat. His breath was heavy and sweat drenched his pillow. Diem was still sound asleep.

After catching his breath, he thanked God that it was only a dream. Additionally, he thanked God that he was never actually shot by the green Afghan soldier that day, and that in fact, that sniveling green puke met his maker with haste as Blaze successfully neutralized what was a military and political cluster fuck. If he could, he would bring that ANA bastard back to life just to have the pleasure of killing him again as extra punishment for the trouble he had helped cause.

He remembered the charade in the press after the incident. Afghan President Hamid Karzai claimed sadness and no knowledge of the impetus of the inside attacks from green on blue. The US generals all claimed that the majority of the Afghans were "still with us" and did not share the rogue mentality of the wayward turncoat Afghan greens. Blaze doubted it. He suspected there were more Afghan soldiers who didn't have the balls to go rogue than the US would ever know or imagine.

Blaze rose out of bed and made his way into the kitchen as he tugged tight on the tie of his navy blue bathrobe. Diem had fresh coffee brewed and ready. *God Bless that woman.* It was steaming, inviting, and precisely as Blaze liked it. Hot and black. He sipped it with a sense of relief as he saw his wife walk into the kitchen. He stood by the counter. Blaze had only slept five hours. Along with the lingering terror of the nightmares, he also suffered a slight sting of a headache from having enjoyed a tad too much Glenlivet the night before. Single malt scotch and late night reading always paired well for Blaze. The hot cup of joe seemed to help alleviate the ailments caused both by his nightmares and the scotch.

He was thirteen years deep into his blessed marriage with Diem. She was a lovely Chinese woman who had put up with his catalogue of idiosyncrasies with more tolerance than one could reasonably expect. Only her beauty exceeded the width of her tolerance.

As Diem reached for her coffee, Blaze gently grabbed her arm and intercepted her as he confessed, "Last night was one of the rough ones. The nightmares again. They hit hard." In his dreams, there was no fog of war. The images were full color and high definition and he had no nocturnal remote with which to make them stop.

She nodded with understanding and gave him a hug as she said, "You don't have to worry about any of that stuff anymore, baby."

Shaking off the terror of his night, Blaze settled into his customary seat at the family table while clutching his hot coffee mug with one hand. Although he was in no mood for an unexpected, introspective life talk with his bride over cheerios and a handful of much needed aspirin, he was happy to be awake. Happy to be away from his night terrors. And very happy to be peering at the beauty of his faithful wife.

Diem sat across from him bearing an expression that signaled she had something to say. He looked at her and smiled as he continued to sip his coffee. She began to speak.

"Blaze, I know you miss being in the field, but I really do feel so much safer and happier that you're home now and doing what you do." Diem took a slow sip of her coffee.

As aspirin frolicked down Blaze's throat, chased by another unrelenting volcanic gulp of decisively bitter black coffee, Blaze slightly grunted and held his tongue. He had left the CIA about a year ago and had been working as a financial planner ever since. He was not adjusting well to being a civilian. He didn't mind wearing the monkey suit every day and chasing every Tom, Dick, Harry, and Frank around the greater Detroit area in an effort to convince them to give an aeronautical fornication about their personal finances, but his heart was certainly not gung ho. As much as the memories of his time in the Marines and the CIA brought pain, regrets, and sorrow, those memories undoubtedly overwhelmed him moreover with pride, nostalgia, and a hunger for further missions. He wanted back in. His balls hadn't dropped out yet.

"I know you're very happy that those days are over, but please don't talk about them with me like that. Let me deal with my transition emotions in my own Irish way—by burying them." Blaze sounded part Heartbreak Ridge-era Clint Eastwood and part drunken Irish poet with his tone of barely-caffeinated morning gibberish. Imagine Dylan Thomas writing a character sketch of Gunnery Sergeant Thomas Highway all sung by Shane MacGowan of the Irish rock band The Pogues.

"You need to be home more, helping me with the kids and the house. It's good for you. I know it's awkward and unnatural for you, but you'll get over it." Diem leaned over and gave him a kiss on his forehead as she ran her loving fingers through his slicked back, black hair. Blaze hadn't had an oil change for his pompadour yet that morning and his scalp was screaming for a fresh tube of Brill Cream.

His hair cream preference was as outdated as his hairstyle. He had been sporting a fifties style rockabilly greaser look since he left the CIA, but it was starting to become a bit too high maintenance. Made him think about going high and tight again.

"It's definitely not my natural modus operandi. And I'm not so sure it's good for me to be honest." Blaze was actually increasingly very sure that his current life was not good for him at all. The only thing that caused him to resist that feeling was the happiness in Diem's eyes every time she spoke of his newfound regular presence in the home.

Diem was not taking him seriously at all. She reached down to grab her keys from the basket by the door as she said, "Don't forget to pick up some two percent milk on the way home. Half gallon. Oh, and also, remember Shane has swimming tonight."

"Got it. Get two percent milk. I guess that's the closest to a mission I'll get for now."

Diem continued smiling and Blaze granted a reluctant grin knowing she did not appreciate his sarcasm or perceived negativity. Diem left the house to begin her day and Blaze McIntyre retrieved the remote from the counter and flicked on the news on the kitchen TV and poured himself some more coffee.

As he watched the self-important talking heads blabber on with their redundant rhetoric, he was struck with the feeling that the rest of the world was beginning to really suffer economically in the way that Detroit had been for years. The economy had been ever worsening and increasingly unpredictable long after the impotent era of hope and change had dissipated. Not a great time to be selling mutual funds and annuities. People thought 2008 was bad. Over a decade later, it was worse. Blaze was making a living but, given the financial climate, sometimes he felt like he may have been better off grabbing an AK-47 and joining the Somali pirates. Piracy seemed to be the only growth sector these days. The only real skill set needed seemed to be some nominal trigger experience and a penchant for brazen nautical hijackings. *If a nine year old kid in sandals can hang and bang on the high seas, why not me?*

Blaze's thoughts were interrupted by the persistent chirp of his cell phone.

"What do you want, you German scam artist? You lose your lederhosen?"

It was Bernhard Miller, Blaze's partner at the firm. Working as a financial advisor with little time under his belt, Bernhard was the perfect business partner for Blaze.

Blaze was fighting many internal distractions by way of lamenting his past profession as a warrior. This had caused a need for him to be under one's constant mentorship at the office. Bernie Miller was the right man for that job. He was loud, obnoxious, and constantly interrupting people in conversation. Emotionally, he was about as sensitive as a cactus shoved where the sun don't shine. Blaze loved him. Somehow.

"What do I want? Are you ever gonna get your Mick self into work today? My books are looking light and I need you to fill them. You ain't good for much else." Bernie loved to remind Blaze constantly who was driving their business partnership.

"Yeah, I'm making my way. Your old lady just left, Bernie, so I can come in now."

"She happens to be my ex-old lady and if the divorce was actually real, it would've been the best thing that ever happened to me. Unfortunately, the broad won't stop stalking me and running interference on me dating my secretary." Bernie had no shame about the complicated nature of his personal life.

"Life's tough when you're a cocky German pimp in much demand. Good thing you're a Midwestern farm boy, cuz east coast broads wouldn't stand you for a millisecond with your Luke Skywalker grin and Smallville stupidity."

"I hear you, buddy. Finish your potatoes and put your pot of gold in the safe. Then, get your double-grape fruit arse in here so we can make some loot."

"Double grapefruit? More like double boulder. I'm still in rock solid shape pal."

CHAPTER THREE

Langley, Virginia, Office of CIA director

Chuck Gallagher stood at his desk—a stand up desk that had become his trademark workstation. His colleagues chalked him up as a glutton for self-punishment. To Chuck, the tenacious director of the clandestine services, the stand up desk was a symbol of diligence. It reminded him that literally and figuratively it was his job to never sit down. It was his job to stand and be counted. To stand and fight. To remain steadfast.

Chuck's heart rate was up. He had just finished his morning calisthenics. He felt particularly energized from the vigorous jumping jacks he had performed. As he stood at his work desk, he felt a twitch in his right calf—his muscles were still reeling from his exercises. He wiped the sweat off his brow with his right forearm. He lifted the cup of steaming black coffee to his mouth from his left hand. The black liquid warmed his throat and the caffeine shot quickly into his system. His synapses were firing. He had a lot on his mind.

In a nutshell, it was Iran. The same old unnamed head of the snake since 1979. Their defiant, messianic-driven obsession with obtaining nuclear weapons—and a viable missile system to deliver them—kept Gallagher up at night and angry in the morning. The details of his recent briefings were swimming in his head. He began scratching notes on his yellow notepad. *Stuxnet 2.0*—it was almost ready. The Israeli scientists were working around the clock in the Negev desert for the sequel to the ongoing cyber weapon franchise. *Neo Iranian Nazi Party*—another puzzle piece. This group was on the rise. They co-opted uber-Persian Aryan nationalism and married it with cultish Twelver Shia Islamic eschatology. *Arash Jafari*—a new recruit who was a friend of the CIA's best Iranian spy asset, Reza Kahlili. Reza introduced Arash to Chuck and recommended him for recruitment. This op would be a perfect fit for Arash since he was an IT guy at the Natanz nuclear plant. Yet another likely piece of the puzzle. *Esfahan, Busheher, and Natanz*—the nuke plants. The targets. The objective was to find a way to neutralize these three Iranian nuclear sites as much as possible to buy time and delay the production trajectory. *But how?* Gallagher wasn't yet sure. He needed to assemble all the intel pieces, find the right agents, and get a plan solidified.

He scratched his head and then tapped his coffee mug with his pencil several times as if he was trying to force an insight. *The right team.* He shook his head in frustration. *These young agents don't have the instinct. They have the training, the technology, but they're soft. Anaesthetised by modern life. Pampered with misguided politically correct training.* Gallagher was always fighting an uphill battle with the powers that be over the protocol for the agency's new recruit training. He wished he had his top dog back. Blaze McIntyre. There would be no hesitation to place an operative like Blaze on a mission like this. He wasn't as seasoned as Gallagher, but his spirit was that of the old school agent. He used his training, but he succeeded because of his heart. His track record made him the rock star of the agency. Until he left. A day Gallagher still wished never existed. Gallagher took the last sip of his coffee as he stared at his notes. The last note he wrote was written in all caps, circled and trailed by several exclamation marks—BLAZE!!!

I have to get him back in the game. Gallagher fantasized—no, he strategized—about a way to persuade Blaze to come back to the agency. He had kept in regular contact with Blaze since he left.

Mostly phone calls, but periodic visits as well. They usually went to a shooting range in the Detroit area, fired off some rounds, and then went to a pub and grabbed a pint while shooting the breeze. Sometimes they went to Blaze's boxing gym, O'Conners. Chuck had always jokingly begged Blaze to come back, but never with any serious pleading. That was about to change.

I'll have to slowly put the bug in his ear over a few visits. Looks like I'll be doing some shooting and boxing in Detroit over the next few months. It was settled. This part of the picture was becoming a bit clearer. *What about the rest of the team?*

Chuck knew picking the rest of the team would prove more difficult. *There's always Zack Batt...nah. He's been too reckless lately. Can't stay out of trouble.* Chuck wrestled over the thought of using one of his most complicated covert mercenaries. Zack was a piece of work and he and Gallagher had a very close but tenuous relationship. *If his head is on even slightly more straight than when I first recruited him, he'd probably adapt perfectly to this mission.* Chuck was still unsure. He resolved to re-visit the idea later. He decided to hammer out the strategy for the op first, then finalize the team.

But that would have to wait. He had a conference call in three minutes. He scribbled the word *TRINITY* at the top of his page of notes. He then ripped the piece of yellow paper off of the pad and carefully folded it into a square and placed it in his pocket. *I think I got something here.* He walked away from his desk and opened his office door. He needed to take a quick leak before the call started. He stood at the urinal losing water weight with one thing on his mind—how to get McIntyre back on the job.

CHAPTER FOUR

First Baptist Church of Detroit, Detroit, Michigan

Sometimes Blaze didn't know who appeared to be more afraid of him—the terrorists that had the pleasure of meeting his fury in the heat of an operation, or average citizens who gazed upon his appearance as if he was a terrorist himself. It was around eighty-five degrees in mid May and it was beginning to feel slightly humid. It was one of those rare Midwest weather days when spring flirted with summer earlier than June. This was an anomaly that Blaze could deal with. He had changed into camouflage cargo pants and a tight black tee shirt before leaving the gym. He had completed a tougher than usual morning workout, complete with TRX training and an intense kettle bell regimen. Given the unexpected warmth of the day, he now wished he had been wearing camo shorts instead.

He parked his worn 2010 Cadillac CTS sedan across two parking spots in an obnoxious and diagonal fashion. He opened the door of his cherished vehicle with a slow push of his hand. As he stepped out of the sedan, he took the final puff of his Perdomo Patriarch cigar. He tossed the stogie onto the hot tar of the church parking lot asphalt. He watched it bounce and twirl for a second or two. The cigar then met its fate under the heel of his black combat boot. As he hurried toward the church building, he used the lower part of his tee shirt to wipe the sweat from his face and neck. Despite a good shower, it was typical for Blaze to expect some residual perspiration within an hour after a good workout. This usually happened as a result of his motor having been just revved up and still running with high voltage. He was still as lean of a machine as he ever was. This particular day, the extreme vascularity in his arms made his physique pop.

Blaze admired the ethereal look of the ornate stained glass designs on the church's front doors as he opened the one to his right. He loved the imagery of the angels. He had a habit of visualizing the reality of attending angels that he sensed had helped him through many hairy battles in the desert. Angels that watched over him during many lonely nights in dark places where he sat awake waiting to strike an enemy. Soon after he entered the church, he caught the horrified face of the new church secretary. It wasn't everyday that a tattooed, muscle-bound secret soldier wearing combat boots waltzed in.

In Detroit, such an intrusion could very well invoke a legitimate sense of fear and imminent danger. That being said, the church never locked the door. Pastor Liam wouldn't hear of it. He was old school. No cell phone, no home security system, just his shotgun and his Bible. He was the quintessential bitter clinger. When former president Obama had unintentionally branded those who took comfort in guns and religion with that label during his first campaign, it was folks like Pastor Liam he must have had in mind. In regard to the Church doors in particular though, it was more of a welcoming thing for the Pastor. In his mind, God didn't close His doors to anyone, criminal or not. Besides, truth be told, there ain't no criminal in Detroit that would not soon regret trying to mess with Pastor McCardle. There are some skills that nothing can stop—be it the cloth of the pastorate or the drag of the whiskey bottle. And it was those skills that the good Pastor possessed that would halt any criminal dead in their tracks long before their intentions could be made known.

After a few speechless seconds, the secretary continued her deer-in-the-headlights stare and waited for Blaze to speak.

"I'm here to see Liam. Is he in?" Blaze smiled.

"Umm, well, umm. Could I, umm, let him know who wishes to see him?" She was horrified as she stared at Blaze's muscles and ink. She was clearly in her early to mid seventies, or possibly older, and was not at all used to seeing so much indelible art on a man's arms. Her expression did nothing to hide her lack of ability to assimilate what she was looking at.

"Please just let him know that Blaze is here, ma'am."

"Um, why, certainly."

She walked with a cautious step down the hall a bit and quietly let herself into Pastor McCardle's office.

"Pastor Liam, um, there is a man here, um, looks like an army man, or something. He calls himself 'Blaze.' Do you, I mean, were you, expecting him, sir?"

Pastor Liam made a quick note in his weekly planner, doggy-eared the page he was currently reading in a biography on Abraham Lincoln, and slowly closed the bottom right desk drawer with the tip of his loafer. He closed that drawer just before his secretary could see the bottle of Bushmills Irish whiskey that hid in there with the cork barely secure. McCardle always favored the protestant whiskey and left the Jameson to the Catholics.

"Why, yes, he's a bit early. But, um, yes, you can tell him to come in. Thanks Betty." McCardle was looking forward to his meeting with Blaze. But, as always, he wasn't quite sure if he was ready for it.

After being retrieved by the hesitant secretary, Blaze walked back to Pastor McCardle's office. He gave two light knocks to the slightly open door and decided to just walk in before Pastor gave him permission. Waiting for permission to see what was behind a door was not Blaze's modus operandi given his past line of work.

"Top of the mornin' to you Pastor."

"Hello, Blaze, have a seat, my friend. It's good to see you." Liam smiled.

"You too Liam. As usual, once I sit my ass down in this seat, I'm sure I'll discover a whole new unopened bag of issues for us to dig into." Blaze could not hold back on his tendency to lay it all out on the table instantly.

"Blaze, please my friend, I've told you before about the language." Liam was really not offended by the nominal use of foul language, but he knew that sometimes Blaze used it liberally in his presence for the explicit purpose of trying to get a rise out of him.

"I know Pastor, you're right. I'm taking baby steps. I'm weaning off the f-bomb and employing damn, hell, and ass like it's a nicotine patch. It's tough to quit cold-turkey." Blaze chuckled lightly.

Despite Blaze's faith, his practice of that faith still had many gaps. Control of the tongue being one of them.

McCardle smirked and waived his hands dismissively. "Enough of that already! Please, tell me, how are things? How can I help today?"

Blaze kicked his booted feet up on the Pastor's desk and leaned back a bit on the chair as he began to exhale after a very telling deep breath.

The Pastor widened his eyes a bit at Blaze's audacity in making himself so comfortable. After a moment, he then relaxed in acceptance of Blaze's boldness. For Blaze's part, it was hard enough for him to open up as it was. It certainly wasn't going happen if he couldn't kick his feet up, kick back, and get fully comfortable. Taking ownership of his immediate environment was Blaze's most unfettered instinct.

"Well, first off Pastor, this whole civilian thing is tearing me up inside. I swear I'm living in another person's body. Like I'm enacting another person's daily routine or completing the drudgery of someone else's boring suburban life. Sarcastic and negative enough for you?" Both men laughed.

"You certainly must think high of yourself to assume you're so special and above the mundane. Is this merely a matter of you needing more time to adjust or is it something else entirely? You've only been out for a year." Liam thought best to start off with a soft challenge.

"It's something else entirely. It's a rhythm deep in my veins that is signaling to me that this ain't right; that I'm destined to return to the service of my country. I've been trying very hard to enjoy the normal life and go about the business of work, family, and the rest of it, but I can't ignore what's tugging at my soul. You know why I decided to retire and come back to civilian life. Diem was incessantly worried. She ragged on me to get out to no end. Then, you compound that with the perpetual guilt and conflict I deal with about the things I've done." Blaze sat quiet for about thirty seconds as he pondered his past.

Then he continued, "You know that I've seen carnage that no one should ever have to see at such proximity. I've held the lifeless bodies of dead friends in my arms so many times that the last incident barely ignited any emotion in me, except guilt—guilt because I couldn't feel emotion. And where is God in all this? My faith has gotten me through many difficult times, but many difficult times have also weakened my faith. It's a paradox that still applies now. Some days I have tremendous trust and I know where I stand. Other days, darkness takes over, I curse humanity and feel abandoned by the Almighty. Sometimes to the point where I doubt His intentions. It makes me feel very, very violent. My mind often plays tricks on me." Blaze began to shake as he revealed the dark terrors of his soul.

"Blaze. This tugging. Tell me more." Pastor McCardle leaned forward and beckoned him with both hands.

"Truth is Pastor, I'm not happy unless I'm in combat or in the middle of an op. I'm at peace when I'm in the process of searching and destroying. As much as guilt, darkness, and conflict plague me as a result of the violence of my world, it's also the very current that provides purpose and satisfaction."

"The tugging. This is it." McCardle nodded his head.

"It's a sick, sick dynamic, I know. But it's the truth. I was made for this. I was made to fight, to train, to hunt, to kill. Made to protect this glorious republic we call America. My disdain for America's enemies is my gift." A prolonged silence fell upon the room and Blaze stared with conviction into McCardle's eyes as if to cement the weight of his words.

Pastor McCardle finally broke the heavy silence. "I know full well what you describe. My experiences have been less intense than yours. But having been part of the struggle in Northern Ireland, I do very much understand the basic construct of your disposition. God has crafted you for a very specific purpose. One that isn't found in many." Liam leaned in and lowered his voice to a serious whisper. He looked Blaze straight in the eye to reinforce the conviction of the charge he was making. He continued, "Your ability to assimilate the death, depravity, and violence is a gift. It gives you more strength than it drains from you. Most crumble upon contact with that world, yet you engage with it and find your strength there. The world needs you. America needs you. Good needs you. I think you know what you need to do. You're not living within your calling right now."

Blaze let Liam's words sink in for a moment. Then he responded, "I know. I do. I really do. But I'm so weary of fighting with Diem on this. You know how women can be. They're an entirely different species from men. And I'm an entirely different species than even most men."

"This is true, Blaze. They're a different species indeed."

"I don't care how many books have been written to the contrary, but it's common frickin' sense. Girls like to sing, and dance, and wear dresses. Boys like to fight, watch things get blown up, and carry guns. Little girls like Hello Kitty, pretty dresses, and princesses. Little boys like fire trucks, garbage trucks, and plastic AK-47's. The only way I'd ever get Diem to sign on to the idea of my going back into the field would be if her natural, maternal protective instincts were provoked by one of our children being in danger. That's the only time you'll get a woman to become a warrior. You threaten their children and watch out. If those damn Islamo-facists were smart they'd start tapping into that reservoir of power. If my kids were in danger I could get Diem to blow up anything, shoot anyone, and jump out of any airplane. But yet she can't seem to understand that I have the same instincts when it comes to the threats facing our country."

Liam responded with his thoughts on the threats facing the country. "Blaze, you know I've expressed to you before my sense as to what's developing on the world stage. I believe the times we live in now are more than unique. It's been many years since the Cold War, and still a few since we saw Putin re-take power when Medvedev was finished. But this new leader in Russia, this Maksim, he's like Putin on steroids. If there were ever a shred of free press or free speech in Russia in the first decade of this century, it has all been poisoned and eradicated by now. There's no autonomy for any entity, business, or person outside of the meticulous control of the Kremlin. Medvedev and Putin treated Obama with irreverence, but Maksim is outright mocking this Fitz with brazen arrogance. The Kremlin placated Bush, used Obama, and is now laughing at Fitz."

Blaze nodded trying to wrap his arms around the point that Liam was driving at. Then he said, "Oh, I know. Maksim is laughing right in our faces and has been for a while."

Liam continued, "And as goes for this Fitz, true Christian or not, he's driving the country in the wrong direction fast. He really makes Jimmy Carter look like Churchill."

"True Christian or not, he's driving the country in the wrong direction fast."

Liam went on, "Fitz has no clue how to approach the new Russia that is hell-bent on re-establishing the Soviet Empire and is increasingly transparent in regard to its designs on the Middle East. They no longer merely assist Iran in its apocalyptic ambitions and then downplay it publicly. No longer do they simply run political interference at the UN every time an effort is made to hold Iran accountable for its nuclear ambitions. Now Russia is crystal clear in admitting its alliance with Iran. There's no mistaking this partnership, this tightly knotted duo of pending doom."

Blaze interjected, "Liam, what are you getting at?"

"Let me finish, Blaze. I'm describing important things here. As I was saying, Iran also has galvanized strong ancillary support in the region with Sudan, Libya, Turkey, Lebanon, Syria, and others.

They're all standing stridently by Iran's side. The storm clouds are very thick now Blaze. If they were on the horizon last decade, they are now in our face. I can't in good faith believe otherwise than that the War of Gog and Magog that Ezekiel prophesied more than twenty five hundred years ago is right at our doorstep and will soon come to pass. That being the case, your service is greatly needed. This is the point. I don't know God's will, and I pray I'm wrong in my analysis. Maybe there are actions and decisions that can thwart this now and delay the prophecy so that more can come to faith. I don't know. But if there is anyone that ought be in the arsenal of the United States of America's military force or covert op pocket right now, it's you Blaze. It's you."

Blaze did his best to quickly understand the picture Liam was painting. Blaze tried to absorb, but couldn't quiet take it all in on first listen. Blaze tried to explain to Liam how he saw himself, "Look, Liam, I mean no offense by this, but I'm just an ex-Marine and a spook. You always start going down this path of mysticism and prophecy and symbolism, and I just don't know what to do with all that. I honestly ain't buying all that stuff. Who knows what the scriptures really mean in those passages. They could be taken a million different ways. Even if you're right, these things are the last thoughts I can worry about right now. Like I said, I am a soldier, a warrior. I can't deal with end-of-the-world theories, when in my mind, I struggle with my own end-of-the-world realities. I've seen this world almost collapse many times. And the only thing stopping that collapse were my brothers in the Special Forces and my brave colleagues in the CIA. I've put cigarettes out on the arms of terrorists, had to employ water boarding like it was a new attraction at Six Flags, and have held a fellow soldier in my arms while blood shot out of his jugular like Niagara Falls. I've got enough disturbing thoughts to think about. I don't need a scripturally pre-ordained war to add to it."

Liam knew he had struck a nerve in Blaze and that what he was describing was too much for Blaze to contemplate at the moment.

Blaze was too close to the micro of war that an analysis of the macro was not something he could always handle. "Very well then, I'll try to be subdued on such thoughts when we're in session here. I understand that you're overwhelmed with all this geo-political stuff. Despite all the capacity you have to assimilate, the wounds still bite at times. Nonetheless, you can't deny, and I know that you don't deny, the sensitive times that we live in. You also know what the role you ought to play in it is. If you didn't, you wouldn't be here describing these feelings to me as you are. Are you still in contact with Chuck Gallagher at all?"

Chuck Gallagher was the current Director of Central Intelligence. He and Blaze had remained friends after Blaze stopped working for the agency. They still met frequently to shoot the breeze and pummel each other in the ring.

"For sure, Chuck and I get together pretty regularly and spar over at the boxing gym. We rarely talk shop officially, given the confidential nature of his position, but we keep each other informed of our personal lives. That, and of course, beating the hell out of each other and calling it exercise."

"I'm sure then you've expressed your frustrations with civilian life with him?"

Blaze could see where McCardle was going with this. "Well, that's just it, I've kept that close to the chest. Reason being, I know the minute I tell him, he'll hassle me to no end to get back in the game, and he'll likely have a very specific game in mind for me. I can't let him know how I feel until I've made an absolute decision about what I am going to do. Of course, the sticking point there is still how the hell I am going to deal with Diem on the issue."

"Well, yes, that is the heart of the matter I suppose. You haven't quite said it outright here today, but I think you know in your heart that this matter is decided; now it's just a matter of acting on it. In regards to handling the conversation with Diem, this is where I leave you with God. As you know, I've often confessed my inaptitude for dealing properly with the mind of a woman."

Blaze laughed, "Who knew? I've looked death and destruction square in the face while spitting in its proverbial eye, for years on end, and yet the thought of talking to my wife about a serious issue gives me trepidation beyond belief. Go figure."

Liam laughed and then offered advice for the next step, "Well, maybe you should start with Gallagher. You let him know what you're thinking, and as a result of his excitement and subsequent pressure on you, the ticking of the clock will force you to deal with Diem."

"Yeah, you might be right. I've always done better when there is the pressure of a ticking time bomb. Except, usually the real ones are a lot easier to diffuse than my wife."

Liam smiled. "Well, I shall do my due diligence and lift up that explosion in prayer my friend."

"Good. I'll need it"

"I'll see you then in two weeks?"

"Yeah, if Diem hasn't buried me yet. Oh, and next time, try to keep the cap on the bottle before I get here. You gotta stop this policy of only drinking on days that end in 'y.' I know we're saved by grace, and I know in Gaelic the word whiskey means 'water of life,' but given your profession, I think you should concentrate more on what the Bible refers to as the 'water of life.' I swear, you probably had more to drink this morning than every Mick in the phone book had on St. Paddy's day last year combined."

McCardle knew they'd never part on a serious note. Not that his drinking problem wasn't serious. "I can see your tendency toward blunt confrontation is truly natural outside of your relationship with your wife. Consider your admonition noted and accepted. I'm working on it. However, the ethnic slur is entirely unnecessary,"

Both men laughed as they shook hands and Liam began to walk Blaze out of his office. "Yeah, yeah," said Blaze. "You know I love you Liam, but you can't muzzle me. I'm a Mick too, so sue me. It's all in good fun, and don't seriously try to tell me the Irish don't like to drink."

"Blaze, enough. I think you better move on with your day, you have plenty to think about now."

"Alright, Pastor. Hopefully, I was the worst of it for you today."

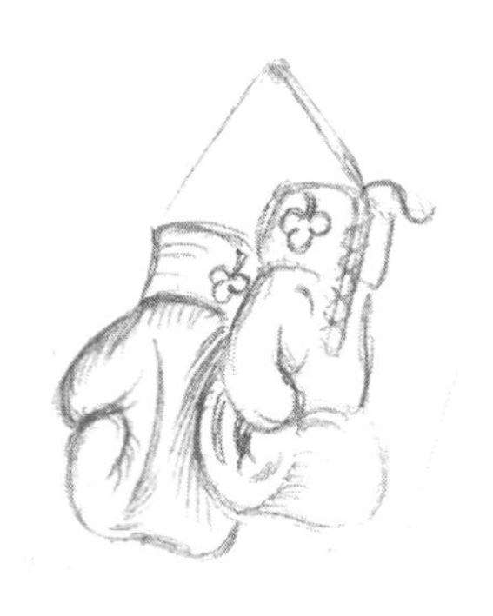

CHAPTER FIVE

O'Conner's Irish Boxing Club, Detroit, Michigan

O'Conner's was teeming with energy. The sound of grunting was constant and everywhere. The smell of sweat and the feeling of male tension hung heavily in the air. The fast, rhythmic tapping of feet echoed throughout the club.

Blaze's thoughts were in a purgatory of sorts. Stability teased him periodically and then laughed its way out of his mind. It was with this strange body-mind dynamic that Blaze pounded away at the heavy bag at O'Conner's Irish Boxing Club in downtown Detroit.

The force of Blaze's gloves crashed against the bag with a thud that syncopated with the whisper and snap of the jump rope four feet behind him. He blinked the sweat out of his eyes and looked around the club for a moment. *This place is packed today.*

As he fought to find an appropriate ebb and flow with his movements, more sweat dripped down through the corner of his left eye. He paused for a second and wiped off his brow with an already well-worn gym towel. His mind began taking him back to the time he was held captive in Yemen. The stench of the cellar, the pain of the beatings, and the confusion of the languages spoken around him seemed tangible even in this moment. It was probably the last time his body had been so beaten down and his soul so demoralized to the point of near resignation. It was after that incident, one in which he was rescued just before his finger nails were poised to be ripped out one by one, that he went home to a frantic bride who was so terrified by his torture experience that she then gave him a stern ultimatum about his occupational future—*no more CIA, no more missions.* Shortly thereafter he learned of Diem's pregnancy—another reason Diem sited as to why Blaze needed to make a career change. His children he adored, the career change not so much. Blaze resisted Diem's plea for a career change for years before finally giving in.

The blasting sound of the bagpipes hit his ears like a tornado of triumphant sound through his iPod ear buds. The fist-pumping cadence of the music served to inspire several intense minutes of relentless assaults on the heavy bag. While his musical tastes were diverse and his iPod full of tunes of all genres, it was the Dropkick Murphys that most often found its way to the top of his selection when he was at O'Conner's. For the moment, it helped him take his mind off the myriad of past glories, current regrets, and future hopes that constantly occupied his mind. DKM always drove him to the peak of intensity in training as it filled him with a deep sense of his warrior nature, his working class roots, and his pride in his Irish heritage. Outside of being a warrior by nature, Blaze was, at the core, a solid product of a working class Irish-American upbringing. This was the perfect soundtrack and battle cry anthem to be set as a sonic backdrop to his unique life's tapestry.

In Blaze's eyes, the Dropkick Murphys represented true patriotism with their songs about struggling soldiers, the rigors of raising a family, and the trials of the increasingly obsolete workingman. Blaze recalled a news story about how the band dropped off a tour with the band Anti-Flag because DKM could not bear their nightly anti-American ramblings any longer.

Blaze slowed his stride as he heard his name yelled in a cocky tone from across the warehouse-like boxing gym. Blaze smiled to himself, wiped more sweat off his brow, and draped his towel over his sinewy, muscular shoulder as he turned to greet his old ball-busting friend,

CIA director Chuck Gallagher.

"How's the world treating you Chuck?" Blaze was always genuinely happy to see Chuck. He had not only been a tough boss who never let Blaze be anything but his best self, but he was also a hell of a friend and mentor.

"Like a baby treats a diaper old friend." Chuck's charm never ceased to amaze.

"I can see your outlook ain't changed a bit mate." Blaze smiled widely as he vigorously shook Chuck's hand.

"Still a heart-breaker, life-taker, and grave-maker. Through and through."

"Well, I hope you're wearing your Depends old man, cuz I'm about to kick the shit out of you." Blaze loved to threaten people as he looked them in the eye with a smile.

Chuck's laugh echoed throughout the club.

"Let's get rollin' pally, 'cuz I ate my Wheaties this morning and had my Viagra last night. Your going back to kindergarten." Small talk was over. Gallagher was ready to throw down.

Chuck Gallagher was a dinosaur. Old school. Obstinate. Hard-nosed. He was also tirelessly devoted, down to the core of his being, to his country and all that might be necessary to protect it. There's not a search party in existence that could find a soft emotion in the man. But contrarily, he was *all* heart. And everyone who knows him, knows it. Chuck's military career started in the Marines, much like Blaze's, and it ended up in the CIA. In very little time, Chuck clawed his way into the director's seat with the vigilance and ferocious ambition of an enraged tiger. Chuck had always been well known for his inability to be flexible. His tirades, pissing matches, and knock-down-drag-out disagreements with colleagues—no matter their rank—were well known, public and beyond legendary. Blaze McIntyre was one of the only individuals that, because he had dominated beyond expectations in all his missions, had earned the respect of Chuck Gallagher. So much so that although standard ball-breaking applied, all-out character assassination was spared.

In his late fifties, although he was ever the quintessential crotchety old man in spirit, Chuck Gallagher was in golden athletic shape. After the customary warm ups and friendly banter, Chuck threw the first punch in the sparring match. Body shot, blocked. With equal force and comparable form to Gallagher's shot, Blaze retaliated. Strike to the head, also blocked. The ping-pong of strength and skill continued for about twenty minutes while both men proceeded to sweat pure passion, aggression, pain and devotion in a deadly serious, but pragmatically playful, manner. As the two men tired of throwing hooks and jabs, they began chatting.

"Chuck, I have some things on my mind." Blaze was catching his breath as he began to open up the conversation. He mopped his soaking head with a fresh towel as he spoke.

"Oh yeah? So what's new? If I killed as many as you, I'd have more on my mind than I have already." Insensitivity was natural for Gallagher. Blaze never held it against him. It was a pre-requisite for Gallagher's position.

"Yeah, well, those things are hidden way deep. I save those for the bartender, the pastor, and the shrink. Not a grumpy old man who lost his touch in the ring."

"Good, because I'm none of those things and I don't venture to help in that area. It'd be the blind leading the blind anyhow."

"Yeah, well, my mind is more occupied with directional issues my man. I want back in the game…I think. But, I ain't got the balls to tell Diem."

"Wow. Now you're striking a chord pal. The pencil pushing ain't doing it for you anymore, uh? You can't tell me shit like that without me being on your ass about follow through. I'm like a pit bull on steroids when you tease me like that." Blaze was making Gallagher's task easy. Gallagher didn't even have to lead him to water.

"I suppose that's why, other than McCardle, you're the only one I've shared this conflict with." Blaze looked Chuck straight in the eye, sending a legitimate signal that he was on the short list of men he trusted.

"So you're practically begging me to break your balls for follow through?" He was gonna break his balls with relentless follow through anyhow, but confirmation would eliminate the chance of any guilt about it.

"Yeah, I suppose that's exactly what I'm doing." And indeed it was the reason Blaze had brought it up.

"Well, good. Now you're gonna be hard-pressed to not break the news to Diem, because I think I got a mission that has your name written all over its bloody path." Chuck smiled with wide eyes.

"Do tell."

"Let me finish the groundwork and then I'll gladly brief you on the skinny."

"Next week? Same place, same ass-whoopin'?"

"Sure, as long as you're clear that it's your ass that'll be whooped." Gallagher knew Blaze was beginning to feel like his true self again.

"Don't count on it Grandpa." Blaze's respect for Gallagher was deeper than he would ever let him know.

CHAPTER SIX

Client's home, Detroit Michigan suburbs

"Guys, I know we've been discussing these ideas for almost nine months now. I know you've done a lot of work and put a lot of time in, and I appreciate that. I'm still just not sure yet."

Blaze and Bernie sat at Frank Barnes's kitchen table for what seemed like the tenth time, but was likely the third or fourth. They'd been stuck in neutral in their efforts to make Frank a client and at the onset of this meeting, their hopes had already been dealt a blow.

Frank Barnes was a doom and gloomer talk radio junkie. His voracious appetite for news and information caused him to constantly be absorbing media—particularly talk radio. Although conservatives dominated talk radio ten years prior, the airwaves were filled equally now with the ever-increasingly dominant views of the multi-layered progressives—left and right. Frank gave thanks for all of this to the former FCC associate general council Mark Loyd. As a result of his influence, the rules of the airwaves were now governed by regulations that made the fairness doctrine actually seem more fair than fraudulent in Frank's opinion. All the progressive voices on the airwaves gladly reiterated the severity of the financial crisis, Frank reckoned, because the fear it caused ultimately helped to advance their globalist agenda. The freedom-loving and libertarian voices on the airwaves spent hours exposing the crisis and, of course, blaming both Democrat and Republican progressives. Yet since freedom proponents had been so defeated in recent years by the machinery of soft tyranny, they had lost hope that anything would change anytime soon. This environment of perpetual financial fear made it very difficult for Blaze and Bernie to gain and retain clients.

Frank had been wildly successful running his textile factory and had amassed quite a fortune. Always the renegade with an independent spirit, Frank managed all his wealth by himself until now. It took the unending tumult of the last nine years to finally get him to the point of consulting with financial advisors and estate planning attorneys. Blaze and Bernie's firm was just one of many that Frank had been flirting with over the past twelve months. Blaze and Bernie had to continually go the extra persuasive mile to try to close this case.

Frank continued, "I know I'm going to sound completely out of my skull, and this is way outside the realm of the stuff we're here to discuss, but hear me out. After absorbing everything that has happened in the world over the past ten years, I increasingly get the sense that there's a high possibility that the United States as we currently know it, define it, and love it could very well be on its way to ceasing to exist." The doom boomed and the gloom glimmered. Frank was off and running with another theory of death.

"What gives you that sense Frank?" asked Blaze, knowing full well what he was in for. This would not be the first time Frank embarked on a long political rant that was altogether tangential to everything Blaze and Bernie had met with him to discuss. Blaze didn't mind so much, but it drove Bernie nuts.

Frank began excitedly rubbing his chin and rocking slightly back and forth on the wobbly wooden chair. He was winding up for a verbal onslaught. "First off all, it's no secret that I was never a fan of Obama—not that I loved Bush or wanted McCain or Romney. You guys know that. Both Bush and Obama and many of the presidents before them have long been laying the incremental groundwork for globalism that has come to supersede our collective sense of nationalism as priority. Our current president, this Fitz guy, is not subtle about it. I personally think he's wet behind the ears. Obama was slick, but this guy? Buffoon with a capital B. He's blatantly accelerating my worst fears. The push for a global currency that faded with a whimper in 2009 is now back with full steam and it looks like, at the very least, we'll see a continental currency sometime this year. The government now runs banks, healthcare, the auto industry and they're damn near close to taking over housing and the trucking industry. This is increasingly not the country I love, although I undoubtedly still love it. Not to mention, the threat of radical Islam has steadily increased regardless of the 'new tone' we've been naively promoting. ISIS, Al Qaeda, Boko Haram and Hamas are certainly not on the run. Dovish diplomacy hasn't made us safer one bit. Our enemies have been playing us the fool with more vigor, intent, and tenacity than ever before. And now we have this Fitz character ..."

Frank's elbows were digging sharply into his kitchen table as he continued to pontificate, with charismatic hand gestures, on all the elements of the global political climate, and the specific trends in the US that clearly aggravated him and gave him pause to trust in any political party, leader or institution, financial or otherwise. His faith in the US currency, in the future sovereignty of the US and in future of his significant wealth was all clearly shaken.

Bernie, who was the poster boy for A.D.D. obnoxiousness, somehow always remained calm, patient, and rational in the midst of a business meeting. Having voted for both Obama and Jack Fitzsimmons, he disagreed with almost of all of Frank's worldview, but he would never allow Frank to know. Bernie responded, "I understand that all these uncertain global changes are huge. The things our government is putting on the table and taking seriously could be seen as unprecedented and downright scary to one of a conservative mindset. I get it. But what choices do we really have here? If what you fear will lead to an erosion of all that we know and trust, does it matter where your money is? Likely not. Even if you shove it under the mattress, in the culmination of all you fear, the dollar isn't worth much anyhow. And we've already discussed the gold idea which you've made clear is only going to remain a portion of your portfolio. So we can't reasonably plan on any such doomsday notion. That being the case, let's continue this proposal with trust that the tax laws will be the same as they've been for over one hundred and fifty years and that our plan will accomplish the ongoing tax deferral you so desperately need."

Frank chuckled a bit. His diatribe was largely a way to vent all of his feelings and concerns. He knew that regardless of whether his fears were legitimate or not, it made sense to go forward with Blaze and Bernie's plan. After an hour and a half of end-of-the-world speculations, and an additional hour and a half of actually reviewing the merits of the financial recommendation, Frank finally inked the deal with Blaze and Bernie. The two said their goodbyes and expressed their gratitude to Frank and headed out to their cars for the usual post-meeting colleague banter.

CHAPTER SEVEN

The Roosevelt Room, The White House, Washington, DC

"I'm beginning to think that Mahoney and Sapp are onto us, Gabriella," said President Jack Fitzsimmons, the 45th President of the United States.

"Jack, you need to relax. There's never been any suspicion as to why I'm here. All through the campaign, not once did we sense that we'd been discovered. Besides, you're the president. Who's going to speak up against you from your inner circle? It's not as if I'm in here flashing a thong like Monica. This is quite more serious. I'm only your therapist." Gabriella Mancini was beginning to feel less like a shrink and more like a babysitter. Managing the emotions and whimsicalities of the President of the United States was beginning to become a larger chore than expected.

Fitz took a deep breath and leaned back in the soft brown leather chair as he shook his head in agreement with his shrink. "I know. I know. I'm just so damn overwhelmed with everything. I'm beginning to wish I called for a recount to see if by some divine chance I really wasn't meant to do this. Talk about being careful what you wish for. I was told by my predecessor what the pressures would be like once I became aware of all the briefings and intricacies of the office, but six months into it, I'm still feeling like I'm on my first day at the job and there's a proverbial stain on my collar." Fitz knew he was veering off into complaint town simply by the look on Gabriella's face. She took the opportunity to change the subject.

"How's Emily, Jack? How's she adjusting?"

"You know her. She lives for change and hustle. She's always been one step ahead. If she wasn't such a piercing, nagging interference, I might actually take comfort in her ability to adjust. But she's been reinforcing my anxieties more than relieving them." When it came to the dynamic between Jack and his wife Emily, it was clear to Gabriella that Jack not only did not wear the pants, he had no pants. This emperor had no clothes because his wife took them.

The first lady was more than a handful. She was all details and no heart. She was a type A go-getter who lacked any shred of emotional intelligence. As the president continued to vent to Dr. Gabriella Mancini, his shrink since the campaign began, she could not help but replay a multitude of scenes from the old television sitcom *Everybody Loves Raymond* in her mind. Emily Fitz's personality was much like Deborah on the show. Emily walked all over Jack when the camera was off and the door was shut. She treated him like a child. Too many times Dr. Mancini had to make valiant efforts to keep a serious countenance while listening to Fitz because inside she was laughing hysterically at the DVR playing inside her mind.

"We spoke last time about the idea of you focusing on your history of strengths, proven skills, and internal locus of control. When you speak like this about the extent to which you've allowed others to affect you, it's clear to me that your focus is off. I know you love Emily, and I know it's difficult for you to remove emotion from the effect she's having on you, but you need to."

Jack interjected, "You're right Gabriella, I just get beaten down so much by her that it's hard to brush aside how she makes me feel."

"The position you're in doesn't allow you to be weak in these areas. Ignoring your wife's behavior and refusing to allow it to effect you negatively doesn't mean you're any less devoted to or in love with her. It simply means you're independently strong and secure.

This will obviously apply to many of the relationships you're beginning to develop with congress, world leaders, and the ever-intensifying relationships with your own staff." Gabriella was suddenly feeling like she was grossly, and damn near criminally, underpaid.

"When I'm focused on God, and the destiny He's called me to embrace, I do feel that sense of internal strength that you speak of, but lately those moments are rare. I'll work to be more cognizant of my tendencies this week. I'll certainly need such an emotional shield given the pressure cooker I'm in." Jack Fitzsimmons rarely revealed the fabric of his faith when speaking with Gabriella.

Gabriella was well aware of the brand of Christianity that the President espoused. She knew he was prominently associated with the emerging religious left. She thought of his faith as a combination of Carter-era feel-good Christianity blended with the contemporary sensibility of young Christians who harbored many socially conservative ideals but identified very strongly with the big government, social welfare driven compassion mantra of the "I am my brothers-keeper" doctrine typified by the post Obama age. All of this, she felt, was piggybacked by the uber-positive, gushingly empathetic sentiments of popular mega-preachers like Rick Warren and Joel Olsteen. She knew that Fitz, too, harbored many socially conservative ideals. He was personally not for gay marriage. He personally abhorred abortion. But when it came to policy and action, he clearly sided with his constituents on the left and publicly championed choice and gay rights. Gabriella understood that to Fitz, these issues were matters that largely would be settled beyond his humble judgment and be left to the intimacy between an individual and his or her Creator. At least, she suspected, that is what he rationalized in his own mind to mitigate the conflict that simmered within his heart over these issues.

Moreover, Gabriella observed that Fitz's core, driving beliefs and agenda aligned primarily with his vision for global equality and global synergy. He viewed borders as nothing but imaginary lines that sinful man had manufactured to create barriers and divisions. He very much was devoted to the "cult of multi-culti" as the right would mock. He intimated to her in sessions that he was actively lobbying and pushing for a global currency. Although he couldn't say it explicitly, she knew he truly envisioned a world in which all nations co-governed. He confessed to her that the idea of eradicating the sovereignty of the United States would be a tough sell. Because of this, he told her he could never reveal this desire publicly. Instead he detailed his belief that the incremental fusion of international infrastructure and commerce could bring about a virtually borderless and seamless world without any overt relinquishment of sovereignty. He knew that as such a plan progressed, over time, the idea of merging nations into wider continental unions would be naturally and effortlessly achieved. He often explained to her that this was his utmost passion as President.

"I have a meeting with Sapp and Mahoney in five minutes, Gabriella. I hate to cut this short, but duty calls. Time waits for no man." Bob Sapp was Fitz's high-strung chief of staff, and Hank Mahoney was Fitz's vice president, the man who truly kept him from coming apart at the seams. His daily meetings with these two key staff members were the lifeblood of his productivity as a fairly green president.

"Understood. Remember—emotional shield, but not emotional insensitivity. Feed the internal locus of control."

"Thanks Gabriella. See you next week."

CHAPTER EIGHT

Natanz, Iran

Arash Jafari sat at his desk sipping tea and clearing his head. He needed a break. He needed to gather his thoughts on the day. And on his life. He had been bouncing around troubleshooting all morning and he was exhausted. Typically, he found himself confined to the expanse of the underground structures of the Natanz nuclear facility, but today he was busy putting out a host of IT fires in the above ground area, particularly the centrifuge assembly plant. Every time Arash thought he had the system wired and bulletproof, another unintended consequence arose. Today was especially taxing since his boss was riding him to fix the glitches quickly. There was a lot on the test schedule as a result of a shipment that arrived that morning and contained a fresh batch of centrifuge components to be put to use for assembly and testing. The shipment was, in truth, many shipments that had arrived that day from a multitude of government-owned entities that had been feverishly producing the necessary centrifuge components to keep the Mullahs satisfied.

Arash had been experiencing volcanic heartburn lately. He was taking medicine for it, but he knew that it was a futile effort and really only helped as a psychological balm. The heartburn was psychosomatic.

Arash Jafari was constantly worried that he would be revealed, or worse yet, that as a result, his lovely wife and two daughters, eight and five, would be slaughtered as punishment to a traitor of the regime. Arash was indeed a traitor. He had been working with the Israelis via his work with the CIA. He had helped to refine a new strain of the Stuxnet computer worm intended to utterly and completely destroy the Iranian nuclear program, at least the tentacles of which they were aware. The first deployment of the worm in 2009 successfully harmed the program enough to retard its progress by wiping out a fifth of the program, but the final blow was still yet to be struck.

Like the computer malware, Arash Jafari himself was also a worm. He was a worm planting a worm. He was snugly nestled inside the personnel infrastructure of the Natanz nuclear facility and so far as he could ascertain, he had been undetected and unsuspected. But his belief that he'd gone undetected didn't assuage the persistent anxiety that plagued him. Nothing could assuage that. It was part circumstance and part the makeup of his nervous nature.

Arash's journey into espionage started oddly and dramatically with a vision. A religious vision. And not an Islamic religious vision. *Jesus.* Clear as could be. Strong, loud, and shock-inducing.

And with His appearance, Arash felt his flesh heat up as if he was locked in a dry sauna with the temperature kicked up to the max. Yet, he felt no pain or discomfort, as if he had been shrouded in a protective fire to which he himself was immune.

He later processed this experience by considering it an immersion in the supernatural fire of truth that manifested itself to him in a physical and real way.

The Nazarene spoke to him in direct terms about his then fanatical obsession with the imminent re-appearance of the Mahdi; the glorious Islamic Messiah—the eagerly anticipated Twelfth Imam—who was to rescue the world from chaos and establish a glorious Caliphate once and for all.

The Nazarene rebuked this fascination in Arash and scolded him for believing in and looking towards the coming of a false Messiah. Boldy, the Nazarene quoted scripture that referred to false Messiahs in the days of last things. He made it abundantly clear that the worship of Jesus, the great I Am, was the only pathway to paradise and peace. He gave Arash glimpses of the future war that would take place in conjunction with the claimed return of the Mahdi.

Arash became filled with poignant and vivid mind pictures of these future times and the chaos and confusion that would mark them. Arash fell prostrate and worshiped the Nazarene with a passion and fervor that far surpassed any of the feelings he had ever expressed for the figure of the Mahdi.

Arash had changed in an instant. He was now an outlaw Christian in the land of the devotees of the Mahdi.

It took Arash several weeks to come to grips with the experience and to even begin to feel comfortable in his new skin, and with his newly transformed soul.

He felt like a fraud and an imposter everywhere he went, particularly when with his wife. He continued to lay his prayer rug next to hers and pray with her daily at all the requisite intervals, only he was praying to who she would only recognize as the Mahdi's chief deputy, Jesus Christ. She had no clue what had transpired within him.

Arash had only confided in one person regarding his conversion. It was a person who he had known was critical of the Islamic doctrine surrounding the Twelfth Imam, and of radical Islam in general. It was his dear childhood friend Reza Kahlili, who at the time, served in the Iranian Revolutionary Guard, and unbeknownst to Arash at the time, was also a full-fledged spy for the CIA.

Arash told Reza of his conversion with great trepidation. Even though Arash trusted Reza intrinsically, he knew that he was revealing one of the most damning stories a man could tell in the Islamic Republic of Iran. What came out of Reza's mouth following Arash's confession was astounding. Arash would have never suspected that Reza was not only a secret follower of Jesus also, but was one of the CIA's top assets in Iran to boot.

Reza had penetrated deep into the guard and was funneling all he discovered back to the Americans, and by proxy, as needed, to the Israelis. The two men swore confidentiality to each other's secrets, and their bond and friendship grew stronger as a result.

Several months had gone by after that conversation and Arash had become more and more engrossed in his faith and had experienced many encounters with the Spirit.

He was both petrified and nervously excited by what he felt the Lord was telling him. *Me? How could I possibly be a spy? I'm afraid of noises in the house when I'm home alone, I don't think I could have the faith or ability to be a spy? I'm just not that slick. I'm a clumsy, over-weight middle-aged tech guy.* His doubts were huge and persistent. But so were the nudges he felt from the Almighty.

The Bible was replete with stories of great heroes, prophets, and messengers who felt wholly inadequate for the callings they had received. Arash supposed he was no different. He mustered the fortitude to speak with Reza about what he was feeling.

Within a week Reza had linked Arash with Chuck Gallagher and the wild journey into the lonely labyrinth of a spy's life had begun. Arash had been living each day entirely on purpose ever since. Eternal purpose.

Arash had met Chuck at a safe house in Iran per Reza's instructions. Arash recalled the conversation vividly, as if it was currently still occurring. Chuck Gallagher commanded a presence. Arash remembered the strength of his introductory handshake and his forthright way of getting straight to the point.

"We're calling it Operation Persian Trinity", said Chuck Gallagher to his newly acquired high-tech Iranian asset.

"What's the meaning behind the name?" asked Arash.

"Natanz, Esfahan, and Bushehr. That's our trinity. They're our targets. We've been gathering a butt-load of MASINT on these disguised nuclear facilities since their inception, and we're ready to deploy our attacks very soon. Natanz is all yours my man. Do you wanna be called the Father, the Son, or the Holy Ghost?" Gallagher threw it all right at him.

Arash was now confused as well as overwhelmed. He remembered thinking *Am I really the guy for this job? Really, Lord? Me?* He knew he was wet behind the ears. It was unavoidable that he would have to ask questions that revealed just how wet. "What is MASINT?", he asked Chuck.

"MASINT is the data we collect on industrial activities and weapons capabilities on our enemies, in this case, your country of birth. We get this data from our airborne IMINT and SIGINT gathering systems. We also utilize a lot of TELINT and ELINT to throw into the INT salad," Gallagher replied to add to Arash's confusion. Gallagher smiled, knowing he was making Arash's head spin.

"Now you're really losing me." Arash smiled sheepishly.

"Don't worry about it boss, I'll get you a handbook on our intelligence catalog to get you up to speed on the vernacular." Gallagher gave Arash a strong pat on the back.

"Good, sounds like I'll need it." Arash was moderately comforted.

Gallagher went on to explain in that early briefing with Arash exactly what type of attack they were planning. "Our pals the Israeli's have been cooking up this stew in the Negev Desert for quite some time now. We've been working with them on this joint effort via their nuclear facilities in Negev. You know, the one that doesn't exist. The big Snuffleupagus of the Middle East. They've replicated the centrifuges that your country possesses. Those damn centrifuges have been the most tested lab rats known to the history of man since in our hands. What're we testing? Stuxnet worm 2.0. That's what. And this one will have teeth. This is what we have on the docket for you and Natanz. The other facilities will have different attacks."

"What is a Snuffleupagus?" Arash was confused.

"You don't know who the hell Snuffleupagus is? I guess you wouldn't unless they're airing old Sesame Street reruns in Farsi. Let's just say it means something that no one knows exists, but yet it exists anyhow." Gallagher had just made things more perplexing for Jafari.

Arash shook his head and mumbled, "Okay, if you say so."

Gallagher then continued to detail the history of the Stuxnet worm and their hope for its future. Arash confirmed that he could be of assistance as a consultant throughout the testing and development phase of the virus.

Arash's imagination was engaged and he was beginning to feel an excitement and sense of divine purpose percolate deep within him.

Gallagher continued to give Arash the lowdown on the history of Stuxnet.

The Stuxnet worm was originally discovered by a firm in Belarus. Its basic function was to infiltrate key, valuable infrastructure and record all its inner workings while simultaneously co-opting and maligning those programs with a wicked re-structuring. The Stuxnet worm was the quintessential cyberweapon that re-invented the practical applications of malware for war purposes. Stuxnet's ability to spy, infiltrate, and re-program was ambitious enough, but even more amazing was its ability to leave no traces of its work.

When the Stuxnet worm was first deployed in 2009, it was successful in wiping out approximately one fifth of Iran's nuclear program. This blow served to significantly stunt the program's development. This, in combination with some Israeli hits on targeted Iranian scientists, was a major victory for America and Israel. But the final victory was yet to come.

Since then, the Iranians had recovered and continued to press on with their nuclear goals. They managed to develop a significantly less bulky and temperamental centrifuge.

In Negev, Israel and America were busy with the preparations for their second attack. They had managed to keep up with the progress of the Iranians and were testing replicas of their upgraded centrifuges in real time.

Digital warfare was, in part, a patience game. The nerds at Negev were working diligently and thoroughly. They were determined to make the next one count, like killing a mosquito with a sledgehammer.

Gallagher explained the helpful role that the German company Siemens had on the back end. They, as it turned out, were the suppliers of key equipment that ended up being identified as part of the Iranian nuclear program. They worked with Idaho National Laboratory, a division of the Energy department, to discover hard-to-detect holes and vulnerabilities in their systems and equipment.

Siemens publicly claimed these tests to be routine Q and A. Privately, however, they were working with the Unites States government to pinpoint precise ways that their product could be crippled by Stuxnet to shut down the Iranians in their apocalyptic nuclear tracks. Stuxnet 2.0, like its predecessor, was the result of a sophisticated collaboration by a number of geniuses spread throughout a number of continents.

"So where do I fit in Mr. Gallagher?" Arash was hungry for specifics.

"You? Where *don't* you fit in? ...You're our eyes and ears inside Natanz. Along with your technical consulting, you'll keep us abreast of all upgrades made to the centrifuges, any hints of movement of product or materials, and any sense of possible new production or mobilization plans. You'll confirm facility layouts and construct detailed schematics. You'll begin feeding us well-crafted dossiers on everyone who plays any significant, or insignificant, role of regularity on a day-to-day basis inside that plant. You'll also be the human instrument, particularly given your IT role inside the plant, to install the worm inside the system. This worm will secretly record all the normal operations of the plant and feed those visuals back to us even as it simultaneously shreds their program limb from digital damn limb."

"That's a tall order for a short man." Arash had not yet learned that humor was pretty much foreign to Chuck Gallagher. The awkward stare and look of annoyance he received quickly brought to light this truth.

"Don't sell yourself short, Arash. We wouldn't be having this conversation right now if my colleagues and I weren't one hundred and ten frickin' percent sure you could handle this."

"I only hope to be able to maintain such confidence." Arash offered a genuine smile.

"You can go ahead and hope, and in the interim, I will simply see to it."

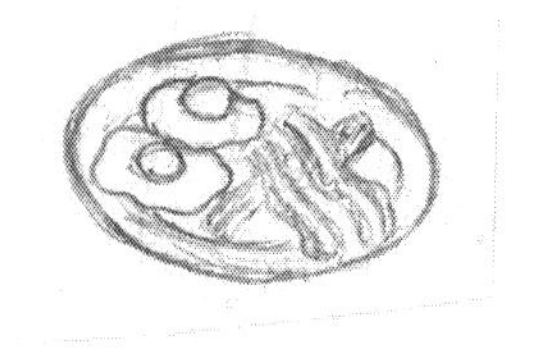

CHAPTER NINE

Ramona's Diner, Detroit, Michigan

Blaze was huckin' fungry. It was rare that he could keep his appetite under reigns past 11 am. Especially if he had to do so while conducting a meeting. His stomach was rumbling hard as he and Bernie entered Ramona's diner. The roadside joint was adorned with nostalgic Americana and pop culture posters, tins, and nick knacks. The patrons were salt of the earth for sure. Blaze and Bernie were certainly out of place in their three-piece suits and pea coats. Trucker hats, flannel shirts, big-ass belt buckles, and even sweatpants would have been more fitting. They sat down eager to place their orders. An attractive waitress walked over to their table. She wore a very tight tank top that revealed her belly button ring and showcased the ornate full sleeve tattoo work on her right arm.

Blaze gave the gal his order. "I'll have three eggs over easy with hash browns. Cheese and onions on the hash browns. Wheat toast with that. And black coffee and ice water."

The waitress nodded and turned to Bernie to begin taking his order until Blaze called out with an additional request. "Oh and also a side of sausage."

"A side of *what*?"

"Sausage." *Sasidge* was how he said it. It was a strange northeast slang pronunciation that Blaze could not shake saying for the life of him. He'd picked up the vernacular from his old warrior pal Zack Batt.

"Oh, okay, sausage. Sorry, you said it weird." The waitress smiled and turned once again to begin getting Bernie's order.

"I'll just have the eggs benedict and some coffee…and your phone number." The waitress smiled at Bernie and laughed him off. He asked her the same question every time, and by observing how her smile grew warmer upon each attempt, it was reasonable for one to be hopeful that one of these days Bernie would get her digits written on his check.

As they waited for the food Blaze felt agitated and his hunger grew. Diem always accused him of being an anxious eater, because the lower his blood sugar got, the more jumpy and irritable he became. In such a state, he often rebelled against his late grandfather's policy of dining vs. shoveling. Shoveling was entirely inevitable for Blaze in such states of hunger.

Finally, the food came. Blaze began digging in immediately like a starved Viking famished from a hard fought battle. Bernie paused first to admire the rear view of the waitress as she left their table, and then he dug in.

After his initial hunger pains were relieved, Blaze began to speak. "I'm glad that case finally closed. Great guy, and I respect the due diligence he put into it, but it sure did seem to take forever."

"For sure. A boost like that will certainly help our numbers, and the plan will really help him keep Uncle Sam away going forward. I dunno though, I don't think I can handle any more speeches on the coming global financial collapse when it comes time to do our first quarterly review with him. I just don't understand that kind of paranoid mindset." Bernie was not prone to imaginative negativity about the future. He didn't lean to any extremes that Blaze could identify.

Bernie Miller was, above all else, a self-described pragmatist when it came to financial matters. He had described himself to Blaze as being a social liberal and a fiscal conservative. He usually voted Democrat but often vocally criticized the party for promoting loose fiscal policy.

In terms of his personal finances, Bernie had done remarkably well in his eighteen-year career as a financial advisor. He had acquired substantial wealth spread decisively and prudently across many asset classes. But you'd never know it if you saw him driving up to a cheap restaurant in his beat up Ford escort. You'd know it less after seeing him emerge from that vehicle with his hand feverishly digging into his cheap suit pocket to fetch a buy-one-get-one-free coupon. All for a meal he'd write off anyhow.

This, of course, was the key to his success in many ways. Frugality was one thing, but Bernie's brand was unparalleled. Blaze wondered if he ever even enjoyed what he had earned. He worried that Bernie's focus on preserving and growing his wealth superseded any impulse to loosen his belt and lighten up on even the most benign spending indulgence. This personality trait, which on the surface was admirable and worthy of emulating, seemed to be, beneath the surface, a restrictive characteristic. Blaze suspected that it might impede Bernie emotionally in his relationships. Partly an overreaction to the spendthrift habits of his whimsical ex-wife, and partly just the way he was naturally wired, his scrooge-like attitude was deep and penetrating.

"Frank's a tad paranoid, but he's right about a lot of things. The signs are everywhere. I don't know if it'll all play out exactly the way he describes, but there are definitely some bad things looming." Blaze dipped his toast into the runny yoke of his eggs and waited for Bernie to respond.

"What? Are you one of those whacko doom and gloomers now? C'mon, all you need to do is take a rational and objective look at the history of the market, the history of the country, and the history of the ebb and flow of the economy, and you'll see that all these things go in cycles. We're just riding out a particularly prolonged downturn that has been exacerbated by do-good politicians. Their meddling hands have extended the pain. But that don't mean that the pain can't be reversed." Bernie had no tolerance for alarmists and conspiracy theory psychos.

Blaze was used to hearing Bernie's views on the financial markets. He was also used to finding ways to open up Bernie's perspective a bit. Blaze replied, "I know that your mind works in linear patterns and with the dominance of left-brained deductions. I get it. I know that unseen forces and probabilities don't enter into your mental framework. That's not how you're wired, but..."

"*Linear patterns*? Blaze, I don't even know what the hell you're talking about."

"Look, you need to understand that there are many factors of the modern age, the global nature of our economy, and the rapidity of the infringement of globalism that make this downturn very, very different from times past. Not to mention the powder keg of radical Islam and the threats it poses to us. We're extremely vulnerable to a perfect storm that could sink the proverbial US ship very quickly if certain things converge simultaneously." Now Blaze had really poked the bear inside Bernie.

"C'mon. *Globalism*? *Really*? *What does that even mean?* I don't see it. I hear you on radical Islam. That, I get. But this whole dramatic new world order fear? I'm not buying it." Bernie stuffed a large bite of eggs benedict in his mouth and jammed in some toast as well. He continued his refutation while still chewing. "Look, I believe in God just like anyone else. I know many arrogant Protestants don't think Catholics are really Christian, but I'll have you know that we are."

Blaze threw his hands in the air in a defensive posture and interrupted, "Bro, I got love for the Catholics as much as anyone else. I dunno what you're talking about."

Bernie ignored the comment. "Anyway, I know that you got that drunken preacher friend of yours feeding you all of this apocalyptic hogwash. I know how that plays into your vulnerability to believe the worst about the future."

"You're right about Pastor McCardle, Bernie. He does strongly believe that we're in the end of days and the Holy Spirit is not the only spirit he has a weakness for. I ain't buying all of it yet either, but I do respect him, and I reserve the right to change my mind."

"Blaze, you need to understand that every time in history when war strikes, or hard economic times emerge, religious people of certain ilk come forth with panic-induced apocalyptic warnings. I just ain't buying it."

"Dude, stop yelling and eating at the same time. It's frickin' disgusting."

Bernie's beat went on. "Whatever, I'm gonna keep investing, keep working, and keep living. I ain't gonna take seriously all these fringe conspiracy theories that every superstitious whack job with a blog, a pulpit or a microphone puts forth." Bernie never minced words with his opinions and he was on a roll with his refutation of Frank's mindset.

Blaze smiled and lowered his voice, in an attempt to lower the temperature of the conversation, as he responded, "I only know so much, and most of that is probably bullshit, but..."

"Now you're being honest."

"Shut up you wise ass. Look, you ought to adopt a more humble attitude yourself. None of us truly know how the future will unfold. Maybe you should stop focusing so much on money and wealth and get in touch more with your spiritual side. Life is like a blink of the eye when compared to eternity, pally. I learned that well in the Marines and the CIA. I'll never take a day for granted again. Every day is a gift."

Bernie looked at Blaze as if he was from outer space.

"You gonna finish that frickin' toast or you gonna continue to get sappy with me like the Jesus freak that you are?"

"Jeez, you German bastard. I thought you were a good Catholic? Believing in JC don't make no one freaky."

"Just give me the toast you ballbreaker. We've got to get back to the office and make some money. The world ain't coming to an end today."

CHAPTER TEN

China (memories)

She could smell the air—pollution and all—like it was yesterday; the ancient feel of the cities and thunderous awe of the countryside. She had not grown up there, but Diem had felt as if she had. Her multiple visits to China were ever-present in her soul and ubiquitous in the deep enclaves of her heart.

She recalled all the times her grandfather told her stories in Mandarin as he sat rocking back and forth in his chair. She received those stories from him in her youth. Now as an adult, the roaring waves of her imagination had washed those old memories ashore. Visceral, beautiful memories. Now, just the slightest smell of second hand cigarette smoke would take her mind instantly to those story-telling sessions her grandfather weaved so effortlessly while chain smoking in his favorite chair.

As Diem grew up, she knew that her family always held an obvious affinity for many things of the old country. Yet their decision to ultimately come to America was not one that wrought any regret. Instead, they regretted the fact that the reason for their departure—Communism—existed in their beloved country in the first place. She understood the ramifications of all of that, but chose in her adulthood to focus on the preservation of the valuable and noble trimmings and underpinnings of Chinese culture and familial tradition, not the political context surrounding it all.

It was on one afternoon in autumn, after she passed by a man smoking on a park bench, that her mind was carried back in time to her tenth anniversary with Blaze. An anniversary for which Blaze agreed to accompany her to China for a visit with her extended family.

It was Blaze's first time in China, and it was there that Diem saw a side of him that she vowed to capture and foster in him forever. The warrior exterior that Blaze carried with him like a medieval suit of armor was beginning to melt. This exterior enveloped even his most shallow of surface emotions. But it had finally been penetrated when he settled into the Chinese interlude he and Diem shared.

Several days into the trip, Diem had realized that Blaze had not once discussed anything in regard to the realm of his work or any related current events connected to his all-consuming occupation. This had never happened before. His mind was always elsewhere. Usually in places he was not at liberty to share with her. Places he wouldn't burden her with even if he was at liberty. Ten years into their marriage, this phenomenon prompted her to fall more in love with Blaze than ever.

She became hopelessly smitten by the man he became when his professional persona fell away completely. His humor was light and ordinary. He smiled easily and frequently. His step was easier and without tenacious guard. She squeezed his hand tight as they explored the land on long walks. She felt herself behaving like a flirtatious schoolgirl for the first time in years.

When Blaze's mind was free, his guard dismantled, and his soul disarmed, he was downright fun—even boyishly awkward and handsomely clumsy. In those moments, Diem could not imagine him doing the things in the cover of darkness that she was told she wasn't allowed to imagine him doing.

If he only knew the jokes that her relatives were making about the awkward white guy she'd brought over, he'd have been blushing the entire time. This vulnerability was not a trait of a career CIA assassin. His all-consuming professional mission was to jettison vulnerability of all kinds in perpetuity. Diem did not know all the details of his job, but she knew the overarching elements and saw the underlying effects. This knowledge, although only a small taste of the full truth, was almost too much for her to carry.

She had carried this newfound mission, of preserving this side of Blaze, for some time after the trip with a fierce evangelical fervor. Ultimately, Blaze's temperament had been successfully chipped away at by her determined Chinese assertiveness. As Shane and Dennis continued to grow, the leverage was too strong for him to resist. She convinced him that he had a patriarchal duty to resign from his front post at the center of harm's way. In direct opposition to his innate bullheaded Irishness, he eventually hung his hat and had been trying to find his way in the business world ever since.

The truth was, though, that Blaze was not very good at navigating through civilian life and normal working life. It showed clearly in his face and resounded audibly in his voice. Diem was happy he was now safe and home with the boys. But she also knew he was slowly dying inside. She secretly was beginning to understand what he meant when he claimed he was born to be a warrior. She fought the instinct to sympathize with Blaze's desire to go back in the field. She was not quite ready to come to honest grips with that realization.

The boys were still very young and the way Diem saw it, Blaze could keep on dying inside for quite some time before he would need any rescuing. For now, she decided, harm's way was going to have to give way to Diem's way.

CHAPTER ELEVEN

Laredo, Texas

Juan Herrara belched. His large belly was full. Two big macs and large fries. Three beers. *Time for a smoke.*

Juan inhaled the cigarette smoke slowly and exhaled with relief. His room was a mess. Nowhere really to sit. Just a mattress on the floor. Shit everywhere. Laundry, empty cigarette boxes, random electronics, wires, and a low rider bicycle with a missing front wheel. He sat on the floor and leaned his ass and lower back against his mattress, exposing his plumber's crack. He was playing Call of Duty on the XBOX. Rap music filled the air. He could hear his mom and her drug dealer having sex in the room next to him. The walls were thin. He leaned over to turn up the music. *Fucking whore.*

Juan really didn't like the fact that his mom was banging a white guy. It was bad enough when other Mexicans were giving her dope for sex, but now Blanco was in the other room laying pipe. Not that he really cared that much. He hated her anyhow. She'd been a slave to heroin and anyone who could supply her with the drug for almost the entire eighteen years Juan had been alive.

He could hear them getting louder. It made him sick. He banged on the wall. "Shut the fuck up!"

They kept at it. Harder, faster, louder.

Then he heard a crash. Glass breaking. His mom screamed. Blanco was yelling.

"You're not finished yet bitch. You want your fix don't ya? We're done when I say!" Blanco shouted.

Juan got up and ran to bust open his mother's bedroom door. She was under the covers. Crying. Blood dripping down her face. Green pieces of a broken Heineken beer bottle shattered beside her.

Blanco stared at Juan with raw anger. He lifted his arm and waived Juan away. "Get the hell out of here kid. This is between your mother and me. Go back in your room you fat shit."

Juan ignored him and shook his head in disgust. He didn't even care if Blanco killed her. He just wanted them to both shut the hell up. He gave up on caring about her years ago.

Juan's mom wiped the blood and tears from her face with the bed sheets. "Just go back to your room honey. We're okay, just a little fight baby, that's all."

"Whatever, Mom." Juan shut the door.

Juan went back to his room. Back to Call of Duty. Back to the blaring hip hop. He cracked open another beer. He wished she would just die already. *She doesn't do anyone any good anyway. Lazy bitch. She don't care about me or Marie.* Juan took care of his sister Marie, not his mom. Now eleven, Juan had practically raised her. He'd do anything to take care of her. He treated her like she was his daughter. He prepared her lunch every day to take to school. He walked her home from daycare. Anything she needed, he'd get her. Even if he had to steal it. She recently began menstruating and Juan researched on the Internet what a parent should tell a young girl going through puberty. He gave her the talk. Then he stole her a shit ton of tampons and pads from the drug store. *Thank God Marie is at Gramma's tonight and doesn't have to hear Mom banging Blanco and getting her ass whooped.*

Juan took another swig of beer. His prepaid cell rang.

"Yeah?"

"What's up? You comin' with us tonight. We're heading to the clubs. Gonna act up. Find some chicas. Fuck up anyone who gets in our way."

It was Angel, one of the neighborhood guys that Juan just began hanging with. Angel used to bully Juan. Used to beat him down in front of everyone. Humiliated the hell out of him. He once gave him a huge wedgie and ripped his underwear. Right in front of Juan's sister. Juan couldn't walk right for days. He couldn't see right for days either. Angel gave him a huge black eye that day. It was one of many.

"Hell yeah I'll go. What time?" Juan was psyched.

"Be at my crib at 9pm. We'll all roll down together. Don't come without your protection. Shit could get ugly at this club."

"Word. See you then."

Juan smiled. He was excited. He stopped thinking about his mom. He stopped worrying about Marie. And he had long forgotten any wrongs Angel had done to him.

Angel and his crew were now Juan's friends. They still teased him, but that was all right. They had his back. They were his brothers.

The last time they went to the cantinas across the border Angel and the crew pushed back a bunch of dudes from jumping Juan. Juan was protected. Juan had beef with one dude that night and beat him near dead with a cue ball in a dirty sock. He earned mad respect from Angel and his crew. Since then, he'd been fighting every weekend.

Maybe I'll score tonight. Been a minute since I got some.

Juan put on his baseball cap, put his cell in his left pocket and his switchblade in his right pocket. He slammed the door on his way out. Not a thought given to the tattered mother he left behind. It was time to go drink and fight. And maybe get laid.

CHAPTER TWELVE

The office of President Hadi Samani, Tehran, Iran

There was no comedic irony to be acknowledged by Iranian President Hadi Samani in regard to the death of his life's mentor; his spiritual and political role model, Mahmoud Ahmadinejad. As honored and humbled as he had felt to assume his mentor's position when he had passed, thus fulfilling the meaning of his name—guide or leader—he still simmered with unspeakable rage when he thought of the audacity of his mentor's killer. Samani was a close friend of his mentor and an integral part of his cabinet. It was not only an audacious act, but one carried out by someone who, in Hadi's mind, should had been executed a long time ago. It was an act carried out by one whose social status was such that his success in killing Hadi's mentor was the ultimate embarrassment in the eyes of Islam.

When it was reported that Samani's mentor and his driver were blown up by a car bomb detonated remotely by cell phone, that was devastating enough. When it was discovered that the attack was coordinated by the group known as GALOI, or Gays and Lesbians of Iran, the magnitude of the insult became unbearable. The act was beyond shameful. The infidels worldwide mocked Iran's loss and championed the efforts of the homosexuals. There was no doubt that many homosexuals in Iran, while denouncing the murderous act, still felt some vindication that Mahmoud Ahmadinejad was in fact terminated by one of the people he claimed did not exist in his country.

Unfortunately for members of GALOI and other homosexuals in Iran, Hadi Samani's vengeful hand proved to retaliate in a couple of very unpleasant ways. First, he had anyone who stepped out of the closet executed by public hanging. Additionally, he developed a law enforcement agency whose sole purpose was to defend Islam by reaching into that proverbial closet and dragging Iran's gays and lesbians kicking and screaming to their inevitable hanging. There were a rapid series of small group hangings as well as nationally televised executions by large group firing squads. These televised events featured audio narrators reading the Koran during the executions, and hailing the imminent coming of the Twelfth Imam. Also known as Imam Al-Mahdi, the Twelfth Imam was lauded to be the One to put an end to such immoral sexual perversions with the coming Caliphate. More homosexuals had been executed in the first six months of Samani's presidency than the entire reign of his mentor, Mahmoud Ahmadinejad. Gay rights activists worldwide had come to view A-Jad as Santa Claus in comparison to Samani.

As the newly elected president of Iran, Samani held his first cabinet meeting at a sacred section of real estate. It was there that all his cabinet members had signed their written pledge of loyalty to the Mahdi. Samani and his cabinet members were all faithful members of the Hojjatieh Society. Hojjat means 'authoritative source' and refers to the Mahdi.

This sacred site was not only the burial ground of his beloved mentor, Mahmoud Ahmadinejad, but it was also the spot where the tomb of Imam Reza, the fourth Shiite Imam—the only one that had been buried in Iran—lay in rest. The gravity and weight of purpose that enshrouded this first cabinet meeting was truly one of destiny and purpose that further validated the strong conviction that Samani held.

Samani was deeply convinced that it was indeed he who had been divinely chosen to pursue *taajil* in such a way as to see the glorious un-occultation of his beloved Mahdi on his presidential watch. *Taajil* is the sacred notion amongst the Shiite Islamic Twelvers that the return of the Twelfth Mahdi can be encouraged and hastened—but not forced or controlled—by the actions of the followers of the Mahdi. The Mahdi, or the Twelfth Imam, who had been in hiding, or 'occultation' since 874 AD, was the One who was to come and erase the yoke of humiliation from the collective neck of mankind. Of course, this process of the stripping of the yoke would naturally occur by the removal of infidels, or the quick conversion of them. As Samani saw it, the Caliphate was at hand and all that was needed was for the conditions to be arranged for the Mahdi to return and take His destined seat of authority in Kufa, Iraq. Iraq is the country of the Mahdi's birth, and it is to Iraq that He will return to administer his rule of the worldwide Islamic caliphate that Samani and the faithful had been feverishly preparing for with diligent, defiant, and faithful hearts.

Samani had not showered in three days. As he walked into his office he threw his work gloves, which reeked of garbage, promptly in the trash. Three days was sufficient, he reckoned, for the neglect of bathing. He was beginning to disdain his own smell. He had concluded that his abstinence from bathing and participation in the lowly activity of collecting trash, alongside the common government workers of Tehran, were for the moment complete. He had duly offered these actions of humility and sacrifice to his beloved Allah. Samani believed such expressions of humility were absolutely crucial for him to continue the sanctification process of his soul. He was convinced such actions were needed if he was to remain positioned to be, as he believed he was ordained, one of the 313 chosen believers who were to join the Mahdi in His return. The beloved Imam Al-Mahdi would return with his chief deputy, Jesus of Nazareth, by his side to help him initiate the commencement of the long awaited global Caliphate.

Samani showered quickly and proficiently in the manner with which he purposefully completed all tasks. After he dressed in his customary plain tan clothes, that to the western eye looked more like a generic version of a UPS uniform, he lit up his thirty-five inch hookah pipe. The expensive pipe was vastly ornate with diamonds and crystals. Samani began reflecting deeply about his rise to power. His countenance grew more pensive as his thoughts percolated. He continued pondering as he let the aromatic smoke of the vanilla flavored tobacco slowly leave his mouth and lead his breath into the air to transform the fragrance of his office. He gazed at the two digital counters that hung on the wall adjacent to the large window overseeing the city. One digital counter was placed there by his teacher, Ahmadinejad. The other, he had installed upon taking office. Ahmadinejad had ordered the installation of the first counter as a means to make tangible the reality of the coming of the Mahdi. It also stood to remind him and others of the importance of living each day in accordance with the expectation of His return. That counter displayed the cumulative days that had passed since the beloved Twelfth Mahdi had gone into hiding. As each day passed, and that number grew, so did the anticipation of Samani that the return was near and imminent. The second counter was of lesser significance but certainly dovetailed with the sentiment of the first. The installation of this counter was ordered during the first week of Samani's presidency to illustrate the absurdity of length in which the imperialist satanic entity of the west had been occupying Iraq, the beloved home country of the Mahdi. It had now been fifteen years and counting.

Although their role was extremely diminished and their official position was that they had pulled out, the Americans were still in Iraq. The country had since been thoroughly transformed economically and had become a site of extreme interest for tourists. Violence was now at a level only slightly higher than surrounding nations, and the economy had been growing with leaps and bounds. If Beirut was the city dubbed the Paris of the Middle East, Iraq had now become the country of the Middle East with an equal allure. It was now recognized by most as an emerging center of global commerce.

Samani, on the one hand, was very delighted by this prosperity, particularly because many of his Shia brethren, who were brutalized by Saddam for so long, were finally sharing in the wealth and prosperity. On the other hand, Samani resented that the Sunnis and the Americans had their hands in the affairs of the country.

It was Samani's mission to extract the western infidels from the Iraqi equation. If the Mahdi were to return to reign in the Iraqi city of Kufa, it would need to occur under certain conditions. Those conditions would certainly dictate the absence of the Americans and the Sunnis. The removal of these elements was just one piece of his efforts toward Taajil.

It was Samani's divine duty to encourage the conditions that would hasten the return of the Mahdi. Unfortunately for the people of Iraq, who had finally obtained a certain level of peace and security, one of those general conditions would be the intensity of chaos, war, and bloodshed. Even in the land of the Mahdi's birth and the site of his eventual rule. Samani was more than prepared to help facilitate these conditions.

Samani desperately missed his dear mentor. He still remembered the day he met him at a meeting for the Hojjatieh Society. The Hojjatieh Society was a secret fraternal group that was mystical in nature. The members devoted themselves to the cult of the Mahdi as led by the groundwork laid down by its founder, Sheikh Mahmoud Halabi. Ahmadinejad instantly recognized and rewarded Samani's intellect, enthusiasm, and devotion. Ahmadinejad made extra effort to take Samani under his wing and make it a priority to direct Samani in the ways of the Mahdi. As much as Samani despised Western Culture and Hollywood, he couldn't help but imagining, in his quiet moments, that his relationship with Ahmadinejad was much like that of Obi-Wan Kenobi and Luke Skywalker.

Hadi sat back in his leather office chair and exhaled some smoke from the hookah pipe while praying to Allah for the strength and wisdom to continue Ahmadinejad's legacy. He knew that Allah would pave the way for this to happen, and ultimately pave the way for the return of the Mahdi. As Hadi reached for yet another puff from his hookah he was interrupted by the ring tone of his cell phone, which was an Islamic prayer sung over acoustic guitars. It was brother Samere.

"Samere!"

Samani put down his hookah so he could fully focus on his conversation with Samere.

"Good morning President Samani!" Samere's excitement was audible.

"How are you today my friend?" Samere was Hadi Samani's most faithful employee, and liaison for all things Messianic.

"I'm well. I have good news. The construction has begun for the train line. It will be a direct line from Tehran to the Jamkaran Mosque. Just as you wished." Samere was extremely proud of his role in this progress.

"Excellent. I'm very pleased with the expedience with which this project is launching. The time of reckoning for the Zionists and the Arrogant Ones cannot come to pass until we have prepared the proper infrastructure needed to receive the Mahdi." Samani fully trusted Samere's leadership when it came to preparation and planning for the Mahdi's return.

"I fully agree. The Jamkaran Mosque is where the great Mahdi briefly appeared in 941 AD, and it stands to reason that we must increase the reverence brought to this site by the Iranian people as a pleasing gesture to the Mahdi."

"Yes. We must continue to create an atmosphere of honor and reverence in our great Republic to entice our Messiah's hastened return. He deserves our utmost efforts." Samani felt a slight chill in his bones as he thought of the return of his beloved Twelfth Imam.

"To that end, President Samani, I've increased funding three fold for the World Toward Illumination program, as was your wish. It'll be televised more frequently and for longer duration as to further increase the awareness of the Mahdi's near return in the hearts and minds of our people."

Samani was extremely pleased with Samere's work. He only wished his mentor could witness these amazing advancements. "Mahmoud would be proud of us. We must continue to honor his name and carry out his devotion to the Mahdi."

"We must." Samere, of course, readily agreed.

"We must indeed. Continue to keep me updated. The day is coming."

CHAPTER THIRTEEN

Somewhere along the streets of Detroit, Michigan

Blaze had felt fully ripe and alive. He could feel his true soul rising out of the mundane parameters that had confined him for so long. Blaze walked slowly down the cracked Detroit city sidewalks outside of Ramona's Diner. He wanted to take some time to think before meeting Bernie back at the office. The wind was howling and the vibrant autumn leaves swirled majestically around the worn concrete with a musical rhythm. He pulled the brim down tight on his grey wool scally driver cap to further keep his head from the wind. He cupped his hands tightly around his cigar, preparing to light it. He then sat on a non-descript city bench and observed the downtown Detroit passersby while he took inventory of himself. He loved this time of year; crisp, full, and emblematic of abundance and plentitude. Abundance of life, hope, and vision. His skin felt like his own again. The only action that was left that would fully make him feel one hundred percent again, would be to break the news to Diem that he was getting back into the game. *Diem…yeah….not quite sure how to attack that yet.*

He sat for several minutes without the ability to muster up a coherent string of conclusive thoughts. The rich, aromatic cigar smoke bellowed beautifully around him as he admired the profound art and aesthetic of the band glued at the base of the cigar. The smell of the cigar was half of the pleasure, and that smell took on unique nuances that differed from season to season. Cigar smoke mixed with autumn air was one of Blaze's favorite. Blaze had cut down to only a few times per week for this indulgence, and found that the infrequency magnified the pleasure.

Finally, the inevitable had been achieved. Relaxation simmered upon Blaze's tumultuous mind as he pondered some of life's dualities. Flashes of brisk, quick acts of violence jabbed within his mind against the juxtaposition of memories of familial harmony. Memories such as throwing Shane in the air, when he was a toddler, and catching him on his way down with a smile that melted all notions of pain and death. He recalled the sweet kisses that were given freely by Diem on their tenth year anniversary trip to China. He could feel her therapeutic lips on his cheek even as he exhaled the rich smoke that burned through the Madura wrapper of his Perdomo 20th Anniversary cigar.

His mind, playing ping-pong on the dichotomy of pleasure and pain, continued: fingernails yanked from the skin of the fingers of a terrorist's family member, a joyful hug from a two year old on Christmas day, blood gushing from the sweaty jugular of an embattled terrorist, the first base hit by an eight year old little leaguer, shrapnel embedded deep in a colleagues shoulder as he flounders to his tragic death, the joy of signing papers with Diem to purchase their first home, his heart beating at an inhuman rate as he dismantled a bomb in an Israeli movie house, his son Dennis showcasing his newfound skills on an electric guitar, a phone call from a colleague's wife asking him why he couldn't find a way to save her husband—and why he was forced to leave her husband's soon-to-be obliterated body behind.

He began to reach the beginning of the final puffs from his cigar and tried to encapsulate the totality of his thoughts. He focused in on acceptance. Acceptance of the sharp contrast. Life…Death… Life… Death… Life… Death. He lived this rhythm so that the world at large wouldn't have to. He was ready again to embrace it. He was ready for the fight. Ready for the call. Ready for the terror. Ready for the risk. Ready for the purpose. And he was finally ready to make this all now clear to Diem.

CHAPTER FOURTEEN

First Baptist Church of Detroit, Detroit, Michigan

The good Reverend Liam McCardle's morning started much the way his life had unfolded—full of contradiction and opposing sentiments. He had his worn, torn, and prolifically marked Bible open in one hand to the beloved Psalms, from which he started each morning's meditation. Resting in the clutches of his other calloused hand, even while the clock boasted the early time of 9:13 am, was his life's vice and soul's curse—whiskey; Johnny Walker double black blended scotch whiskey to be precise.

Pastor Liam McCardle undoubtedly and unequivocally retained a deep, searing passion for both of the items he held in his hands. He relied almost schizophrenically on the power of each item to bring him daily pleasure, to accentuate his joys, to aid as elixirs of life and also to powerfully neutralize, clarify, and mediate his pain.

Pain was more than a familiar friend to Pastor McCardle. It was an unrelenting force that had been so normal for him that it may have well been crafted into his DNA. After years of serving in the Police force's CTSA (Counter Terrorism Security Advisors) unit in his native Belfast, Ireland, he had learned to assimilate the pain of life quickly and efficiently. His living room wall was not big enough to host the photographs of all the fallen brothers he'd served with, nor the friends and relatives who had been unwilling participants in an ethnic fight that persisted like a never-ending virus.

Reverend Liam closed his eyes as he sipped from his glass of Johnny Walker Black. A half-melted ice cube lingered on his tongue and slowly disintegrated as his mind wandered from the provocative text of Psalm 151. Images of men he had shot in the heat of urban battle surged to the forefront of his mind. Young men. Maybe twenty or twenty-one, no older. He remembered distinctly one such man. A face he would never forget. It was in the heat of an operation when the young man had momentarily pulled up his black ski mask to wipe his brow. Liam saw and felt the intense trepidation in the young man's eyes. The terrorist's identity had been compromised and his position severely weakened.

Liam thought of his own son in retrospect as he downed another sip of Johnny Black. *Why Lord? Why were these young men so attracted to the violence? Why this young man and not my son?* He knew the reasons. He knew all about the depth of feelings, the long documented historical and cultural strains, the obstinate family ideologies and the clear, impassioned logic that hid behind, and fueled the fire for, the fighting in Ireland. His eyes circled back to the words of the Psalm as he sipped yet some more scotch whiskey prior to his 10:00 am marriage counseling session that he was quite unprepared to lead.

I went out to meet the Philistine,
and he cursed me by his idols.
But I drew his own sword;
I beheaded him, and removed reproach from
the people of Israel.

Pastor McCardle recalled how he fell to the ground that day with a bleeding, wounded shin as the young man spat in his face. The bullet had taken him down to the ground that day, leaving him vulnerable to the young IRA terrorist. Liam remembered how alert he felt at that moment with the young man hovering over him with a sense of absolute impunity and false victory. Liam's ability to think and act quickly in the heat of an operation was by far the greatest ability the good Lord had ever bestowed upon him. He remembered the curse words that hurled from the young man's lips as the kid spat on him. All the while, Liam's temperament remained untouched by the mockery. Instead, his situational agility rose to a heightened state of acute observation and patience.

The lifting of the black ski mask was the boy's fatal mistake. As the terrorist reached to wipe the sweat from his brow, Liam swiftly lurched up, and forward, to grab the kid's gun right out of his loose hand. In one unhindered, continuous motion he stared straight into the kid's countenance and shot him square in the head.

That recollection struck Liam McCardle with more intensity than he could handle on a Monday morning as he weighed the parallels between that memory and the last words of the 151st Psalm. He had drawn his enemy's own gun. He had put a bullet directly in his head—a modern day beheading. His stated goal was to uphold the honor, and remove the reproach, of his people of Ireland.

He remembered when that incident hit the papers in the days of The Troubles. He'd never forget his wife's tears as she threw a milk carton at him and screamed at him hysterically as if he had done something wrong in the ordeal. The heart of a woman, he even then knew, was a mysterious and altogether different thing than that of a man. To his wife Kathy, it was his fault. His fault that he wasn't a bloody mailman, or a carpenter, or some pencil-pushing attorney or business executive. It was his fault, he recalled her saying, that he had to aspire to work as a police officer. It was especially his fault that he chose to train for the CTSA. This was all his fault. To Kathy, the fate of the world was not nearly as important to watch over as was the fate of her beloved husband. It seemed to Liam that not a week had passed by in his nineteen years on the force in which she didn't beg him to quit. *Stubborn as I was, she should've known there was no talking to me back then.* An empty glass stared back at Liam as he held that regretful thought for a slight moment.

The irony of his pouring his third glass of whiskey prior to 10:00 am while reading the good book did not strike Pastor McCardle. What did occur to the good reverend was the irony of his wife worrying, for almost twenty years, that he'd become a casualty of the force, and yet in the end she was the one who died suddenly and painfully of pancreatic cancer. It was not an irony that was at all likely to shed light on, or make him cognizant of, the irony of his simultaneous drinking and praying. The reality of that irony would take an ever-distant back seat. Likely until he met his Maker.

CHAPTER FIFTEEN

Somewhere in the suburbs, Detroit, Michigan

"Bernie, pull over," Blaze blurted out as they were cruising down the road.

Blaze and Bernie were on their way back to the office after a lunch meeting with a client.

Bernie glanced at Blaze but didn't lighten his foot from the gas petal. "What? We have like forty minutes to get back to the office, prep the next case and get to our next meeting. What the hell do you want me to pull over for? Got a corned beef craving or somethin'?"

"Nah. Just shut up and pull into that candy store. I need to get some chocolate for Diem." Blaze knew he'd need to make an effort to get Diem into a mood where she would even hear him out on going back to his warrior life. Chocolate always constituted effort.

"Since when do you get all sweetheart on me midday?"

"Don't doubt me. I got strategies." Blaze wasn't about to explain.

"You ain't got strategies, you got stupidity."

"Another crack like that and you'll be realizing your own stupidity after I re-define enhanced interrogation techniques on your ass."

"Alright, make it quick. I don't think they're gonna have chocolate covered potatoes in there though."

"Very funny. You're killing me with the leprechaun humor." *If you're gonna bust my stones for being a Mick, at least be funny about it.*

The time bomb was indeed ticking. Blaze knew deep in his soul that the time of spousal confrontation was soon coming, and if he knew Diem, a little dark chocolate could go a long way—even if she later realized its strategic purpose. He couldn't do this civilian job much longer, and his soul ached on account of him knowing what he needed to do. McCardle was right. His nation needed him. And he needed to once again become the hunter.

The financial planning duo entered the chocolate shoppe and were immediately greeted by the enthusiastic owner, a well-groomed man with a friendly smile.

"Hello, thir, may I help you? I thust love that suit. Very handsome."

Wow. Holy flamin' purveyor of fine chocolate. The flamboyance was unabashed and quite comedic—especially the lisp and the exaggerated inflections. Unfortunately, it didn't do too much to help tear down any stereotypes. Blaze got a kick out of such characters.

"Thank you. Glad you like the suit. I, myself, would be just fine with a tee shirt though." Blaze smiled.

"Oh, I bet you would!"

Wrong response. Ouch. "Well, I just need something simple. A small collection of various dark chocolate truffles for the little lady. You know, the kind with different fillings. Gonna be dropping some life-changing bombs on her soon and this can ease the pain a bit. Know what I mean?" Blaze was trying to make this as quick and as simple as possible. He was hoping Bernie would not ask what the life-changing bomb was all about it. Luckily, Bernie barely heard Blaze's mention of it.

"Oh, yes, I do. My partner is the same way. A little chocolate and he is thust all ready for whatever I got to say!"

"Yeah, well, then I guess you're the guy to help me then. Whaddya suggest there cap'n?" A box of chocolates was all Blaze wanted, but he sensed he was getting a much larger experience during this purchase than he had asked for. He had a feeling Bernie would not help the situation.

Blaze caught Bernie with a juvenile smile on his face. Blaze almost lost it but was able to hold in his laughter. Luckily, he had been in enough tight situations around the globe that called for him to restrain the expressions of various emotions that he could handle withholding furious laughter. Even when confronted with a character that made Rupaul seem like John Wayne.

"You two got so much in common, maybe you should buy chocolate for each other." Bernie teased while showing a devious smile. All three men were on the verge of raucous laughter.

"Well, that'd be fine with me, but clearly he has a fine woman at home who needs it more!" interjected Mr. Happy Chocolate vendor. He was fully picking up every ounce of the nuance flying around. And he was eagerly having fun with it. You could tell this chap did this all day and it was an art form. Blaze would've bet he sold more chocolate than a hetero any day.

"Alright, alright, enough outta you Bernie or I'll make sure my friend here passes out your cell number to all his buddies." Blaze shot an elbow to Bernie and looked at the man purveying chocolate with an apologetic nod.

The man smiled widely. He was having fun with this verbal mischief.

"Oh, yeah, they'd thust love that! You better watch it there Mr. Bernie!"

This guy is a riot! God bless capitalism and the various mechanisms that propel it. "So what'll it be? You got a collection of chocolates for my broad or what?" Blaze really wanted to move this thing along and get what he came for.

"Broad? Oh thir, that has got to be offensive to her, don't you thay?"

"Nah, she knows I adore her. 'Broad' ain't no different than calling a guy 'dude', and you can call me 'dude' anytime you want—just don't call me *your* 'dude'." All three men began laughing hysterically.

"Don't flatter yourthelf! I got a beautiful partner already! Anyhow, I got the perfect mix of chocolates, for your, umm, broad..." The man laughed lightly as he began to pack up Blaze's box of chocolates.

The playful entrepreneur frolicked behind the counter and delicately arranged a small gold box with eight dark chocolate truffles of various types. A raspberry filling here, a lemon there, and some almond littered ones to boot. Blaze handed him his debit card and the chocolate master proceeded to gift-wrap the box.

"Thank you sir. You've got a wonderful store here and you're very kind, and I have to say, quite funny as well. I wish you all the success in the world." Blaze meant it.

Chocolate King laughed heartily and replied, "Well thank you thir! You're welcome here anytime! Even your grouchy friend can come! Take care of that broad of yours! We have new free thamples weekly! I thust know your broad will love them!"

Blaze and Bernie continued laughing as they began to exit the establishment. Bernie kept shaking his head in comedic disbelief of the entire exchange as he held the door for Blaze. They walked fast to the car. The two men got in quickly and shut their doors simultaneously.

Bernie quickly offered his assessment. "Looks like you got a new friend there Blazey boy. Seems like he definitely lights your fire."

"Shut up you jerk. He's a nice guy trying to make a living like anyone else. He's a frickin' quintessential small business success story. Probably would kick your white-collar ass anyhow. And bury you in chocolate. Then kiss you."

CHAPTER SIXTEEN

Federal correction institution, Fairton, New Jersey

This wasn't the first time. But Zack Batt sure as hell prayed it would be his last as he sat in reflection waiting for his visitor in the fenced outdoor area of the prison. The time prior, it was maximum security. This time he was being treated to minimum security. He wouldn't be in federal at all for this incident had it not been for his active, and rather fresh, parole status. Hell, he even got to be on the 'camp' side, which boasted a very non-prison veneer and was altogether less intimidating to visitors and inmates alike, at least in its visual design.

The hole was a surprise he did not expect or find amusing in the least bit. Cold, damp, and horrifying stone walls enveloped him in a six by eight foot fashion. A dilapidated steel crapper stared him down. A meager set of disintegrating bed sheets, with requisite soiling, taunted him with a mock welcome. Sunlight was bullied from entrance. Airflow was neglected from the cell's fraternity. Handcuffs escorted him out once a day for a brief hour of sunlight. Human contact was withheld. Diginity was a faint ideal. Loneliness, like an eternity's roll, caved his mind and swallowed his soul. Three damn days. All because there was no beds available upon his arrival.

He now sat patiently in the peaceful picnic area outside the camp's main core. The gentle breeze lapped against his face as Zack sat enjoying a cold Coke Zero, waiting for his visitor. It had been only two weeks since his arrival. It had been three days less than that when he was sprung from the hole and assimilated into "gen pop", or general population. It was a release that felt like a messianic resurrection from the gnarled depths of darkness to the breath of blinding light. Yeah, gen pop was that much better.

Zack was not a monster, but he was thoroughly troubled and screwed up beyond belief. His childhood alone produced enough issues for a shrink to be able to bill for decades in order to unpack. He wiped the sweat off of his forehead with the back of his right hand as he dropped his head into the clutches of his hands and thought about what got him where he was. *Domestic violence? That's not who I am. I was just trying to stop her from hitting me with a lamp. I wasn't trying to hurt her.* The judge didn't buy it. He was not impressed at all by Zack's clandestine, patriotic interludes.

Skinhead. History of violence. Gang associations. Prior time in maximum security—albeit brief. The guards were left scratching their heads when he'd gotten out early. Only Zack and his current visitor knew why and how someone who rendered another paralyzed from a street fight gone wrong could get out so quickly.

Zack lifted his head and found himself staring squarely into the eyes of his grin-faced, smart-assed visitor.

"What the hell kind of cockamamie stuff runs through your head? Uh? Why the hell do you always end up in a place like this only for a poor pathetic bastard like myself to fool himself into bailing you out?" Gallagher took no measures to temper his true feelings.

"Hi Chuck. Great to see you too you old artifact bastard." Zack expected such a greeting, and was completely un-phased by it. He was, however, very happy to see his proverbial wicked military stepfather from the CIA.

Chuck Gallagher had a soft spot in his heart for Zack Batt. Even though Batt didn't deserve a lick of his unsolicited mentorship, Gallagher felt an attachment to the wayward street thug. Somehow

Gallagher saw beneath his thuggery and his attitude to a redemptive quality waiting to emerge. He also recognized Zack's very real potential use to the US government. Zack was the prodigal son, time and time again—although he was light on the humility and heavy on the iniquity. He always apologized to Gallagher after each incident, but his commitment to truly change his ways was always ambiguous.

But Zack Batt was an undeniable asset of the United States government. Of course no one outside of the CIA inner circle could ever know it. If ever prodded, there was no chance in hell that the association between the two would ever be admitted to by anyone on Uncle Sam's side. Zack was one of the government's best private mercenary contingency assets. And Gallagher had honed him from the get-go for exactly that purpose.

"I'm gonna get your ass out of here Batt, but with a price of course. I need your help, and as always, your country will be highly grateful." Gallagher never let one of Zack's personal crises go to waste. The quid pro quo was an integral part of their relationship.

"What's it this time? Offshore interrogation? Need me to do another hit on a radical activist in Latin America? Not sure if I'm still your guy, seeing that I'm rotting here in prison." Zack still couldn't believe he was behind bars again. He swore he wouldn't screw up this time. He had made so much progress. Figures, it'd be another wayward woman that he'd tangle the wrong way with that would get him into trouble again.

"What's the story this time? Something about roughing up some broad? What the hell is wrong with you?"

"Trying to defend myself against my girlfriend."

"Aw, you poor defenseless bastard."

"Hey, bitch pummeled me with a lamp." He pointed to a barely healed gash on the side of his face.

Gallagher took Zack's face in his hand and turned it to get the best light. "Not so bad."

"Nearly knocked me cold."

"But you somehow managed to come back on her?"

"I—well—she had a broken lamp in her hand and was still charging, so yeah, I had to pop her."

"Which broad is it this time? That same whack job with all the jewelry in her face or that cute Armenian-Italian one? Helluva mix she's got." Gallagher could not keep track of Zack's women. For a veritable compulsive screw-up, Zack Batt still found a way to persuade hot women to spend time with him whenever he was on the prowl.

"Neither. A whole new ball of wax I don't care to explain, and hope to never see again. I suppose a mission would distract me from my disastrous luck with the ladies." This was true. Zack was at his best when he was in the thick of operational danger. When he was between assignments, somehow he wasn't as good at avoiding danger.

"Good. I'm glad to know where you're head's at now, because if it was latched onto some whacky broad, I'd be moving right along here and letting you rot in this cell." Gallagher did not chuckle. He was deadly serious. He needed Zack's head clear.

"So what's the angle this time." Zack was calm now and ready to get into the real deal briefing. His tone and facial expression made it clear to Gallagher that he was serious about jumping into a new mission.

"Aryans. Of a slightly different stripe." Gallagher knew this was gonna throw Zack for a loop.

Zack jerked his head quickly—mouth agape and eyes wide. He proceeded with his response, talking rapidly like a machine gun, as was his customary street-bred speech pattern. "Aryans? Damn, fighting them has historically got me into a hell of a lot of deep shit. I suppose now's as good of time as ever to wade back in though. What the hell do you mean by different stripe anyhow? We're talking about *Aryans*, right? There is only one damn stripe for an Aryan—white, European decent and nasty as hell." Zack was game, even though he was already confused as to what exactly this game was going to be.

"Not these ones. Except for the nasty part. These Aryans love

Allah and fashioned the name of their nation via a suggestion by Hitler and his buddies. I'm talking about the Iranians." Now Chuck knew he'd really be confusing the hell out of his young protégé.

"What the hell do the Iranians have to do with Nazis?"

"The word Iran means 'Aryan' in Farsi. The name came out of the many meetings Persians had with the Germans during WWII. Persians are just as Aryan as anyone in the Third Reich. And some of them are hell-bent on emphasizing their claim to the master race by targeting the Jews."

"Sounds like fun. An insane ideology meets an insane theology. When do I clock in and where is my employee handbook?"

"Let me pull my strings and get your ass out of here first." Gallagher knew Zack would be a perfect fit for this mission.

"Good. Please move fast on that pally. Look around the yard here. I'm not exactly with the honor roll here." Zack waived his arms motioning towards the lovely co-habitants he had been surrounded by.

"Oh, and you're so refined and full of dignity and scholarship? You got a friggin' spider web tattoo in your inner ear and you're griping about these fellas?" Gallagher cracked a smile.

Zack chuckled and gazed around the small grassy area that was littered with a scattering of old picnic tables and populated by inmates in bright orange jump suits sitting around with visiting friends and families. Zack and Gallagher were sitting to the side on a bench with their backs against a wooden fence.

"See that dude over there." Zack pointed to a large, muscular black man across the way in the visitor's area. "That's Mohammed. Original name, right? Right. Well, Mohammed has been in the system for twenty years and was one of the many African American inmates to convert to Islam. Mohammed has no qualms about making known his pure disgust for white people. He hates me more because I have Jewish blood."

"So whaddya expect? You're in federal prison not daddy day camp." Gallagher insisted on giving Zack absolutely no slack.

"Well, homeboy decided I was unworthy to work out in the weight room one evening and began throwing forty-five pound plates at me out of nowhere." Zack took a sip of his Coke Zero.

"What the hell did you do?" Gallagher always liked to hear about a good scrap.

"I grabbed a ten-pound weight and zipped it at him like a Frisbee. It nailed him smack dab in the side of his head. It was a modern day David and Goliath prison riot for sure. One up for the half Jew, and one down for the Philistine." Zack's face contorted with intensity as he finished detailing the story.

"Alright. I get the picture. I still think you deserve to be in here and that you ought to become Mohammed's personal assistant—if you know what I mean, but that's just me." Gallagher chuckled sadistically.

"Yeah, I love you too, you old bastard. How are those social security checks treating you?" Zack began chuckling along with his old hard-assed mentor friend.

"Damn good. I'm spending them like a good drunken sailor should with the pleasant knowledge that your generation will never have the luxury." More laughter emerged from both men simultaneously.

"You see that Rumpelstiltskin freak over there?" Zack waved his arm in the direction of an old man with straggly gray hair limping with a cane. He was trotting towards one of the picnic tables in his orange jump suit. "See how he is limping? Well, that limp is his little backtrack mechanism. You see, the other day I was getting out of the shower covered only by my towel. That old bastard came out right in front of me completely naked, with a full erection, and asked if I could help walk him over to the bench to get his cane. He had that look in his eye. You know, that I'm-game-if-you-are homoerotic prison look. I made it very clear that I wasn't game and that he better learn how to walk real quick on his own and get the hell out of my face, or he was going to be real damn sorry. He later came up to me in the yard and tried to play it off like he really had a legit need for help with his mobility. I tell you, I need to get on the outside, and quick. Or I promise you, I will hurt someone in here." Zack was not laughing. His hostility was clear and palpable.

"Alright, you sold me now with that story. Now I have compassion. I'll expedite the process. You'll be out in days." Gallagher was no longer laughing either. He wished such incidents on no man.

"So tell me more about this Persian Nazi thing."

For the next twenty minutes or so Gallagher gave the cliff notes version of the historical connection between the radical Islam of the Iranians and the radical anti-Semitism of the Nazis. Of course, Gallagher's vernacular made for an interesting and entertaining weaving of the tale.

He noted the decree made by the Reich Cabinet in 1936 exempting the Iranians from any of the restrictions of the Nuremberg Racial Laws due to the common Aryan ancestry of Iran and Germany. He explained the lavish gift from the German government to the Iranian people that consisted of over 7,500 books that were carefully selected to emphasize and reinforce the common heritage and Aryan culture that existed between the Iranians and the National Socialist Reich. "It was the freaks with the funny mustaches sending a literary French kiss to the whack jobs with the crazy beards".

Gallagher then went on to explain how Nazi literature constantly praised and referenced the virtue and commonality of the Shah of Iran and Hitler. The common, oppressed class of Iran felt a special kinship to Hitler and heralded him as one of the greatest men in the world for destroying a 200-years old plan of the Jews against nationality in the world, against nationalism, and particularly the Aryan races on earth. Hitler, they believed, had created a new day for the new world.

The two cultures had mutual admiration for the swastika. It had been a symbol for Persia for 2000 years before the birth of Christ and was viewed by Germans and Iranians alike as an indelible symbol of

Aryan triumph. It was not only the Persian under-class that embraced this Aryan mutuality, it was also the Persian elites and intellectuals who fostered the notion of Aryan racial superiority.

After a visit by the Persian ambassador to Germany in 1939 to meet with the German Chancellor, the Persians took to heart the German suggestion to change their name. Hence, Persia became Iran, the Farsi word for Aryan. At the time, Reza Shah proclaimed, "We considered Germany the chosen representative of this race in Europe and Iran its representative in Asia. The right to life and role was ours. Others had no choice but submission and slavery."

In the 1930's, the official Iranian Nazi party was born, also referred to as the Iranian National Socialist Party. At the mention of that, Gallagher warned Zack, "Well, wouldn't you know it, as anti-Semitism is now rearing its ugly old head of age-old hatreds again with a flame as fierce and as hot as it did in the thirties, the good 'ole Iranian Nazi Party is officially back and gaining strength and membership exponentially through the help of social networking websites."

"So what exactly do you want me to do? Now that I have officially been schooled on the back story to this match made in hell."

"We need to infiltrate the nuclear plants at Natanz, Esfahan, and Bushehr. These bastards are way too close to accomplishing their goal of forcing us all to meet our makers. We have a source on the inside. His name is Arash Jafari. We know we can trust him. He's been working for us ever since Reza Kahlili began spying for us. Now that Reza has defected to the US, Arash is pretty much the only asset we have over there that is producing.

"That said, there is only so much intel he will be able to feed us. In this race against time, we need more assets over there fast. These fruit bags in the Neo Iranian Nazi Party are well embedded within the nuclear plants.

"With your skinhead appearance and overall approach on life, you're going to have to hide your Jewish heritage and tuck away that small piece of you that is of English decent. And then you need to embrace that one fourth of your ancestry that hailed from Germany with a big smiling Nazi skinhead face. You're going to join the Neo Iranian Nazi Party. First, you will do it online and develop as many relationships as possible through social networking. The main relationship you will cultivate online is with a guy named Hamid. I'll get you his dossier. He's all gung ho on the Persian Aryan thing. More importantly, his cousin, who is also a NINP member, works at Bushehr. He's a researcher. He's our objective. When the time is right, you will make a trip to visit your new digital Persian buddies. Then the real fun will begin."

"Hacking away on a computer isn't exactly my idea of a mission. Hopefully I can get off the nerd and into the field quickly so I don't die of boredom. Who else is in on this?" Zack was thankful for the history lesson but more interested in hearing about the part of the mission in which he would actually engage the bad guys.

"Blaze."

"Blaze? I thought he was out? I thought he turned into a suit and was doing the civilian family man gig?"

"Yeah, well, the beast inside has come out again. He's back with a vengeance. Well, pending approval from his wife of course. But he's working on that." Gallagher smiled big as if he was gloating about his own flesh and blood.

"Now I'm excited. When Blaze and I get together, near death experiences and unexpected twists and turns become the order of the day. Hopefully we'll survive this one like the ones back in the day." Zack was smiling ear-to-ear and ecstatic with the thought of being re-connected with his old warrior pal Blaze McIntyre.

"I'll relay your enthusiasm. Now let me get the hell out of here and work on getting you out of this rat hole. Stand by for more instructions and a hotel address."

"Roger that." Zack was not only relieved to be sprung from the slammer, but amped up beyond belief about the reality of going on a new mission side by side with Blaze.

CHAPTER SEVENTEEN

Henry Ford Hospital, Detroit, Michigan

The tubes were everywhere. Blaze struggled to open his eyes. Once he did, he grappled with attaining some sense of cognition and consciousness. His vision was hazy and shifty. The pounding in his head was piercing and rhythmic. At first he had hoped that it was merely a hangover. If only that's all it was. The sight of the tubes negated that thought and sprinkles of lucidity began to emerge. No stranger to pain, Blaze instantly tried to discipline his mind to assimilate the agony he was feeling.

The nurse came in to give him another shot of narcotics.

"Did you have a nice visit with your family? Your wife is so beautiful and those kids are just darling."

Blaze cocked his head up to notice some flowers next to him that appeared to be dancing in his vision. He had no recollection of his family's visit whatsoever.

"Oh, yeah, thanks. I'm very thankful for them." Blaze was still trying struggling to make sense of why he was lying in a hospital bed.

"Well, I'm sure you are. Your wife told me stories about your past. She made it clear that this wasn't the first time you've found yourself in a hospital bed. This one though, she said, was unexpected since you're not presently involved with anything for the military."

The nurse smiled at Blaze with an obvious admiration and appreciation.

Blaze rendered a slight smile and a nod to acknowledge her comments while simultaneously signaling that he was too weak to respond fully with words. His mind began racing in a million different directions. The recollections were fragmented and volleyed back and forth between indiscernible visions of potential realities and apparent figments of his wildly inconsistent imagination.

The driving he remembered. He was by himself on his way home from the office. He remembered the flames. But they came from *inside* the vehicle. Blaze swore that happened before the crash. But yet he remembered more. Flames, that is. He was certain that these flames were *outside* the vehicle, after the crash. Swirling, furious, and shrouded with thick smoke and bursts of blazing red, purple and orange movement. He remembered Harry. Again, he struck. *Damn it.* And now, here he was in the hospital as a result of what he tried to rationalize as 'war-induced psychotic mechanisms' that his mind triggered randomly as therapy for his buried, tortured past. He knew it was common for his brain to play tricks on him. Hell, Harry had been dead now for almost *ten years*. It would only be natural for him to have occasional visions of him. But it sure as hell wasn't natural what he saw. Or had been seeing. Regularly.

The ghostly visitations started shortly after Harry passed away—from a nasty heroin overdose. Harry Saylor was one of Blaze's closest and most influential childhood friends. He walked to the beat of his own drum. When got into something—whether it was weight lifting or shooting heroin—he committed more fully than almost anyone Blaze knew. He was one of the most extreme and unpredictable people Blaze had ever met. Harry carried an intensity with him that was coupled with courage, bravery and unfortunately, recklessness. Harry also had one of the most eccentric and bizarre senses of humor you'd ever come across. Blaze remembered sitting in the cafeteria in high school and hearing a small explosion coming from the bathroom near the cafeteria. The women's bathroom. As the explosion went off Blaze glanced over at Harry. Harry cackled loudly. The laughter was devious and was emblematic of his juvenile hooliganism. He had commissioned a very popular and gorgeous cheerleader to set off a series of M80's in the bathroom. She was clean as a whistle in her scholastic reputation and would never draw the slightest bit of suspicion. He had devised the perfect cover. Harry's life was littered with such pranks and tomfoolery. Never a dull moment.

Harry was an outcast, a misfit, and a rebel. He was feared by many on two levels. Most feared his physical strength and reputation for fierce street fighting. Others feared that he'd recruit them as pawns in his various plots, schemes, and trickery. He had his own code. Looking back, it struck Blaze that Harry was much like Jack Nicholson's character Frank Costello in the film *The Departed.*

But as is often the case with those who possess strong propensities towards eccentricities and extreme behavior, self-destruction ultimately clawed its meat hooks into Harry's soul. From the first shot of the needle, Harry fell head over frickin' heals in love with H. He went from being a master of various domains and realms of life to becoming a dependent, sick slave within months. But it lasted for years.

Somewhere along the journey, Harry came to grips with the depravity of his life and sought deliverance. Although jail was a place he knew well, and he wore the ink to prove it, his conversion to faith was not one of the jailhouse variety. During a brief period of relative lucidity, during which Harry had been off smack, but on methadone, he and Blaze had gone mountain biking for the day. They had stopped to take a drink of water, and for Harry to smoke a cigarette, and they discussed life. But mostly they discussed death. Harry's death, to be precise. Harry may not have been high on heroin at the time, but he was far from recovered. His profound obstinance had been an asset in his fight against his addiction, but it was going to take more than that, and he knew it. Blaze knew it too.

Harry and Blaze sat down on a rock. Harry took a deep drag from his Camel cigarette. He then proceeded, in a moment of typical forthright vulnerability, to describe some episodes in his life in which he saw angelic visions. Harry explained that while he was using heroin, and was fully under the drug's control, that the angelic voices felt like torture and mockery in a sick psychotic sense. He did not recognize them for what they were. It wasn't until after his last stint in the joint, where he was forced to detox, that Harry finally saw the angels with his eyes wide open, even if not everything was clear.

Although the visions were for the most part fragmented and unclear, a host of things were clear about the mysterious angelic appearances. They were terrifying. They were from God. They warned of Harry's future death. They lamented the future of the world's system. And they were real. So real, in fact, that Harry, while sitting there on the rock, amidst the scintillating scenery of the surrounding woods, enjoying his cancer stick, spoke plainly about these experiences with a visible fear in his eyes. He detailed the transformation that his soul went through as a result of these terror-filled, yet redemptive, angelic hauntings. He professed to Blaze that although the furious demons of his heroin addiction were still very much battling for the domain of his affection, he had given his soul to God that very afternoon as a result of their conversation.

When Harry finally lost his battle with heroin, Blaze took deep comfort in the notion that his friend had won the protection of his eternal soul through his submission to the Almighty. That submission was something he was constantly reminded of by the frequent, haunting encounters with Harry's ghost. These visits hovered around Blaze's consciousness constantly and the visions seared his soul with a teasing and brazenly prophetic urgency.

On this occasion, Harry's ghost did not arrive with the preferred temperament with which Blaze would choose to have him return. He arrived with agony, fury, indignation, and murderous pleading. This particular sighting—the one that prompted him to end up in a hospital bed—was extremely violent and frantic. Harry's intrusion into Blaze's vehicle was sudden, urgent, and altogether jarring. The pieces of Blaze's memory were starting to join together as the narcotics they pumped through him loosened their grip.

Before the crash, Blaze was thinking about Diem and his children. He was praying that they would remain safe in this increasingly uncertain world. He knew first hand about the fragility of the globe. Hell, he'd been commissioned to gallivant around it while neutralizing unseen bad guys for over a decade. Also weighing on his mind were the various events and political changes he had been hearing about in the news. He had been stringing the developments together in his mind as he filled in the gaps with all the intel he possessed from years in the field. He was convinced by the rise of global villains coordinating against the welfare of the United States that something more and more wicked was this way coming.

It was when his trepidations and meditations focused on this ominous thought that he peered upward as he drove. He then saw the droplets of blood slowly dripping onto the dashboard after originating magically out of thin air. He blinked several times, banged his chest to test his alertness, and cursed incessantly for several seconds before he witnessed a wrist dangling, again out of thin air. The wrist hung from the interior roof of his vehicle just a few feet in front of his eyes. There was a star of David tattooed on it and a nail had been driven through it. It continued to stand alone in the air dripping blood like some whacked out cartoon image—one that would freak out even the most wasted of acid dropping slackers seeking such a visual thrill.

Blaze had swerved several times while trying to maintain composure. He tried to assure himself that this vision was nothing but a result of his sleep deprivation, his stress, and years of seeing things in war that no man ought ever need see. He was wrong. And he knew it as soon as the wrist revealed the body connected to it. The body was Harry's earthly body in ghost form. The image was like the holograms he saw in old sci-fi films; like Princess Leah emerging from R2D2.

Harry's ghost began speaking in a violent, ranting gibberish. Blaze remembered some phrases and general themes that Harry was shouting about, but nothing real specific. He recalled many passages quoted from the Old Testament book of Ezekiel, but couldn't remember which ones or even if they were quoted in their entirety. Harry repeatedly heeded Blaze to be a watchman. That, he urged throughout the visit. Harry raged about a coming war and spoke in strange ways about evil rising in the nations.

He then began pontificating on personal things that related to Blaze. He seemed to be consoling Blaze and urging him to embrace his loneliness and sadness. Blaze had not a clue what the hell he was referring to. Harry told him to move on with honor. He spoke about Blaze's family as if they were no more. This confused Blaze and horrified him to the core.

Harry also railed against world leaders in his raving rants. The ghost continued on and on, eventually weeping for the poor, the lost, the addicted, and the foolishly proud.

And as Blaze recalled, almost fully recovered now from the haze of narcotics, Harry had disappeared mid-rant as furious flames emerged within the vehicle. He then exploded before completely disappearing. It was in that sudden burst of flames that Blaze had passed out and smashed his vehicle into a tree. Blaze always knew he never wanted to be a tree hugger. He could now say he had tried it, and it wasn't a lick of fun. Nor were the lingering messages he wished he had not internalized from the ghost of his long dead friend.

CHAPTER EIGHTEEN

Laredo, Texas

Juan Herrera was fat. Because he was fat, and was always fat, those around him suffered from the cruel wafting stench of his demonic body odor. He was teased practically from the time he was in diapers. Teasing eventually led to bullying, and bullying took the form of real, street-thug issued beat-downs by the time he became a young teenager. By the time he was sixteen, Juan was determined to reverse this dynamic and find a way to exert not only his masculinity, but also his forceful dominance over others to compensate for his feelings of inadequacy. The deep-seated feelings of inadequacy that plagued his youth did as much damage to his psyche as his body odor did to all who came close to him. Now eighteen, Juan was full of piss and vinegar.

Juan loved playing Assassin's Creed on his XBOX. Sure, it was an older game, but he took what he could get, when he could get it. This game was handed down to him from a cousin. Juan's family was royally screwed up and he knew it. His father was a ghost that disappeared at Juan's earliest memories. He was barely around past his initial sperm donation.

The section eight housing was deplorable and most of the time Juan was alone. His younger sister was eleven and usually was at daycare or a relative's house. Juan got the privilege of staying home by himself from age thirteen on, and primarily spent the time in a daydream world of video games and rap music. When he did get out, he would hang out with the only two older kids who accepted him in the neighborhood. They still teased him of course, but they would beat the living shit out of anyone else who dared to tease him. He was *their* punching bag, no one else's. This gave Juan a sense of a safe cocoon of protection he had never felt before in his life. He would do anything these kids would ask. They were the only people in the world that ever stood up for him. His mother couldn't even stand up for herself, let alone him. She was a junkie whore, and Juan knew it, and understood the horrible implications of his mother's addiction as early as age five.

When Juan went out to the clubs and cantinas across the border into Mexico with his mentors in the neighborhood, he was able to escape the fact, and temporarily forget, that his mother and all her stupid bullshit even existed.

Juan's mentors were all in their early twenties. Juan was their young protégée. They would protect him even when he would begin to provoke fights with other kids. This was entirely new for Juan. He was used to being bullied, not doing the bullying. Now, he was insulated from repercussion and could feel the invigorating rush of pushing others around, just as he was pushed around his whole life.

He began to feel like some sort of Superman, and he loved the feeling. His acts became more and more brazen, and his respect amongst his buddies, and anyone that now knew him, began to grow exponentially in a very short period of time. It was only a few weeks ago when he commanded the respect and attention of some serious players across the border.

Juan was kicking ass at Assassin's Creed as he waited for the orders from his new business associate, an anonymous member of the Mexican Gulf Cartel. Juan was wooed and lured with all kinds of promises of money, glory, prestige, and affiliation, but none of that was even really necessary. Sure, he wanted to make some money to take care of his sister and get her and himself as far away from that whore of a mom he was cursed with, but he would have agreed to work for the cartel regardless. He had come to love the feeling of violence, regardless of where it pointed, because he internally used it as a reconciling force for all the shit he had been through in his life.

The order he was waiting on would be his initiation directive and he couldn't have been more stoked to get going on it. He had no idea what the target had done to deserve the hit, and he did not give a shit at all. He had a buddy, who introduced him to the cartel, who was ordered to do some real crazy shit. Straight-up beheadings. No shit. *Heads rolling on the streets of the freakin' United States of America.* Juan could only imagine the thrill.

The only thing he knew about this hit was that he was one of many new and recent recruits that were being commissioned to do hits on a particular group of people in the states. That's all he knew. He didn't know the common affiliation or the offense that earned the targets their brutal consequence. He fantasized that it would be a heroic, high profile hit like the one that was attempted on the Saudia Arabian ambassador back in 2011. If Juan got such a job, he swore he wouldn't screw it up.

Finally, his cell rang.

"This is Juan."

"Juan, pay attention. The address for the target will be delivered to you shortly, along with a description. You'll be given a van with a motorcycle inside of it, and clear instructions. Your instrument will also be in the van, with instructions. Use it carefully or it will harm you as well. You'll need to plan some reconnaissance time to successfully execute this job. Observe your target thoroughly before you attempt the mission. Failure on an initiation order could result in your own elimination. Remember that."

The messenger hung up and Juan was simultaneously excited, jacked, and about to soil his boxers. An electricity surged though his veins like he had never felt before in his short life. He could not wait for the instructions to come. It was time to stop playing video games and get in the real game.

CHAPTER NINETEEN

The office of Bernie Miller, Detroit, Michigan

"It's almost 10:00 am and you're just now getting your keester in the office? Did the whiskey get the best of you last night you incorrigible Mick?"

Bernie was in rare form for a Monday. Blaze could feel his balls breaking before he even set foot in the building, let alone found his way inside the office to hear the taunt of Bernie's blue Monday office banter. Civilian business life had left its proverbial track marks on Blaze. It had taken a toll. Blaze had resolved to cut the cord. Sure, he hadn't exactly told Diem yet, but that was all right, he could do a test run on Bernie.

"Yeah, yeah, I know pally. Just sit your overgrown German ass down cuz I gots to talk to you about some stuff." Blaze knew that trying to get personal and serious with Bernie was much like trying to explain quantum physics to an infant. It was going to be tough.

"What stuff? You still crying all night from your imaginary nightmares of battles gone wrong in lands far away?" Bernie held deep respect for Blaze's honorable exploits for his country. The problem was that the respect was so deep that it never surfaced. Only sarcasm, half-brained wit, and straight up idiocy actually surfaced.

"Yeah, that's it pal, and your shoulder looks as good as any to cry on. Bring it in here for the real thing and give me a big giant man-hug." Blaze was right, this was definitely gonna be tough.

"Alright, alright, cut it out you bastard…or I'll take you down to that chocolate shop to go be with your friend." Bernie's charm and humor never seemed to surprise. It was always out of line and out of control.

"You really are gonna burn in hell, aren't you?"

"Easy, I told you already I have no tolerance for the theological stuff before noon. So break it to me Blazey boy, what's the matter?" He wanted the meat of the talk now.

"I'm getting' out partner. I'm getting' out and I'm going back in."

"Back in what pal? The nut-hut? The looney-bin? What the hell are you even talking about?" Bernie knew exactly what Blaze was talking about. He was half wishing Blaze was full of crap, and half being his normal ball-breaking self.

"I'm talking about ending the lie I've been trying to tell myself that this racket is gonna work for me. It's been fun. Really. But I'm done. I've been slowly dying inside ever since I began doing this. I ain't a salesman and I ain't a financial advisor. I'm a damn warrior, through and through. There's no getting around that." Blaze wasn't sure Bernie would really understand, but he was pretty sure Bernie would respect his decision.

"So what are you gonna do then, uh? Go start some wars in third world countries? Go play GI Joe all around the damn globe until you feel good about yourself?"

"It ain't like that pal. War is a growth industry in this day and age and I'm an opportunist. And I'm a friggin' patriot." He spread his hands out in an appeal for understanding, and then waved his partner off when it was clear he wasn't getting anywhere.

"Alright, I know, sorry for breaking your balls, but whaddya expect? You get what you get with me, you know that. I understand what you're saying. You gotta do what you gotta do, and for you, I do see that this really is what you gotta do. You have been a lousy drag around here lately anyhow."

The two men laughed and continued filling each other in on both the vitally important happenings in their lives, as well as sharing some of the completely irrelevant and useless thoughts that sometimes enters the minds of strange men who are rapidly approaching middle age.

Blaze resigned on the spot. Bernie accepted the resignation and wished him luck in future endeavors. The blessing, of course, came with additional friendly verbal abuse, sarcasm, and comedic ball-breaking of a high order.

Blaze said his good-byes to his ball breaking business partner. He then proceeded out the door to prepare himself to greet his wife at dinner and somehow explain his utter excitement over his newfound unemployment. Somehow, just the thought made him feel like his balls were breaking yet again.

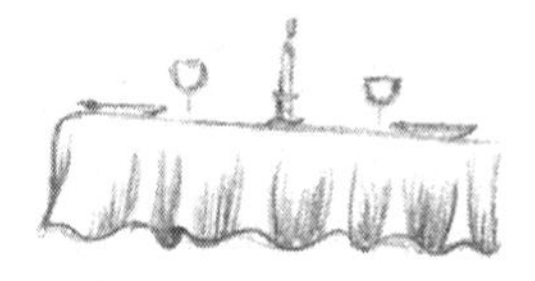

CHAPTER TWENTY

Cliff Bell's Restaurant, Detroit, Michigan

Diem's smile had eased as she took the last sip of her first glass of Pino Grigio and stared into the strong contours of Blaze's face and oceanic blue eyes. The gift-wrapped box of chocolate didn't hurt in easing Diem's smile either. Her almond skin upheld her smile with a distinct beauty that was cradled perfectly by her surrounding black hair.

Blaze was already a sip or two away from finishing his glass of Blanton's bourbon on the rocks and he could tell Diem liked seeing him loosen up. The conversation, thus far, had been light. Diem enjoyed Blaze's recollection of the fine merchant from whom he purchased her chocolates. Blaze ordered a well-done eight-ounce filet mignon accompanied by potato gratin, surrounded by wild mushroom cream and balanced out by blanched asparagus. In contrast to Blaze's turf, Diem chose a delectable arrangement of grilled Atlantic salmon supported by Israeli couscous all embellished by fried okra and tomato saffron broth. The lovely couple's appetites were burning as they digressed into teenage-like flirting. And they were hungry as well.

Without warning, Diem's tone and facial expressions telegraphed deep concern and care. She couldn't help but feel the need to address

Blaze's recent behavior. Her smile disappeared and she put her hand on Blaze's as she made her thoughts known. "Blaze, you need to know, that I've not been the same since your accident. I'm thoroughly worried about you. I wonder about your mind. Seeing visions of Harry? All this mythical religious stuff? Are you okay? What goes on inside your head?"

"Diem, I'm fine. Really. Relax."

"Look, I know you don't let me in on everything you're thinking. But, you could've been killed. I know you've been places and seen things I can't imagine. I know you'll always carry a lot with you, but can't you someday be somewhat close to normal? Will it always be like this? Can you at least let me in so I can try to help you?" Not knowing usually helped her cope, but now, the not-knowing was beginning to tear at her sanity.

"Diem, don't worry yourself over me. These are the crosses I carry. I was designed to carry these crosses. We all have ours to bear. Mine were specially designed, as am I. As for being close to normal…."

Blaze's eyes shifted nervously peering from one end to the next of Cliff Bell's fine dining establishment. The pleasing rhythms of the live jazz band performing that evening helped to fill the conversation void as Blaze fought for the courage to speak his tortured heart. Diem stared lovingly and waited patiently for him to struggle through his words.

Blaze continued "…this is just not me. The whole *normal* thing. The whole *regular guy* act. I know it sounds dramatic and ridiculously barbaric, but I will say it again. I am a warrior through and through. I've not been simply slowly dying inside, but rather I've been getting murdered inside with every passing day. I can't ignore the overwhelming drive and urge of my heart to once again serve my duty. To fulfill my true purpose. Diem, I'm going back in." Blaze gazed in her eyes as the bomb was dropped. He tilted his head downward as he braced for the fallout.

Diem's face lost color and she sat staring at him, frozen, for several seconds that lingered like a multitude of incomprehensible eternities. Her wine glass slowly slipped through her fingers as she managed to, at the very last minute, save it from crashing to the table. She knew this day would come. She could sense it in his voice more and more as of late. Drudgery was eating him alive. Normalcy and mundane living did not wear well, or at all, on Blaze McIntyre. For some unknown reason of divine insanity, it was pain, chaos, extreme risk, and strategic violence that wore well on him. She hated this truth as much as she loved the man for whom the truth befit.

Diem suffered a quick, dashing moment of internal wrangling. She wanted to simultaneously cross her arms, literally and figuratively, and refuse the idea all together. But at the same time, she sympathized with the impact of his realties and she wanted to nurture him through his resurrected path. After her thumb and index finger reclaimed a reasonable grip on the stem of the wine glass, she finished now her second glass before mustering up a response to Blaze's pronouncement. Jazz music filtered through the air like a comedic tormentor all the while.

"How could you make this decision without talking to me? What do you mean you're 'going back in'? Who did you talk to? You didn't quit your job with Bernie at the firm... *did you*?" Blaze's guilty countenance signaled the obvious. "Have you thought at all about Shane and Dennis? About *me*? Do you want them to be fatherless? Is this how you show your devotion to me? By sentencing me to the inevitable life of a widow?" Diem's tirade drew the stares of other diners and the attention of the waiter. Diem knew she was causing a scene. She knew her protest was ultimately impotent. She began to calm.

Blaze took a deep breath, the kind he would take in the heat of battle when his steps continued swift, silent and effortless as he approached an unsuspecting target. He wished he could tell her differently. He wished he could live differently. Work differently. Be different. He spoke slowly and softly, " I didn't make this decision alone. I've been wrestling with this issue for many months. I've brought it to God in prayer. I've talked through it endlessly with Pastor McCardle. And I finally discussed it with Chuck Gallagher." Blaze knew the mention of that last name would ignite a new volley of anger from Diem.

"Well, of course Chuck Gallagher is all for it. He doesn't have a family. What does he know about this decision?"

"Diem, he knows me. And so does Pastor McCardle. And I believe, so do you. I know this hurts. I know this isn't what you want. I wish I could say it wasn't what I want, but I don't know how to make myself not want to do what I'm convinced deep within my soul I was born to do. I'm convinced this is my calling and duty. My integrity and honor will be fleshed out by my living this calling." Blaze felt a surge of truth burn through him as he spoke his heart.

"Do you know the terror *I lived with* every night? Tossing and turning wondering if I'd get a call to hear your voice? Or, if the stars aligned, maybe we'd talk on Skype so I could see your face? Only to then wait in vain for hours of silence. And then I'd pray all night for you while I cursed your name at the same time. And the boys? Do you know what it's like to constantly revise your response and back track your previous answer when they ask when Daddy is going to be back? Where's daddy? Why can't he be home more? Do you have any clue what that's like? Do you know the joy and peace that has come to me since you've been home and the boys have been seeing you on a consistent basis? Do you know how important it is that you're more than a voice on the phone to them? Do you?" She felt her frustration recede, as she was able to vent each bullet point of her list of previously unspoken grievances.

Blaze had heard every word she said, and he felt her pain deeply. But it did not change anything. "My love for you and the children is unquestionable. I would fight a thousand armies to protect you and the boys. I love spending time with them, and I'll continue to spend time with them. Extended quality time in-between missions. Diem, I need to do this. I can't fight it any longer."

"So now I need to fight it instead? So I get to be the one who is home, alone, cursing the country I love because it has become my husband's mistress?" She knew she sounded a tad absurd, but she truly felt a deep jealousy of Blaze's passion for serving his country and ridding it of its enemies.

Blaze sighed gently and took Diem's hand. His eyes penetrated hers as he gently removed a strand of hair from her eyes. He leaned forward and kissed her lips gently. While his left eye shed a slight tear, he passionately assured Diem. "No one, or nothing, takes your place. Not a one. Not a thing. You know that."

And with that, she became disarmed. And her resolve to resist was shattered. She knew who he was. A warrior through and through. And it was time to be a warrior's wife, once again.

The wind was chaotic that night. Much like the perpetual state of Blaze's soul, or the world around him for that matter. He could hear the trees flailing with momentum and vigor as he lay on his back enshrouded by their king size bed. Diem laid her head on his chest and reveled in a sense of serenity and bliss.

They had made love with a wild, combusting energy. A whirlwind of emotions had sprung from deep within each of them as their souls also intertwined. Their bodies thrusted rhythmically in search of each other's pleasure and delight.

After satisfying the itchings and twitchings of their flesh, and the misgivings and forgivings of their hearts, the warrior and his wife were one. Her soul lay at rest, while he slept with one eye open as his mind raced frantically. He was eager for the next step. But anxious. Blaze McIntyre had an eerie sense that the road ahead would be fraught with snares and traps that would emerge in entirely new and frightening ways.

CHAPTER TWENTY-ONE

The Kremlin, Russia

He had kept the mug. It sat boldly on the shelf in his office, on the wall adjacent to his desk. The proud Russian president stared at the mug in a reverent and worshipful way as he stood beside his desk allowing his body to lean lightly against the bookshelf. Every time it caught his eye he felt a jitter and stir deep within his soul. For Maksim Koslov, a rigid hearted-man in his late forties who had never taken a bride, the jitter and stir was the closest he every came to feeling love. And love he indeed did have—a tremendous love for the skull-shaped mug and all that it meant to him; his legacy, his heritage, his future, and the destiny of his beloved Mother Russia.

Discipline and diligence were characteristics that were woven into the fabric of Maksim's being; trademarks, that in his mind, were the guard rails that had enabled him to fulfill the meaning of his name—"the greatest." He never saw the meaning of his name as irrelevant and mere trivia. He endeavored, from as early as his boyhood years, to live up to it. His imagination as a young child surpassed that of all his peers. He, even at the young age of six, was mesmerized by Russian history, particularly that of the great Czars, with such an intense, visceral fascination, that his family often held him in greater esteem above his siblings. They highly encouraged Maksim's dreams to someday become a great warrior of Mother Russia: a warrior and a leader. And, whether they knew that they were fostering the notion or not, a Czar.

Maksim always started his day with a review of its agenda. He coupled this with other meditations. This took place during his coveted morning quiet time in his office. In this solitude he often found himself studying the czars of Russia's past. He also focused on strengthening his knowledge of his Scythian ancestors. Both threads served to inspire Koslov in his ongoing aspirations. This office time was brief but meaningful. Usually thirty to forty-five minutes at most. On this particular morning, as he stared at the mug that was a physical symbol of his dominance and ambition, he lamented that his quiet time was over as he readied himself for his morning swim.

Maksim made his way to the pool within a few minutes and wasted no time jumping in. He assumed a strong pace in no time at all. Maksim's mind was racing in a myriad of directions as he swung his arms in a precise arc with perfect rhythm. The water temperature of the pool was perfectly set at seventy-two degrees and he was engaged in an unusually vigorous swim. His heart was brilliantly beating and the currents of his mind mimicked its pace and intensity. He reminded himself to be measured with his excitement so as not to misstep. Maksim was ever-cognizant of the folly of emotionalism and its potential to cloud objectivity and derail action. No one could ever accuse Czar Koslov of emotionalism—fervor and spirit, yes, but not emotionalism.

However, he was so unusually pleased with the rapidity of unfolding events that aligned with his plans, that, he pondered, for this particular day it was quite possible that his emotions may truly gain a foothold with him.

He had reached the center of the pool and was swimming over the painted image of a bear imprinted at the bottom of the pool. He loved that image. It was a design that he had replicated from an ancient Scythian artifact he had acquired. His Scythian heritage was one of his most profound interests and Scythian motifs were present in many of the items in his vast art collection. The source artifact was a golden warrior helmet with a bear sculpted upon it. The bear painted on the pool's floor was flawlessly done. He had demanded that precise image be painted on the pool floor in the Kremlin so that he would be reminded, each morning as he swam, of the emerging strength and power of the country he so loved. Russia had once again become the bear. It was a long, twisted, and sordid path, but one worth taking.

Maksim completed his swim and hurled his sinewy, muscular body out from the pool. After sufficient drying, he made his way to the breakfast room covered by his robe. There were no scheduled guests to join him this morning, so a robe would be fine for him to take his breakfast in. The staff heeded his request that American jazz music be played as he ate. This morning it was primarily Miles Davis, but a dash of Coltraine was mixed in for good measure and strong impact.

Maksim's mind was jogging backwards as he slammed steaming black coffee down his throat to chase his last bite of toast. *It's furiously wonderful how events have transpired. How circumstances have given way.* The sounds of John Coltraine prominently filled the air. *Damn, I do love good jazz.* This thought was a trite interruption of his glorious recollection of his rise to power. But, yes, Maksim did love jazz. It was the only thing he found redeemable of American art and culture. *The Americans. What a sad story they've become.* He dabbed a tickling bead of water from his hairline with the sleeve of his robe. His mind then again became transfixed on the sequence of events that led him to the Kremlin, where he so happily enjoyed eggs over easy at the moment.

He had become a reluctant fan of Vladimir Putin for a time. Putin had set in motion many actions that Koslov later aspired to perfect and intensify. He had watched with glee as Putin systematically dismantled all traces of Boris Yeltsin's progress toward democracy, free elections, freedom of religion, and free market enterprise. It had eventually become difficult to believe that Yeltsin had any role in encouraging or grooming Putin, particularly as Putin maneuvered to erase the election of governors and instead appointed all eighty-nine of them himself. Koslov felt a tickle of jealousy of that move as it served to mark the evolving narrative of Russia's history. A narrative Koslov wanted to earn credit for. A persistent narrative that embodied the nation's character once described as a "riddle wrapped in a mystery inside an enigma" by Winston Churchill. The narrative was not entirely disagreeable under Putin's rule as Maksim would assess. Just too tame and slow in its approach. Maksim had in mind a timeline for Russia's re-emergence on the global stage that was more broadband and less dial-up. It was that crucial difference that led to Putin's necessary demise.

He likely couldn't have pulled off the coup without the help of his lovely, disgruntled friends of the Solntsevskaya brotherhood. He couldn't thank Putin enough for cracking down on these thugs and jailing many key members. Those hard-line, law enforcement actions, although done more to protect political power than to smoke out lawlessness and corruption, helped Maksim solidify an enemy of his enemy. And they became Maksim's friends real quickly as Putin declared himself the enemy of the Solntsevskaya brotherhood strain of the Russian mafia. It was a great boasting right for Putin. But little did he know that the enemy he made would help initiate the coup that would leave him taking a dirt nap.

It was only 6:15 am as Maksim completed his breakfast. He savored the last few notes of the Miles Davis track that had been playing as he made his way into his art studio. He would spend the remaining forty-five minutes of his pre-workday routine there until 7:30 am rolled around and the day would begin to more thoroughly engage him.

Maksim was unusually gifted at many things. Whether it was business, communication and the art of persuasion, individual sports of a high-octane physical nature, writing, or political prowess, Maksim was no stranger to various states of excellence. Painting was no different. He had dabbled in painting as a teenager, but didn't excel at it until his political career began to blossom. He had found that the busier and more complex his political career became, the more therapeutic and necessary his painting became. Along with morning swims and evening kickboxing sessions, the painting was a tremendous release valve for Maksim.

Maksim's mind was often a pile of raw thoughts and ideas during the onset of each painting session. He often likened his mind to a sausage factory as he would paint, swim, or kick box. Every event, thought, pending decision, and handful of variables floated around his head in an ugly, messy sea of simultaneity and disarray. But like the ugliness of making sausage, when the process was over, he emerged from the other side with a proverbial eatable product—however unhealthy in its eventual effects—in the form of a clear, decisive mind. This morning was no different. His morning swim began the process, and the painting he was now applying effort to would likely complete the circle of his thoughts. When his aides would ask him how swimming, painting, or kickboxing was on any given day, he often replied, "the sausage is complete." He never explained. He just let them stand there perplexed and smiling awkwardly.

This morning would constitute his second session on this particular painting, and he reckoned he would need at least three more sessions before it was due for a frame. It would be, as was his custom, an extremely ornamental gold frame. This was precisely the way he envisioned his Scythian ancestors to have packaged their art. The fascination and excessive use of gold was a key emphasis in Scythian culture. Maksim honored this tradition.

In regard to central and definitive motifs of Scythian culture, the horse was undoubtedly one of the most prominent. It is widely attributed that the Scythians were one of the first, if not *the* first, groups to tame and ride horses in Central Asia. It was the development of their equestrian skills that enabled the Scythians to become monstrous warriors and conquerors of an unquenchable nature. The horse thus became a strong and clear symbol of a voracious appetite to conquer. This was his inspiration and purpose for conveying the glory of the horse through his painting. If he did not think it such a lowly and detestable art form, he might just consider getting the symbol of a horse tattooed on him.

Maksim sipped from his coffee mug as he allowed a momentary pause from his painting efforts. His mind became focused on the details of how he conquered the Kremlin and swiftly eliminated Putin.

The impetus for his coup had been a statistic that had been released at the time. It was Putin's second reign of power, to which he re-emerged after Medvedev's term was up. Years prior, in Putin's first reign of power, a poll was taken of the Russian people that indicated one in four citizens would actually vote for Stalin if he was alive and running for president of Russia. At the time, the world was shocked by the implications.

By the time Putin re-emerged for his second reign, the Chechen problem had grown and persisted beyond a controllable grip. This thwarted the hope that Russia's increased coziness with Iran would somehow serve to help diffuse the Chechen problem. This reality drove the Russian people to desire safety and strength above all else, regardless of how iron the fist that ultimately ruled them might be. When the same poll was taken again during Putin's second reign, it revealed the results that three in four Russians would vote for Stalin if he had been alive and running for president. This prompted increasing suspicions in the international community about the state of the collective Russian mindset.

For Maksim, the survey results were a glowing green light and an electrically charged trigger for his long-schemed revolutionary coup. He knew that at least three in four Russians were eager for his rule; his iron clenched fist. It was his time to strike.

The brush gently stroked the canvas as fine hues of brown began emerging. These hues formed free-flowing hair on the horse image. As his mind continued to linger, with an enormous sense of inner satisfaction, on the sequence of events that brought him to power,

Maksim saw the strong image of the skull-shaped mug crystallize in his mind.

Although the mug physically remained in his office safely on a shelf, its significance was always held deeply within Maksim's heart; its image lodged securely in his mind's eye. It did, however, leave the shelf, and serve utilitarian purposes from time to time. These purposes were of a nature that embodied the full value and meaning of the mug. The last time the mug was put to use was the day Putin died.

Maksim had finally achieved his goal of legitimizing the LDPR (Liberal Democratic Party of Russia) in the months and weeks prior to the coup. Since its founding, the grossly misnamed Russian political party had been steadily gaining traction. Its founder, Volfovich Zhirinovsky had been a visceral focal point for the party. Zhirinovsky spearheaded the development of the party's ideas, vision, and its gradual coalescing with the Russian man on the street.

But the founder was also easily dismissed and ridiculed for a bold flamboyance that was at once comical and dangerous, but moreover, an easy discredit to the legitimacy of the ideas he attempted to give trajectory to. As Zhirinovsky's influence faded, due to inner-party struggles and his increasing weakness for Vodka, Maksim slowly, and slyly filled the void. But unlike Zhirinovsky, Maksim's charisma, scintillating oratory skills, brazen leadership and overall magnetism gave instant and heavy credence to the vision of the LDPR. The wind was at his back, and momentum was building in such a way that strength repeatedly gave birth to renewed and increased strength. As each press release and subsequent media report captured the interest of the Russian citizens, the popularity of the LDPR continued to skyrocket. His only roadblock was Putin.

It was a crisp autumn morning when he settled the Putin problem. Maksim's tentacles ran deep in the Kremlin and he had secretly built alliances and paid off the majority of Putin's administration. Those who were not on board were simply poisoned like cheap journalists. Maksim recalled the glory he felt in the marrow of his bones as he walked nonchalantly into the Kremlin that day accompanied by the loyal thugs of the Solntsevskaya brotherhood. Everyone in the building knew who they were and why they were there. And everyone promptly looked the other way.

Maksim walked into Putin's office with a sense of destiny. He was not ushered in and he did not knock. Putin's face instantly revealed his understanding of the situation the minute he saw the mafia thugs he had been politically crucifying walk into his office as if they were invited. He had heard that Maksim was building an alliance with them, but he had not had confirmation until the moment he saw it less than ten feet in front of him. In his own office no less.

The execution did not take long and was not difficult. Putin demanded an explanation for the presence of the brotherhood thugs. Maksim closed the door, smiled, and thanked Putin for his service to Mother Russia. He then politely informed him that his services, and his life for that matter, were no longer needed. Then, in the ultimate gesture of insult, as his thugs held Putin still, he lifted Putin's personal marshal arts swords off the wall. With a sword in each hand, Maksim lunged forward to pierce upward and diagonally through Putin's abdomen, to form the shape of an 'X' with the swords, as he hoisted Putin off the ground. Putin's weight slowly fell into the swords as he succumbed to his death. He uttered only the word "bastard" as he transitioned into an unknown eternity.

Then, to the shock and repulse of even the onlooking mafia thugs, Maksim stepped forward toward Putin and kneeled in front him. He drew from his coat pocket the glistening, golden skull-shaped mug. He had been waiting for this moment of consummation. He almost giggled at the arrival of the moment. The excitement was not containable. His Scythian ancestors had used the actual skulls of their enemies. Maksim had conceded to the sufficiency of the symbolism of the skull-shaped golden mug. The blood was pouring steadily and with thickness and rapidity. As chaotic as the bloodletting was, channeling a good sufficient stream into the mug was effortless and completed within seconds. Also completed within seconds, was

Maksim's taking of the blood-filled mug and gulping it down like a shot of vodka.

He felt the warmth of Putin's blood slide down his throat and he imagined the power his Scythian ancestors must have felt when they drank their enemies blood out of their actual skulls. Maksim had then felt power and dominance like he had dreamed of since he was a young child. His day had come. The Byzantine Empire was on the precipice of re-emergence.

The next day, the Russian media reported Putin's suicide. They had also informed the public of the emergency appointment of Koslov as president by Putin's cabinet. Maksim Koslov wasted no time cleaning up the blood, occupying Putin's office, and placing the golden skull-shaped mug on the shelf. All eighty-nine of the governors Putin appointed throughout Russia had 'disappeared' over the course of the next three months. The disappearances were not reported in the Russian media, and they barely made the bottom text scrolls on the cable news channels in the west. The majority of the newly appointed governors had long expected their new positions. The fact that many were prominent members of the Russian mafia was barely reported and elicited complacent shrugs from those who did become aware. The new dawn had come, and Russia was indeed hailing it.

The intercom alerted Maksim that it was now 7:00 am and that he'd better proceed to the steam room and the shower to prepare for his 7:30 am meeting. He cursed the interruption of his recollections. He quickly assessed the progress of his painting before he hurried off to the steam room. It was coming along quite nicely. Hell, Hitler's paintings never looked this good. He thought to himself that if he was a better painter than Hitler, it stood to reason that he would indeed also be a better conqueror than Hitler. He washed the paintbrush, took off his robe, and hurried with purpose to the steam room to renew his pores, his mind, and his focus. The day was new, and like Russia's future, full of promise.

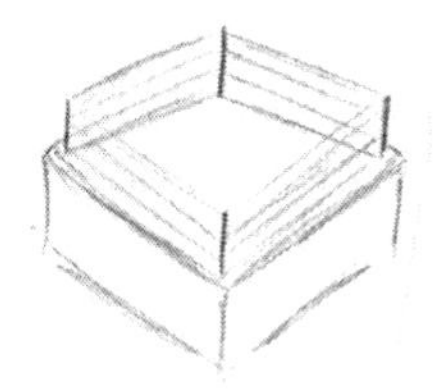

CHAPTER TWENTY-TWO

O'Conner's Irish Boxing Club, Detroit, Michigan

From the viewpoint of any unsuspecting outsider who might happen to walk into the back office of O'Conner's Irish Boxing Club at 6:30 am on one fine Thursday morning, it would be instantly thought that Chuck Gallagher was bizarrely intense and intensely bizarre. Chuck was preparing both for his sparring match and subsequent CIA meeting with Blaze McIntyre.

Chuck Gallagher stood behind his stand-up desk in the back office space O'Conner's had made available for both Blaze and Chuck to hammer out their business. To the eye, the damp, cold aesthetic of the gunmetal grey office seemed to visually swallow up his presence in the room. He was wearing athletic shorts that bordered on offensive. They were of the variety that one with a better sense of fashion would avoid. Anyone who harbored a sense of juvenile jocularity would certainly describe them as hoagie huggers.

Chuck Gallagher did not give an aeronautical fornication about fashion, and the notion of sitting down to work was anathema to him. Classical music filled the air as Chuck furiously scribbled notes in preparation to lay out his plan for Blaze's first mission back in the game. His forearms twitched and flexed as he manhandled a number 2 pencil with a hard-nosed, old school tenacity. The sight of Chuck displaying singular focus on the scribing of his notes, while standing with perfect posture in front of his stand-up desk, resembled a distorted, hybrid image of Clint Eastwood, Donald Rumsfeld, Henry Rollins, and the animated character of Mr. Buzz Cut.

Blaze was finishing what was to be the final few minutes of his early morning calm commute. His Cadillac found its way into a prime parking spot at O'Conner's and he sat with the car running for just a minute or so to finish listening to the end of the song "South Australia" by The Pogues. The melodies and words were festive. The tune always helped relax him and take him to his happy place. But now it was time to turn off the good feeling driving music and boot up the good bruising fighting music.

Blaze stretched his legs on the steps that sprawled forth from the side door of O'Conner's. For the most part, Blaze had shaken off the remnants of pain from his injuries. His stubborn commitment to working out against his doctor's directives proved to be a good decision and his strength and endurance were hovering around ninety percent. His hamstrings were a bit tight, but the rest of him felt good and limber and ready to engage. He bent over to tie tight the laces on his Lonsdale sneakers and then headed in to find his old pal Chuck.

Chuck emerged from his office just as Blaze set foot inside the gym. Blaze could hear the classical music from Chuck's office fill the air.

"You old Spartan bastard. Up early this morning to greet the sun and spit in its eye?" Blaze was shadow boxing as he greeted his mentor and friend.

Chuck laughed. "Damn right you pansy bastard. I don't even need an alarm clock to rise and shine like your weak generation. Did you get turned down by your old lady last night, cuz you sure don't look ready to fight to me?" Gallagher was prepared, at least in the caverns of his own mind, with a firm capital P.

"Oh, I'm ready. I'll tell you what I'm not ready for though, and no human in their right mind should be ready for, and that's the ungodly sight of that banana hammock you call gym shorts wrapped around your sorry loins. No one needs to see form-fitting junk garments on an artifact like you."

Chuck had no idea as to what was the issue with his shorts. He had been wearing these shorts for over thirty years and was not about to stop now. *How does Blaze even move in those baggy shorts? Damn things hang down past his knees.* "Go warm up for a few minutes you Irish swindler and I'll be out before you know it to knock the potatoes out of that thick head of yours."

A quick two to three minute warm up was all that Blaze reckoned Gallagher would afford him. With his iPod ear buds securely in his ears, Blaze pressed shuffle on his collection of albums by the New York Hardcore band known as Madball. The music was heavy and hard. The persistent underlying grooves coupled perfectly with boxing rhythms. The lyrics to the songs injected an urgency and strength within Blaze. The track *Adapt and Overcome* filled his ears. The song spoke of fighting all odds and improvising in tricky life situations. It typified Blaze's mentality. Blaze felt strong today and his feet were obeying his mind's wishes. He was ready for a damn good sparring match.

The two men wasted no time. Both were already gloved up. They walked to the ring as they continued to verbally abuse each other. Chuck was first to wiggle his body through the ropes and into the ring. He bounced on his toes and jabbed at the air as he continued spouting threats.

"You better get used to getting beaten, pushed around, and sent home dizzy. This here sparring match will be only the beginning. I got a hell of a mission for you this time, pally. Of course, no pressure—the cornerstone of western civilization is the only thing that hangs in the balance."

Blaze lifted the rope and swung his body underneath. Once in the ring, he immediately began shadow boxing with a feisty bravado.

"Thanks for the heads up. Let me go change my underwear and I'll be right back to oblige you in this match." Blaze laughed.

"If I thought you were actually kidding, I'd afford you a laugh."

Gallagher was clearly done with the talking and ready for the hitting.

"Save the laughs for me after I leave you bleeding on the mat." Blaze was ready to get this show on.

"Enough of the chatter there cupcake, let's do this."

Blaze wore baggy Under Armor gym shorts. Gallagher was, of course, wearing something verging on disgusting and quasi-pornographic.

The sparring started off uneventful and heated up slowly as Chuck and Blaze warmed up. A few minutes in, Blaze began breaking a sweat. His sweaty muscles and tattoos glistened under the overhead lights.

Gallagher appeared as if he was going to loose his breath, and his step, early on. But it was a false hope for Blaze. Chuck exploited every mistake his opponent made and he got several sequences of good shots in on Blaze. Blaze took the punches and absorbed their shockwaves while focusing on holding his ground, waiting out Chuck's energy reserves, and planning his own succession of hurting bombs to lay on his old friend and mentor.

But Gallagher kept at it and managed to land several more shots in quick succession. Blaze felt twitches of stinging pain that apparently still lay await deep in his bones. It was the ten percent of him not yet pruned for re-emergence into physical training. He fought through it to the endorphins rush that so defined the pattern of his life—pain births struggle, which then yields perseverance and forward movement.

It was about twenty minutes in. Blaze's feet tapped with perfect synch. He spotted Chuck yield to a momentary pause. With the speed of mythically enhanced lightening, Blaze landed two strong body blows and one triumphant headshot. Sweat leapt from Chuck's forehead like ocean waves catapulted from a tsunami. He winced with pain and then smiled with a sick look of sadistic pleasure. A small stream of blood trickled from his mouth. Chuck nodded to Blaze. He was done for the day.

"Alright, you got me this morning, you muscle bound Mick, "

snarled Gallagher.

"Your damn right I did you old Mick bastard. Just a foretaste of what is coming for America's enemies." The sparring match was now serving as a foundational pow-wow to psych up each man in their coming challenges.

"We're going to need a whole lot more than your measly fists to neutralize them." Gallagher was now exhausted.

"Let's go get some coffee and talk about that." Blaze was eager to get talking about the heart of the matter—his comeback op.

"Roger that."

The two men walked about a half of a block to their destination.

It was a mom and pop corner coffee shop in downtown Detroit. The walls were painted with bright oranges, yellows and mocha browns. The décor dripped with uber eco-conscious modernity. Abstract art, with vague earthy aesthetics, adorned the walls. The tables were full with a collection of patrons who appeared to be the quintessential sampling of the great unwashed. Right beside where Blaze and Chuck stood in line, a twenty-something white guy with dreadlocks and a Che tee shirt spouted off about W's blunders. His corduroy-wearing girlfriend nodded between sips of what appeared to be a mocha cappuccino.

The line moved a bit and they were able to better see the menu. Chuck squinted with frustration as he read it. Blaze just shook his head and waved his hand in the air dismissing the menu. Chuck Gallagher and Blaze McIntyre just wanted a damn cup of coffee. Instead, they were inundated with a myriad of fanciful options to enjoy their needed caffeine fix.

The line moved again and it was Blaze and Chuck's turn to order. Blaze looked up at the menu again as the young, cute female clerk awaited his order. He pointed at the menu again and waved his hand in rejection.

"I don't speak French. I just want a large cup. I don't know what all these things are on this cockamamie menu. I just want a regular cup of coffee. You know, the brown kind." Blaze was all together perplexed and frustrated with the unnecessary maze that was the menu options at this modern coffee house.

The cute twenty-something girl with a streak of red dye down the one side of her brown hair looked at Blaze and smiled. She then glanced at Chuck. She eyeballed him from his head right down to his gym shorts. She restrained herself from launching an outburst of all out laughing mockery. Her face showed how she felt. Tough old bastards like Chuck cared not. The girl responded to Blaze's menu rebuttal, "Well, yes, I suppose I could find a way to get you simply a large cup of brown coffee. You sure you don't want any whip cream or anything?"

"It's 9:30 am, ma'am. I don't eat desert that early." Blaze figured his logic was common on this matter.

"Okay, and just so you know, we don't have any senior citizen discounts so I apologize to your friend, but he'll have to pay full price for his cup," She winked at Chuck—it was an obvious, irreverent jab.

Chuck uttered a light growl as Blaze burst out into laughter. The young girl smiled big and winked again at the old dinosaur.

The two men sat down at a small table with their cups of joe. Neither took cream or sugar. Piping hot, black and straight down the gullet as God intended.

"So did you break it to the old lady?"

"Sure did. And for the record, Diem is still young and vital. I'm her old man, she ain't my old lady." Setting the record straight, as Blaze should.

"Yeah, yeah, yeah. Alright Prince Charming, so what did she say." Gallagher just wanted to cut the crap and cut to the chase.

"It was a tough conversation as you can imagine. My having been out of harm's way recently has been the fulfillment of all her prayers in years gone by. She's the mother hen. She wants a stable and full household. She fears she'll be a widow. She fears Shane and Dennis will end up fatherless. She also admitted that she recognized the crumbling that has been going on inside of me. She couldn't deny the reality that every day that I pretended to be a good civilian, a piece of me died."

"You think she'll really be able to handle it?" Gallagher was hoping this all was a real green light.

"I wasn't sure at first. But since I broke the news to her, she's been nothing but supportive and understanding. She knows who I am. You can take the boy out of war, but you can't take the war out of the boy."

Gallagher nodded his head in agreement, fully understanding the truths that Blaze was speaking. "Well Blaze, the timing indeed seems providential from where I'm sitting. These nut bags in Iran are on the cusp of having full-on global leverage with high flying nukes and a butt load of messianic ill intent."

"So this mission…it's got to do with the Iranians? Figures." Blaze had assumed that given the climate, any mission he'd be embarking on now would likely somehow involve the Iranians.

"You're damn right. They're the unnamed, ignored boogey man of the last two decades. You're up to speed on this Samani fruit, right? He's ten times worse than Ahmadinejad. And ten fold more pissed off."

"Yeah, I know all about him. So what are we looking at here." Blaze wanted the skinny.

"We need to find a way to disable, or severely retard, the progress and processes at Natanz, Esfahan, and Bushehr. These are three of the most important nuke plants. We don't really know how far along they are in having operational nukes, but if they've progressed the way they have in the realm of long-range intercontinental ballistic missiles, we're in for a world of hurt." Gallagher was now intensely looking Blaze straight in the eyes.

"How the hell are we going to infiltrate these plants, let alone dismantle the operations?" The task, at first hear, seemed entirely overwhelming to Blaze.

"I'm assembling a team and have concocted some possible approaches. We already have a source inside Natanz and close to the Iranian Revolutionary Guard. His name is Arash Jafari. He's a Persian national who has been working with us. He was working hand in hand with Reza Kahlili before Reza defected back to the US. Arash is still fully secure and undetected. He'll be our starting point."

"What other grunts do you have in mind?"

"Well, for one of them, I'm in the processing of pulling some strings to bust him out of the joint." Gallagher began chuckling.

"Wait…what? The joint? The only other valuable grunt I can think of who would be crazy enough to somehow be doing time in prison would be Zack Batt. You're not serious, are you?" Blaze loved working with Zack, but knew full well the escapades and shenanigans that colored Zack's personal life.

"Dead serious."

CHAPTER TWENTY-THREE

The Oval Office, The White House, Washington DC

It had been quite a long time since President Jack Fitzsimmons had attended college. It was soon after grad school that he met Emily. At the time, she rendered him smitten and beholden in just a few short weeks. That magical glue of infatuation had lasted for the majority of their marriage. The strength of that infatuation served to totally transform in Fitz the houndish sexual behavior that typified his early collegiate years. For the most part.

He sat sternly and quietly at the Resolute Desk, staring pensively into the corner of the room that at one time, prior to Obama's presidency, hosted the famous statue of the bust of Winston Churchill. As he stared, Fitz agonized in prayer with open eyes over his teasing yearnings to be with a woman other than the first lady. Fitz still found Emily extremely riveting in appearance, and quite the lover when he did manage to get her focused in the bedroom. But it was her other traits that erected barriers against their marital intimacy. Like the permanent scowl that plagued her demeanor towards him in private. Or her incessant soulless ambition—that very easily had eclipsed his own—that left him starving for her affection. All of this had left him seeking, at least in his imagination, a different bed to lie in.

Fitz did not have the brazenness, nor the tactical sense, to actually act on his wandering desires in the form of an extramarital affair. That said, he readily confessed to God his shame and regret for looking at internet porn sites in his weaker, albeit infrequent, moments. In fact, it was the crushing guilt of one of those moments that had prompted his current prayers as he sat at the Resolute Desk. A prayer that was cut short by the ringing of his landline.

Fitz rolled his eyes as he reached for the phone. He knew who it was. "President Fitz. I trust you are having a productive and efficient morning. This is Maksim Koslov. Do you have some proper time to talk?" It was clear that Russia's new strongman was all business this particular morning. Certainly not a deviation from the norm for Koslov.

The Russian Czar had not yet been outfitted by the media with his proper functioning title. But President Fitz sensed full well the inertia that was pushing Mr. Koslov towards increasing grips on power. Power wielded by a Czar. It was this inertia that gave Mr. Fitz a bit of the nervous shakes upon hearing Koslov's voice.

"I'm doing quite well today sir. How are things there in Russia?" Jack knew that things in Russia were just fine for Koslov. Maybe not so much for the people of Russia.

"Well, I'll tell you, I'm well. My staff is well. And the people of Russia are full of hope and promise. This is what I have always promised, and they now know I am delivering." Koslov's voice exuded with pride. He had more than a high opinion of himself.

"I gather that your sense of your own approval rating is rather high. I wish I could speak of myself with such pure confidence." Fitz attempted to deflate Koslov's over-confidence. The Russian President decisively ignored the comment.

"Mr. Fitz, you and I have always agreed more than we have differed. It's the bedrock of our understandings that I wish to continue to develop as we speak even today." Koslov wasted no time to get to the heart of his call.

"I feel the same way Maksim. What exactly do you have on your mind today?" Fitz's eyes rolled again. He wasn't sure if he felt the same way at all, but didn't know what else to say. He was curious to hear Koslov's perception of their overlapping mutual understanding.

"You and I have often spoken about our sense that the world is becoming a smaller and more integrated place every day. We both agree that in the future we'll see proper nation states become almost obsolete. The world already possesses a slew of travel and communication underpinnings that will make it natural to move into a new structure of continental states. This, in time, shall give way to a global government acceptable to the citizens of the world." Maksim aimed to instantly engage Fitz with his broad-brush strokes on globalism. A deceptive tactic coming from a man hell-bent on reviving the Soviet Empire.

"Maksim, you and I share much of the same vision in terms of the broad framework of a global future, but we do have many differences about certain movements, methods, and detours along the path to that end. Where is this line of thinking going exactly?" Fitz leaned back on his office chair as he swirled around to face the window, scratching his head with his free hand all the while.

"You Americans are always so eager to jump to the bottom line so quickly. No appreciation for the art of conversation I suppose. Well, I will tell you, that as much as I share this vision, I don't think it will happen without the ability to make decisions along the way that otherwise would not be made."

"What kind of decisions are we talking about?"

"I speak very much here of the countries of the Middle East. Israel. Our Persian friends." Finally, Koslov hit the heart of the matter.

"*Your* Persian friends, not ours." Fitz straightened his posture as he made his point.

"You don't need to posture with me. I know the official position of the United States. Your Secretary of State has been very clear about this. But I also know that you have larger goals that may supersede your desire to punish the Iranians."

"Maksim, no one here wants to attack Iran. That's the farthest from our intentions, but we also can't allow their nuclear activities and incessant threats to continue. We need unified international action. We need some sanctions with teeth." This was about as hard as Fitz ever got.

"That's why I'm calling. I'm not asking you to share my position that the Iranians need the bomb to be an equal deterrent to the Jewish strength in the region. I still believe a cold war posture of mutually assured destruction will work just as effectively with Muslims and Jews as it did between atheists and Christians."

"Are you asking me to back down on the Iranian sanctions?"

"I'm making the case that such sanctions won't neutralize the problem or bring us any closer to our vision of eroding national borders. They won't advance us towards the eventual installation of a peaceful global government. We've not always been the best of friends with the Iranians either. They still haven't forgotten when my Scythian ancestors repelled the invasion of King Darius in 513 BC. History sticks with the Persians. For this reason, we always tread carefully with them." Now he was speaking truthfully. Russian-Persian history was full of issues.

Jack Fitzsimmons' voice stiffened as he found his spine and replied, "I've not decided how I'm going to proceed with Iran. The fact that there is ample evidence emerging that suggests that your country is working in absolute tandem with them isn't making my decision any easier."

Koslov face turned red with frustration as he struggled to keep his cool. "Again, may I remind you that some decisions will need to be considered, by all of us who share this vision, that would otherwise not be made. If we don't employ such flexibility for the greater long term good, the world will always be divided and at war. This goes to the heart of the Israeli difficulty. They've been a clear and regrettable stumbling block to the world for years and years. A counter-balance is needed."

Fitz was never one to be accused of being a Zionist or

warmonger. In fact, it was a miracle he got the Jewish votes that he did. It was his conviction that because Christ chose to be of meager means and to die violently on the cross in a victim's posture, that it was God's intention for Christians to champion the cause of all victims. Fitz didn't see Israel or the Jews as victims in the Israeli-Palestinian conflict. His sympathies were strongly aligned with the Palestinians and Israel's Arab neighbors as a whole. This sensibility also extended to his complex feelings about the Iranian issue. He always secretly felt as if the Iranians were behaving the way they were because of some wrongs somehow done to them in the past.

"I appreciate the call Maksim and I understand your concerns. I will consider your suggestions." His mind was now fully considering the implications of Maksim's words.

"Enjoy the rest of your day Mr. President. I'll wait eagerly for your further thoughts as you wrestle with these issues." Koslov knew he had made an impact. He sensed the change in Fitz's tone by the conclusion of the conversation.

Fitz hung up the phone. He was no longer in a mood in which he could resume the prayer he had started prior to Koslov's call. He felt as if he should focus his prayers on the Middle East instead. Yet he couldn't get any real focus to engage in prayer. He didn't know why, but he always felt it tough to pray about Middle Eastern affairs. *Where would one begin anyhow?*

CHAPTER TWENTY-FOUR

Federal Correction Institution, Fairton, New Jersey

Zack was happy to see Chuck, even with having to endure the obligatory ball breaking. He went back to his lonely cell looking forward to getting sprung in the next day or so per the old man's promise. He reflected. *What a helluva journey. This life I've lived. Who knew? A skinhead thug rises from the projects and the streets and ends up being on the CIA's short list of third-party mercenary assets.*

His motto was 'if you can't grow hair right, don't grow it at all'. But despite that motto, and the stark reality of his receding hairline, Zack Batt would have shaved his head anyhow. From the days in which he dropped out of high school, at the age of seventeen, in his hometown of Charlestown, Massachusetts, to the current time in which he spent his days trying unsuccessfully to stay out of prison in between obliging to covert CIA missions as a highly paid contracted mercenary, Zack Batt was a skinhead.

He sported a crisp, shaven head that sat atop a long sinewy body—a body strewn with muscular striations and scars of both the intentional and unintentional variety. He stood a towering, six feet three inches and had a chiseled physique that drew immediate attention, and usually fright, from most onlookers.

On the side of his neck was a wonderfully colorful and detailed tattoo of a roaring Lion. A menacing image of the angel Gabriel, sporting a fedora hat, and manning an AK-47 lay tattooed upon the top of his right hand. Spider webs adorned his right elbow, as well as one tattooed awkwardly upon his inner ear. Across his knuckles, one word per set, the words 'SKIN' and 'HEAD' were etched in traditional tattoo script.

On days that he wasn't locked up wearing a bright orange jump suit, he was decked out in the requisite skinhead attire: ten hole Doc Martin boots, Levi's blue jeans, polo shirts and plaid shirts made by brands such as Fred Perry or Ben Sherman, and a variety of attire made by the English boxing company Lonsdale. To the uninformed, he was a seemingly walking paradox. Zack Batt was indeed a skinhead with Jewish blood.

Zack grew up in Charlestown, Massachusetts. He grew up hard. He grew up fast. At a very early age, he was ostracized for having no Irish blood. He lived with his mother in the projects. No matter how hard he tried he could not get along with the hoodlums in the neighborhood. His father had left when he was three, and the memories Zack had of him were not worth recalling.

Drugs, crime, a widespread plague of moral depravity and the terror of youth violence ran rampant through the projects that young Zack called home. Zack was often the victim of mocking, teasing, and randomly issued beatdowns by the strong Irish contingency in the neighborhood. This was most the case in his pre-pubescent years before his physical strength, and subsequent confidence, grew immensely.

His mom worked days in a factory and waitressed most nights at the local bar. Guidance was minimal at best, and usually non-existent, for young Zack. Zack never took to drugs because it was the drug users, and their predatory dealers, that made his life a living hell. He wanted nothing of it. But what he did want, was revenge.

He immersed himself in punk rock and hardcore music as a means to vent his angers and frustrations. It became a sonic backdrop that served to increase his confidence levels so he could bravely face each hellish new day in the concrete jungle that surrounded him. In this culture, he found friends. These friends became like family.

He discovered two strains of this counter culture that he chose to embrace simultaneously: the puritanical rhetoric of straight-edge hardcore punk which preached clean living and abstinence from drugs, alcohol, and tobacco coupled with the working class, street anthems of Oi! skinhead music. Zack married the two ideologies and styles and made them his own. He was as comfortable and zealous with the straight-edgers, as he was complicit with the skinheads.

He upheld his straight edge ideals in terms of his lifestyle practices, but over the years he began to more and more identify with his skinhead side. When he was eighteen he joined a group dubbed SHARP or *Skinheads Against Racial Prejudice*. The group was adamant about repairing and reshaping the image of skinheads in the media. Their mission was to wipe out fascism and Nazism from the skinhead motif. Combatting years of narrowly reported media coverage of sensational events surrounding racist skinheads, this proved a difficult task. From the Nazi skins beating up Geraldo on his talk show set in the eighties, to the images of the movie *American History X,* the average man on the street had only one impression as to what a skinhead was: Nazi.

For Zack, joining SHARP was more about channeling a general boredom and lack of direction into something somewhat organized than it was about any real passion for high ideals. Being part Jewish, it was easy for him to embrace the goal of wanting to stomp out racism and clean up the image of what a skinhead was, but truly he just wanted some like-minded friends to hang out with and roam the streets, clubs, and pubs of New England.

SHARP was big on trying to educate the public on the true roots and culture of skinheads. They emphasized the role that Jamaican immigrants to Britain played in the creation of the skinhead phenomenon in the UK. They traced the fashion trends of the skinhead lifestyle. This originated with the British mods (moderns), who were known for sharp dressing, riding scooters, and listening to soul, ska, bluebeat, rocksteady and early reggae music.

SHARP would denounce the unfortunate infusion of politics and race into skinhead culture and site it as the regrettable divisive wedge that had spoiled the skinhead image. Originally, skinheads were apolitical and racially tolerant, made up of black Jamaican immigrants as well as British nationals. Over time, skinheadism became a broader and broader tag that applied to a variety of related strains.

Skinhead groups representing politics both on the far left and the far right and everywhere in-between emerged, both in Britain, and eventually in the US and worldwide. Music and fashion preferences were also diverse. The one seemingly consistent thread for most skinhead groups was an identification with the street-tough sensibilities of the working class and an obsession with skinhead fashion: boots, braces, Harrington jackets, Fred Perry polos, bomber jackets, sideburns, tattoos, and plaid shirts.

Zack's unexpected slip into the never-ending vortex of CIA covert recruitment was born out of the fallout of his first significant prison sentence. He was contacted by Chuck Gallagher while serving three to five in federal for paralyzing a neo-Nazi at a punk rock show in New Jersey where the internationally renown non-racist Oi! band, known as The Business, performed.

The victim had shamelessly been sporting a tee shirt with the logo of the band Skrewdriver on it. Skrewdriver had been the seminal neo-Nazi skinhead rock band from England that was mandatory listening for any neo-Nazi recruit. It had been rumored that before the band went public with their abhorrent ideology, that they had toured with mainstream rock bands such as U2 and Motorhead.

Zack was taken up in the wild spirit of indignation that he and his fellow SHARP friends were feeling. They were appalled by the audacity of this Nazi to so obviously make known his beliefs. But Zack's reaction was far more extreme than any of his SHARP friends. Zack once again drifted into his untamed violent nature. It wasn't long before words flew, pushing and shoving proceeded, and ultimately, Zack got a hold of a nearby folding chair. That folding chair took on a life of its own in Zack's hands, and became the near-death instrument that repeatedly pounded the skull of the neo-Nazi.

The crowd scattered and Zack paid no mind to the emptying of the room. He only proceeded to beat the Nazi harder and harder. Zack's internal justification was based on the notion that he was defending his Jewish heritage and fighting the forces of racism and evil. This was indeed part of the truth.

The other part of the truth, was that Zack struggled with an unhealthy pleasure in committing violence for the sake of it. This part of the truth drove him to continue swinging the chair long after his point had been made. And long after the Nazi was rendered powerless. The victim was beaten to the point of paralysis by the time Zack caught his breath and came to his senses.

Zack looked around and saw that his friends had split. He did the same. This time though, unlike in the past, he didn't get very far. He was captured and arrested within an hour of the incident.

Chuck Gallagher was given a dossier on Zack by a buddy of his within the agency who knew Zack's family. The dossier was complete with the clippings from the Rolling Stone magazine article written about the chair-beating incident. The article showed a picture of Zack shackled in an orange jumpsuit as he appeared in court. Gallagher was taken back by Zack's appearance in the photo. *What the hell are these jackass kids thinking when they get tattoos on their necks?* Gallagher read the article and it intrigued him as much as every other bullet point he had read on the subject's dossier.

Gallagher was told of Zack's tenacious fighting skills and his misguided love of his country. It was too late to get Zack into the military given the mess Zack had made of his life. It wasn't too late to offer Zack a deal to get out of prison, entirely expunge his record, and mold him into one of the deadliest and effective mercenaries the CIA had in their arsenal, but denied ever knowing. That's exactly what he did. And Zack thrived with the new identity and renewed purpose.

Zack's first mission, after Gallagher bailed him out of jail the first time, was to assassinate a radical communist activist in Argentina that was gaining far too much influence in the South American continent as a whole. Zack's approach was pragmatic and direct. He studied the movements, patterns, and habits of his target. He did his due diligence thoroughly and applied his natural gift of extreme situational awareness. Once the building blocks had been arranged correctly, the hit was easy.

Zack's marksmanship was like a heroic verse from a Marty Robbins ballad—impeccable and executed with an appearance of effortlessness. The most troubling observation Zack made about himself, after his first hit, was how much he enjoyed it, and that the event left him completely without inner conflict and at perfect peace with himself. This lack of guilt puzzled Zack, but also confirmed that he was made for this.

Gallagher thought of Zack as one of the biggest blessings, and one of the best-kept secrets, that the CIA had ever been given. And he also felt often like the gift of Zack Batt was the biggest curse the agency ever received.

To the point, the ramifications of Zack being a curse largely fell into Gallagher's lap to manage. He was Gallagher's project. So it was, of course, Gallagher who had to continually clean up Zack's messes. Gallagher had run the cost / benefit analysis on Zack a million times and every time he swore to himself when he concluded that Zack was still too valuable to abandon.

In-between missions, Zack inevitably wandered back into gang life, succumbing to his unhealthy addiction to danger and violence. This concern never left Gallagher's mind.

SHARP had long ago ostracized Zack because of his uncontrollable violent nature, so Zack naturally embraced his straight-edge sensibilities to compensate. He moved out of Charlestown, MA to the lovely streets of Kensington in Philly. A prominent chapter of the nationally syndicated, radical straight-edge street gang known as FSU was situated in Philly, specifically Kensington. FSU was an acronym for many things. Publicly known to mean *Friends Stand United* but privately, on the streets, and painfully felt by the group's enemies, it stood for *Fuck Shit Up*.

The group held high virtues of straight edge living and anti-racist ideals. Of course, these were fine attributes and admirable in and of themselves. Unlike a biker gang, the IRA, or a neo-Nazi gang, FSU did not deal drugs, run guns, promote prostitution or engage in the traditional revenue-generating activities of the typical street gang.

FSU largely subsisted by running extortion scams. They reveled in a sadistic desire to apply their boiling, testosterone fueled machismo violence senselessly to as many as possible. Backed by an extreme Puritanical philosophy, no one was really safe—because few could measure up to their high standards of behavior.

Drunks were routinely beaten. Drug dealers and defenseless addicts were damn near killed. Frat boys, out for a good time and few hits from the beer bong, found themselves in the hospital.

FSU's notoriety reached such heights that they were rewarded with their own special on the History Channel's *Gangland* series. Luckily for Gallagher, Zack never appeared in the final edit. Apparently the History Channel heard Gallagher loud and clear on his informal, confidential request.

It took Gallagher years of stern lectures, idle threats, physical confrontations, and aggressive prayer to a God he struggled to belief in, to finally see the day that Zack left gang life. Since then, Zack's relapses into jackass tomfoolery had been minimum, and his contributions to the CIA's needs had been maximum and fruitful.

Gallagher was thankful beyond belief that the only reason Zack had landed in prison this time was because of a tiff-gone-wrong with one of his nut-job girlfriends.

CHAPTER TWENTY-FIVE

The office of the Prime Minister, Jerusalem, Israel

It was the day after Passover and Chaim Simmons, Israel's larger-than-life prime minister, still reveled in the joy of the celebration.

Prime Minister Simmons was a man for whom controversy, scourge, negative press, and straight up reality show-esque drama did not deter nor detract. The finger-pointing political pundits had a hard time figuring him out, but he certainly knew how to play the game. And deep down beneath the ever-outrageous show he loved to star in, there were some real, core beliefs.

The ever-increasing threats from Iran kept him up at night. The increasingly neatly packaged alliance formed between Iran, Turkey, Lebanon, and the nations of North Africa kept him up even later. The fact that Russia had been blended into this geopolitical cocktail from hell damn near made his heart stop.

But at the moment, Chaim was basking in the freedom, albeit fragile and elusive, that the nation of Israel had been feeling in recent months. He felt as if he was among the Jews of old having just been freed from Egypt. The ramifications of Israel's newfound wealth and prosperity were vast. Massive oil findings had catapulted the nation into an era of self-sufficiency that would have been an outright laughable notion just years prior. The narrative of the nation of Israel continued to surprise the world. One hundred years ago, the notion of a re-established Jewish state was mocked as a fantasy.

Now, Israeli citizens were discovering prosperity and opportunity like never before. Entrepreneurship now dominated the nation's new psyche. Israel had developed the ultimate and supreme ownership-based economy. As Chaim took a sip of some very fine home-pressed red wine, plucked carefully from the vast collection he kept in his cellar, he pondered the juxtaposition of Israel's prosperity with the lingering threat of her organized and motivated enemies. He resolved that barring verification of Iran's rumored nuclear capabilities, Israel was indeed safer now, and strategically more secure, than at any other point since her re-birth. That said, the premise that Iran did not either already possess these weapons, or were inches away from possession, was one that many challenged. Including Chaim.

As Chaim concluded his reflections, the silhouette from the kitchen disappeared and its source figure appeared before him in the study. As he reclined in his favorite brown leather chair, she placed an ashtray on the adjacent end table.

"Thank you Abigayil." Chaim smiled with gratitude.

Abigayil smiled seductively as she walked slowly out of the study. Chaim gazed at the short skirt that hid her rather attractive backside for longer than any modest man would venture to stare. Chaim reached up to flick the switch on the overhead exhaust fan. Then he lit his madura Crown David cigar. It was one of his favorites. He had picked up a box of them from a small cigar boutique shop outside of Philadelphia once after he had given a speech at a conference in a hotel near St. Joseph's University. The cigar shop was called SJ Cigars and was owned by a nice Israeli entrepreneur who was more than pleased to have Prime Minister Simmons visit his shop.

As he exhaled the first puff of his cigar and enjoyed the lingering taste on his palate, he chuckled to himself as he thought of his colorful relationship with Abigayil. She was not his first mistress. And if in his heart of hearts he were to be honest, she would likely not be his last. Chaim Simmons had a problem with women. The discipline he practiced in his work life did not transfer over into his personal life into the complicated realm of his relationships.

Chaim's problem had always been well known and had earned him the nickname of 'the Jewish Clinton', though sexual permissiveness was the only thing he had in common with the former US president. After the huge amount of controversy and press that resulted from his last wife, of a mere four years, leaving him upon discovering Abigayil, Chaim had been trying to tell himself that he would finally settle down. Three divorces was enough, he reckoned. If he ever did marry Abigayil, which he knew she would be soon pushing for, he would try to hold this one down.

As he pondered this internal promise, cigar smoke bellowed upward and the thick aroma saturated the study. He knew he was weak in this area. But for now, the tabloids had finally been leaving him alone and he would enjoy this time with Abigayil and, day by day, try to focus on fidelity.

And also for now, he would enjoy the peace and prosperity of his nation. Even while he prepared to counter or, more provocatively, pre-empt the evil and terror he knew was still bubbling up furiously within the nations that so tightly surrounded his beloved Israel.

CHAPTER TWENTY-SIX

The office of President Samani, Tehran, Iran

Hadi Samani peered out his office window at his beloved city. A city rich with history and significant meaning. President Samani often fantasized about the imminent return of the Twelfth Imam descending in glory upon his cherished metropolis.

The World Toward Illumination project had now been in full effect for months, and Hadi Samani was more than pleased with the influence it was having on the wonderful people of the Islamic Republic of Iran. The Promised One was indeed nearing His arrival. The preparations were becoming increasingly feverish and anticipatory. Some truths Hadi knew unequivocally—deep within his ever-patient soul. He knew with certainty that he had been chosen for this point in time. He knew he had been chosen to facilitate the global conditions necessary to hasten the imminent return of his beloved Twelfth Imam.

Hadi was pleased with the coalition of nations that was forming in his favor. It was absolutely necessary to squelch the illegitimate pigs of Zion. It was all coalescing perfectly according to plan. *Praise be to Allah.* The root connectors of the coalition had been percolating for years. But it wasn't until the uprisings of 2011, and the subsequent shifts in power from Sunni to Shia throughout the Middle East and

North Africa, that the coalition really began solidifying. It had grown to take on a more pure and focused coat of devotion towards the end goal of wiping Israel off the map.

Sure, the world applauded and hailed the U.N. peace treaty with Israel, that gave birth to a nominal Palestinian state, as the end of all strife in the middle east, but no one in the Islamic world truly had any intentions of holding to that agreement. The clouds of jihad had continued to gather, despite the news reports to the contrary, and despite the newfound feeling of peace and security that Israel had felt for the first time since its illegitimate national birth.

While the world basked in a false sense of peace, the soldiers of the Mahdi and devotees of Allah planned for the coming Caliphate with diligence, patience, and cunning strategic forethought. Allah knows Hadi Samani had no love in his heart for the atheists to the north, and that ultimately, they would be targeted very shortly after the Saturday people and the Sunday people were dealt with, but for now, the dealings with the bears of Russia were necessary and crucial. Hadi took a deep breath and dialed his secure phone to call Maksim Koslov for an update on their joint venture efforts.

"Good afternoon Maksim. How are things in Russia this fine day?" Hadi was adamant about maintaining manners in communication even if they were clearly sterile and performed only out of duty and formality.

"Well indeed Hadi. The wind is at our back, and we're rapidly accomplishing a myriad of goals that we have set long ago. How are things in Iran and what shall we talk about today?" Maksim was in a good mood and felt no anxiety as he launched into his call with Hadi.

"Things are progressing perfectly here. Our people are anxious for the justice of Allah. I know you don't understand such sentiments, so let's talk about common matters. When will your scientists be arriving at the plant to help us with the finishing processes needed to be online? The day is nearing, and having full nuclear capabilities and delivery abilities is paramount." Hadi Samani was, if nothing else, a driven taskmaster. He obsessively monitored every tentacle of his operations and made sure every element was constantly feeling pressure to maintain its pace and meet its goals to his pleasure.

Maksim responded to Hadi's concerns. "A week from Tuesday they will arrive in Tehren. So I'm told. Take heart, Hadi, we're almost ready. The Israeli's have known no boundaries with their incessant boasting. Ever since they struck the black gold of hidden treasures in the sand near the Jezreel Valley, they've been pronouncing to the world that they are enjoying an age of prosperity greater than that which was enjoyed in the days of Solomon. They're fools to think that simply because they've discovered large amounts of oil that they have the right to now bully the world economically. So they are experiencing an unprecedented boom of construction and building. And they've adjusted to a relative veneer of calm with the Palestinian state that they've begrudged for years. All of this will blind them with arrogance. They'll continue to oppress their Arab neighbors and control politics and economics in the US. But we'll not sit idly by as they hide behind their borders and seek to humiliate the rest of the world with their extreme indulgences."

"Indeed, there's too much injustice in the world for one nation to hoard such wealth and contain such prosperity. You know full well this is their nature. It can't be changed without force. Persuasion and reason have never worked with the Jew. Only imposition and war has ever put them in their place and eliminated their arrogance. Just because they have dug their treasures near Megiddo, does not mean they will rule Megiddo. Our book tells a different story as to who wins the battle of Armageddon. Praise be to Allah." Hadi was now losing Maksim's attention. Maksim's threshold for religious speak was notoriously low.

"Well I spoke with President Fitz by phone last week. I've begun to lay the groundwork to nudge him in our direction. As we've agreed before, he's very weak in his mindset and is prone to following, particularly when two or more agree internationally on an issue. Fitz is very reluctant to go against anything seen as a global consensus. His vision of a peaceful new world order is also very helpful in getting him to cooperate, or at the very least remain uninvolved, with our plans." Hadi Samani and Maksim Koslov had the same read on President Fitz. This helped to solidify their working relationship.

"Very good to hear. Please keep nudging him Maksim, and work that angle. As you know, he's not able to speak to me, and I of course, would be loathe to ever engage in a conversation with him. Allah forbids me. But we do need him neutralized if we are to confront the Zionists. I now have other matters to which I must attend. Let's plan to speak again after the scientists have finished their work next week."

"Until then." Maksim rolled his eyes at all the religious talk.

"Goodbye Maksim." Hadi was aflame with excitement about the progress of Iran's nuclear progress and the increasing sense of anticipation he harbored for the re-occultation of the Twelfth Imam.

CHAPTER TWENTY-SEVEN

First Baptist Church of Detroit, Detroit, Michigan

It had only been approximately thirty-six hours, give or take a few. Pastor McCardle had, for the most part, gotten through by staying on task and keeping busy with his studies and sermon preparations. The more frequent hospital visitations to the most senior and infirm elements of his flock also soaked up the time. He took lunch at his desk. It was rare that he left the building for lunch. As he took a bite of his leftover meatloaf, he was painfully aware that it was meal times—altogether before, during, and after meals—as Churchill had enjoyed, during which he had the hardest time resisting the urge to twist the cap and pour himself a stiff drink.

His current moratorium on alcohol was far from perfect. In a way he was like some churchgoers. He'd managed to stay away from the booze the way many stayed away from church. But there was always Christmas and Easter. Everyone had to worship once in a while.

Yet, in Pastor McCardle's mind, any movement towards lessening his reliance on alcohol was a step in the right direction. Regardless of how feeble and indecisive the step. He prayed God would help nudge his steps more and more. He knew full well his own ability to guide those steps was minimal and weak. As he pondered the nuances of his current fight against his cravings for booze, he heard the familiar and deliberate steps of Blaze McIntyre in the hallway leading to his office. It was rather divinely ordained timing. He had been staring at the bottle of Laphroig scotch he had in his lower right desk drawer. And he was intent on pulling it out until Blaze walked in.

"McCardle, whaddya say pally?" Blaze was very happy to see Liam.

"How are you Blaze?" Liam, likewise.

"Doing good. Doing good." Blaze rarely repeated his words for the sake of emphasis. This time, however, he really was doing quite good and felt the need to say it twice. After saying it, he was reminded of his friend Johnny who was always mocked by his cigar-smoking peers at the lounge for saying everything twice. The habit didn't make him at all as cool as Jimmy Two Times from *Goodfellas*.

"Come. Sit. Talk to me my friend." McCardle motioned for Blaze to take a seat.

As usual, Blaze took full liberty to kick his boots up on McCardle's desk as he prepared to launch into a purging of his heart and mind.

"I haven't seen you since the accident. When I came to see you in the hospital you were going on about a great number of random and incoherent things. Are you more clear now? Can we talk about the details of what went through your mind during the accident?" McCardle was both sincerely concerned for his friend's mental well-being and personally intrigued as to the nature of Blaze's mental disturbances.

"Well, I'm all healed up now. I was lucky to have such a quick, full and successful physical recovery. I'm even back to sparring regularly with Chuck Gallagher. But I'll tell you more about that here in a bit. As for mental recovery, that's a bit harder to diagnose. Maybe you can help."

"What do you mean Blaze? Explain." McCardle's interest now fully peaked.

"I crashed because I was having another vision. Harry's ghost again. This time it seemed more real than ever. And ten times more haunting." Blaze didn't really want to talk about it, but knew that he should.

"You'd mentioned that in the hospital. Tell me more." McCardle was fascinated by these episodes that Blaze was experiencing.

"It was extremely cryptic. Almost apocalyptic. He was laughing and then crying and then pleading. He was manic and maniacal. The ghost was hanging upside down in thin air. Blood dripped from his wrist. A nail was spiked through his wrist and a tattoo of the Star of David was etched upon it. He began quoting the book of Ezekiel repeatedly and with a fury I've never heard before in my life. He kept going on about rising evil in the nations, the poor and the lost, and future wars. He went on and on about the watchmen of Ezekiel and urged me to be one. He told me to find, and hold onto, my honor. He wept for me and spoke to what seemed to be a future version of me. He spoke of my family in the *past tense,* Pastor. I can't shake that from my mind."

Pastor McCardle stared at Blaze momentarily, as if trying to put the finishing touches on his thoughts, and then replied cautiously, "I'd love to tell you that your vision was meaningless and nothing but an hysterical figment of your tortured imagination and war-weary soul. But I know you wouldn't believe me, nor would you believe that I believe that."

"I know. So what do I do with what I saw and heard?" Blaze agreed, but still needed some direction.

"I'm not sure. As you said, most of Harry's words were fragmented and cryptic and his ramblings shifted in tone and content from sentence to sentence." McCardle was still trying to wrap his arms around Blaze's narrative.

"Right, but nonetheless, I feel like I was meant to hear something from all of it." Blaze knew deep inside that each visit from Harry was somehow providential.

"What does your gut tell you that you were meant to hear the most?" McCardle was trying to drive Blaze to the heart of this matter.

"I suppose the most pressing messages I took away were

messages of affirmation of my recent decision to get back into the fight." This was true.

"And what else Blaze? What else?" McCardle's job was in part, to prod people to dig deeper and think more comprehensively.

Blaze shook his head. "All the stuff you talk about I suppose. Gog and Magog. A war against Israel. Evil rising in the nations. Rumors of War. You know, all the end-times stuff. As a warrior, I try not to connect too many of the larger dots, only the necessary dots to complete the mission at hand at any given moment. But, now, I feel like I may need to know all the connecting points of data. I feel like Harry was urging me to know more and to be more." Blaze realized the weight of this admission.

"What more could he be asking you to be?" McCardle sensed real purpose in Harry's last visit.

"A watchman." Blaze felt a heaviness in this thought.

"What does that mean to you?" McCardle was beginning to understand this line of thought.

"I'm not yet sure. But my eyes are open to discovering what it might mean. I have a sense that this pending mission with Gallagher has something to do with that discovery process."

"Have you informed Diem of the decision?" McCardle had to make sure the obvious question was asked and sufficiently answered.

"Oh yeah, you can put that on the to-done list." Blaze said with a sense of accomplishment.

"Really? How did *that* go?" McCardle was a tad startled with the ease in which Blaze pronounced this new development.

"She was feisty and resistant at first, but she now gets it. She knows who I am. She knows I am a warrior through and through. She worries most about the boys. So do I."

"This is understandable. You'll have to wrestle with that worry as you go down this path. There is no easy approach to that piece of things." McCardle knew the seriousness in which this issue would weigh on Blaze and Diem.

"I know this. Such is the nature of the cross I carry." Blaze said this with a knowing smile.

"So how did your last meeting with Gallagher go? How much has he told you about the mission?" McCardle was excited for Blaze in regard to the bold decisions he was making.

"The meeting went well. As you know, I can't say much about what he's briefed me on so far. But, I'll tell you it seems to fit in somewhere with the prophecy narratives you endorse and warn about. God willing, I can be used as a strategic instrument to delay the inevitable outcomes of such foretold events."

"Blaze, tell me more about what you mean by delaying the outcomes?" McCardle's curiosity was piqued.

"The way I see it, if your interpretation of the prophecy regarding the Ezekiel war is accurate, there isn't much we can do about the fact that it *will* happen."

"I would say that's accurate."

Blaze nodded and continued. "And although there are many pieces of that picture that seems to be coming together right now, that doesn't mean the good Lord isn't going to delay the fulfillment. He gave us free will, right?"

"He sure did."

"And He is always looking to graciously give people as many warnings and as much time as possible to figure out the truth, right?"

"It's in His very nature."

"Right. So it stands to reason that maybe these promptings I've been getting have something to do with God intervening to delay the war of Gog and Magog. Maybe, maybe not. But if my skill set can at all help that possibility, I gotta suit up and show up."

"I think you're showing some wise discernment."

"Call it what you will Pastor, it's just the way I see it."

"Given the news lately on the dictator in Turkey and increasing Neo-Ottoman posturing they have been displaying as of late, I'd imagine any mission you were to embark on would rightly have something to do with combating the forces of the coming storm heading Israel's way. I hope and pray that somehow you indeed can be one instrument in God's hands to delay the coming event for just a bit more, if not a lot more, time." McCardle was keenly aware of the daily developments in the Middle East and North Africa and the relationship these developments had with Israel and America.

Blaze gave a pensive look and began to elaborate on his reflections, "Ever since Egypt fell into the hands of The Muslim brotherhood and the subsequent movement towards a Caliphate accelerated, the stability of the world has been increasingly threatened. As much as I'd like to not think about the ramifications, I can see how this might fit into the events described in Ezekiel 38 and 39. The alliance described sure seems to be forming." Blaze could see McCardle thoroughly digesting his observations.

"Let's be on guard as if the times are truly unfolding, even as we pray that we are wrong. For your part, Blaze, you need to fight as if you fear you're right, even as you pray that your fight will effect things in such a way to prove that you're wrong." McCardle's words lingered in Blaze's mind for a bit before he responded.

"Wise council my friend. Wise council indeed." Blaze felt as if his path was becoming more and more clear.

"Blaze, I'll be leaving later this week for a trip to Northern Ireland to visit family. I'll be gone for a few months, but we must keep in touch as much as possible. I'll be constantly praying for you and your family."

"I appreciate that, Pastor. Let's meet via videoconference while you're away. I'll certainly need more sessions like this as things continue to rapidly progress. Are you going to be okay in Belfast with all that down time? I'm worried about your weakness for the spirits mixing a little to seamlessly with a boatload of downtime—in Ireland of all places." Blaze raised his eyebrows to belabor the point.

"Your candidness is brazen my lad, but your concern is real. I am working on the drinking. Keep me in your prayers in that regard. You're one of the few I confide in about the issue." McCardle was grateful that Blaze cared and that he could speak to him with courage about his struggle.

"No problem. Mum's the word. Be safe and enjoy your visit."
"May the road rise to meet you, Blaze."

CHAPTER TWENTY-EIGHT

The office of President Hadi Samani, Tehran, Iran

It had taken a bit of time for Hadi to clear the cluttered realm of his mind and heart to focus on his midday prayers. There was much to do lately, and he never seemed to feel quite on top of the ever-increasing workload that he chose to create for himself. His ambition was insatiable and his fervor knew no relent.

Hadi finished the last drop from his cup of tea and forced himself to physically push away from his desk. He would engage in his midday prayers in his office today. His prayer rug was new, and he attributed a great deal of superstitious favor to it as it was a gift from the Ayatollah. He kneeled facing Mecca and began his recitations.

"Oh Allah, I invoke my entire being to Your command. I submit all my resources and faculties to Your control and purposes. I pray that You hasten the emergence of the Promised One, the beloved Imam Al-Mahdi. The deliverer of Islam in this wicked world. The one who will cement the burgeoning Khalifa that You so desire, and have forever promised. I beg of You, Allah, use me in any way You prefer to assist in the quick return of the mighty Twelfth Imam."

His mind focused for several seconds as he pondered the implications of the prayer he had just uttered. He began to shiver and shutter in eagerness for the coming of the Mahdi. Hadi Samani knew, beyond the shadow of a doubt, that he was born for the very purpose of being a key instrument in the implementation of global conditions that would quicken the return of the Mahdi, Islam's Messiah.

His work with the Russians and all the allied Islamic nations of the Middle East and North Africa had continued to accelerate towards that end, and he could feel the pleasure of Allah in his heart. As his inner joy intensified and he continued to utter further expressions of devotion to Allah and the Mahdi, an intense heat enveloped him. His eyes opened and felt an intense pain as a bright light pierced them. His head pounded with what felt like a migraine from hell. His heart began pounding maniacally. He became dumbfounded and was full of palpable trepidation. Something supernatural was occurring.

Blinded, Hadi screamed in pain and fear. A voice began to speak with a profound authority, "Hadi Samani, servant of Allah, true follower of Mohammed, faithful devotee, it is I, the Mahdi. I have come to make myself abundantly known to you so that you increase in strength and purpose. I am returning shortly. You will play a pivotal role in the facilitation of my return. Do not stop the good work you have begun. Carry it through. Push harder and stronger with all your plans. I am lurking and am near. The world will soon know the power of Allah by the miracles I will bring. The infidels will meet their just fate and the world will see the natural rise of Islam as Allah has always coveted. The caliphate will be fulfilled, but first, the world will suffer a necessary cleansing that will shake the very foundation of creation."

Hadi struggled to catch his breath. Even as he was still unable to see, he replied to his Messiah as best he could, "Oh beloved Mahdi, I groan with hunger for your return and your rule over the world. Destroy the infidels and redeem Islam for Allah's joy. Use me to the fullest. Show me the signs of your coming and the marks of your reign."

The mystical Messiah continued talking. "My return will be as described in the Hadiths. I will return in glory with my chief deputy,

Jesus of Nazareth. The infidels of the world will be confronted with the choice to see the precious face of Allah and convert to truth, or resign to their death as enemies of goodness and peace. There is no other way for those who refuse to submit. The nations of the earth will also submit. There will be no leader, no tribe, no country, and no religion that will be spared from submission to Allah and the caliphate. Nations that fail to conform will be collectively sacrificed just as the individual infidels that resist. Jesus of Nazareth will dutifully eliminate the infidels that remain, in wonderful service to Allah and my return. Those who resist and refuse will face the beheadings they deserve and that Allah commands. Jesus of Nazareth will make clear the folly of those who mistook him as deity and he will seek out all Jews who refuse to submit to Allah until only a few are left hiding behind rock and trees."

Hadi got curious. "Imam Al-Mahdi, subject of my devotion, how long will it take to restore the world to Islam when you return?"

"It will be accomplished within three and one half years. The world will, at that point, be re-ordered to the fullness and complete authentic glory of Islam. No impurity will be permitted. Jews, Christians, and all who have refused to convert will have been eradicated. Sharia will be the law of the entire world with absolute perpetuity. The official, and only, day of rest will be Friday. No longer will Saturday and Sunday be regarded as they have been by infidels. The Islamic calendar will be the only measure of our days, weeks, months, and years. The Gregorian calendar will be banned from use as an irrelevant tool of the infidels."

"Oh beloved, where shall you set your post and make known your wishes?" asked Hadi with a trembling voice and a shaky posture.

"One of the cornerstones of the caliphate will be rooted in Al-Quds, along with my commanding seat in Kufa, Iraq. The city shall no longer be referred to by the blasphemous name of Jerusalem. This shall be accomplished by the shedding of the blood of our enemies, the enemies of Allah, the stubborn and cold infidels."

Hadi was able to finally see a slight view of the Mahdi's face. It was glowing with a vibrancy that he would never, ever be able to shake from his mind. It was entirely not of this world. He continued, despite his sense of awe, to ask Mahdi questions. "Mahdi, beloved subject of all my desires and hopes, how will you persuade the world to your truth and Allah's laws?"

"My miracles will be many. From the moment of my emergence on a white horse blessed by the hands of Allah, I will show them Allah's power with my control of the weather and my dominion over the crops of the earth. All will bow to my abilities and to those of my deputy, Jesus of Nazereth. He will also display miracles that will be undeniable and will show any man of a right mind that it is only with Allah that real power and peace can be attained."

"Oh Mahdi, please tell me more." Hadi was salivating with the inside knowledge being intimated to him, despite his strong personal grasp on the prophecies detailed in the Hadiths.

"The Jews will first be lured into a peace treaty that we will agree to as a matter of necessity to accomplish the Caliphate. It will be executed with a Levite. It will be a seven-year agreement that we will never abide by. Yet it shall pacify Allah's enemies to the advantage of ultimate peace and satiation of Allah's will. However, the Zionists will strengthen their resolve against my rule when they are aroused by the Dajjal, who will be of Jewish blood, and will fool many with false miracles and deceptive speech. Take heart and press on with strength. I am coming soon, Hadi Samani."

In a flash of light and smoke, the ghostly vision of the Mahdi disappeared and Hadi Samani collapsed into a pool of sweat on his prayer rug.

His body felt drained as if he had just run a marathon. His muscles burned and twitched. He struggled to catch his breath. He felt exhaustion deep in his bones and elation deep in his spirit. He lay there completely still on the rug for forty minutes basking in the afterglow of his first supernatural encounter with the Mahdi.

The time was near and he could taste the glory of the Messiah's return. It was Samani's duty and passion to prepare the Islamic

Republic of Iran to receive its Messiah and lead the world towards the coming Caliphate with blood, confusion, deception and unspeakably horrific chaos of all varieties.

CHAPTER TWENTY-NINE

Arash Jafari's home, Natanz, Iran

Arash's wife, Atoosa, had gone to bed. He sat in his comfortable armchair and pondered the state of his marriage. He adored his wife. He looked down at the Quran in his lap. He knew it inside and out, and used to pour through it regularly, but now it's only value was to hide the Bible covered underneath—the Bible that he was just now beginning to really understand.

Arash had been staying up late almost every night and feeding on the words of the scriptures. His appetite for learning the Word was voracious. His attention to his wife, was as a result, waning. And he knew it. He was deeply conflicted. His new love was drawing him away from his first love.

His first love—Atoosa—his princess. They had always been a great team. They had always treated each other with immense kindness and love. His passion for her had always persisted. Until now. Now, it wasn't passion he felt for her. Now he felt concern, love, and compassion. He could never tell her. She would never accept his new faith. She would reject him along with it. But Arash wished he could tell her. He wished she would have ears to hear and a heart to understand. But he knew that was unlikely. In his prayers, he felt promptings to continue to hide his faith from Atoosa.

Betraying those promptings could jeopardize everything.

Arash meditated on the words of Romans 8:35-39. "Who shall separate us from the love of Christ? Shall trouble or hardship or persecution or famine or nakedness or danger or sword?" Arash feared these conditions could soon fall upon him as a result of his faith. He continued his meditations. "As it is written: 'For your sake we face death all day long; we are considered as sheep to be slaughtered.' No, in all these things we are more than conquerors through him who loved us. For I am convinced that neither death nor life, neither angels nor demons, neither the present nor the future, nor any powers, neither height nor depth, nor anything else in all creation, will be able to separate us from the love of God that is in Christ Jesus our Lord."

Arash held these passages close to his heart. He knew that it would be his faith in the reality that nothing could sever him from his Savior that would ultimately sustain him. It was Romans 8:35-39 that Pastor Saeed Abedini held onto for strength when he was tortured in Evin prison. Arash had strongly identified with the story of Pastor Abedini and his courage as a persecuted Christian leader in Iran. He prayed that God would equip him with similar faith, strength and endurance for whatever the future may hold.

Arash prayed he would never suffer for his faith even as he feared he would. He was willing to if it was God's will, but he prayed that he would be spared. Somewhere within him, he knew the prayer was likely futile. He sensed his day of persecution would someday come.

Arash worried that Atoosa would catch him reading the scriptures. He worried how she would react. He was certain that she would turn him in to the mutawwa. Her devotion to Islam and the Mahdi was her greatest commitment. Arash knew this well—he had encouraged her in it! He recalled how close he felt to Atoosa when they really began growing in their knowledge of the Mahdi and their passion to see the return of the Twelfth Imam.

As he thought about the marital harmony he felt before his conversion, he had a twitch of doubt about his current faith in Christ. *Is any of this real? What if I'm wrong? What if the Twelfth Imam is the true*

Messiah? What if this Jesus is a false messiah? What if my vision of the Nazarene was from the spirit of Dajjal? What if there is no Messiah at all and I've been fooling myself since the beginning and all of this is folly?

His eyes circled back to the passage in Romans. He felt the presence of God fall strong upon him and he doubted his doubts. He began to pray for strength. He also began to pray for Atoosa.

He heard a shuffling from the bedroom. Atoosa began walking into the living room. Arash quickly covered the Bible in his lap with the Quran. Arash sensed her looking at him questioningly as the Quran settled atop the Bible.

"Why don't you go to bed? You're always staying up late. Come lay with me. I miss you. I miss falling asleep with you holding me." Atoosa was half asleep as she questioned Arash. She looked at him curiously, still confused as to why he insisted on staying up late reading.

"Okay, my dear. Give me a minute and I'll come to bed. I just need to finish up my reading. I won't be long."

"Okay, but hurry. I don't want to fall asleep without you."

Arash smiled and began reading the Quran in his lap that covered up his Bible. He read through some passages. He now saw the words of the Quran through a completely different lense. He saw opposite messages of the Bible everywhere, particularly in the description of the Islamic Messiah.

Atoosa walked back to the bedroom. After she left the room, Arash placed his Bible back in the cabinet below his bookcase. He locked the cabinet and placed the key underneath the armchair cushion. As he lifted his head up after placing the cushion back in place, he saw Atoosa staring back at him.

"I'm coming honey. I'll be there in a minute." He didn't think she saw what he was doing. He prayed he was right.

Atoosa smiled and replied awkwardly, "Okay honey."

Arash held Atoosa tightly that night. She slept calmly. Arash laid tense—sleepless for hours—his mind and heart swirling with tumult and anxiety. He didn't know how long he could continue this double life.

CHAPTER THIRTY

Belfast, Ireland

The restaurant was more like a modified home. Its décor and aesthetic exuded the essence of closeness and love that McCardle's now reunited family had for each other. A tremendous waft of goodness filled the air for all to smell long after they had finished their meals. Good food was in abundance. Stews, bangers and mash, pub sandwiches of all types, and the most delicious meatloaf in the entire world were all part of the menu for the evening's festivities.

Everyone was well dressed and in good spirits. And good spirits were also in good supply. The venue was a modest one, but a familiar one. Warm, boisterous, and teeming with the sounds of family and friends. The fire was burning to the right of Pastor Liam McCardle as he smiled wide and endured the mix of praise and admonitions that were pouring out of the mouth of his dear old mum.

Liam did his best to hear every word his mum was saying as he leaned his ear closer towards her and attempted to block out the increasingly loud volume of the music that was filling the establishment. He recognized all the music that had been playing that evening, save some modern Irish rock oriented picks. It was The Dubliners classic "Whiskey In A Jar" that was playing at the moment.

Liam sure missed home. He sure missed his family. He missed hearing Irish music in Ireland. And truth be told, he sure missed whiskey—in a jar or otherwise. His heart was forever green, but his liver had been blackening by the day.

"Son, you know your father would be so proud of you. He always bragged about your preaching, your intellect, and that his boy was living in America and doing the good Lord's work, far away from the divisive struggles and strife with the Catholics. There was no shortage of pride in you, had by him, when you were here fighting the IRA either. That said, when you got out of seminary and moved to America, your father, and myself as well, were so relieved to know you were out of harm's way. Far away from the remnants of the Troubles." Liam's dear mum was full of genuine love and pride as she expressed her heart to her visiting son.

"I know he was proud of me mum, and I always strove to do him proud, as I did for you. I am very happy in America, but I must tell you that it is wonderful to be home and see everyone that I love and care about." Liam smiled and transmitted a deep feeling of sincere warmth and love to his mum.

"Well, we do miss you. Things haven't been easy since your father passed away, but I'm happy. Your sisters have been helping me and so has your Uncle. We're very blessed." As Liam's mum smiled, she showed some slight tears. The memories of Liam's late father were rich, strong, and emotional.

His mother, who had the liver of a Viking, pivoted on her chair to grab a shot of whiskey off the tray that a nearby server was balancing. She gulped it down like a sailor who hadn't seen land in forty years. Liam laughed, as this was not an unfamiliar sight. She wiped her chin with the sleeve of her sweater and continued her thoughts.

"Why don't you come home son? Come home and find a church here. Hell, come home and start a church!" She put her arm around her son and looked him straight in the eye. She had the you-better-listen-to-your-mum kind of stare.

"Mum....stop. Please. Really."

"Don't 'mum' me. It's a great idea! Think of how happy you would make your sisters and I. You still haven't found a woman since Kathy passed. You know that you need an Irish girl. There are plenty still here for you son. I can see by the look on your face that you think about it." She gave a persuasive smile.

"Of course I think about it mum, but that doesn't mean its God's will or my preference. I'll lift it up in prayer some more on account of your pushiness on the issue."

"That's my boy," she said as she pinched his cheek.

As Liam's mother finished that thought with a big smile, she grabbed yet another shot of whiskey, stood up, pushed her chair in and made her way to the dance floor. That woman did not slow down with age. Now in her early seventies, she could drink and dance like she was still in her twenties—and still be up at the crack of dawn the next day and keep the cleanest house in all of Ireland.

Liam shook his head and chuckled. His mother was full of life and it was an utter joy to see. Suddenly he felt a strong hand pat his back, and a strong voice soon followed.

"Good ole Liam. How the hell are you?"

It was Johnny Leary. He hadn't seen Johnny since his days working with him on the force.

"Johnny Leary! It's great to see you my friend! How's life treating you?"

"Frankly, like a dog treats a fire hydrant, but I won't bore you with the details."

Both men roared with laughter.

"Your mum told me you'd be home visiting. I heard you're exporting Protestant fire and brimstone to the states these days and lighting up the pulpit. God Bless you Liam. I always thought you were a bit of a wind bag!"

More laughter erupted and the two men continued to catch up and reminisce on old times, old operations, and some of the bad times as well— fallen comrades, deaths in their families, and the lingering political problems that still existed in Ireland. They held a conversation for several minutes until Leary's glass was empty and he pardoned himself to go fetch another pint. McCardle wished him well and walked towards the dance floor.

It didn't take him very long to see her. Erin McNeil was as striking as ever. His heart instantly began pounding and he felt a boyish nervousness he hadn't felt since his teen years. *Maybe mum was right. Where else does a man find an Irish rose but in Ireland?*

And what an Irish rose she was… blooming magnificently right before his very awe-struck eyes. She shuffled and swayed and took over the dance floor like no other female in the joint. Her reddish brown hair was radiating with beauty and bounty. She was laughing and giggling with a lust for life that was only a few steps ahead of the lust that Liam was beginning to feel as he gazed upon her like a hopeless voyeur.

His smile began to widen and grow as she glanced his way with a wide smile of her own and a genuine look of surprise and excitement at his presence. Liam felt a burning inside that usually only occurred when he gulped down whiskey too quickly.

Liam had known Erin McNeil presumably since his birth. Their mums used to walk together in the late mornings with Liam and Erin respectively in the strollers side by side. They had been given baths together as toddlers. Play dates with the two of them were frequent long before the term 'play date' existed. As they progressed into their tween and early teen years, the two had always been close even though they ran in different circles.

As young adults, they had secretly each kept a close ear to the street on the others doings, but had never maintained a tangible relationship to speak of. Under the circumstances, their mutual sights in mind were clearly sparking unbridled, pent-up fondness beyond the pail of normalcy.

Erin managed to gracefully, and playfully, meander over to where Liam was standing so boyishly as he studied her every dance move, suggestive or not.

"Well, well, well…if it isn't the red, white and blue preacher making an appearance back in his home country." She shook Liam's hand as he bowed to kiss hers.

"Very, very nice to see you Erin. You look wonderful and I've been thoroughly enjoying your exploits on the dance floor." Liam's eyes locked on Erin's with a magnetic gaze.

"Thank you Liam. You know, I often wonder about you, what became of you, how you're doing, what's life dealt you. Are you doing well? Has happiness nestled inside of you?" She peered inquisitively as she asked.

"My dear, the good Lord has blessed me beyond compare, and I've been given the exquisite privilege of ministering to so many wonderful folks in America—albeit in the rough and tumble urban context of Detroit, Michigan."

Erin changed the subject. "I heard about Kathy…and your father. My condolences."

"Thank you Erin. I'm doing well considering and appreciate your concern. How's life been treating you?" He had not gotten as many reports on Erin as she had on him.

"Life's been good…well, it's becoming good…I separated from Patrick a little over a year ago…that was tough. My McKinnis is now eight years old, and she's darling. Taking care of her is a lot of work, particularly when I am all by myself, but she's a true joy. Work is steady, the best that an Irish gal can hope for."

She had overcome life's obstacles and come out the other side with grace and charm. "Well, it's wonderful to see you. The way life moves so fast, it's a miracle and a pleasure that our paths have even crossed again at all."

"We could cross some more if you dared to get your ass out on the dance floor…"

And with that, the preacher went head over heels into a long-gone nightlife he had been far removed from up until this evening. He danced with vigor and passion for hours with Erin and engaged in various forms of flirting, both subtle and intense, and both verbal and physical. They ended up back at her place.

His life at the pulpit, his memory of his wife, his gnawing fear of the prospect of Ezekiel 38 and 39 unfolding—all those backdrops—had all submerged into a foggy, grainy background. For the moment the carnal, hopeful, uninhibited drawings of his soul dominated him.

He spent the night with Erin and made love to her in such a way that his entire being felt as if it was transported to an entirely different ethereal realm. His flock in Detroit, his lovely deceased wife, and his concern for the dangerous mission embarked upon by his friend Blaze McIntyre were as far from his mind as the Earth from the Sun. Leave Ireland to the Irish. As they say.

CHAPTER THIRTY-ONE

The Hampton Inn, somewhere near Fairton, New Jersey

After pulling some strings and springing Zack Batt from the slammer, Gallagher bought him dinner and got him a hotel room. He paid for the hotel room for several days in advance, and ordered him to get some "serious damn shut eye" because we have "some serious damn work ahead of us". Zack, weary of the rigors of prison life, insisted on a suite that had a hot tub and allowed smoking.

As soon as he swiped his key card and entered the room, Zack immediately undressed and began drawing the water in the hot tub. His head was thumping something fierce, and the rest of his body was fatigued to the core.

The clicker lay on the bed. Zack reached for it and turned on the large flat screen TV. He scanned the channels until he found something worthy of his attention and that would agree with his mood. The old FX show *Justified* caused him to stop channel surfing and he settled on watching a re-run of one episode of the program from Season 3. He remembered seeing this episode back when it aired in 2012.

He had a deep affinity for the portrayal of the main character, Federal US Marshall Raylan Givens, and he enjoyed the tension between Raylan and his primary nemesis, Boyd Crowder. Zack absorbed every nuance that oozed out of the badass, gun-slinging Southern lawman that was personified by Raylan's character. It was the perfect show to help him ease into a post-prison soak in a Jersey hotel hot tub.

Zack leaned back in the hot tub, enjoying the movement of the whirlpool mechanisms, and lit a cigarette. He had taken up the habit recently despite its obvious contradiction with the straight edge ideals with which he associated himself. Sometimes, he reasoned, life had a way of eating away at your ideals. To him, straight edge was largely about avoiding highly addictive hard drugs. He rationalized that cigarettes didn't count. He inhaled slowly, but deeply, and enjoyed every second of the drag.

He was beginning to feel like a human being again, and was trying to shut out the horrible memories of being in the hole and all the rest of this most recent prison visit, including the crackpot broad who threw the lamp at his head and put him in the joint in the first place. He chuckled to himself softly as he intently watched TV. The dialogue that ensued in the episode of *Justified* he was watching was phenomenally written. It reminded him to make sure to get back to finishing the Elmore Leonard novel he was reading. *Justified* had inspired Zack to go back and read the work of the author who inspired the show. He'd begun to read Leonard in prison. As he watched, smoked, and soaked, he also began to download and unpack all that Gallagher had told him about his mission. The mission that was his get-out-of-jail-free ticket.

The whole notion of a Persian Nazi group emerging at all, let alone gaining support and ascendancy, astounded him. He had never imagined such a strange thing to exist, let alone with such strong historical context. The dots that Gallagher had connected for him in regards to the Aryan makeup, the anti-Semitic tendencies and the true history of Iran and its connection to Germany circa WWII completely blew him away. As appalled as he was at the existence of such a group and its relevance to assisting the enemy government of

Iran, he was still monumentally stoked to have been commissioned to infiltrate it.

He felt a new surge through his being. It was an adrenaline rush akin to that sought by the most avid of thrill junkies. He purposed to begin his research and digital outreach to anyone he could find connected to the group online first thing the next morning—after consuming what had become a highly anticipated room service breakfast delivery.

Morning came slowly. Zack slept like a hibernating bear. He awoke with new and refreshed thinking. The contrast was extremely enjoyable. *Yesterday I was stuck in a prison with a bunch of numb nuts convicts and today I am relaxing in a robe in a nice hotel room paid by the generous taxpayers of the United States of America. Life sure has a funny way of forcing a roller coaster ride.* Zack sat at the provided desk in the hotel suite surfing the net in an eager attempt to spark the first connection to his new mission. He sipped the strong, black coffee with a deliberate sense of pleasure. Such a luxury had not been part of his morning routine in quite some time. He had hoped that he would have the patience to savor every bit of the eggs benedict and hash browns he ordered from room service, but his jailbreak appetite got the best of him and he devoured it with a vulture-like intensity. He was well rested, and now well fed, for the first time in a long time.

Prior to retiring the previous evening, he had managed to quickly set up Facebook and Twitter accounts for his new identity and he sent some preliminary messages out to some hopeful online targets, including this guy Hamid that Gallagher had given him intel on. Zack's undercover name was *Douglas Schmidt.* Common, but German as hell. It gave not a hint of the reality of his half-Jewish heritage, and was a fine fake name to wrap his newfound Nazi Skinhead persona in. He took another sip of his coffee and felt the surge of the caffeine. He sorted through a slew of irrelevant junk messages until he finally stumbled on a tweet of interest. *Hot damn.* It was Hamid. Hamid wasted no time to show a clear lack of respect for keeping anything to the chest in his response to Zack's—*Doug's*—ranting tweets the night before.

"Finally, an American who gets it. Down with Zionism." The tweets to follow were even more lovely, that is, if you fancy hate-filled anti-Semitic bigotry. The subsequent tweet read, "No one likes a pig in their house. Death to non-Aryans." The rest of this man's tweets reeked with similar non-eloquence. The last of the turd-filled shorthand prose proclaimed, "We will finish what Hitler started. Allah willing." The man's opinions were completely devoid of subtlety or nuance.

Zack saw many Facebook messages and Tweets fly by that were anti-Semitic, pro-Jihadists, and favorable towards the desire for a Caliphate, but the tweets from Hamid were the most incendiary. His tweets mentioned the word 'Aryan' more than any others. That was the key word Zack would focus on to try to bridge a connection. Zack smiled with satisfaction. He needed to know more.

"Being American is irrelevant. A pig is a pig." Zack knew he'd have to tread slowly and develop a rapport with this ghost tweeter for a while before digging in deep and finding a way to use him to infiltrate NINP—the Neo Iranian Nazi Party group. It would take even longer, and likely prove to be much harder, to try to find a way to leverage himself into a trip to Iran to meet with the group.

Zack followed up quickly with another tweet. "Aryans worldwide unite. The time is now." He had to continue to find ways to build on the 'Aryan' emphasis.

After Zack tweeted his call to arms worldwide for Aryans, he sat back and took a deep breath. *What drives these people to seriously embrace such extreme ideologies and theologies?*

Zack had always engaged in his share of extreme behavior. He knew his internal questioning of the jihadists and the Persian Aryans was somewhat oxymoronic, but he also knew there was a huge difference between extreme behavior of a wayward street thug and a global jihadist hell-bent on a Caliphate and the elimination of all non-Muslims.

With the bubbling angst and alienation that had been a persistent thread throughout Zack's tumultuous youth and young adulthood, faith was not something that he ever managed to get a handle on. He went through times in which he flirted with embracing one faith or another, but he never really pulled the trigger on anything. His inherent distrust in people, any organized body, and the state of humanity in general always became a last-minute roadblock to his becoming a full believer in any truth claim.

Stemming from his affinity for reggae music, he came very close to cloaking himself in Rastafarianism, but despite his respect for Bob Marley and the Bad Brains, he still saw way too many gaps in both the theology itself and the lives of those who called their God 'Jah'.

There was also his curiosity about Hare Krishna. He knew many kids in the hardcore punk scene who had converted to this offshoot of Hinduism and were instantly zealous about its virtues. Mostly they were wooed by the preaching of Hare Krishna punk bands like Shelter, 108, and Cro-Mags. The notion of rejecting materialism, embracing physical health, and prioritizing stewardship of the earth all appealed greatly to Zack. But when it came down to Zack considering giving up eating Philly cheesesteaks to become a strict vegan or believing in reincarnation, again, he became lost and was disenchanted with the idea all together.

Christianity had always seemed like an unnatural fit for Zack because of his Jewish heritage and he was heavily inculcated with noise about the hypocrisy of the global Christian church and individual Christians who were in the public eye. That said, Zack's personal interactions with those who claimed Jesus as Savior were all positive and he had a great deal of respect for Christians.

As a half Jew, Zack was simply not inclined to explore the merits of Islam. That said, he did have several strong friends, one of the Lebanese Shia variety, and another an African American convert he met in prison, that he had grown very close to in hard and strange times. Through them, it had been confirmed to Zack that the Islam that was so distorted by the radicals and the terrorists he now hunted and killed was far from the peaceful brand lived by many the world over who called Allah their God and Mohammed their prophet.

To Zack the most attractive faith was Judaism, and he did gravitate towards a loose and infrequent interlude into the faith cherished by half of his ancestors. In his mind, he was attracted to the pragmatic, civilization-building tenets of Judaism. He viewed these tenets as the common sense relational and societal building blocks for a prosperous world. The prevailing worldview, and every day directives, of the Talmud spoke to Zack. It was the idea of being subservient to an invisible force in the sky that Zack still could not wrap his arms around. He still did not, in his moments of intellectual honesty, fully belief that a God of any sort actually existed. As a result, he still remained an agnostic who was open to evidence of ultimate truth.

As Zack thought about the lunacy of the rhetoric of the Jihadists, the Persian Nazis, and the Twelvers, he pondered the one Old Testament scripture that he conveniently held onto and took pleasure in as a highly-skilled mercenary of the US government: *An Eye for Eye…a Tooth for a Tooth.* Zack harbored no guilt in applying this policy, as he knew that it was actually a progressive step away from the previous policy of *You take my eye and I will kill your entire family, and your family's village.*

Both of Zack's eyes were firmly intact, and his vision was clear. In his vision, he saw himself successfully infiltrating this Persian Nazi group and using them to penetrate the nuclear facilities at Bushehr and disrupting the progress of America's most ambitious enemy. Zack's current policy was a revision of the Old Testament retribution standard: *Before you come near my eye, I will destroy your entire arsenal and shut you down with extreme and uncompromising force.* That was Zack 1:1.

As Zack chuckled at his arrogant thought of writing his own batch of scriptures, he got up from the desk, tightened his robe, and placed his room service tray outside his hotel door. He walked back to the desk and took a big gulp of ice water and once again checked his Twitter feed. Bang! There it was! His new pally from Persia was taking the bait and eager to chat it up like a schoolgirl that had too much fun on the weekend.

"Jews have nuke. Aryans need one. No justice, no peace." Zack couldn't believe his eyes. This guy was a piece of work. There he goes, co-opting social justice lingo to help with his neo-holocaust agenda. Zack shook his head in disgust at the obvious incestuous relationship that had developed between the global radical left and radical Islam.

Zack played along, happily, and instantly tweeted back. "Iran deserves nukes. Nothing should stand in the way." So far, so good. He just needed to keep prodding this guy on so he could build a stronger relationship.

"America stands in the way. You are problem." *Wow. This guy is on his toes. Does he tweet 24-7?*

"I'm not American. I'm Aryan. And proud." Again, Zack had to keep pounding home the Aryan emphasis.

The next tweet volley came back to him twelve minutes later. "Are you organized?"

Bingo. Now we are getting somewhere. He wouldn't ask if I was organized, unless he was already organized. Time to get him talking about NINP.

"Not organized. Want to be. Need to be."

Zack waited for a solid twenty-five minutes for a reply. Nothing. *I guess this guy does actually know how to do something else other than tweet hate all day.*

Zack's impatience got the best of him and he decided to hop in the shower and begin to get ready for the rest of the day. If he had to bet, he would wager on a new tweet waiting for his perusal by the time he got out of the shower and dried off.

CHAPTER THIRTY-TWO

Esfahan nuclear facility, Esfahan, Iran

No matter how many times he had to endure it, Blaze never got used to disguises. He was a warrior, not Sherlock Holmes. He'd much prefer an all out face-to-face gunfight, or fistfight for that matter, than the detailed planning of espionage. The problem, however, was that regardless of his preferences, Blaze McIntyre was damn good at espionage and ops that required disguises.

His skin had been cosmetically darkened and he was feeling as Persian as his Irish self was ever going to allow. His credentials were impeccably prepared for him and he felt as if he was all set to flex his multi-lingual muscles and rock some Farsi. Still, he preferred to go as unnoticed as possible. Minimal human contact was the goal. Maximum destruction to the target would follow.

The delivery truck was identical to the ones that hustled in and out of Esfahan on a daily basis. Although every op was loaded with unforeseen peril and risk, Blaze felt confident he could pass for the deliverymen who dropped off raw materials at Esfahan.

In 1984, a year that Blaze singularly associated with the title of one of Van Halen's best albums, the lovely Chi-coms assisted the Iranians in getting the Esfahan Nuclear Facility up and running with three small research reactors. Purported to be a multi-purpose research center, Esfahan has come to be primarily important as a stockpiling site for uranium taken from mines, which are used to produce uranium fluoride gas. From Esfahan, the gas was shipped to Natanz to feed the centrifuges for uranium enrichment.

Blaze was finishing his prep for the op at one of the Iranian safe houses he had been given access to. Everything was almost ready. As Blaze carefully planted C-4 strategically within the wooden crates purported to carry raw materials to be housed at Esfahan, he recalled the day Gallagher briefed him on this op, even though it was rather recent.

Gallagher was talking four hundred miles per minute and Blaze was trying to just settle into the atmosphere. The color brown was everywhere. Brown leather chairs. Brown leather adorning all of the couches. Light brown walls adorned with escapist images of Havana. Brown liquor settled in crystal glasses. And most prominently, robust brown cigars with long ash extensions.

These fine brown stogies rested in the hands of every gentleman that populated the Anchor's Away Cigar Lounge, an exquisite establishment nestled conspicuously in the Midwest rust belt city of Toledo, Ohio. Gallagher had insisted that this would be the perfect venue in which to meet.

Gallagher loved Anchor's Away, as it was his periodic escape from the intensities of his job. Under most circumstances, Gallagher was able to spend a few hours at Anchor's Away without giving a thought to the perilous world of being America's spymaster.

The patrons of Anchor's Away came in all stripes and found unity amongst each other with ease. You had business owners and clock punchers. Blue-collar ruffians and white collar number crunchers. Left-wing creative types and right-wing military types. Young punks and old farts. Every race, color, and religion. All finding laughs, sharing stories, and strengthening the natural bonds of male camaraderie in the ultimate public man cave. Whether all the men sat silently puffing on their cigars while watching *Family Guy* or were boisterously swapping stories about fishing, broads, fighting, golf, or being over-served, Anchor's Away rarely knew a dull moment. If one spent any time at Anchor's Away, they would walk away with the conviction that the cigars themselves deserved the Nobel Peace Prize for all the peace and unity they had inspired.

The two men were in a private back room that had been swept for bugs and made sound proof and secure per Gallagher's instructions.

The owner of Anchor's Away was one Butros Rshtuni. Butros was a burly middle-aged man with a thick full beard, a roaring sense of humor, and a counter-top salesmanship that rivaled any burgeoning tobacconist. He was born in Lebanon and was half Lebanese and half Armenian. He was also a devoutly patriotic US citizen who had been assisting Gallagher and the CIA for years in all things related to Lebanon.

As a Lebanese Christian, Butros was eager to engage in what he saw as an ideological struggle that was perpetually damaging and threatening his country of origin as well as his country of adoption. This struggle, of course, being the global struggle against radical Islamism and the terror it produced. From Butros' perspective, the least he could do was to occasionally convert a back room in his cigar lounge into a CIA safe meeting room. The most he could do was provide some free cigars and top shelf liquor when those meetings occurred.

Butros liked to gab and would talk about anything and everything to his customers as they purchased their cigar stashes. Butros was known for pontificating about his love of AC/DC, fly-fishing, and Mediterranean cuisine. He was also well known for his passionate political views, particularly, in regard to the nations from which his bloodline sprung—Lebanon and Armenia. Above all issues, he was most known for expressing his outrage at the lack of global attention given to the history of the Armenian genocide.

When not engaged in discussing those topics, Butros usually had the effect of making everyone he came in contact with laugh hysterically. His humor was legendary, his impressions impeccable, and his comedic audacity unmatched.

Blaze leaned back deep in the brown leather chair. He proceeded to puff and rotate his Perdomo Reserve Champagne Sun Grown cigar as he lit it. As he smoked, he sipped from his glass of Woodford Reserve bourbon on the rocks as he waited for a good time to put the kibosh on Gallagher's small talk and cut to the heart of the matter.

"...and that was the least of what that son of a bitch had coming to him. Had it been earlier in my career, he would've suffered a thousand hells. Did I ever tell you about the time that…."

"Chuck. Zip it pal. I know you could go on and on forever detailing past glories, but we're here to discuss how we're going to deal with present dangers. Let's get into it old man."

"Alright, you high-strung bastard. Fine. Here's what's on the table. We're finally launching Operation Persian Trinity. We've already commissioned the Father at Natanz, have a meeting lined up for the Holy Ghost to spook the freaks at Bushehr, and you my friend are the Son that will shock and awe the scientists and uranium shepherds at Esfahan." Chuck really thought he was clever at naming this op and its participants.

Blaze rolled his eyes at the contrived delivery. "Esfahan uh? Iran…always a challenge. I guess a disguise will be in order? What else is involved?"

"You'll get all of that, your encrypted sat phone, and all the necessary weapons and assets for the op soon."

Blaze nodded. "Right, so what's my job on this?"

"Despite years of multi-national warnings and the surprise Israeli hit on the plant warehouse in 2011, Esfahan is still churning. Right now, we need to buy us more time to tweak the improved Stuxnet worm before we unleash it at Natanz. To that end, we'll first stunt the supply chain of raw materials being funneled through Esfahan so that Natantz is starved of the materials it needs to feed the centrifuges for uranium enrichment. The stunt mechanism is going to be good 'ole fashioned C-4 buried in crates full of raw materials delivered by your fine Irish self. Although, we plan on making you over to look more like the Prince of Persia than the owner of Murphy's Pub."

"So I take it I'm a delivery guy. How soon will the truck be ready for me once I get into Iran?"

"The truck is already there. A safe house is set up as well. Various vehicles and motorcycles will be strategically placed for your acquisition. You'll find them in tight alleyways as you're traveling southwest out of Esfahan. This should help to facilitate your clean getaway to the safe house should hell follow you."

Blaze nodded, as he constructed the op's storyboard in his head.

Gallagher exhaled a large, bellowing cloud of cigar smoke and leaned back with a pensive, almost worried, look on his face. He then looked Blaze square in the eye and asked, "Are you sure you're ready for this? It's been quite some time you know…"

Blaze was ready. His flesh practically screamed with agony from civilian boredom. The withdrawal he experienced during his brief time away from the field had been torture.

"Hell yeah. More ready than I've ever been. My time off did nothing but grow my hunger and fan the internal warrior flame. My personal training regiment has continued and I'm sharper and more prepared than ever."

Gallagher smiled a subtle devious grin of faint fatherly pride, took a sip of his Crown Royal on the rocks and barked back with a militant tone. "Roger that. Now, back to my stories…."

Gallagher's stories, although highly relevant, seemed world's away, as Blaze continued prepping his mind and soul for yet another new adventurous and dangerous op.

CHAPTER THIRTY-THREE

The office of the Prime Minster, Jerusalem, Israel

Abigayil had kept him up the night before. A "predatory tigress who was volcanic in the sack" were the exact words that he used to describe her afterwards. She took that description as a flattering compliment on both her nature and her performance. As it was intended. Chaim Simmons struggled to remain calm as the flashing images of his wild night receded from his mind and the content of his morning briefing took hold. The smile from his morning afterglow died. The Prime Minister's lips tightened together and his brow furrowed as he digested the update on Iran and its lunatic leader, President Hadi Samani.

It was only a matter of time, Chaim knew, that this freak show would claim to have had an actual interaction with this Mahdi boogeyman he kept calling to return. The problem was, Chaim didn't believe for a second that Samani ever uttered a lie concerning his belief in the Mahdi, or his intentions to ignite global chaos to usher in the Mahdi's return. Chaim knew sincerity of belief when he saw it, be it benevolent or nefarious in nature.

Hadi Samani was a devout and utterly insane follower of the doctrine of the Twelfth Imam. It was his sincerity in belief and pure honesty in his vocalized intentions that the world had been missing.

This was no ploy invented by the Mullahs to arouse fear in the world. This wasn't a giant blackmail scheme. No carrot in the world would tame this belief, this determination, this evil regime. *Haven't we learned anything from the Holocaust? Hitler told us exactly who he was and what he planned to do. The world ignored him until they were forced to engage him. How could the world be so blind as to make yet the same mistake?* He asked these questions to himself, but knew the answers. He did not expect any bright light to pierce the world's opinion and change their perception.

The briefing staring back at him told him that President Samani had proclaimed to the Iranian people, and to the entire Muslim world via Al Jazeera, that he had been blessed with a personal visit by the Mahdi himself. Furthermore, Samani announced that the Mahdi intimated to him that this was indeed the year that He would return and set up a worldwide Caliphate. Chaim's blood boiled. As much as he expected to wake up and read such a briefing some morning, he was still not prepared for it, nor did its thrusting reality alleviate even a twitch of its haunting implications. Experience told him to calm himself, reflect on the news, and formulate a position and a decisive strategy before discussing it with anyone—be it his staff, the media, or particularly POTUS.

He slapped experience square in the face, deliberately ignoring its wisdom, and immediately dialed to get POTUS on the line.

"Mr. President, how are you this morning?" Chaim didn't give a rat's ass how Fitz was really doing. A raving lunatic who denied the first Holocaust and was planning a second just announced his Messiah was on his way—a Messiah who according to prophecy would reign in Jerusalem after annihilating the Jewish people.

"I'm well Chaim, is something the matter? It's highly unusual for you to call without scheduling in advance. Should I be worried about something?" Fitz didn't like the sound of Simmons' voice. He was already rolling his eyes, pinching the bridge of his nose, and thinking to himself, *Oh no, here we go with the war mongering again. Never a dull moment there in the desert. I can't believe I have to deal with this guy almost every day.*

"You're damn right something is the matter. Have you gotten the latest news out of Iran? Samani has announced he's been paid a ghostly visit by the Twelfth Imam. Do you know what that means? He says the Mahdi has told him that this is the year of His return. How do you think I'm going to digest this news?" Chaim was steaming pissed. Not just at the news, but also by the ever-growing apathy he perceived coming from President Jack Fitzsimmons. Their relationship had never gained real traction since Fitz took up residence in the White House.

"Chaim, this news just hit the wires. Don't jump to any conclusions or do anything rash. We still don't really know what all this means."

"What? What the hell are you talking about? We know exactly what this means! Samani, and Ahmadinejad before him, have been telling us for years *exactly* what this means. It means its go-time for the Iranians. It means they're moving forward with their plans to wipe Israel off the map and destroy America, the big Satan. Guess what? We're first, and I plan to do all I can to stop it." Chaim's face burned as red as a fire truck. The tension was thick and growing thicker.

"Joint covert ops between our two countries are being executed even as we speak to seriously interrupt, delay, and potentially destroy their progress on the nuclear program. Sanctions are being advanced and intensified and diplomacy is being wielded to its fullest to neutralize the threat. There's no need to irrationally go cowboy on the world right now." Fitz was extremely adept at not reacting to Chaim's temper. He was also adept at not fully understanding the immediacy and severity of a whole range of impending crises that faced his nation, and the world for that matter.

"Do you think that I haven't thought for years about what I would need to do when this moment arrived? Do you truly believe that we, as a nation, don't have a well-developed, and highly debated strategy to implement for this very scenario? We're not impulsive. We're students of history, particularly Jewish history, and the history of the world that has ignored the Jews and ignored the real threats made by the enemies of the Jews."

"Samani is not serious about all this hocus pocus Mahdi stuff. This is just his tool to rally his people and get them to follow him. This helps him detract from their domestic problems. Samani doesn't really want the world washed in blood. It doesn't make any sense. Iran, and millions of Muslims, would be equally as effected as Israel and the West." Fitz felt as if a rational, human application to the issue was needed.

"Samani and the Twelvers in Iran don't respond to rational, earthly fear or normal negotiations. These are not the atheists of Russia during the Cold War. They're an extreme apocalyptic death cult hell bent on the utter destruction of all Christians, Jews and non-Muslims. Think David Koresh running a country and being on the verge of having a nuke." Chaim's face was redder than hell and his voice rose in intensity with every syllable.

"Chaim, c'mon now, do you remember Waco? It was a disaster. If Samani is Koreshian in nature, the last thing anyone should be thinking about is storming the compound. It doesn't end well." Fitz smirked and leaned back on his chair.

"Okay then, if diplomacy and sanctions are the way to go, how come you haven't had an inch of success in pushing your Russian friend towards condemning Iran's nuclear program? Or your Chinese buddies?"

"I'm still working on my relationship with Maksim and making much progress. I think I can get him to come around on Iran very soon. You have to trust me on this. These things take time."

"Time, huh? Like that's in great supply. How much 'time' will it take with the Chinese?"

"That one is more difficult, but I think can change if I am successful first with Maksim."

"I doubt it. China is not going to be swayed by you. You're their debtor. They own you. The Bible is clear 'The borrower is slave to the lender'."

“I don’t appreciate you’re arbitrary application of scripture to insult me or my country.”

“Look, I’m sorry if I seem slightly out of line here. But you need to understand the position I’m in. Israel is at risk more than any other nation.”

“Chaim, I know you’re on high alert and you’re frustrated, but we’re still your allies, I wouldn’t dismiss anything at your peril but we need to tread carefully on this news, just like all news and developments out of Iran. We have different views on how to approach this, but we have to come to a consensus.” Fitz was pleading at this point.

“Maybe, Mr. President, maybe. However, for now, I must assume that present circumstances will continue to be consistent with the narrative of my people throughout history. We’re alone, and must act as such.”

Fitz never managed to have his rebuttal heard. The dial tone mocked him instead.

Chaim slammed the phone down and immediately opened up the Talmud sitting on his desk. His hands were shaking. He had not picked that book up in months. He didn’t even know where to start.

CHAPTER THIRTY-FOUR

CIA safe house somewhere near Esfahan, Iran

Blaze had finally snapped out of his retrospective daydreaming. He was settling into his preparation routine at the safe house Gallagher had provisioned for him about forty miles from Esfahan. He refocused his mind away from his recollection of the day Gallagher presented his mission to him at Anchor's Away cigar lounge and toward the task at hand—preparing to embed C4 explosives into wooden crates. He packed the C4 into viable, barely visible cracks and holes within the wooden crates.

He felt an extreme exhilaration simply in the preparation process. He had missed being in the field deeply. From soup to nuts, he thrived on the entire process. *This sure as hell beats watching FPS Russia on YouTube, competing twice a year in Tough Mudder, and reading Ted Bell novels just for a taste of the life.* Blaze finished the prepping of the wooden crates and headed to the bathroom to double inspect the fullness of his Persian disguise.

He really hated the way his skin felt with the damn coloring. It itched like crazy, but this was all part of the game. He took a good, hard look in the mirror and nodded. *You're all set. No one here in the Aryan land of Persia will ever suspect you're an American Mick. And a deadly spy to boot.*

Next, he double-checked the vehicle he was to use as his Trojan Horse in the op. He diligently inspected the basic functions of the vehicle and concluded that all was well and ready to go.

He heard a slight chirping and promptly retrieved his encrypted sat phone from the pocket of his olive green Dickies work pants. It was Gallagher.

"Hey you Mick bastard, you all ready to go another round here or what? I've been sweatin' your involvement in this and not sure how to feel. You got me nervous boy." Gallagher treated Blaze like a tough father would a son he loved.

"Boy? I'm quite the man, although not an artifact like you. And yes, this Mick bastard is quite fine, and in fact, quite prepared to kick some Persian ass with a good ole fashioned American boot."

"You got the C4 planted? You inspect the vehicle? Double-check the disguise? Take inventory of your weapons?" Gallagher rapidly rattled off this series of checklist questions with no real intention of allowing Blaze to actually answer.

"Everything but the weapons. I'm about to hand-pick my tools here shortly."

"Okay. Godspeed on this one Blaze. This is crucial to the larger goals of Operation Persian Trinity. And we're counting on you."

"I know that. I'm all in and I'm strong and on." Blaze assuaged Gallagher's fears with the confidence of his voice.

"Roger that. Be careful Blaze."

Blaze spent the next hour or so meticulously planning his approach in his head and doing his best to think outside of the box. He imagined any and all potential contingencies. He knew that op plans often morphed, changed, and recreated themselves minutes into their execution. This being the case, it was vitally crucial to have an adaptable mindset, and even more necessary to have a grab bag of contingency plans to pull from at any given moment.

He traced, in his mind, the locations of the strategically placed contingency vehicles that awaited him along the southwest path out of Esfahan, towards the safe house arranged for him. He thought about various combat circumstances that could arise and what weapons would be both effective and practical. Of course, Blaze also had his sentimental favorites. These particular weapons, which acted as roadmaps to his warrior life, had an easy path into most of his arsenals. He narrowed it down to just a few.

First, he decided on one of his favorite pieces of fine German steel— the Walther P99 Limited MI-6 edition. He knew its origins stemmed from a shameless, cheesy tie-in to the James Bond film franchise, but he cared not. He grew up with an addiction to Bond films, and this particular gun had somewhat of a history of being a good luck charm for him. Many a tight spot in the heat of battle had been opened thanks to the Walther P99 MI-6. Blaze, although full of traditional Christian Protestant faith, still harbored an irrational sense of superstitious Irish luck that he admittedly applied to his attachment to this weapon. Therefore, the piece was unquestionably included as part of his arsenal for this mission.

The second piece was, in his mind, slightly under-developed, but badass nonetheless. The G.R.A.D. was a genius invention that burrowed a .22-caliber gun under a knife. It was full of practical application in times of heat, and it was fun as hell to train with. His only misgiving was that he hadn't yet gotten his hands on the prototype that combined this with a cell phone gun. Now *that* would be the trinity to use in Operation Persian Trinity. Maybe next op.

Next, he chose several M67 fragmentation hand grenades to keep him company in the event he had to lob them at some unwanted trailers following him out of the Esfahan facility. The grenades weren't mind-blowing but they did the trick and he had always found them easy to carry, quick to unleash, and deadly.

Last, but by no means least, Blaze packed the Glock 18. He accessorized his G18 with the requisite suppressor and extended mags that always proved useful in times of need. When it came time to choose the ammunition for his beloved G18, he sided with the Buckingham variety; incendiary ammo had always impressed Blaze and he never tired of employing it.

As he carefully assembled the G18 and its companion accessories for portability and concealment, he was hit with a flood of memories. He had been in a multitude of situations in the early part of his service as a Marine in which he was forced to kill with this firearm. Lately he'd only used the G18 while playing Call of Duty on his son Shane's XBOX. While playing, he often wished he could jump inside the screen and take charge himself.

By all measures, Blaze was ready to stand up and be counted. T's were crossed, I's were dotted, and the blood in his veins was pumping with an intense patriotic ferocity. The overwhelming sense of undeniable purpose that surged inside him would yield to nothing but a driven, destined satiation of his truly calling. Iran's bomb be damned. America's favorite Mick was on the job.

The morning of the op broke like that of any other day in Iran. At Esfahan, workman picked up their tasks and projects right where they had left off the night before. There was no unusual tension in the air. It was with this favorable backdrop that Blaze drove the makeshift delivery truck up the long, guarded gate of the factory of Esfahan.

Blaze had felt a cool, deliberate confidence fall over him shortly after he lifted up the mission quietly and silently in prayer. His disguise had worked out unusually well and he was satisfied with its effects. This helped add to his confidence.

In the distance, he could see several guards smoking cigarettes, talking, and laughing. It was a tad after 6:00 am in Iran and Blaze was counting on encountering employees who were still in the slack mindset of wishing the morning alarm did not come so soon. As Blaze began rolling closer to the gate he could hear the high volume of the chatter between the security guards. They barely acknowledged his truck. The guards may have been soldiers of Allah at heart, but at the gate of Esfahan, they were mere soldiers of the time clock.

As Blaze reached the gate, the guard motioned him towards the electronic ID scanner. Blaze swiped the ID as if he'd done it a thousand times before. Nothing happened. No beep.

One guard looked at the other and then back at Blaze. He told him in Farsi to swipe the card again. Blaze swiped the card as he was asked, this time slower. His heart began to beat quite a bit faster. The machine beeped. Blaze nodded his head, holding back the smile inside, and was permitted to pass through the gate.

As soon as the rear wheels of the truck passed through the gate, Blaze quickly reached his encrypted sat phone and send a text to Gallagher. "I'm in."

Gallagher's reply came quickly. "Watching."

Aerial back up was lying in the wait in nearby Iraq to facilitate an extraction should things get hot.

Blaze did a quick visual sweep of the area. He quickly noted all pathways, windows, and high concentration points of vehicles and personnel. Then, swiftly, he catalogued in his mind the low vertical thresholds of which he would be able to scale if needed.

He then took a second, slower look around while his truck crept towards the wing of the facility that housed the raw materials he was purportedly delivering. Everything fit with the schematics and aerial photos.

Blaze backed the truck into the bay for unloading. He heard the shuffle and hustle of the crates being unloaded and he could see the men methodically doing their job from the side view mirror of the truck. He waived casually as workers walked by the truck. Blaze sat in the truck with the engine running for precisely twenty-two minutes until the unloading was finished. The C-4 had been burrowed within the second row of crates that were pulled from the back of the truck. The C-4 crates, were by now, nestled perfectly within the rest of the truckload inside the bay of the raw materials storage warehouse.

Blaze began to pull away from the truck when, suddenly, he saw one of the warehouse workers running out of the bay towards his truck. He was urgently waiving his arms for Blaze to stop, as if he had forgotten something. Blaze wasn't sure if he should stop, but he decided that it was best to see what the guy wanted to avoid any suspicion.

The man walked to the side window of Blaze's truck and launched into some kind of diatribe in a regional dialect of Farsi that threw Blaze off for a minute. He felt as if he was being interrogated.

Blaze was seized by a wave of panic. He froze. Blaze had taken some precautionary crash courses in Farsi before the op, but maybe he brushed through them too quickly. He was way more focused on other aspects of the op. *Note to self: don't cut corners on foreign language reviews. Particularly basic Farsi prep. Gonna take Rosetta Stone a bit more seriously next time.*

"I don't know," said Blaze in Farsi. Every time the man paused, Blaze repeated the phrase. It was all he could think to do. He tried to act as the annoyed, indifferent delivery guy.

The crates had real raw materials in them, and if they had pried open any one of them, they would have discovered the real deal. *What could this guy be freaking out about?* Blaze tried to listen more closely to pick up on some of the man's words this time, as the guy reiterated his apparent grievances. But this time, he spoke even quicker, and with an increasing sense of frustration, and anger. Blaze suspected his clear lack of understanding of the man's Farsi gave him away. The guy was on to him.

Amidst the yelling, Blaze finally recognized some of the words being shouted. The man was demanding Blaze's name and reason for being at Esfahan. Although the intensity and fragility of the moment would naturally call for a serious and calculated response, Blaze instead reacted instinctively by harkening Fletch-era Chevy Chase wise-assery. "The name is Simmons. Gene Simmons. Here to rock 'n' roll all night and party every day."

And with that, the party had begun.

The man angrily turned to waive over several more guards. The back up guards started toward the front of Blaze's truck at a jog—which was fortunately pointed outwards towards the exit of the facility. Then they began to run vigorously.

The yelling man's head was still turned, as he focused on recruiting back up. In the flash of an instant, a knife was jammed with full extension into the side of his neck, killing him instantly. Blaze yanked the knife application of his G.R.A.D. from the man's pulsating neck and watched his entire body unwind and flop to the ground, like a slinky falling off a balcony.

Now he had the back up guards to contend with. The party never ends.

Several dudes got within a few feet of him and were trying to apprehend him. Blaze could see the fear and confusion in their eyes. As they reached out to grab him, his hand-to-hand combat skills manifested with ease and success. The two men were quickly subdued and eating concrete.

Blaze look up and saw four more men quickly gaining ground towards him. A bit more alarming was the swarm of guards and speeding forklift trucks trailing close behind the four grunts. Blaze quickly drew his Glock 18 and shot two of the four men in the torso without effort. He reached into his backpack and grappled for an M67 frag grenade. Once he was able to get his paws securely around one, he pulled the pin and threw it about one hundred feet out. It landed within ten feet of the forklift trucks and the charging men. *Bye-bye fruits.* Blaze wiped the sweat off his brow in a brief expression of relief.

Before he could turn to begin heading back towards the truck, he felt a strong arm curl around his neck. *Damn it, I thought I got them all.* A guard had him in a strong headlock. *Always a straggler.*

Blaze herked and jerked and tried to get loose to no avail as he wrestled with the straggler. Sweat and blood smeared the two men as they struggled about with neither getting a clear upper hand. Finally, the guard gained leverage and hurled Blaze off his feet and smashed him to the ground. Blaze blocked the fall with his right arm, saving his head from some serious damage.

The man pinned him down, Blaze's hands now behind his back. Vulnerable. Bound. No play in sight.

The guard pulled Blaze's hair to yank his head back and sideways, as Blaze lay on his stomach. Blaze managed to speak. "So this is how you party in Esfahan, uh? I can only imagine the gig we could have if we unleashed those centrifuges." With a swelling, bleeding face, Blaze smiled big for his new captor.

And then with the thud of a gun butt hitting a hard, stubborn Irish head, everything went black.

CHAPTER THIRTY-FIVE

The McIntyre residence, Romeo, Michigan

Instead of Blaze's face being the last thing Diem saw before she hit the sack, it was the 9mm Beretta on her nightstand. The pistol didn't give her quite the same comfort as her man by her side, but it was the next best thing in his absence. She didn't always keep it out and loaded, but she had a premonition and was feeling particularly vulnerable. The whole day had seemed draped in heavy malaise and she felt a gnawing, irrational sense of pending terror since morning. She would lock the door before lying down to sleep. She didn't want the boys to be able to get in with the loaded gun lying out in the open.

Diem felt a chill to her bone. Outside her window, the wind was roaring and the trees were blowing. She sipped some hot chamomile tea. It warmed her body but did nothing for her soul. She stared at the gun. She hated the thought of having to use the gun, but yet that is all she found herself thinking about. Diem was a good shot—Blaze made sure of that. But she was prepared only out of necessity. Her mind was reeling.

Is this what I'm in for again? A cold piece of steel keeping me safe at night instead of the warm flesh and blood of my husband? Lord, why did I let him go back in? I should've fought him. I should've stood my ground. I should've trusted my instincts. Why did I let him convince me? Why am I supporting this? I'm alone. Again. Diem tried to shake her doubts. The wind blew stronger. She glanced at her iPhone on her nightstand to check the time. 11:21 pm. *Will I ever get any sleep tonight?*

She took some melatonin pills and sipped more tea. She began to feel small, exposed. Her loneliness was creeping with strength. She didn't feel safe, even with the firearm by her side. She tried to force her mind to focus on pleasant things—cooking, sunny days, nature, and ice cream. She tried this for a few minutes and gave up. The tactic did not work. She wished her life could be simple again, like when Blaze was home. *Blaze doesn't like simple.* This contrast had been a barrier in their marriage from day one.

She decided to change out of her flannel pajamas. She walked to the closet and undressed. She stood in her purple lingerie as she began to reach for her silk robe. The moonlight hit her figure directly. She turned her back towards the window, concerned of how visible she was.

She heard some shuffling outside her window. She grabbed a flashlight from inside the drawer in her nightstand and walked over to see what it was. She saw nothing. She heard it again—the crackling of sticks, ruffling of leaves and scuffling of dirt and rock. She felt uneasy. *Is there someone out there? Is it some terrorist coming after me to get revenge on Blaze? A burglar?* She felt silly for having such thoughts, insane really. She brushed off her paranoia. *Must've been a squirrel or some braches falling.*

Still she felt funny. *Is someone from the agency out there? Someone checking up on me? Someone Blaze sent to watch after me? …or is it someone from the agency spying on me for some other reason? Maybe someone at odds with Blaze?* Diem didn't trust the CIA or the federal government. If it wasn't for her trust in Chuck Gallagher, she doubted she would've signed on to Blaze getting back in to the game. Blaze had always stressed to her that they needed to be guarded against the potential malice of the bureaucracy. He'd seen too many strange things happen to colleagues. He knew that the CIA, and the government as a whole, had large pockets of corruption just like any other power structure. He was always watching his back. He knew that moles got in. Diem knew one of Blaze's biggest fears was that the ultimate enemy would emerge from within the agency. Blaze was known, and usually mocked, by his colleagues for his paranoia about moles in the agency.

She walked away from the window. *Its nothing. Just the wind. I need to get some rest.* She got under the covers, turned out the lamp on her nightstand and laid her head on the pillow. As soon as she closed her eyes, she heard a knock on her bedroom door. She quickly rose out of bed and went and unlocked it.

"Shane! What's wrong honey? Can't you sleep?"

Shane stumbled in the bedroom rubbing his eyes. He was clearly upset. He ran to hug his mother. Diem scooped him up and propped him beside her on the bed, after putting the gun away in the nightstand drawer. Not that the sight of a gun was at all unusual for the McIntyre children.

"I had a nightmare, mom. There were wolves chasing me. Flying monsters too. I couldn't get away from them. I was screaming. One of the wolves was just about to eat my leg. Then I woke up."

"It's okay honey, even adults get scared sometimes. Really. We all do. But it's okay. We have nothing to be afraid of. We're safe here. The Lord is watching over us and He'll give us strength to protect ourselves from any harm. Including your bad dreams."

"Thanks mom. That helps, but I wish dad was here."

"I know, honey. I do too. We all do. But right now you need to get back to bed. We all need to get some good rest."

"Good night, mom." Shane kissed her on the cheek.

"Good night, Shane. I love you."

Shane went back to bed and Diem did the same. Diem fell asleep quickly, barely getting through half a prayer. She had felt about as safe as she was going to feel for now. Rest could no longer wait.

CHAPTER THIRTY-SIX

Esfahan, Iran

Blaze shook to it and gained consciousness to the piercing sight of an overhead hot lamp bearing down on him. Temporarily blinded, he could see nothing else, but could hear frantic arguing in Farsi between the two men in the room with him.

As his vision adjusted and recovered from the hot lamp, he got a visual on the men in the room. One was the prick guard that head locked him and gun butted him. The other looked to be a supervisor of sorts based on his wearing a different uniform. Both looked like they didn't know what the hell to do about Blaze.

Blaze felt disoriented and lightheaded from the trauma of the gun butting he endured, as well as the other abuse of the scuffle. He rolled his neck several times to attempt to get his blood flowing and psych himself up for a viable plan to get his ass out of Esfahan. *Fuck this. I ain't gonna die in some two bit, half ass Iranian nuke joint. There's gotta be a way to jam up these ass clowns trying to hold me here.* As he rolled his neck maniacally, he noticed out the window to his right that his truck still sat exactly where he left it. *If they ain't moved the truck, I couldn't have been knocked out very long. Maybe fifteen or twenty minutes.* The place was clearly on lock down, but they still hadn't managed to move or quarantine his truck. *I bet they're in the warehouse going through the crates. I gotta get outta here before they find that C4.* Blaze peered down at his feet, which remained unbound. His arms were still tied with rope.

The ass clown supervisor-looking-guy turned and smirked at Blaze and said, "You will die in here, I hope you know."

Asshole speaks English, good to know. "Is that right? I wouldn't be too sure about that, ya meatsnake."

Supervisor guy walked towards Blaze and kneeled down to whisper in his ear. "Allah has given you to me and me alone. You understand? None of my superiors even knows you're here yet. You are all mine to kill how and when I see fit."

No sooner did he finish annunciating his last carefully intimated word in Blaze's ear, when Blaze snapped his neck around and went full blow Mike Tyson on this poor chap. He bit the ass clown's ear clean off and spit it on the floor in fury.

The supervisor screamed for his bloody life as he curdled in shock. The other guard began to charge. Blaze quickly lifted his arms up surrender style, leapt as high as could, and landed the free rope in between his bound arms directly onto the coat hanger above him, suspending him. Now hanging firmly from the coat hanger, back against the wall, feet securely free and elevated, he crunched his legs upward and kicked the incoming guard squarely in the face before the ass clown knew what hit him. He then issued one final brutal punch in the face to the crouching, bloodied, earless supervisor, just to button things up with closure.

With both ass clowns out of commission, Blaze ran like hell towards the truck. On the way out, he busted a window and used the edged broken glass that lay in tact to cut loose the rope that bound his hands.

He managed to get to the truck without being stopped. He hopped in and fired it up without hesitation or mistake and slammed his boot on the gas pedal. Steering with his left hand, he reached under the seat and grabbed the C-4 detonator with his right. *These bastards are going to have their noses deep into my payload right as it reaches out to bite them.*

As Blaze's vehicle sped toward the gate, he just missed plowing over some guards heading towards him—all while being inundated with a hail of undisciplined gunfire by guards late to the party. Several bullets hit the windshield, leaving it just short of shattered. Only one whizzed passed his head. Other bullets pounded the side of the truck. His truck was still fairing well, thanks to it being bulletproof. His boot stomped heavily on the gas pedal and floored it just as a slew of even more guards began heading towards the truck with automatic weapons fully engaged.

In his rearview, facility vehicles were now heading after him with vigor. Two trailed him neck to neck and were closing in behind his truck within fifteen yards. Shouting and chaos blossomed all around him. He shot two guards while his truck swerved all the while. He was fast approaching the gate. Smoke, fire, and now blood coalesced throughout the facility as Blaze's gunfire connected with his enemies via his Glock 18. His arm extended out the passenger side window as he pulled the trigger on his G18, a few yards away from the gate. Another guard met his fate with Blaze's bullet. Straight through the heart.

As if on queue, the C-4 finally exploded at the precise moment that the front grill of Blaze's truck met the locked gate at the exit point. Although he could not afford to look back, he heard the explosion of the raw materials warehouse as he crashed through the gate fleeing the now-chaotic Esfahan plant.

Alarms rose above the sounds of the chaos. Blaze smiled. *It's safe to say there ain't gonna be any uranium fluoride gas comin' out of Esfahan for a while.* C

Blaze waited until he was heading southwest on Rt. 51 near Garmase to call Gallagher and give him the 411 on the happenings.

"What the hell happened Blaze?" Gallagher knew that some hiccup was bound to occur on Blaze's first comeback op.

"Language issue. They speak Farsi, and I failed to. Red flags went up and bullets flew. And they had me caught and bound for a minute. But I out played them and broke free. They still have me in hot pursuit though. I'm on my way to secure the getaway vehicle now. Gotta get my ass to that safe house ASAP." Blaze was out of breath and talking with a concise, fast cadence.

"Everything's all prepared. You know the plan."

"Gotta go. Talking is slowing me down."

"Roger that."

He could hear the helicopters, although they trailed. He wasn't far enough ahead of the ground vehicles pursuing him to create the cushion he needed for the next vital step in his escape. He stepped on the gas heavily as he made his way to the getaway vehicle. Blaze bobbed and weaved through the unsuspecting traffic that clogged Rt. 51. He could see quite a few angry faces screaming at him as he put all vehicles around him in complete peril. Horns were honking all around him. Exhaust smoke filled the air. Tension, sweat, and anger was palpable.

Miles later, Blaze had managed to put the traffic behind him while those who followed him were apparently entangled in it. He banged a hard left into the tight alleyway that harbored his getaway vehicle.

He parked the truck, double-checked the second batch of C-4 packed in-between the passenger seat cushions, and hopped on the waiting motorcycle hidden behind the atrocious smelling industrial garbage dumpster. He stifled a gag as his nose filled with the smell of rotten butcher trimmings.

Wow. Blaze had heard about this bike, but seeing it and sitting on it gave him an entirely different sense of awe than merely hearing its description. The bike was a modified version of the Dodge Tomahawk. The military engineers had enhanced it for the CIA with a host of button-ready weapons and distraction functions. With 500 BHP, a Viper Engine V 10, and a slick, futuristic design slapped with sharp chrome and black accents, Blaze felt as if he was unworthy to sit on this thing without a cape. It was the closest thing on earth to Batman's bike in *Dark Knight.* With all its functionality and power, it still maintained a relatively sleek design, which Blaze suspected would come in handy as he proceeded to the safe house. The bike was documented to have reached speeds as high as 300 mph in its testing. As enticing as that stat was, Blaze vowed to keep it under 120 mph as he didn't trust his own judgment at any speeds, in any vehicle, above 120.

Blaze's slack-jawed, fan-boy reaction to the bike did not last long. A black Cadillac Escalade was doing its best to enter the alleyway and it did not give him a good feeling. He backed the bike out from behind the dumpster and re-positioned it towards an open forward path with one quick movement—a turn of the handlebars and a re-positioning of his feet.

Just as he pushed the start button, he heard quickening footsteps and the sound of an AK-47 assault rifle, which was apparently the preferred weapon of his enemy. In the bike's left rearview mirror, he saw the three men charging from the black Escalade .

Blaze had planned for this. The bike rocketed forward like a metallic cheetah made in the factory of the War Gods. As the Tomahawk screamed with triumph, Blaze's second round of C4 decimated his truck and rocked the Escalade while hurling the mangled bodies of two of the assaulters into the side of the vehicle. The other was launched onto the hood. Their pursuit of the imposter at Esfahan ended in a spiral of smoke, fire, auto parts, and debris. All three died instantly upon impact.

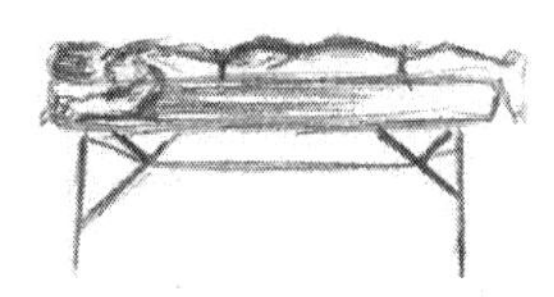

CHAPTER THIRTY-SEVEN

The Kremlin, Russia

His hamstrings were extraordinarily sore from the brutal and intense kickboxing sessions of the past week. A deep relaxation fell over him, along with a profound sense of therapeutic satiation, as the massage therapist continued to perform deep work on his hamstrings.

The massage therapist had managed to work out all the troublesome knots that accumulated within the taut tendons and muscles of Maksim Koslov's hamstrings, and from the rest of his warrior's body.

Maksim found his weekly massages to not only be pleasurable but a necessary alignment of both body and soul. The massages centered his highly fertile mind and ultimately enabled him to more effectively tackle the simultaneity that encompassed his very busy schedule.

Maksim closed his eyes and felt himself floating on air as he allowed his body to reach new heights of relaxation—the therapist's hands briskly working his muscles all the while. It was in this state that he often found clarity on issues he was wrestling with—or that his mind would finally crystallize on an approach for an upcoming meeting.

This particular day, it was his approaching call with Hadi Samani, the president of Iran, that occupied his now loose and limber mind. He knew what Samani wanted to talk about. The attack at Esfahan. They had not had a formal conversation about the implications of the attack yet and Samani was eager to do so.

Koslov thought about the situation. *Samani's terribly impatient. His religious insanity is beginning to become more than just a tolerable annoyance. He'll be frantic over this set back and try to push for unrealistic recoveries on the timeline.* Koslov's mind drifted away from his thoughts on Samani. He had already resolved to manage Samani's expectations with reserved caution and vague answers. His mind now wandered to thoughts of his over-arching goals.

If he could accomplish his goal of neutralizing—or liquidating as Samani would describe it—the Jews, and get Israel out of the picture, Russia would have a strategic role in the control of the Mediterranean and all the resources and advantages it boasts. Russia had already made great strides in controlling the flow of gas throughout Europe. Koslov knew that similar resources, and the ambition to acquire and control them, would be the key to Russia's continued reemergence.

If the Americans keep electing naïve Presidents like Fitz, maybe we can even talk them into giving us Alaska back so we don't have to take it from them. Either way, we will get those resources. Alaska should never have left our control. Just like Ukraine. The thought almost made him chuckle. *For years now, we've had the Americans in the palm of our hands—sucking up and giving it up. Weak and apologetic, just the way we need them. They are their own worst enemy. They are a skeleton of their former strength.* For a nanosecond he almost felt bad for the Americans.

Koslov did not take his time to get up off of the massage bed as was often suggested to him by his therapist. He was sufficiently fixed up and was eager to make his call to Samani and move on with his day.

After he dressed, he strode to his office and promptly dialed Samani to get on with the inevitable.

"Good afternoon Hadi." Maksim loudly said—an extra bit of strength in his voice after his rejuvenating massage.

"And good afternoon to you Maksim. I trust all is well at the Kremlin. I am happy to hear from you and eager to discuss the important matters at hand." Hadi had not been the same since his mystical encounter with the Mahdi. His ambition was more feverish than ever. He could almost taste Israel's destruction, and he could smell the downfall of America and the West like an aroma rising from his tea cup.

"I understand. I know you must have some serious concerns regarding the unfortunate attack at Esfahan."

"Yes, I do. We're taking as many precautions as we can think of to ferret out gaps in our security there and at Natanz and Bushehr, but those Jews are tricky. We should never underestimate their deceitfulness, particularly when matched with the ingenuity and technology of the Americans."

"There's no doubt that the Jews will never give up on their attempts to thwart our plans, but they'll never stop us. You know that." Koslov was attempting to reassure Hadi, knowing it would likely do nothing to soften Hadi's impatience.

"Of course they'll never stop us. The Madhi is returning imminently and there's no force that can stop his implementation of Allah's plans. The Jews can try all they want, but their time is running short. I'm not concerned about them stopping us, but I'm frustrated with them slowing us down and making things difficult. We need to accelerate all plans to overcome this setback, and we need to do that immediately."

"Hadi, please, you don't need to speak to me with such firmness. We have the same interests. I'm doing what can be done to overcome as much of the setbacks as possible, but it's challenging. Realistically, I think we can expect to overcome a third of the setbacks. We'll likely still experience a net setback of six to nine months if we're fortunate." Koslov knew this would not sit well and he did not care. Yes, they had the same interests in terms of antipathy towards Israel, but they had vastly different motivations. Koslov's timetable didn't have to keep pace with the religious-driven urgency that Samani possessed.

"Maksim, I appreciate your analysis, but I think you're being wildly conservative in estimating your abilities to affect the situation. Please rethink this scenario and find a way to hasten the process. A six to nine month delay is simply unacceptable." Samani, caught up with religious fervor, felt no sense of having over-stepped his boundaries.

"Let me remind you of your limited options for completing the development without Russia. If we can't reasonably work together, maybe we shouldn't be working together after all." Koslov was clearing bluffing, but felt compelled to drive home the point.

"Do what you can, but please stay on this with diligence. Of course we'll continue to work together. We're of one purpose on this." Samani did not take the bait, and backing down and being apologetic was not feasible for a megalomaniacal theocrat.

"I'll keep that in mind as we continue to run political interference for you on the world stage. Which, I must remind you, isn't always completely in our interest."

"I understand Maksim. The Islamic Republic of Iran is grateful for our relationship and we honor your loyalty. We'll continue to reciprocate that respect." Samani was done. He had made his point and was no longer interested in talking.

"I'll report to you next week the status of everything. Have a great rest of your afternoon Hadi."

"You as well Maksim"

In Moscow, as Maksim hung up the phone he peered reverently at the skull-shaped mug in his office and hung his mind on the grand nature of all of his plans. His Scythian ancestors would be proud. A revived Soviet Empire was within his reach.

In Tehran, as Hadi Samani hung up the phone he peered anxiously at the digital counter hanging in his office displaying the number of days that had passed since the beloved Twelfth Imam had gone into hiding. Samani knew that it would truly not be long at all until that counter was no longer needed. The Mahdi was in transit and the Caliphate was on the precipice of emerging, and Hadi Samani could not wait to assist in the bloodshed necessary for this phenomenon to reach completion.

CHAPTER THIRTY-EIGHT

Natanz, Iran

Arash Jafari was trying to settle into his work day. He decided to organize his office and clean up his desk before digging in. He was unsettled inside and thought that maybe if he got more organized he could calm down a bit. His new life continued to jostle him. It was nerve-racking enough to have been thrust into the role of a spy. It was downright horrifying to be a spy in one of the most brutal and risky countries in the world. Not just a spy, but a traitor. It was even more brazen to embark on such activities just weeks after Iran's facilities at Esfahan had been attacked, by what President Samani insisted was a joint Israeli-American effort.

Gallagher had coached Jafari endlessly on his approach, and attempted with his own brand of pseudo-interpersonal skills to instill in Arash the confidence he would need to cleanly complete the mission. Arash tried his hardest to assimilate the encouragement, but was ultimately still plagued by strong, persistent waves of insecurity and fear that tugged against his internal sense of purpose.

"Treat it like any other day at Natanz. You're going to work. You're troubleshooting IT issues. Along the way, while taking a working lunch, you happen to casually hack into the system you know so well and plant the Stuxnet Worm in-between bites of your khoresht."

"I'm glad you think so simply of my mission. I'm afraid I feel a tad differently about the seriousness of being a traitor against my country—particularly being a traitor by working hand in hand with the big Satan and the little Satan simultaneously," Arash reminded.

"All you need to be concerned with are the risks of your immediate surroundings when you go in to accomplish this mission. You needn't worry about the larger risks at the time of application. It'll interfere with what I'm telling you is the simplicity of the task. Focus. Simplify. Complete. You'll succeed and you'll clock out like any other day."

Arash nodded his head accepting the advice. Gallagher's words were finally breaking through. "Okay. If you say so, then so it will be. I'll get it done as described. No use talking it through any more. It's go time, as they say."

Arash Jafari recalled his own words the one day he had clocked in for his normal 7 am to 3 pm shift at Natanz. It was like any other day at the plant, except for the fact that everything had changed since the attack on Esfahan. Production schedules were reduced, even suspended in some departments. Arash's work had slowed down as a result of the decreased activity, all stemming from the attack on Esfahan and the resulting production disruptions. He had heard it said that the attack would set back Iran's overall nuclear plans by a minimum of six months. Arash knew that if he was successful he'd add a much greater delay.

Arash still couldn't get used to carrying a pistol. He was never a gun enthusiast or a military guy, and he'd never gotten into so much as a schoolyard scrap. Confrontation was something he had avoided all of his life at all costs. Arash made no attempts at covering up the fact that he had pretty much lived the life of an out-of-shape computer nerd since his youth.

The pistol he carried, however, did not need to be hidden, as it was issued by Natanz, not the CIA. Natanz decided to arm all employees, even IT, after the debacle at Esfahan. This, he saw as a blessing, because he may very well need the pistol, and he wouldn't have trusted his ability to successfully hide the gun had it been a gift of the CIA. Of course, he now had to wrestle with the fear of his gun-carrying colleagues, but he tried not to think about that.

Shortly after Arash logged onto his computer and settled into his office chair, his office landline began ringing. It was his superior, Dabir.

"Good morning Sir." Arash did his best to hide his nervousness.

"We're on high alert still, Arash. I expect total vigilance from you. Are you keeping your eyes open? We can't afford to be attacked like Esfahan."

Arash could here the contention and condescension in Dabir's voice and he wondered where this was all coming from. It had been weeks since the attack occurred at Esfahan and Dabir had never taken such a tone with him like this. *Have I aroused suspicion somehow? Had he sensed disloyalty in me in someway? Or was this just some sort of erratic and arbitrary paranoia that had randomly struck Dabir?* Arash did not know.

"I fully understand sir. I'm conscious of my surroundings and am fully on guard."

"Good. We can trust no one, and nothing, in times like these."

Arash didn't like the potential inferences in Dabir's last comment. Of course, Arash recognized his own unusual sensitivity in interpreting such comments, given his newfound covert activities.

After hanging up the phone, Arash wiped a few drops of sweat off his brow. *I need to really lose some weight, my fat sweats don't go so well with my new life as a spy.* He did his best to recall a verse from Psalm 25 to reinforce confidence within himself. His memory was rather good, as he did not have the luxury in his country of carrying around a Bible for quick retrieval of needed scripture. His Bible had to be carefully tucked away. The verse came to him. "Guard my life and rescue me; let me not be put to shame, for I take refuge in You." He felt the comfort of the Holy Ghost immediately upon recitation of the Psalm.

For several hours that morning, Arash proceeded with his normal tasks. He had to finish a few reports, double check on some amended issues from the previous day, and run some routine security tests. All the while, he was waiting for an opportune moment to hack into the system and plant the Stuxnet worm 2.0.

Throughout the early morning hours of his workday, various colleagues came in and out of his office in the usual way. Strangely, more than ever, it was talk of the Mahdi on the lips of many that morning. Praise and reference to the Mahdi was commonplace, but this particular morning it seemed more frequent and more intense. Arash wondered what the impetus for this might be. 'He is coming soon!' some said. Others uttered 'I feel the Promised One might even now be upon us!' And yet others proclaimed 'Allah's wrath be to the infidels! The beloved Mahdi is coming and the Caliphate will emerge!'

It was not long ago that Arash had such religious thoughts stemming from a different source. He would have never guessed in a thousand lifetimes that instead of lifelong devotion to the Twelfth Imam, he would instead become a committed Christian and a spy against his Persian homeland. Life sure had a funny way of carving its on path, particularly once he put his life in the guiding hand of the Nazarene.

As his colleagues and co-workers expressed their Messianic fervor throughout the day, Arash enthusiastically faked a perceived zeal for the coming of the Mahdi, while retaining a deep devotion to Jesus Christ in his heart.

It was shortly after the whistle blew for the normal line workers that Arash sensed the perfect window to begin his daring task. He quietly closed his office door, even though his office was enclosed entirely by walls fully made of windows and all passerby could clearly see in. Nonetheless, he wanted to give the impression that he was hard at work concentrating and did not wish to be disturbed.

He sipped from his cup of tea and began typing. He was indeed the proverbial fox with the key to the hen hound. His passwords gained him access as usual, and he began taking the necessary digital steps to cover his tracks as he embedded the well-tested and well-researched Stuxnet worm into Iran's centrifuge-controlling computer systems.

His heart slammed against the interior of his chest and the fat sweats were indeed now coming on strong once again. The moment in which he triggered the installation of the worm had felt entirely surreal.

He could not believe he was risking his job, his life, and his family's well being as a result of his newfound belief in Jesus as Messiah and his bizarre partnership with Israel and the CIA. *My parents would shun me fiercely if they were alive to see and know about this.* He knew deeply just how radical were the decisions that had brought him to this point; initiating a bold digital warfare attack on Iran's beloved nuclear weapons program.

The fix was in, but the job was not over. The worm would just now begin recording all operations of the plant while slowly tearing the program apart. The quickest the nerds at Negev were able to get the worm to begin to tear apart the program was estimated to be five to seven days. This was where the tough part began. Arash had to play it cool, and play stupid for a while until this cycled through. He prayed for the discernment, wisdom, and steadiness of mind to see it through.

The rest of the day was uneventful, just as his friend Chuck Gallagher back at Langley had assured. Arash clocked out at the end of his shift as he did any other day, and went home to greet his wife and quietly pray to Jesus while kneeling to Allah; a duplicity that had become second nature to the burgeoning overweight spy.

CHAPTER THIRTY-NINE

The Oval Office, The White House, Washington, DC

It was time for their weekly Monday morning meeting with the President. Bob Sapp arrived just a step before Hank Mahoney. Bob smiled and extended his arm to motion Hank to enter the Oval Office first. Neither of the men had yet to shake the weekend off their minds. And they were each not ready to begin discussing the issues surrounding Israel and Iran.

"Thanks Bob." Hank said.

Hank Mahoney, Fitz's VP, never lost his cool. Never. He was the minty, calm and collected voice of reconciliation that managed to talk everyone off the ledge. This was not widely known about him in the press. From their standpoint, he was a curiously uninvolved and useless veep.

But those inside the white house and close to POTUS knew Mahoney put out fires on a daily basis. This meeting would prove no exception to the utility and value of Hank Mahoney's temperament. He would once again act as the firefighter.

Had a drunken sailor been present, even he would have been offended. Bob Sapp, the president's bulldog-like chief of staff, had no couth. Zilch. Zero. F-bombs were a breath of fresh air coming from his vulgar mouth compared to the litany of other more explicit obscenities that hurled from his lips. And this was the case before he even got angry. Once his anger was awakened, Lucifer himself would blush at the hellish vernacular that ensued.

Sapp's extreme character flaw never served to officially and fully alienate his colleagues. Sapp's vulgarity was tolerated because, underneath the layers of linguistic slime, his insight was on the money. He was a truth teller.

And for this Bob Sapp was one of the most valuable people surrounding the President. Even if it was quite possible he was slowly killing the President with second hand smoke all the while. Rush Limbaugh may not believe that second hand smoke has any power to kill, but President Fitz and his Democratic colleagues did—and their turning a blind eye to Sapp's furious chain-smoking, anywhere and everywhere, was a noticeable anomaly.

Amidst the smoke-filled Marlboro haze that choked the oxygen out of the oval office, Hank Mahoney sat pensively. The blasphemous language rang throughout the four walls. The topic of the Iranian nuclear threat was front and center. Hank was waiting for an appropriate moment to interject his thoughts. This wasn't quite the moment.

"I don't care what your damn religion is, what their damn religion is, or what the bastard Republicans think or don't think. Truth is truth, and the truth here is that if those nutjobs in Iran get the bomb they'll use it. They'll use it against Israel and they'll use it against us. This is horrible for everyone, future generations not excluded." This was the first set of consecutive sentences shouted by Bob Sapp that weren't laced with eye-bleeding obscenities. Mahoney thought this would be a softer moment to interject his thoughts on the debate. But he didn't yet get his chance.

Fitz threw up his hands in frustration. "Whose side are you on? You sound like one of them! Why don't you go be chief of staff for a Republican! You might as well. You sound like a hate-filled warmonger, you might as well go work for one. I don't pay you to act like a pissed-off paranoid conservative. I pay you to run my staff and advise me on *my agenda*, not your turncoat opinions. I don't blame the Iranians for wanting the bomb. Everyone knows Israel has it. What's to stop Israel from attacking Iran because of their support for the Palestinians? Pakistan has the bomb and we aren't talking about going to war with them, are we?"

"Gentleman...," Mahoney finally found a spec of dead air. "...please. This isn't about paranoia or taking sides on the Palestinian issue, or who's a Republican or who's a Democrat. This whole issue needs to be approached with common sense, balance, and a tread lightly attitude. Chuck Gallagher already has a covert CIA op in play with a top-notch team to help stunt the growth of the Iranian nuclear program, and potentially set it back to its inception. We must continue to carefully support and engage in the economic sanctions against Iran without being perceived as insensitive to the Palestinians, and more so, not be perceived as being inseparable on all levels from the Israelis. We don't need to take Iran's side, nor do we need to carpet bomb them at this moment either. Many multi-pronged efforts still need to play themselves out to effectively neutralize this problem."

Mahoney had done it again. He had parted the roaring red sea of the ongoing debates and disagreements between Sapp and Fitz. He was the third element in the dynamic that always brought the two together in a rational compromise and unified approach.

Sapp looked at Fitz and exhaled a large cloud of cigarette smoke and began to chuckle. Fitz smiled and chuckled to himself. He walked over to Sapp and patted him on the back. "You know I always appreciate a vigorous debate, and damn it, with you I know I can always get one. Good thing we have Mahoney here to referee and bring us both back into reality each time."

"It's a good thing. You and I can't afford an endless knock down, drag out. We have too much on our plates and too many enemies, political and otherwise, that seek to destroy us, to be always fighting each other."

"You're right about that. Okay, we'll continue the covert ops and hold fast on the sanctions. We'll treat this Iran thing in a way that doesn't alienate the relationship I am building with Koslov and also doesn't piss off the Muslim world too much by them thinking we're nothing but pawns of Israel. We'll straddle the line." summarized President Fitz.

"Gentleman, I'm glad you've come to an understanding." Mahoney could barely proclaim this with a straight face and they didn't receive it with a straight face either. They both patted Mahoney on the back and began to tease him for his never-ending even-keel, peacemaker approach.

CHAPTER FORTY

Natanz, Iran

Arash's nerves had calmed considerably since the bold day in which he deployed the Stuxnet 2.0 worm developed by the Israeli technicians at Negev. Work was, once again, just work. Even Dabir had been extremely civil, and even affirming towards him as of late. He had even commented on Arash's excellent propensity towards efficiency in his work. Life at the Natanz nuclear facility seemed to be as normal, and as such, Arash's guard was down.

It had been two weeks since that nerve-racking pivotal day in which Arash pulled the trigger on the Stuxnet 2.0 attack and officially became a true hidden enemy of the Islamic Republic of Iran. The worm began immediately recording the data inside the centrifuge systems, but it took about a week before it began the process of systematically, and incrementally, destroying the program. That progress remained in motion and Arash was anticipating the resulting breakdowns and difficulties to begin emerging very soon. Likely, within a week or so.

During the past two weeks, Arash had been occupied with feeding back info to Gallagher. He had prepared and transmitted dossiers to the CIA on all the key managers, supervisors and employees at Natanz. The dossiers included photos, family information, religious status, formal associations to various political and religious organizations, military history and/or status, and detailed descriptions of their daily and over-arching duties and responsibilities at Natanz. Additionally, Arash prepared updates to his original report on the production schedules within the plan, the daily flow of deliveries and employee movement. Since the Esfahan attack, much had changed, and he needed to revise his report so that Gallagher was up to speed on the new dynamic at Natanz.

Arash had not experienced heartburn in quite some time and was very thankful for the peace his body now experienced. Life at home had seemed fine, despite the gnawing guilt he felt for living the double life of a spy and for being a covert convert to Christianity in a land where people were arrested and killed for such things. If his wife Atoosa was to discover any of this, he feared how she'd react.

He loved her very much, and prayed for her daily, but she was deeply devoted to Islam and fiercely loyal to her country and her family. She was increasingly fervent about the coming of the Mahdi and had been increasing her prayers and Koran readings in recent days and weeks. Her memory of the Hadiths was impeccable and she was becoming quite scholarly with her faith—an unusual achievement for women in Iran. Only Arash could feel, and know, the growing distance between them. Atoosa had no clue that deep in his heart Arash had drifted far, far away from her as a direct result of the changes in his life.

Arash was having a hard time focusing on his work, as he was overwhelmed with his thoughts. It seemed as if his life had changed so much so fast—a life that continued to radically change internally, even as the exterior of life remained unchanged and seemingly mundane. He was preparing some reports for Dabir at his desk and sipping tea when he peered through his office window and saw some police walking through the plant. They were being escorted while wearing hard hats and being directed to be careful around the heavy equipment that populated the plant. Arash wondered what was going on. *Have they discovered what I have done? Do they know about Stuxnet? How did they track me? Had they somehow tapped my calls with Gallagher or Reza? Oh Lord, please protect me, rescue me from the adversary.*

His heart leapt as he gazed upon the entourage of law enforcement making its way up the steps of the plant towards the offices. He watched as the group of lawmen stopped and had, what appeared to be, a very serious conversation with Dabir.

Dabir glanced towards Arash's office. Arash could tell by the look on Dabir's face that the fix was in. *Why did I trust Gallagher? A simple operation, uh? Not so simple now. Have I simply been a pawn of the Americans and Israelis? What danger have they put me in? I'm so stupid. I should have trusted my fears and never ventured forth into this spy thing. Who do I think I am?*

There was nowhere to run, and running would only make things worse. Arash sat in his swivel chair and stewed with fear, rage, and horror as he watched the situation unravel slowly before his eyes. The minute or so that it took for the party of cops to reach his office seemed like thirty.

Dabir ushered the police into Arash's office and glared at Arash with a piercing look of utter disdain. The police marched in promptly and one held up a Bible in his hand. Arash was shocked at the sight of his personal Bible held before him like a hot murder weapon.

The cops shouted and hurled accusations at Arash of being a traitor to Islam. Arash attempted to play ignorant.

"What's going on? What's that?"

"You know what it is. Don't play stupid. We know what you're hiding! You've joined the infidels!"

Did they know everything I was hiding? Do they know about my spying and the Stuxnet worm? Or just my faith? Did Atoosa turn me in? Did she see me place the key to the cabinet—where I keep my Bible—under the chair cushion? Arash had no idea how deep he was in it for.

A surge of testosterone and brazen defiance burst through Arash. He grabbed his Natanz-issued firearm and shot the cop directly in front of him right in the groin. The cop's face clenched as he screamed in agony. He held his wounded crotch as he fell to the ground. A puddle of blood oozed from his pants. The other cops instantly pounced Arash, subdued him, and began beating him mercilessly. He didn't scream, but he felt each hit with excruciating pain. The fists flailed like heavy rocks against his head and body. Nightsticks pounded against him at any open spot. He curled up fetus-style to try to blunt the impact, but was unsuccessful. The pain was penetrating, quick, repetitive and unrelenting. Arash struggled to absorb and endure. He still did not scream. He didn't want to give them that pleasure.

Arash had been viewed as a timid, harmless tech guy. No one expected such a violent, irrational reaction. Neither had he. He could not believe what he had just done. He felt defiant, strong.

You can beat me, you can defile me, you can torture me to no end, but my faith in Christ remains. It will never die. Kill my body and I live on eternally with Christ… and the Stuxnet worm will churn on and shred your plans of death for the world limb from digital limb. From digital limb to failed digital limb.

CHAPTER FORTY-ONE

The Hampton Inn, somewhere near Fairton, New Jersey

Zack was eager to get back online and check his Twitter account. Lo and behold, his new Persian pal had left a mountain of messages. His new pal, simply known as Hamid, had even visited his manufactured Facebook page for his cover persona, *Doug Schmidt.*

After reading some Facebook messages in which Hamid praised the Nazi skinhead rhetoric that populated Zack's Facebook page, *Doug* responded in kind with some lavish praise of Hamid for his devotion to the Aryan cause. The two of them finally decided to engage in a private instant message chat in which they arranged to share a common email account. To avoid being tracked or detected, they agreed to leave messages in draft folders for each other to read, but to never actually transmit any emails to each other through the account. The last thing Hamid wanted was his messages being intercepted by the infidel's digital spying tools.

As much as Zack was on board with wanting to ensnare this guy and utilize his information and contacts to try to weave some disruptive inroads into Bushehr, he really resented the fact that he had to pose as a Nazi skinhead to get the job done. He had spent a good portion of his life trying to foster an anti-racist image of skinheads, and his current cover just reinforced the false view that skinheads were largely white supremacists. That said, who was he really interacting with? Just some nutjob extremists in Iran. *No worries.* He thought to himself. *I'll use any cover to try to stop those psychotic theocratic freaks.*

Within a few hours, the conversation that had developed in the draft email folders was beginning to get somewhere. *Doug* had asked Hamid if he was planning on attending the upcoming *World Without Zionism Conference* in Tehran. This annual event of absurd anti-American and anti-Israeli rhetoric and hate had become a growing focal point for bigots and anti-Semites the world over. If David Duke was welcomed there while waving his KKK flag, then why not a little known Nazi skinhead named Doug Schmidt? *Secret agent skinhead in effect, baby, here we go!* The chorus to the song "Secret Agent S.K.I.N." by the punk band Murphy's Law was now churning in Zack's head.

It didn't take long for Zack to hear back from Hamid. He was indeed planning to attend the conference. *Doug* expressed how he had always wanted to go to the conference. As hoped for, Hamid said he would help get him access and assist in planning his itinerary. Bingo.

The email draft folders filled up with enthusiasm over the now planned meeting between the two new digital friends. Brazen anti-Semitic rhetoric and chest-thumping Aryan pride rants permeated all of their exchanges. Zack deliberately probed Hamid about the progress and status of Iran's nuclear program. *Doug* voiced his opinion that Iran had every right to have the bomb, particularly since the "dirty Jews" had one.

Once again, Hamid took the bait. Hamid explained that he wasn't sure exactly how far away they were from the bomb, but that they were close. He confessed that the Stuxnet worm and assassination of their scientists was setting them back, but not catastrophically. Of course, he had no idea that as he typed, the new and improved Stuxnet 2.0 had already been deployed at Natanz.

Hamid revealed that he had a cousin who worked at Bushehr and a brother-in-law who worked at Natanz. *Doug* inquired more about these relatives to get a good sense of Hamid's inadvertent reach into the nuclear development world of the Iranians. Gallagher gave him the intel on Hamid's cousin Azad at Bushehr, but he had no idea about the brother-in-law at Natanz. The useful info kept flowing and Zack was rapidly putting the pieces together in an attempt to flesh out a strategic plan of infiltration.

The exchanges began to taper off for the day, and Zack decided to shut down the nerd for a bit to assess all he had learned and analyze the situation and how to proceed. He had made tremendous progress in an amazingly short period of time. Just as he began expanding upon his notes and getting a mental grip on the trajectory of his cyber recon, his sat phone rang. It was Gallagher.

"So whaddya got so far you hooligan bastard? Don't tell me you ain't got nuthin' or I'll have you locked back up again in a heartbeat." Ever the pleasant conversationalist, Chuck Gallagher laid on his usual charm from the conversational get-go.

"Nice to hear your voice, Chuck. I really missed your bulldog approach to human relationships in the short day or so since last we spoke." Zack chuckled a bit.

"Yeah, I'll bet you did. This doesn't mean we're gonna be touchin' tongues in the shower any time soon, hot shot. I don't roll that way."

"I don't care who you swap spit with pal, as long as it ain't me. Keep your tongue to yourself. Anyhow, yeah, some strong progress here. Real strong. Got Hamid on the hook via Twitter and we've now taken our chats to a whole new level with some email folder draft drops. Keepin' it on the down low so he feels warm and fuzzy."

"So what's the logical next step?" To the point as usual, Gallagher wanted results.

"The *World Without Zionism* conference, that's what. Get my credentials prepped asap boss, cuz I'm going to Tehren. Hate-a-plenty! Maybe I'll get a chance to get my photo taken with David Duke. Who knows, maybe I can get an autographed Member's Only jacket from A-jad to keep me warm too!"

"The World Without Zionism conference eh? Perfect excuse to get your ass over there to snoop around. I like it. Keep me posted as you draft the particulars. Good work, you no good criminal." No compliment could ever go forth from Gallagher, unless paired with an effectively negating insult.

"That was my thinking. I was just reviewing my notes and trying to hone in my plans as you called. I'll have more for you in the coming days." Zack had been accustomed to ignoring Gallagher's insults as they were flung. However, he often reflected upon them later and laughed out loud as he recalled each one.

"Good, while you're working on that, you need to noodle the rest of the operation as well. Lot's of shit going down. We got some trouble with Arash Jafari. The poor bastard went postal the other day when the *mutawwa* confronted him for having a copy of the good book in his home—and not Mohammed's good book. His own wife, a devoted Twelver, turned him in for having a Bible. The *mutawwa* stormed into his office at Natanz and arrested him. He freaked out and shot a guard right in the stones. A new form of birth control I suppose. Anyhow, we're very vulnerable right now with him in custody. He's no doubt being tortured and interrogated Iranian style as we speak. A hot extraction is urgent. And you and your old pal Blaze are just the dynamic duo to pull it off."

"Damn, Jafari is new at this too. It probably won't take much for him to cave, right? And what the hell is the mutawwa?"

"Mutawwa is the Iranian religious police. And yes, Jafari is new, and him caving would be the prevailing opinion, except that his dossier makes it very clear how much he now despises the regime and sees their theology-driven apocalyptic agenda as utterly demonic. Being a converted Christian, his faith may actually be the mechanism to help him keep the secrets inside. We'll see. Torture has its way of breaking down even the strongest of faith. Especially Iranian torture. We need to get him out before he cracks."

"Okay, well, get me to Iran as soon as possible so Blaze and I can bust out Arash before I hob nob with A-Jad and David Duke at the conference."

"I got everything set to go." Gallagher assured.

"Anything else? Shall I single-handedly fight the North Koreans and conquer China before lunch as well?"

"Quit crying cream puff. You can handle it. If you couldn't, you'd still be rotting in jail."

"Your candidness never ceases to amaze me, Gallagher. You old, crumpled up artifact of a man. I love you too."

Zack chuckled and Gallagher grumbled and the two men hung up and got back to work for the good of the country.

CHAPTER FORTY-TWO

Dr. Gabriella Mancini's office, Washington, DC

"Hi Gabriella."

The President showcased a countenance that hinted towards a sense of subtle deflation in his spirit. It was evident in the tone of his greeting.

"Hello Mr. President. What do we have to look forward to today?"

Gabriella was chipper and ready to dig in as usual. She was an extremely smart and energetic therapist and her inherent personality strengths often served to help her clients more than her actual words.

"Oh hell, I don't know Gabriella, my world is full of all kinds of snares and pickles."

Jack Fitzsimmons wasted no time in revealing his true state of mind. Jack often played the flustered, disgruntled world leader.

"You signed on for it Jack, hell, you *campaigned* for it," reminded Dr. Mancini.

"That I did…that I did", pondered the President.

"Where do you want to start? What is weighing the heaviest on your mind?"

Jack thought for a moment. He decided to initially stray away from the personal stuff—his struggles with his wife, his attraction to internet porn, and his larger spiritual battles. He thought it proper to start with work, specifically, his recent reflections on the Iranian nuclear program.

"Besides all the personal stuff, I'd have to say the entire labyrinth that is the issue of Iran is in the forefront of my daily thoughts and concerns."

Gabriella didn't expect the discussion to start there, but why not? It was, in fact, probably one of the most important challenges facing the globe at the moment.

"Tell me more."

"Well, a very heated discussion occurred this week between myself, Mahoney, and Sapp. For the record, it all ended up well and good, and I'm thoroughly satisfied with the unique dynamic and healthy tug and pull interplay that exists between the three of us, but it was quite a discussion. Sapp was unbelievably hawkish on the issue, so much so, that I began to seriously wonder if he was a neo-con mole. He insisted that we needed to pursue aggressive measures of all sorts to stop Iran from getting the bomb. As usual, this position was advanced amidst a haze of unwelcome cigarette smoke and swearing that would make the *Sons Of Anarchy* blush."

Gabriella never watched television. She was a bit of a recluse and a nerdy bookworm. She had absolutely no clue in the world who the *Sons Of Anarchy* were, but she nodded her head and went along with his line of thought anyhow.

"How did you react?"

"I instinctively came from the other direction. I've been more and more leaning towards the notion that Iran having the bomb would not be the end of the world. Pakistan has the bomb and they are Islamic. Israel has the bomb and no one, save the Islamic world, really challenges them. And of course, we have the bomb. I just don't think that starting a war would be a better option than trying to diplomatically handle an Iran with the bomb. I know they have an extreme religious slant with the whole Shia Twelver thing, but at the end of the day, I just refuse to believe that they're anything but rational. I don't believe that they can't be managed with a reasonable batch of carrots and sticks, like any other rogue nation."

"So you're weighing the known risks of war versus the unknown risks of allowing Iran to get the bomb. Keep in mind, I am your psychologist. I can't give opinion on policy, nor should any of my comments be interpreted as such."

She knew he understood this, but it had to be continually re-emphasized as a matter of requisite CYA.

"I know Gabriella, it goes without saying."

"So what has shifted your thoughts? Last time this issue came up, you were leaning towards doing whatever you could, short of going to war, to stop Iran from getting the bomb."

Her face crinkled with a feigned look of confusion.

"I haven't moved from that position. I'll continue to support aggressive sanctions and covert actions to stop them. I've already just commissioned a series of new covert actions against their nuclear development efforts. That said, in my heart of hearts I am bracing for the reality that all these efforts may only slow them down. I suspect it is simply a matter of time, which means that I have to imagine a world in which Iran has the bomb, and strategize how that inevitable reality might best be managed."

"That's quite a stark realization." Gabriella deliberately contained her own thoughts on the matter, which were quite different than the President's. But she knew her role. He paid her to listen and to prompt deeper reflection, not to interject with her own beliefs and opinions.

"I suppose. I'm not sure how a thinking person can come to a different conclusion."

"Who else shares this sentiment?"

"Well, Maksim Koslov does, but that's to be expected. For as many areas where I can find agreeable overlap with him, he's still by and large not a certified friend of the United States in the eyes of many, and he clearly minimizes the Iranian threat. However, we've both been very open about our desire to see a unified world in which borders are eroded and a centralized, fair global governance emerges."

A silence fell over the room for about twenty seconds or so. Fitz stared off slightly upwards and to the right as he pondered the magnanimity of his vision. Conversely, Gabriella sat with a neutral look on her face, while internally she was horrified with what she was hearing. She thought of the biblical and historical traces of global unity and one-world government aspirations. The Tower of Babel came to mind first. She couldn't imagine that the fleshing out of Fitz' utopian vision could possibly end any differently.

"Do you truly think that such a vision of a unified world is not only achievable, but inherently benevolent and a worthy goal? Do you really trust that Koslov truly wants that as opposed to a re-empowered Russia?"

She was pushing it with this question, and she knew it. She scaled back her body language and temperament after launching this question. She hoped to disarm Jack by signaling to him that it was nothing more than a naturally challenging question intended to provoke him to more deeply scrutinize his own ideas.

"While I suspect Koslov is a nationalist at heart and will always care about Russia first, he still sees the need for larger global cooperation and unity. Gabriella, the growing consensus among the world's power brokers is that this is a necessary and inevitable structure the world must move towards in order to preserve itself in this current information age. The world is getting smaller by the minute. Processed information makes the world go round. Divisions, hate crimes, and prejudices are condemned by the citizen's of the globe. In order to continue to manage such social threats, along with terrorism, we need a comprehensive global structure. We have global banking, global trade unions, global commerce, but yet we have failed to install a global currency or a global government? It's a normal progression. Those who stand against might as well get back on their horse and buggy and get out of the way."

"It sounds like you're convinced on this."

She was diametrically opposed to the notion and didn't buy for a second that Koslov was doing anything but using the global governance rhetoric to bend Fitz his way. It was times likes this when it was extremely difficult for her to keep her thoughts to herself during a session.

"It's one of the main goals I purposed to strive towards upon taking office." Fitz's face was full of perceivable focus.

"Do you trust the intentions of leaders like Koslov when it comes to the coordination of such ideas?"

"Everyone knows how Koslov is. The rumors of his unseen brutality and dictator tendencies are ubiquitous. I've no illusions about him. That said, it wouldn't be the first time in history in which two leaders, or nations for that matter, joined together for a positive common purpose despite the inherent flaws or unfavorable actions of either individual leader or nation."

His naiveté was astounding to Gabriella. It was as if the clear lessons of history were completely lost on Jack. Gabriella struggled to fight her instinct to further challenge his thinking. *I'm a citizen of this country right? Do I not have the right, or even the responsibility, to challenge him if I think he is way off course? Is he delusional? Is he living in some sort of fantasy world? Peaceful global governance? Really?* She fought her internal thoughts and struggled for an appropriate way to get her point her across without overstepping. She couched her warning in her extremely soft, soothing voice. "As long as you're on guard. You're in a position of extreme power and many will attempt to influence and manipulate you if you're not perceptive of their true intentions."

"I hear you loud and clear. Koslov is always a concern of course, but my main target of scrutiny remains Samani. This conversation has been helpful, but I still have much to pray on, if I could find the focus."

With that Gabriella informed the President that the hour had come to an end. The President thanked her as usual. He walked out with a sense of validation in all that he had been contemplating, oblivious to the true thoughts that his therapist would have loved to share with him in response, had she had the appropriate chance.

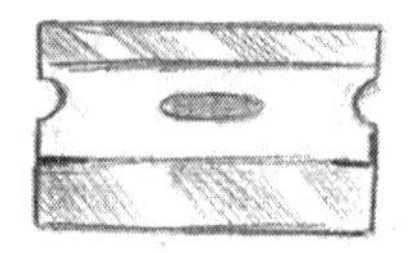

CHAPTER FORTY-THREE

Evin Prison, Iran

Horrific screeches of incomprehensible agony curdled within Arash Jafari's ears. He laid on his stomach, naked. On the dirty floor of his cell. He listened intently to the sounds coming from the other cells—vile and torturous. The sounds were so awful he'd almost rather he was one of the prisoners screaming in agony, than one of the cellies having to listen to it. The pleas of the prisoners prompted mockery from the guards—and further beatings. Arash heard the diabolical exchanges in full, loud and clear Farsi. The begging never stopped. The torturers didn't relent. Neither did Arash's misery.

His cell was no larger than a bathtub. Walls kept him trapped in with heavy, menacing cement blocks. They crushed his soul as he stared at their cold affront. The luxury of a window could not be found. The doors were built of thick, impenetrable metal. Two ventilation holes could be spotted in the ceiling that hung a claustrophobic distance of a mere six meters high above.

Arash rolled over slightly to one side. He reached down and gently touched his sore testicles. They swelled with pain. He felt more excruciating pain lingering in his lower abdomen. Earlier that day, his guards had laughed at him and his faith as they beat his balls with a nightstick repeatedly. It was payback for the bullets he shot in the officer's crotch back at the plant.

Having been in Evin for several days—Arash didn't know how many—he had been amazed both at the immense cruelty with which he had been tortured and with the miraculous stamina that he had somehow summoned to withstand it.

He had been mumbling prayers since he had been dumped into the Godless abyss and he had been holding onto the spirit of Shadrach, Meshach, and Abednego as inspiration to get him through. He would not sell out. There would be no trial in Rasht for Arash, just secret torture in Evin.

His captors constantly reminded him of his offense as they administered their tortures. He was still fully naked and had been since he was placed in his cell. His flesh burned with an undying sting that was exacerbated by the salt they had rubbed into the razor cuts. The razor cuts came the night before. Food and sleep deprivation screwed with his sanity. The lights in his cell were kept on twenty-four hours per day. When Arash would finally find a momentary interlude of rest, the guards would promptly beat him until he was awake. Even when they stuffed his face in a toilet full of feces, he held fast and did not denounce his faith in Christ. Instead he quoted scriptures from the Psalms and Ezekiel with a wild and maddening howl. He was deprived of sound, other than the piercing screams of his fellow inmates. This only proved to help Arash push through the physical realities plaguing him and meditate on eternal truths and strengths.

The stories and rumors about what occurred at Evin had always troubled Arash, even when he was a devoted follower of the Mahdi and a believer in the regime. He knew full well what he still may have in store for the duration of his stay.

Tears dripped from his eyes and merged with the blood that coagulated randomly all over his face. He prayed to God that he wouldn't next have his fingers broken and the webs of his hands and feet cut with razors. He feared that such measures were coming, even as he prayed for a miracle. Specifically, a miracle involving the CIA, and this Blaze McIntyre character Gallagher spoke so much about. The one he was told had filled the wires and the war rooms with enough combat folklore and third party storytelling to intrigue anyone within earshot.

CHAPTER FORTY-FOUR

CIA safe house, somewhere in Iran

When Blaze was assigned to an op, he insisted on signing off on every detail of the plan from surveillance, to communication boundaries, to weapon preparation, to every item stocked in the safe house. He required everything that would be needed to recover from what were often tumultuous battles, extractions, and assassinations fraught with snares and snafus of all imaginable varieties. Blaze preferred controlled environments and he took an active hand in forcefully crafting as many environments as he could. This was particularly true in his downtime because in the heat of an op there was only so much you could control. The rest you often had to leave up to God and your arsenal of firearms.

When the safe house was introduced into the conversation of planning the op at Esfahan, Blaze knew where his head would be at post-op and made the appropriate provisions. First, he requested some choice food to be stocked in the kitchen: whole wheat bread, brown rice, fresh chicken, pulled pork, broccoli, collared greens, green beans and a plethora of different hot sauces, protein powder, coffee, barbeque sauces and spices. He also demanded a variety of California red wines, and several Italian ones. Moving on from the soft stuff, he made sure that there would be at least two bottles each of Red Breast Irish whiskey, Sailor Jerry spiced rum and Blanton's bourbon. Better to be over-prepared, he reckoned, as he never knew how long he would need to squat at a safe house after an op.

In the entertainment realm, he always made sure he had a pre-loaded iPod sent with all of the tunes he needed. Loaded with cuts from all different genres—rock, punk, Oi!, metal, hardcore, rockabilly, the Italian crooners, Irish folk, psychobilly, outlaw country, alt-country, and Americana. He never knew what mood he'd be in post-op, so he planned for all sonic possibilities.

His viewing tastes often varied, but for this op, he made sure he had streaming access to old Clint Eastwood flicks such as *Heartbreak Ridge* and *White Hunter, Black Heart.* As for TV series, he looked forward to digging into past seasons of *24*, *Rescue Me*, and the only season made of FX's *Lights Out.*

Depending on what physical state he found himself in after an op, Blaze intended to work out and train as much as he could in a safe house setting. Enemies never stopped training or preparing and neither could he. Heavy equipment conducive to heavy weight training and bodybuilding was an impossibility, so Blaze kept it simple with these requests. An array of small, easily portable functional equipment would suffice; TRX suspension bands, kettle bells, training rope, jump rope, agility ladder, weighted vest, boxing gloves, and the most cumbersome piece, a quality Lonsdale heavy bag. All his requests were accommodated.

The only other unusual request that he made was for a stash of his favorite cigars. They were supplied in a portable humidor and included fine choices from brands such as Perdomo, Rocky Patel, Alec Bradley, Camacho, Oliva, Padron, Room 101 and La Flor Dominicana.

It was with one of these fine cigars that Blaze sat in the tub enjoying on the first evening he arrived at the safe house in Iran. Sitting in the tub, puffing on his much-earned cigar, he felt like Lee Majors in the old TV show *The Fall Guy.* He was in no mood to talk to the agency personnel who were there to receive him. He needed to decompress, clear his head, and analyze what went wrong, *and what went right*, at Esfahan. More importantly, he needed to reflect on what response his actions might have set in motion, and what the response might require of him.

The water temperature in the tub was perfectly warm and soothed his aching bones to the core. Blaze re-traced the images of the op sequentially in his mind and was amazed that he had escaped unscathed. Especially with that straggler guard gun butting him and taking him hostage. There was a strong chance that he could have been caught and captured and that this very moment he would be making love to an electric shock device in some barren, dusty warehouse basement as opposed to enjoying an Alec Bradley New York cigar in a tub at a safe house. Nonetheless, he'd have to soon face the music and fess up to his lack of preparation on the linguistic front.

Not being up to speed on his Farsi was a ginormous mistake and he was already cringing at the barking and verbal beat-down he knew Gallagher was going to give him. Gallagher showed no mercy for preventable mistakes.

The agency knew this was Blaze's modus operandi. Blaze had a history of pulling off hairy, risky ops that no other spook would attempt, and yet he always managed to fail at the simplest, easiest and most basic aspect of an op. He was a natural prodigy as a spy, and an assassin, but had the Achilles heal of strange idiosyncrasies that arose amidst otherwise tactical perfection. He had somehow managed to avoid any real consequences for these troublesome idiosyncrasies time and time again. He attributed it to the fine meeting point where superstitious Irish luck met the pre-ordained Providence of his Protestant faith. A meeting point he knew didn't really exist.

Blaze exhaled some smoke as he listened to the tunes erupting wonderfully from his iPod speakers. He chose a playlist with a diverse mix of artists such as The Marshall Tucker Band, George Jones, The Dubliners, Wayne Hancock, Kid Rock's country stuff, Johnny Cash, Larry and His Flask, David Allan Coe, Nick 13, The

Zack Brown Band, The Head Cat, Blood or Whiskey, Lynyrd Skynyrd, Gene Vincent, Stray Cats, Waylon Jennings, Gordon Lightfoot, and all the Hanks—Hank Williams, Hank Williams Jr., and even Hank III.

But it was The Zack Brown Band that played as he fully felt himself relax. His mind transported itself to far-off and imagined tropical beaches as he felt the deep soak of the bath water and took a sip of the rum and coke cocktail that sat beside the tub on a bench. It was one of his favorite rums. He was a fan of everything Sailor Jerry had done, and the rum bearing his name was no exception.

He had always admired the simple, bold tattoo designs that Norman Collins, aka Sailor Jerry, had created and the way the images spoke of the spirit of the pacific, the pride of WWII Sailors, and the strength of America. Sailor Jerry was also an early pioneer of conservative libertarian talk radio. This was a little known fact that also greatly intrigued Blaze. He was a renaissance man who was full of life—sailor, renowned tattoo artist, poet, talk radio personality, and a man full of art, patriotism, passion, and a well-documented history of being a fun-loving prankster.

Blaze did not stay long in the beach-ensconced fantasy he was enjoying. The reality of where he was, what he had just done, and what tomorrow could bring forced its way back into the foreground of Blaze's mind. He was feeling anxiety about writing his report on the op because he was exhausted and couldn't imagine completing it that night. He would have to get it done early in the morning though because he knew that the day would not get very far before Gallagher would demand a secure video conference to discuss everything. And Gallagher would be rip roaring pissed if he hadn't already read, and thoroughly digested, a report prior to that call. Blaze knew the old warhorse all too well.

Blaze also felt anxiety because he knew this was just the beginning. He had been paying attention while he was living the quiet civilian life and he knew that regular assassinations of Iran's scientists were taking place. Thinking back to recent conversations with

Gallagher he had a sense that he was going to be commissioned for such a task. Gallagher peppered his conversations with vague references to such past exploits and always said it in ways that made it clear that he was testing Blaze's reaction to the concept.

Blaze took another strong puff on his cigar and exhaled slowly. He needed an extra buffer day to unpack everything before diving into writing a report and dissecting the whole scenario with Gallagher on a video call. But this was a spy's life, and an assassin's life, and he was in Iran. Time was entirely of the essence and it waited for no damn man. Blaze included.

Diem was on his mind. A lot. He missed her with an eternal ache. Visions of her and the boys teased his mind constantly since he had been away. He wondered how they were all doing. He wished he could steal a private jet, grab a bottle of Jameson, a bouquet of roses and some gold jewelry—that he couldn't afford—and run to his bride.

Blaze decided against continuing to wish, and he did the next best thing, he began to pray. He pulled up the New Testament app on his iPhone and began meditating on some scripture. He skimmed through the Psalms, but had a hard time wrapping himself up in David's petitions to the Almighty for some reason. He moved on to Matthew and was comforted by the thought that the big Guy would be with him 'even until the end of the age'. Right now, he would settle for the 'end of the mission'.

His eyes eventually focused on the book of Ezekiel and he began to take a deeper look at the passages that McCardle always mouthed off about. As he read through Ezekiel, he saw the pattern of prophecies described and how a good many of them had all ready been fulfilled, especially the ones detailed in Ezekiel 37 regarding the state of Israel. Blaze ingested the words from verse 20-21: "Hold before their eyes the sticks you have written on and say to them, 'This is what the Sovereign LORD says: I will take the Israelites out of the nations where they have gone. I will gather them from all around and bring them back into their own land." Blaze paused and took in the implications of the words. After a moment, he moved on to the 22nd verse: " I will make them one nation in the land, on the mountains of Israel. There will be one king over all of them and they will never again be two nations or be divided into two kingdoms." His mind was fully blown by the specificity of all the prophecies regarding the rebirth of the state of Israel and the convergence of Jews in the land as the end times emerged.

But it was the unfulfilled prophesies of Ezekiel 38 and 39 that he had been trying to avoid. Now he had no choice but to wrestle with their implications. The scenario that was laid out was rather clear. The enemies of Israel were described and identified in such a way that made it hard to interpret them as anything other than Iran, Russia, and a host of surrounding Islamic Middle Eastern and North African nations. He re-read the first four verses of Chapter 38: "The word of the LORD came to me: "Son of man, set your face against Gog, of the land of Magog, the chief prince of Meshek and Tubal; prophesy against him and say: 'This is what the Sovereign LORD says: I am against you, Gog, chief prince of Meshek and Tubal." Blaze knew that it was widely sited that Magog referred to the land now known as Russia, as Magog was the grandson of Noah who had settled in that land.

Blaze read on finally focusing on verse five of Chapter 38: "Persia, Cush and Put will be with them, all with shields and helmets, also Gomer with all its troops, and Beth Togarmah from the far north with all its troops—the many nations with you." It didn't take a scholar to figure out who Persia was. Their pairing with Russia in the prophecy lent credence to McCardle's analysis concerning the remarkable cooperation now between Russia and Iran. Cush was the ancient term for the modern country of Sudan. Blaze knew that one. He looked up the root of the reference to Put and discovered it referred to the lands known now as Algeria and Libya. He then did some research into the mention of Gomer and Beth Togarmah and discovered that the general consensus was that these references most likely were describing the land occupied today by Turkey. That certainly fit the times given Turkey's increasing anti-Israel policies.

As he continued to pour through the text, it became clear that the attack on Israel would be supernaturally thwarted in a horrific and thunderous display of divine strength. Blaze's eyes fixated on the 22nd and 23rd verses of Chapter 38. The passages referred to divine punishment promised for Magog and their allies: "I will execute judgment on him with plague and bloodshed; I will pour down torrents of rain, hailstones and burning sulfur on him and on his troops and on the many nations with him. And so I will show my greatness and my holiness, and I will make myself known in the sight of many nations. Then they will know that I am the LORD.' " Blaze got the chills and his heart quickened.

He thought of all the flash points around the world that Gallagher had alerted him to. Almost all of them were in the nations described in the prophecy and they all involved jihadists hell-bent on Israel's destruction. Russia fit the bill without question. Koslov continued to make Putin seem like a pussycat with his military advances, strong power grabs, and outright bold proclamations. The idea that their assistance with Iran's nuclear program was at all veiled at this point was laughable.

Blaze decided it was best to stop reading Ezekiel for the time being. He was trying to search the scriptures for comfort, but all he found this time was a window into future terror and chaos. He put his curiosities on the back burner and decided to re-visit them the next time he spoke with McCardle.

For now, he would have to access the Lord's comfort through the sung words of Johnny Cash, particularly the Rick Rubin recordings. He would need as much rest as he could get. The next day would bring a tough workout and an even tougher call with Gallagher. And although he longed to speak to Diem, he knew that that call would ultimately be emotionally draining and he was concerned that it might become a distractive wedge in his day. He would call her tomorrow after he wrote his report and talked shop with Gallagher.

Blaze extinguished his stogie, got himself out of the tub, dried quickly, put on a silk robe and climbed into bed.

He logged on to his Netflix account and watched a *Rescue Me* episode from Season 4. Momentarily, he pondered whether he would have been better off being a smoke-eating fireman instead of a covert assassin and spy. He knew the answer. He was born to blow things up and set fires, not put them out.

It didn't take long before he was laughing at the dialogue dominated by Denis Leary's character, *Tommy Gavin.* It also wasn't long before he was drawn in by the dramatic elements of sorrow that occupied his favorite character, Chief Jerry Reilly. It was the episode entitled *Commitment* and Jerry tragically took his own life with a pistol to the mouth. The show had never been the same going forward without him, Blaze thought, as he logged off of his Netflix account, fluffed his pillow, and laid his head down. He dreamt about being stateside and prayed that the safe house would remain safe through the night. Although he tried not to, his sleep occurred primarily with one eye open.

CHAPTER FORTY-FIVE

CIA safe house, somewhere in Iran

Blaze awoke and sprung out of bed with purpose. He put on his Under Amour workout shorts and a white wifebeater tee shirt. He was full of energy and a strong eagerness to get on with the day. He thanked the Lord that he awoke to an alarm clock, and not the safe house alarm indicating they'd been detected. An annoying, persistent buzz was far preferable to a pack of Iranian Revolutionary Guard members storming in with heavy firearms.

He washed down a handful of various vitamins and supplements with a chocolate protein shake as he sipped a cup of black coffee for breakfast. Afterwards Blaze proceeded to the small workout room within the safe house compound. His mind was scattered and he needed the workout not only to train his body, but to organize his mind so he could get a grip on the day. He had many conversations ahead of him with key people in his life and he needed to optimize each one.

He strapped on a weighted vest for extra resistance before starting his training. He was used to vests, but usually his were bulletproof. He wanted to get his heart rate up quickly, so he started with some jump rope for about three minutes or so. Then he hit the agility ladder for five minutes. Blaze grabbed the sandbag and contorted his body to complete various movements. Then he moved on to some rigorous kettle bell swings before finishing his full kettle bell routine. Lastly, he did some heavy rope training for his back and shoulder muscles.

The last twenty minutes of his regimen was consumed by working the speed bag and heavy bag with a battering consistency. All the while his iPod ear buds blasted a mix of various tunes ranging from AC/DC to Everlast to Mastodon to Ted Nugent. Mastadon's *Leviathon* album really summoned the guttural beast within—which helped to effectuate an intense and purposeful workout. The Nuge made him want to hunt down terrorists as if there was a forest somewhere that held every angry jihadist the world over, waiting to become his target. Uncle Ted provided the most appropriate soundtrack for such a sensibility. Everlast helped him find his groove on the speed bag and keep his head cool to plan his day. AC/DC did what AC/DC does; provide soul satisfying blues based rock 'n' roll in a way that none else ever have or will deliver.

After a quick shower, Blaze was dressed in a white V-neck undershirt, with a dog tag necklace dangling perfectly in the space left vacant by the V-cut, and a pair of camouflage shorts. He wasted no time before grabbing a cold water bottle and firing up his MacBook to bang out the report for Gallagher.

He described the prep work, the transportation details, the dialogues he heard and engaged in and every sequential detail contained within the scope of the whole mission. He was still not sure what tipped them off and made him a suspicious element prior to the point in which they discovered his obvious Farsi deficiencies. He hoped that the larger context of his report might somehow provide a clue to an analyst back at Langley as to what might have lead to the initial suspicion. *Was it a flaw in my cosmetic job that transformed me from a Mick to a Persian? Was it my general demeanor? I thought I was pretty slick, believable, and unassuming. It couldn't have been my lack of being familiar. We made sure we impersonated a delivery truck and company that constantly sent new guys as to not make them wonder.* Blaze couldn't figure it out for the life of him.

The real question, the one Gallagher would dwell on, is if they somehow knew ahead of time to be on the lookout. *Had there been a damn leak? A fricken' rat?* Nothing got Blaze's blood boiling more than a rat from the inside. A dirty traitor. Blaze would have to continue to give that mystery a good, hard think over the next few days. For now, he would have to put that question aside and finish his report in earnest.

Although he wished he could avoid it, Blaze confessed fully to his failure to get his Farsi in order as he should have. This was ultimately the main hiccup of the entire op. Had he had that dialed in, he may have overcome the enemies initial suspicions and avoided the capture, the car chase and the subsequent shenanigans in the alley way where he picked up the motorcycle. Blaze chuckled to himself thinking, *but what the hell fun would that have been?* The high speed chase and alleyway showdown was a blast in retrospect, but at the time that he had finally broke free of it all and was out of the woods, Blaze was a tad shaken up—even for an old spook who frequently boasted of maintaining nerves of steel. He was more than blessed to have come out of that snafu unscathed. It was Providence. For sure.

Blaze continued tapping the keys rhythmically for the duration of his report as he focused on the things that went right, including his improvisation and handling of things after they went wrong. *What's a good spy if he isn't flexible? A plan ain't nothing but a rough intended trajectory. The proof of a spook's value comes in the ability to adapt to every unexpected twist and turn that inevitably plagues every op.* And to that end, Blaze was successful. As usual.

Blaze wrapped up his report and promptly fired it off via a secure encrypted e-mail to Gallagher. It was about an hour or so before their scheduled call, so he shot him a quick secure text to let him know that the report had been sent. Blaze's stomach was screaming for vengeance like an old Judas Priest album. It was time for lunch.

After devouring a barbeque chicken sandwich on a whole-wheat roll with a side of green beans, Blaze took a quick minute to mentally prepare for his videoconference with Gallagher. After a quick review of his report, he logged into the secure videoconference portal. It was proprietary software, but functioned pretty much identically to Skype. Blaze logged in and waited about a minute or so before seeing that Gallagher had logged in. Gallagher's edgy, ugly mug popped up on the screen and his trademark intensity was instantly visible.

"McIntyre. I read that damn report of yours. As usual, your literary abilities serve to paint a rosy picture of what happened."

"I paint the picture I see boss, and if you were there, you'd see the same damn picture."

"Alright, alright, let's cut to the chase. I'm glad you got your ass out of there alive and got the job done, but you clearly were playing hooky the day they taught Farsi. Don't think I'm going to overlook that." Gallagher knew nothing else other than to break balls, even in the best of circumstances, no compliment ever left his lips prior to a cascade of unrelenting, insensitive ball breaking.

"Boss, not sure how I would've carried on all this time had it not been for all of your gushing, dripping encouragement."

"Screw you Blaze. It's spooks like you that scare the hell out of directors like me. Criticism, failures, and shit hitting the fan rolls off your shoulders like soft raindrops and you keep rolling on, op after op, surviving and completing missions without even a minute of real self-analysis. I'm hard on you because I'm trying to teach you how to take inventory of your skills and habits. Your success rate is great, but your weaknesses still need to be isolated and neutralized. That ain't gonna happen if you keep glossing over them so you can emphasize and feel good about your strengths. And I'm afraid that, one day, a tiny weakness will either kill you or put our nation in great danger, all because your ego won't deflate for a damn millisecond." For once, Gallagher got to the real heart of the matter. And although he was heated as usual, it was clear to Blaze that there was a truckload of genuine concern in his voice. Also clear to Blaze was that the man had a very good point and his wisdom was deep.

"Point taken Chuck. I'll look for ways to deflate my ego in the future, unless of course I'm stuck sparring with you. Then the ego will be in full effect and I'll whoop your ass like usual." Blaze heard him loud and clear and wanted to move on to the next agenda item, but had to return a round of ball breaking to attempt to keep some semblance of an even score.

"Moving on to other important things. Our asset in Natanz got pinched. But we aren't sure if it had anything at all to do with the actual operation. Apparently, he had converted from Islam to Christianity recently and his own wife found his Bible at his house and turned it in to the authorities. He went ballistic when they confronted him and shot one of the Iranian cops right in the crotch. Needless to say, he was thoroughly beaten and is currently locked up."

"So where's that leave us? We can't leave such an asset in their hands to torture him. The Iranians have a strong history of squeezing every last bit of info out of a prisoner." Blaze knew what was coming next.

"Stay posted Blazey boy, we're working on some preliminary plans for a hot extraction as we speak and it looks like you and your old convict pal Zack will be the lucky action heroes for this little charade."

"Been a while since I worked with Zack, and I'm about due for a new mid-life crisis adventure. Game on." Blaze's voice rose with excitement.

"I'll get back to you soon on the details. Also, I might sprinkle in a few assassinations for you and Zack to keep things interesting. Scientists. We'll probably due it Israeli style. Mossad isn't beyond accepting some extra manpower on this stuff, and it's important we fill in any gaps. We need to put as many nails as we can in the temporary coffin for this nuke problem. Iranians have a way of resurrecting pretty frequently."

"So what you're saying is I probably won't see my wife and kids for at least another year?"

"I didn't say anything of the sorts. You're a professional. You'll get these assignments wrapped up in no time at all and you'll be in Diem's arms before you know it. Godspeed."

"Roger that."

Blaze pondered the implication of the escalation of Operation Persian Trinity and was wondering how it would all unravel. He was excited on a professional level to get some more opportunities to do what he did best, and there was no more worthwhile target of his deadly skills than the Iranian nuclear scientists and the Iranian Revolutionary Guard. That said, he missed Diem and the boys more than ever, and was beginning to doubt the wisdom of his going back into the field. *Maybe I should have just stuck it out with the drudgery of the suit and tie guy life. I didn't need to know Farsi to get home alive every day when I was wearing wing tips. I'm no good to my family if I'm dead.* It only took a few minutes for the reality of who Blaze truly was to creep back into his consciousness. *I am definitely no good to my family dead. And dead is what I was when I wore wing tips. Now, I am fully alive and serving my country as God intended.* Resolved in this affirmation, Blaze's thoughts turned to Pastor McCardle, whom he was fixing to call.

It seemed like Liam was having a helluva time in Belfast. Blaze wondered if he'd ever make his way back to Detroit. If he didn't, Blaze sure as hell couldn't blame him. A city that had its streetlights repossessed wasn't exactly a city that was on a path to retaining happy citizens. If it was struggling before, it was a veritable warzone now.

Blaze was more than happy to have a chat with Liam after the always-abrasive chat he just endured with Gallagher. He logged into the secure video conferencing portal and got connected with Pastor McCardle.

"Liam! How are you my friend? How's Ireland treating you?" Blaze was genuinely thrilled to see Liam's face on the computer screen. He had furnished Liam with access to the proprietary software for the videoconference after clearing with Langley. When you were a stranger in a strange land, acting as an imposter with ill intent, and doing strange things in dangerous places, a familiar and friendly face was a huge mood enhancer.

"Ireland is as magical as I remember it in my youth. Much has changed, but of course, much has also stayed the same. Many old faces, with many old stories, and quite a bit of love remains here. My mother won't stop badgering me about staying here permanently. Although, I've told her that's an absurd notion, I'm indeed going to stay here longer than originally planned. I'm really enjoying myself."

"Well that's fantastic. Any respite from Detroit is a good thing, but an extended trip to the land of your youth to visit with old family and friends is unbeatable. How's the fill-in pastor managing with your flock back in the Motor City?" Blaze might have been right about Liam never returning to Detroit, from the sound of things.

"Oh, you know, the flock responds well to me, but ultimately it's the Lord who steers their ways. I am sure they're doing just fine with my substitute. More importantly, how's your family doing while you're in harm's way poking it deliberately in the eye with a sharp stick?"

"Not totally sure, but okay from what I gather. I have a call with Diem after I get off the phone with you."

"How's your work treating you, Blaze?"

"I can't say too much, but let's just say I had few hiccups but still met my initial objective. One of those initial objectives is remaining alive."

"Good to hear. I've been somewhat disconnected from things going on in the world since being here in Ireland visiting, but I've managed to pick up bits and pieces when I'm able. Good ol' Koslov is not backing down with his blatant political interference on behalf of Samani at the U.N. Koslov has also increased his military presence on the Iranian border guarding the straights of Hormuz. It appears the knots that tie together the allied enemies of Israel, as detailed in the prophesies of Ezekiel 38 and 39, are growing stronger. I'm so thankful to know that you're in a position to be instrumental in potentially thwarting these developments and alliances. God willing."

"Thanks for the vote of confidence. I'll be sure to recall such support next time I'm in the heat of it. Every ounce of positive encouragement helps fortify the spirit. So what's the deal with you staying longer in Ireland?" Blaze had a feeling there was more to this newfound extended stay than just Liam's desire to spend more time with his aging mother.

"Truth be told?"

"You're a friggin' Pastor, it better be the truth that you're about to tell!"

"I became reunited with an old lady friend from years ago and it appears she is quickly becoming more than a friend." Liam still felt strange actually uttering the truth of this reality. Even more so given the fact that he was still concealing a heavy part of the truth of this reality. A reality that was causing him to ache deeply with regret. He could not believe he slept with Erin. It was clearly outside of the context of marriage and he knew better. *How many times have I preached on this topic?* He felt like a traitor to God and to his late wife. His heart still ached for Kathy, but he knew he had to move on. And now was as good of a time as ever. Despite his whimsical sexual failure, he felt a purpose already with Erin, and he was pretty sure it was a purpose designed by the Almighty.

"Wow. God bless it. I'm happy to hear that. A fine lady might be a good thing for you at this point. It could take your mind off of your apocalyptic obsessions and nip away at your lust for the booze. You are staying off the booze, *aren't you?*" Blaze didn't want to ask, but he had to. Liam may be his Pastor, an assumed position of mentorship, but when it came to Liam's weakness for the spirits, Blaze played the role of a makeshift AA sponsor.

"For the most part, I honestly have, other than one pint of beer. But I didn't have a second pint, and I held fast against the whiskey, even though it was flowing freely all around me and my urges were stronger than a Tsunami."

Liam had grown to become comfortable talking with Blaze about this topic. Blaze was almost the only one in the good reverend's life who he let in to know about his struggle with the sauce.

"Good to hear Liam. Damn good to hear. I was getting worried about you when you were popping the cork before noon on weekdays. That just can't end well."

"I know Blaze, God has been kind to me and is giving me strength."

"Well, I gotta pop smoke here and get ready to get on a call with my beloved. I miss her dearly." Blaze felt a twitch of sadness just mentioning Diem in a context of separation. *Am I getting soft? What is wrong with me?*

"Let me pray for us quickly before you go. *Dear Father in heaven, bless my friend Blaze, a warrior for the global cause of good. Protect him with clusters of angels and the impenetrable strength of the Holy Ghost. Comfort him and encourage him and help him to trust You in the darkest of corners and the most threatening of circumstances. In the name of Christ, Almighty God, Amen.*"

"Thanks Liam. Be good. Talk soon."

"Godspeed, Blaze."

Blaze felt refreshed after his brief conversation with Pastor McCardle. He had never felt particularly connected with any church before, and still had a hard time assimilating in such a setting, but he and Pastor McCardle had linked in a way that was clearly divinely appointed.

Liam's warrior past in Northern Island as an anti-terrorist law enforcement member made him uniquely worthy of Blaze's trust. Blaze respected his perspective and found his wisdom to be extremely valuable.

After a conversation with Liam, Blaze usually felt a renewed layer of God's armor around him to help him push on to and through the next obstacle, the next horror, and the next mile marker on the highway of harm's way.

Blaze sat at the leather swivel chair staring at his Macbook computer for a minute or so reflecting on the spiritual thrust that had been guiding his life. He felt an effervescent peace nestle deep within his being. It was time to call Diem.

CHAPTER FORTY-SIX

The foot of the Alborz mountains, Iran

Above and fully surrounding them was the notably narrow expanse of the Alborz mountains. The mountain range was peppered with high peaks and colored with lush green forestry—full of inherent optic beauty and majestic structure. Below them were deep layers of thickened crust. The crust was heavy and formed the foundation that had upheld the mighty mountains for as long as can be known.

The busy pedestrians and floating human element of shoppers and dining enthusiasts of the Saadat Abad district of Evin had no clue, nor interest, in the two men who sat sipping tea in a high-brow teahouse at the foot of the Alborz. They sat inconspicuously on the upper deck terrace that protruded out from the establishment, which happened to offer an exquisite view of the mountains. Other, less obvious, and less exquisite sites were also within visual range from the terrace.

One of the two men had short-cropped hair that was slicked back tight to his head with a slight flip in the front. He looked like he had captured Sha-Na-Na's barber from the fifties and transported him to the future through a time machine. His face and cheekbones showed deliberate definition and contours. His muscular makeup was so distinct that even the sight of his neck displayed taut and firm strength. He wore a black leather jacket, Levi's Blue Jeans, and what appeared to be high-end hiking shoes. Oakley sunglasses adorned his face, as he sat conversing with his friend at the outdoor seating at the popular upscale teahouse. To most he likely appeared to be nothing more than a hiker on holiday from Europe.

The other of the two men looked a little more intimidating. He wore a crisp shaved head, an olive green bomber jacket, Levi's blue Jeans, and black 10 hole Doc Martin combat boots. He caught a few curious looks, but none that lingered with any seriousness.

The two men let their eyes wander everywhere, except to the establishment that was adjacent to the teahouse. This was the one view from the terrace that most never saw because it wasn't obvious or visually attractive. If they did see it, they intentionally ignored it.

Zack Batt did manage a quick glimpse when he bent down to retrieve a scally cap from his backpack to keep his bald head warm from the cool mountain breeze. What Zack saw when he caught his glimpse was precisely as he expected—an extremely forgettable outhouse post with meager signage. It alerted anyone who might care to gaze upon it that it was the location of the 'Evin House of Detention', known to many of its past and present inhabitants as 'Evin University'.

Blaze and Zack were not interested in this outhouse for higher education earned abroad. They had other plans.

From the outside view, the facility did not look like much at all. An unsuspecting observer would not think much to inquire or stop and inspect. But the view from the road was certainly deceptive in its ability to reveal the huge complex of guard towers and cells that lie behind it. Over one hundred solitary cells and innumerable ordinary cells populated the grounds that could handle fifteen thousand prisoners.

Optics aside, the truth was Evin was full of horror. Inside Evin's fences and walls, the terror was large and menacing. Its most prominent inmates found themselves there for their political speech and intellectual thoughts, their perceived religious infractions, or their discovered religious objections—or as was the case for Arash Jafari and many like him, for their specific religious conversions away from Islam to Christianity.

In Evin, those who did not cooperate were tortured in what felt like perpetuity. Rape, as a method of torture and an inducement during interrogation, was an old tradition at Evin. Any universal notion of basic human rights was jettisoned instantly when one traversed the front gate at Evin. And those drinking tea and chatting in Farsi about their shopping finds at the teahouse next door didn't give a second thought to Evin on such a fine afternoon when the mountain air blew so benevolently.

Blaze McIntyre and Zack Batt's thoughts were fully and thoroughly burdened with Evin. And they were fixin' to do a little something about it.

"It's good to see you Zack. I've heard all about your illegal escapades and dumbass heroics in the past few years, but never thought I'd get the privilege of rocking a mission with you side by side again. In all seriousness, it's great to have you here." Blaze let loose a huge smile as he shook Zack's hand and subsequently slapped him on the shoulder.

"It's been a helluva ride for sure Blaze. It's damn good to see you too. Your pretty boy haircut and Tom Cruise silly boy face is better than the musky walls of solitary confinement any day. Besides, who else would be better to hang with on a trip like this? We've got a ton of fun ahead of us on this one."

"Well our employers are blessed to have us both back in the game, cuz its pretty clear there is a ton of game to be had at this point. Hot getting hotter with the clock a tickin'. Speaking of, how is progress on your portion of this shindig?" Zack was confused at first, and then nodded slightly as he realized Blaze was asking about his work to infiltrate the Neo Iranian Nazi Party and get intel on Bushehr.

"Oh, yeah, that. Well, let's just say the fishing is good, real good.

I'm all lined up to hang out with an ocean full of fish after we're done crashing our party. Gonna be chillin' at the *World Without Zionism Conference*. Should be able to meet some friends and relatives of my contact who are employees at my portion of the trinity. Should be interesting."

Blaze put his head down and folded both his hands over his forehead shaking his head in disbelief slightly. "I still can't believe such a conference actually exists, but whatever. This is the world we live in now I suppose."

"By the way, the name is Schmidt. Doug Schmidt. And there isn't any Jewish blood in me. I am 100% German, and 200% Ayran. Got it?" Zack pointed his finger in Blaze's face and cracked a bit of a smile.

"Got it. Just be careful though, cuz I might go Churchill on your ass at any moment you no good skinhead thug."

"Churchill? He was a Brit. Proper. You're a two-bit Mick with a grease ball hair cut. You ain't got the goods."

The two men both began to laugh. Blaze's head naturally turned towards Evin as he laughed, but when his head pivoted back to Zack's sight, his laugh began to soften. The two warriors sensed the weight of their mission and the evil of the 'University of Evin'.

Blaze's face got serious. Quickly. A determined look of purpose. Zack's face followed suit. The two men sensed each other's shift in mood and thought. They nodded their heads in unison.

Finally Blaze spoke. "While we laugh, he screams. Let's get this recon done."

Zack barked back, "Roger that. We're gonna have to put all of our nuts, guts, and glory into this one."

Blaze nodded. "Time to shamrock 'n' roll."

CHAPTER FORTY-SEVEN

Romeo, Michigan

Diem McIntyre could still not believe that she actually had the meat of her day freed up. Her youngest and most-challenging son, Shane, had finally begun first grade—triggering the beginning of her new life. Kindergarten was half day at Shane's school, Crosspoint Elementary School in Romeo, Michigan. It had been a good transitional year to get Shane used to school and to allow Diem a foretaste of daylight freedom from children. But now that Shane was in school for a full day, Diem could finally indulge in some extended 'me time' each day.

It was Shane's third day of first grade and he exhibited no hesitations whatsoever and was full of excitement and energy. He bounced around joyfully making noise in the back seat of the Toyota Venza crossover vehicle that Diem drove haphazardly towards Shane's school. Shane's older brother Dennis was already in homeroom, as his day started earlier than Shane's. Internally, Diem was also jumping for joy. She was excited, both for Shane and herself.

After years of enduring the laborious, anxiety-filled trials of childrearing, Diem was ready for a chance to catch her breath. All day. Every day. At least during the week.

With a husband who was, for the most part, effectively out of the home trenches and stuck in actual trenches of war, raising two rambunctious boys was very difficult. She was a tough woman and she carried her burden with grace, but over the years she faced extreme isolation, loneliness, and late-night fear. Her husband was not only rarely home, but was in dangerous lands doing dangerous things that she was unable to know about.

Instead, she was left to the extremities of her imagination. He rarely was able to contact her while on missions. On a rare occasion, she would get to actually see his face via a secure video conference. *Will he be coming home this time? What if he is caught? Or worse, tortured? What if he is exposed and ends up on the evening news and excoriated in the press by the pundits?* All of these questions teased her during daytime hours. At night, corresponding imaginative visions of worst-case scenario horrors haunted her dreams.

She got through those times in various ways. She leaned on her faith, her family, and her friends, new and old. Blaze's parents and sister stopped by often to help out and keep her company. People at church were always reaching out as well. But one of the mechanisms that really proved to help her, particularly in the solitude of the evening when the boys were in bed, was the friends she connected with via social networking who were all military wives scattered throughout the country. She belonged to several such groups and found immense comfort in the common experiences and perspectives expressed by other wives. Of course, she could never really identify herself and had to use a fictitious online persona. That drove her nuts.

Diem pulled up into the school drop off line. She waited her turn like every other soccer mom—and Mr. Mom. Kids walked with the aid of chaperones from their parents' cars with their backpacks weighing down their small, underdeveloped bodies. Diem tried to be patient. It was hard. She was already slightly disconnected from the mom routine just from the anticipation of another free day. Her thoughts bounced back and forth between a yearning desire to see

Blaze and a sizzling exuberance to finally get on with her third day of freedom.

She was planning to do a bit of light shopping, meet a good friend for lunch, and maybe even take a quick power nap. She had hungered for this season in life for quite some time. It was really like a dream. And dream she did. Daydreaming, that is. While she struggled to patiently wait in the drop off line, she focused her eyes on the volunteer moms helping to receive the kids into school from the procession of minivans lined up before them, she continued to ruminate in the anticipation of her newfound freedom. Her daydream was abruptly interrupted by Shane's voice from the back seat.

"Mom! When will I see Dad again? He hasn't even heard me play the new songs I've learned on my guitar. I want him to hear the new Chili Peppers song I learned." Shane's understood little as to the reason for his father's periodic absences.

"Daddy's working honey. You know Daddy does important work and has to be away for a while at times. He loves you very much and asks about you all the time. He was very excited that you're learning a Chili Peppers song when I told him. He remembers seeing them live at Lollapalooza in Scranton, Pennsylvania back in 1992!" Diem was doing her best to neutralize Shane's temporary estrangement.

"Dad saw the Chili Peppers live? Wow. I didn't know they were as old as Dad." Shane gazed out the window pondering the implications of the probable age of both his father and that of Anthony Kiedis and Flea.

"Your Dad isn't that old, but the Chili Peppers are an old band. Get your book bag together. We're up next here honey."

Diem glanced in the sideview mirror and saw a man on a motorcycle wearing a full leather riding suit slowly throttling a stealth looking sport bike about three car lengths behind her. *That's strange. What's this guy doing? He has no kid with him, and this is the land of endless minivans, not sport bikes.* She quickly pivoted her neck to check on Shane to make sure he was readying his book bag and preparing to get out of the car.

Diem contorted her head towards the back seat and gave Shane a kiss and a hug. While her head was turned, she missed the sight of the motorcyclist coming closer to her vehicle—although she did hear the volume of the engine sound getting increasingly closer.

A flapping, smacking sound emerged with a thud from the driver's side of her vehicle. Something, or someone, had hit or slapped her vehicle. She craned her neck to the left and peered out forward from the driver's side window. She caught a quick glance of the motorcyclist's rear-end. His ass was slightly hoisted above his seat as he sped away from the drop-off line. He left nothing but a nominal plume of exhaust smoke behind.

The vehicle ignited quickly. Diem felt the heat implode within the vehicle. Her skin caught fire and the flames engulfed her in an instant as she watched Shane become swallowed in the explosion. Diem saw it all thrust upon her. She screamed Shane's name and tried to brace the impact. It was no use. The explosion quickly rocked her crossover vehicle in a matter of seconds.

The reverberating sound of the explosion rocked the entire semi-circle drive of the elementary school child drop off line. The whipping, licking residual flames scorched the face of the building. Chunks of black asphalt, auto parts, and horrific airborne body parts of moms and children filled the chaotic air with a panoramic death-wind that was certifiably unfit for benevolent eyes.

The slightly hoisted backside of a random, murderous motorcyclist was one of the last sights seen by Diem McIntyre. One of the last sights after kissing her son. Her young, hope-filled son who perished almost instantaneously with his mother in the blink of an eye.

Elsewhere, a hardened warrior had no idea as to the agony and ocean of revenge he would soon be immersed in.

CHAPTER FORTY-EIGHT

Evin Prison, Iran

The horrid smell of the drill bit merging violently with the vulnerable and helpless flesh of Arash Jafari's right hand still hung in the misty air of his damnable Evin prison cell. It lingered as a constant reminder of a thousand unimaginable hells. His hand trembled as he examined one of the wounds. He knew the bit had pierced his hand completely and he was surprised he couldn't see through it. The hole was now filled with a pulpy mass. He struggled to clench his fist regardless. He winced as the blood dripped from the hole.

This was just one of the unthinkable punishments Arash had been enduring for his crime of being an "anti-government activist"—a catch-all phrase used by the Iranian regime to imprison anyone for almost any perceived offense. In Arash's case, that offense was the possession of the Holy Bible. In Iran, Bibles don't go over too well.

The dementia had kicked in something fierce at this point and Arash had somehow managed to access what was left of his dilapidated soul to reach out to the Almighty. The hallucinations merged with his fragmented prayers and his flesh burned with pain at heightened intervals when he would attempt to cry out to God. His vocal chords projected no sound but his body spasms mimicked a man who appeared to be howling at the moon in agony.

Lord, I curse the day I was born as Job did, yet I believe in the day I will be delivered. I don't know Your plans for me, but I trust that they are plans to prosper. If this is the end, I accept it, but I do not believe You brought me this far only for the purpose of a tortured death in Evin. You giveth, You taketh away....but You also restoreth, replenish, and re-claim. Re-claim me. Rescue me.... Rescue me, Lord of Lords, King of Kings.

A sliver of sunlight crept through a pinprick of a hole that existed in the corner of Arash's seemingly Godforsaken cell. At the moment Arash uttered his prayer, the light began to illuminate and crystallize in his right eye with a beaming intensity. It was so powerful that it drew him into a bit of a trance and he sat there gazing into it with an elated sense of relief, as if God was illustrating His power to penetrate and make the light of His presence known in even the most hidden and darkest caverns of evil.

As the light seared his countenance, Arash was able to push away the culmination of his physical torture, his emotional agony, and his spiritual isolation. He felt God's presence. And although he had mistaken feelings for promptings in the past, he was pretty certain that this was an affirmation of his prayers. His hope for deliverance was buoyed. His belief that he would be rescued was encouraged and his unflinching faith in the God of Abraham, Isaac, and Jacob was cemented eternally.

A large rat scurried past his bare feet and Arash did not move and the rat did not inspect him. Arash sat naked, sweating, bloody, and exhausted. But he sat in a newfound peace that transcended the horrors of his circumstances. It was a miraculous state of spirit, as if he sensed that as was done for Moses during the Red Sea miracle, a proverbial road would be made in the ocean of Arash's circumstances.

His tolerance for pain was suddenly increased to a maniacal threshold. He gazed upon the multiple drill holes in his hands and felt a kinship with his Lord and the suffering wrought upon Him on the cross by the nails that pierced His skin.

After countless sleepless nights, Arash Jafari finally found rest in his solitary cell in Evin. His naked body collapsed peacefully against the cell wall. The toxic cocktail of urine, blood, and rodent droppings that he sat in did not prevent his rest. All current hells were assuaged, and by the hand of God, rest was temporarily granted.

CHAPTER FORTY-NINE

Somewhere on I-75 South leaving Detroit, Michigan

"Have you delivered the groceries?" asked the stern, no-nonsense voice on the other end of Juan Herrara's cell phone.

"Hell yes, meat, veggies, and even desert. All delivered, baby. Done deal." Juan was too young to appreciate the importance of silly code language, but he played the game nonetheless. He was extremely proud of himself and was eager for affirmation from his anonymous cartel contact.

"Good. Follow the plan. Keep moving. We'll deal with the rest." The cartel ghost hung up the phone. No atta-boy, no 'good job'. All business.

Juan was temporarily deflated. He expected at least some sort of appreciation from his invisible boss. Some sort of expression of gratitude or hint of a job well done. He got nothing. Straight up nothing.

Screw it. If the cartel wants to treat me this way, fine. I still kicked ass on this mission and I'll get mad respect from the fellas in the neighborhood. It's my barrio now. My legend has just begun to be written.

Juan couldn't wait to exercise his bragging rights to his friends and enemies on both sides of the border. He'd make sure that he left out no detail every time he told the story. He'd detail all the recon work he did, scoping out the woman's daily routine for days before he popped the bomb on that vehicle. He watched her patterns with the kids and shopping. All that crap. He knew her like he was Google fuckin' earth. He even saw a vague silhouette of her getting undressed one evening with his binoculars. That part would be one he'd have to embellish for sure. *What a body.* He'd describe every inch of her as if he knew it first hand. He'd get a holler out of his boys for sure on that.

Juan had a huge grin on his face and a snide chuckle under his breath as he pulled the white, fifteen-passenger econo-van up to the BP gas station. He had already ditched the sport bike miles back behind a beaten up abandoned old barn in the middle of a cornfield somewhere.

Juan got out, after parking, and strolled into the convenience store. One chili cheese dog, some beef jerky, and a large fountain soda. Road fuel. Lots of miles left. He took off his flannel shirt as he walked back to the van, wearing nothing but a white wife beater tee shirt. His arms were big, strong, but still layered with baby fat. Scattered randomly all over his arms were dark blue tattoos done in jailhouse style.

After filling up the tank, Juan climbed his very large arse back into the van and turned the key. He scanned the old radio to hear the news reports on his work. The first few reports he heard detailed the horrific nature of the attack being on an elementary school and described the unthinkable casualties that were wrought on the children and the moms. Some grandparents and a few dads too.

Witnesses from the scene described the overwhelming explosion and the scarring visuals of the event. One recalled, "There were flailing body parts everywhere…flying scraps of auto parts….death all around." Another described, "Everything was airborne. Everything became like a weapon. Damage was everywhere—cars, people—everything."

One dad from the scene who had been far in the back of the drop off line had made it out unscathed and gave, what the press had considered to be, the most useful description of the attack. This man had described, in about half detail, the mysterious motorcyclist that perpetrated the attack on the Toyota crossover vehicle that had shocked the town of Romeo, Michigan.

Juan grinned with pride as he listened to the man's account of his work. *This guy's description won't do jack. No one saw my face and no one saw me ditch the bike and the suit. I am untouchable.* That thought was interrupted by two other news stories that came in quick succession of each other. One story was about a woman who woke up with her throat slit in Kansas City, MO. Her three children were found lying in their beds with bullet holes in their heads. The other story was about a woman in Provo, Utah. Her neighbors woke that morning to find this poor soul hanging from a tree in her own front yard, naked, with only her underwear hanging beside her on the branch.

What caught Juan's attention was the analysis he heard of these stories. They were both somehow being linked to his attack. *WTF? I was acting alone. What the hell do these two murders have to do with my attack? Their murders don't even come close to comparing to what I did!*

And then he heard it. The broad he blew up, the woman in KC, MO and the lady hanging from the rape tree in Utah all had one thing in common. They were all wives of men who worked for the CIA. Men who made great gains in the war against Islamic terror.

Juan began driving faster and faster as his adrenaline pumped with increasing ferocity. His mind was racing with a chaotic velocity. He tried desperately to assimilate what he just heard. *I just killed the wife of a CIA agent. And her son. Holy shit!! This is better than I thought! I will be an instant legend now.* Juan felt invincible at the moment, as if he was the most badass Tex-Mex outlaw that ever existed. He fantasized about a lifelong career as a hit man and an assassin. He also wondered who the other hit men were and why the cartel didn't tell him that he was part of a larger operation. *Need to know basis, I guess. Whatever.*

What made no sense to him though, still, was why? Why did the cartel have him do this? If these CIA dudes were tracking down

Islamic terrorists, what the hell did the cartel care? *Maybe they were also giving heat to the cartel. Who knows. The job is done, and I kicked ass. Can't wait for my next assignment. This sure beats drinking malt liquor all day and playing Grand Theft Auto.*

CHAPTER FIFTY

Somewhere outside the perimeter of Evin Prison, Iran

The mountain air did not blow and the heat was intense. Two guards paced, with apparent boredom, back and forth outside the entrance doors at the Evin Detention Center. It was just another day for them, and their cigarettes smoked the same as they ever did. Sweat beads formed on their temples as any other hot day, and they alternately swore in Farsi and praised Allah with the same set of lips as they did any other day.

The perimeter of Evin University was littered with an elite team of private mercenaries from the Black Dog Group who were there on hire to support the mission of their respected team leaders, Blaze and Zack.

The Black Dog contingency had all been thoroughly briefed on the surrounding topography, the facility layout, the strategic plan, the back up plan, and the disaster contingencies. Most of the Black Dog group was comprised of highly trained and experienced ex-military professionals. The pack included the best of the best from the Special Forces alumni, Rangers, Navy Seals and Delta Force.

Many of them also worked for SCG International in-between missions, where they trained soldiers in pre-deployment and endeavored to pass their multitude of skills on to young aspiring warriors. They also worked security jobs for entertainers, world dignitaries and politicians, and did high-end security work for powerful CEO's through SCG International.

Most became quite attracted to the plethora of private sector opportunities that awaited them in their post-military life. Danger never left their side, but at least they were flush with cash now for risking their lives day in and day out. A high paid warrior is indeed a happy warrior.

Blaze and Zack felt confident in the team and were impressed with their quick ability to grasp the mechanics of the mission. This was not going to be an easy mission, but it was in many ways a simple one. As long as things went relatively smooth. A hope that often times never panned out.

Blaze and Zack were positioned atop an elevated spot on the perimeter. About fifty feet above Evin. And about a quarter mile from the entrance of the facility. They were surrounded by trees. Cover was adequate.

"How you feelin' Zack? We've been watchin' these pretty boy guards now for hours. No surprises in sight. I think sniping time is soon upon us. Whaddya say?" Blaze was peering intently at the two guards with his binoculars, as he lay flat and camouflaged with utter stillness.

"I think you're right old pal, but caution tells me we ought to give it a few more minutes until we pull the trigger. Confirm the team is ready for back up, and if so, let's get this party rocking in five." Zack was not known for being over cautious, but when one was in Iran, there was no such thing as being over cautious.

"Roger that. Get your Intervention ready."

Both men simultaneously steadied their CheyTac M200 Intervention Sniper Rifles, complete with the necessary Opps Inc 50cal suppressor. Blaze waited to hear from every member of Black Dog that they were primed and ready for the mission. Within a few minutes each member confirmed their position and affirmed their readiness. Blaze also confirmed that the fellas flying the Osprey V-22 helicopters would be in place in time for the extraction. Once he got the affirmative on all operational fronts, he began counting down. And then both men sniped in precise unison.

It started as hoped for; uneventful, quick, and quiet. Both guards transitioned into eternity with only a little bit of blood spray emitting from their foreheads. They flopped to the ground lifelessly.

"I feel bad for the disappointment these boys are now feeling on account of the fact that there ain't gonna be seventy virgins greeting them anywhere anytime soon. Ashes to ashes baby," commented Zack. This brief interlude of stealth would soon be interrupted. The prison's video surveillance signaled back to the Evin staff that there were two dead guards lying outside the front gate.

Game was officially on.

"Time to move." Several seconds after Blaze gave the command, one of Black Dog's finest shot a Simon door-buster from his M-16 Carbine. The Israeli invention was the perfect match for the heavy door that adorned the front gate of Evin. The door was breached perfectly. The collapse was clean. The explosion took the door right off its hinges. The passageway left was perfect. Time for the team to storm in and retrieve the package they had all come for.

Alarms sounded, guards emerged everywhere and all hell had broken loose from the centerpiece of hell on earth, Evin Prison. The unprepared guards were quickly met with formidable opponents. The entire team, accompanied by Blaze and Zack had entered the facility. Black Dog led the way clearing a path for Zack and Blaze as they set out to grab Jafari. Gunfire was everywhere. Smoke and fire filled every hallway, pathway and crevice of the initial labyrinth that followed the front gate's threshold. So far, so good. The team was plowing through the opposition and making great gains into the facility.

Two Black Dog members shouted for Blaze and Zack to follow them as they headed down a hallway that would ostensibly lead to Jafari's solitary cell. Blaze and Zack moved quickly behind them until one of the Black Dog members abruptly went down. The first shot hit his shoulder and the second went to the side of his head. His body fell quick and Blaze saw it rapidly unfold and, knowing he was already dead, made the instantaneous decision to leap over the now dead body and continue running onward. Time was of the essence.

The sole Black Dog merc that continued to lead them shouted and pointed violently to Jafari's cell. Blaze and Zack hurried to reach it, with an entourage of Black Dog assets following behind them watching their backs and dropping guards like a teenager playing whack-a-mole at a Jersey shore boardwalk arcade.

Blaze yelled Jafari's name, but heard nothing. He yelled louder and louder and finally heard a faint grunt. He couldn't confirm it was Jafari yet. He yelled his name again and heard a more forceful grunt. Zack gave Blaze an affirmative nod and the team all stood far back from the door.

"Get back against the wall and cover your ears the best you can Arash. We're getting you out of this hell hole." Blaze shouted with what was left of his hoarse voice.

Once again, the Simon came to the rescue and successfully breached the door to Arash's cell. The explosion rocked the cell. The door fell on part of Arash's body, causing some more injury. Arash was disoriented. His hearing, damaged. But he was alive—battered, demoralized, emaciated, filthy, tortured and bloodier than hell—but alive.

Blaze picked up Arash and Zack quickly radioed the helicopter team for the extraction. All the while, Black Dog assets were wrecking prison guards by the dozens.

The team surrounded Blaze with a hedge of moving protection as they moved to exit the facility. The sound of M16's shooting ahead and behind continued until the team was safely outside the facility and the Ospreys were in clear sight.

The firefights continued as they headed toward the Osprey's rescue. Blaze felt the heat of the enemy's fire whiz past his right ear as he charged hard. Zack crouched as he ran to avoid the heat. Black Dog mercs retaliated creating cover for Zack and Blaze to get to the bird first. Chaos swirled until the Osprey had gotten its primary package—Jafari—and the entire team. In short order, the bird lifted them out of harm's way and over the Alborz Mountain area. Several minor aerial battles ensued on the way out, but before long the team was out of Iran and on their way to safety ala one of the only remaining US bases in Iraq.

Blaze was entirely spent and exhausted but satisfied. He looked out the helicopter window and took a deep breath with yearnings to see his family heavy on his heart.

CHAPTER FIFTY-ONE

The office of President Hadi Samani, Tehran, Iran

Hadi Samani sat by the phone eagerly awaiting a call from Samere, his trusted Messianic advisor and key man in all things related to the coordinated preparation for the coming of the Mahdi. Samani had heard all the news reports both in the West and on Al Jazeera, and he was ecstatic about the results of their recent operation. Samani was more than pleased with the increasing dividends being paid as a result of the ever-developing relationship between Hezbollah and the Mexican drug cartels. The assassination plots were only the tip of the iceberg.

The phone rang.

"Samere!" Samani could not contain his exuberance.

"President Samani."

"It appears we've had great success with our mission?" Samani could feel the strength of the proverbial wind at his back.

"Indeed it was a huge success. All three infidel wives, and some children of our enemies, have been eliminated per our plan. Our message will be received loud and clear when the CIA receives our postcard, which by now, they probably already have received. However, it's doubtful that they'll reveal that they've received it. They'll contain their newfound fear within the agency and likely not pass along that fear to their people. Our alliance with the cartels provokes great fear in them. Allah be praised."

"Allah be praised indeed. What exactly was the message on the card sent to the CIA?" Samani was curious as to the exact language.

Samere explained, "Below the crescent moon it was written the names of the deceased infidels. It was then written on the card that Hezbollah takes full responsibility. They'll get the message. Back off the sanctions, back off the drones, back off the support of Israel. They'll also know from the crime scene patterns as to who we are working with. The rape tree in Utah clearly points to the involvement of the cartel. They know when they see women's bras and underwear hanging from a tree after a murder rape, that the cartel has left their unique mark."

Samani's smile widened, "This is excellent news. Our source inside the CIA has made me extremely proud. He has served Allah and our Republic well. Have we transferred the wire to him yet through the Lebanese Canadian Bank?"

"Indeed, he has received his worthy compensation for his role. We hope to use him again if he doesn't end up exposed. It was difficult circumventing the OFAC regulations with so many masked layers." Samere had always pleased Samani with his swift and prompt execution of business matters.

"Good work Samere. I'm proud of your diligence on behalf of Allah and the Republic. Do keep me posted on all other issues pertaining to the coming of the Mahdi and our ongoing war against both the Big Satan, the Little Satan, and all their deceptive ways."

"As is my pleasure, President Samani. A report will be forthcoming tomorrow."

"Bye for now, Samere."

"Goodbye President Samani."

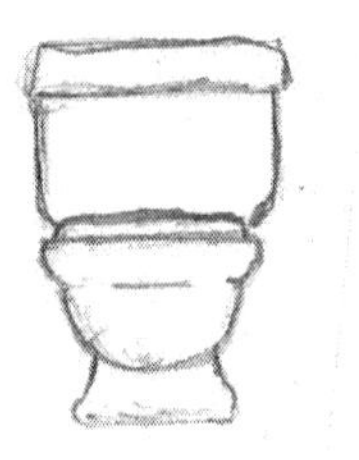

CHAPTER FIFTY-TWO

Somewhere over Iraqi airspace

Amidst the incessant hum of the Osprey V-22 helicopter, Blaze glanced down and managed to notice that his secure sat phone was vibrating. His thoughts of his family receded as he took the call.

"Yeah?" Annoyed, Blaze answered.

"Blaze. It's Gallagher." There was a tone Blaze detected that he had heard before: hesitant and troubled. It was a tone that preceded terrible news.

"What is it Chuck? The mission went relatively well. We lost one merc, Arash is pretty banged up…but he's alive, and they didn't get anything out of him. What in the hell could be the matter?"

"It's bad, Blaze. I can't tell you over the phone. I'll be at the base in Iraq when you land. We'll talk then. Gotta go."

Chuck hung up. A tough old bat like him was used to delivering bad news. But this time was going to be entirely different. When it came to informing Blaze McIntyre about the murder of his beloved, Chuck was not so tough. After ending the call, he found himself on his knees hugging a porcelain Kohler toilet bowl, puking furiously as if he was paranormally possessed.

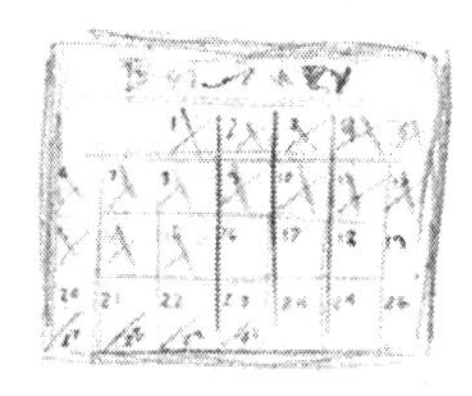

CHAPTER FIFTY-THREE

The Kremlin, Russia

Maksim Koslov was thoroughly annoyed. He had domestic annoyances, foreign policy concerns, and a series of personal ambitions that he felt were not being achieved nearly fast enough. On top of all of that, the international press was reviving an old story about an all female Russian punk rock band that was jailed for two years for voicing their political opinions. Putin had put an end to Pussy Riot with an iron fist, and now that the group was back playing their music throughout the motherland and speaking out against his regime, Koslov was considering turning Pussy Riot into a whimpering prison riot once again.

The icing on the cake of his aggravation was the series of setbacks and hiccups that plagued his ongoing relationship with Iran. He had heard all about the newer, improved Stuxnet-like computer worm that had recently wreaked havoc at Natanz, he was still getting pressure to expedite a cure to the disaster that occurred at Esfahan, and now he had Samani breathing down his neck about the timelines for work at Bushehr.

Maksim picked up the phone and dialed Samani as scheduled.

"Hello Hadi, how are you?" Maksim's tone made it clear the question was rhetorical.

"I'm doing well, our republic is doing well, and our Messiah is approaching his reemergence. The time is near." Hadi Samani knew that Maksim Koslov was highly irritated with any religious references, let alone the blatant theatrics with which Samani routinely presented his faith. But Samani did not care at all, and his brazenness was growing daily as he truly felt the imminence of the Twelfth Imam.

"Moving on here President Samani, what business of ours do you wish to discuss?"

"First of all, I'm sure you're aware of the unfortunate digital attack on Natanz and the immense setback it has caused to our production there. The Americans and the Jews are relentless with their cyber trickery and the fury of our Islamic revenge will scold them for it tenfold when Allah permits. But for now, we must deal with the issue and recoup as fast as we can. Part of this means that I insist on urgent expedition regarding the scheduled deliveries and production timelines at Bushehr. Are you able to move up the schedule of the scientists and technicians? This is imperative."

"We've been meeting all of our promised obligations according to our agreements and all of our subsequent addendums. I'll see what I can do about any increased cooperation." Koslov was placating at best.

"Allah is on our side with or without Russia. This joint venture is an asset for your country, I'd imagine it would behoove you to find a way."

"Iran needs us with or without Allah on your side. Don't prod me on this. I said that I'd see what I can do."

"Are the parts on track for delivery this week as scheduled?"

"Yes, they will be there."

"Excellent. I'm astounded at our recent ability to increase the amount of spent fuel being retained at Bushehr. We've gone from 25% to 35% without the nuclear inspectors noticing. That equates to a great increase in the amount of weapons grade uranium we are able to produce. We are almost at our goal. Our top researcher, a bright young man named Azad, is working feverishly. He will be rewarded greatly."

"Speaking of keeping off radars, you never mentioned to me the Natanz employee that betrayed you. I had to hear about that from other sources." Koslov could not believe the story when it was told to him. The Iranians were not known for allowing prisoners to be rescued. That was one thing that Russia and Iran truly had in common.

Samani's lowered his voice to a treacherous tone. It pained him to think of the incident. He was clearly burning with hot rage inside at the thought of the lost captive. "Yes, well, to our dismay, Arash Jafari was rescued, by what we believe was the American special forces, before we made the connection between him and the computer virus at Natanz. You can bet that our internal security at all the plants have been entirely revamped since. That can never happen again."

"Well you better make sure that nothing of the sort occurs at Bushehr. We have too much invested in this venture."

"I'll see to that and you see to the quickening of our scheduled plans."

"I'll see what can be done. Have a good day Hadi."

"You as well."

Neither men truly wished either a good day. As is for most powerful men, they wished only for their interests to be advanced and secured.

CHAPTER FIFTY-FOUR

The Oval Office, The White House, Washington, DC

Jack Fitzsimmons felt good for the first time in a long time. For a man who sat with great power in the Oval Office, Jack Fitzsimmons rarely felt powerful. The majority of the time he could feel his nervous stomach acids eating away at the lining of his gut as his mind raced blindly in a million different directions. Since he had taken office, he had felt as if he had not had the traction to truly implement any of his own vision or agenda. Instead, he felt as if circumstances, exterior powers, and unexpected inertia carried him to and fro haphazardly like a ship caught in an unbridled Nor'easter.

Not today though. Jack was on his second read of his briefing regarding the covert mission in Iran that he had green-lit weeks prior. His foreign spy asset was recovered without leaking any info about his activities or whom he was working with. The team that extracted him suffered only one casualty, and the Iranians were undoubtedly beside themselves. By now, Stuxnet 2.0 was systematically deconstructing their centrifuges and wreaking havoc on their nuclear ambitions. Samani and the mullahs were acting normal in public—threatening the end of Israel, condemning the big Satan, and claiming the Mahdi is with them. Nowhere in the western press, Al-Jazeera, or anywhere did any sign of turmoil surface in regard to Iran's nuclear path. But Jack reckoned not all was so pretty behind the curtain. They had to be sweating the setbacks that they had been dealt, and one could only guess how much more time had just been purchased by the US and Israel, but some serious breathing room had likely just been accomplished.

Feeling satisfied with some success on something, Fitz took in a deep breath. With that, his expected call came through.

"Chaim! How are you this morning?"

"I'm doing well Mr. President. Very eager to hear your thoughts. I did receive and read your report." The Prime Minister of Israel was all business with Fitz, often times as a means to disguise his inherent dislike of the man.

"Yes, I'm very satisfied with the outcome. Our men have completed several key goals of the Operation Persian Trinity mission. We've caused serious supply interruptions with the raw materials at Esfahan, unleashed the vicious Stuxnet 2.0 virus at Natanz, and successfully extracted our foreign spy asset from captivity at Evin. We still have some 'work to do at Bushehr, but we've already, undoubtedly created some substantial breathing room by our efforts."

"I'm fully aware of these successes and am pleased as well. This is a good and necessary step. But these are only steps. They'll not alleviate the ultimate need for more direct force, and they're only roadblocks in the Iranians eyes, not game stoppers." Chaim tried hard to keep a tone of gentle disagreement.

"Chaim, I understand your position. That said, I do believe we can continue to contain the Iranian problem through constant disruption, subterfuge and targeted assassinations. No one can afford a military attack on Iran's nuclear facilities. The risks and ramifications are too large." Fitz's tone was casual and unconvincing.

"I would love to believe you were onto something with your analysis, but I don't, and you know that. We'll give it some more time, now that it appears we have some. But our end game has not changed, as the Iranians end game has not changed. They're charting the course of this charade. We're simply planning necessary responses to ensure our survival. Thank you for all your work and cooperation with these missions, Jack. The people of Israel are extremely grateful."

"You're welcome Chaim. We'll continue to do what we can, within reason."

"Yes, of course. Hopefully we'll agree with the definition of 'reason' as time goes on."

With that, the call ended. Fitz shook his head with a sense of disbelief in what he viewed as the obstinate nature of the Prime Minister's views. Fitz was never going to authorize an official US attack on Iran and would never publically support an Israeli attack on Iran. Everyone knew this. Fitz still harbored sympathy towards Israel's enemies and resentments towards Israel, but he had to continue pursuing the disruption campaigns. Fitz thought about how different he believed the geo-political landscape would be right now if Israel simply did not exist. In his mind, they were the sticking point holding up so much movement towards progress. All from a country that was the size of Rhode Island.

CHAPTER FIFTY-FIVE

The McIntyre residence, Romeo, Michigan

It was three thirty in the afternoon and the shades were pulled down and no light was permitted to creep into Blaze's bedroom. There were rarely sounds in the house other than the normal creeks that any house ominously makes when otherwise silence allows them to be audible. Blaze lay in his bed, empty. The bed creaked under his burden as he breathed heavy and shifted his weight. He felt as if a concrete block rested upon his chest.

Occasionally, in moments of heightened pain, Blaze would let out a loud scream of terror. He had showered twice only in the two weeks he had been secluded in his room after returning from the base in Iraq—the base where Gallagher explained the losses that had brought him to this newfound hell.

His face wore a full beard: unkempt and unruly. He wore nothing but boxer shorts and a robe and forced himself to sleep whenever God would allow him that escape. It was not even depression that had struck him, but some affliction of mind and spirit far more blunt, far more debilitating and entirely incomprehensible to understand outside of first hand experience. His flesh felt, at times, as if he was literally being poked by sharp objects that invisibly taunted him.

He thought of Job and envied Job's faith in affliction. Blaze had no such faith in this state. Hope was a conspiracy. A will to live was an unachievable attribute. He tried to get angry but failed. It took ambition to be angry.

Occasionally, Blaze would rise to appropriate sparks of anger and punch the walls that enclosed him. These bursts were short-lived and produced no satisfaction. His soul was drained—bereft of any life. On a good day, he would manage to stumble to a chair by the window and stare out into the daylight. He'd lean his elbows on the cold, white tiles of the windowsill—hoping for hope. He tried to pray but could not. He could only muster a weak human wish. He wished that somehow the light would penetrate the darkness that owned him. He would sit and stare and wait. But the darkness never relented. And the light proved impotent.

Moments arose at times in which Blaze mustered up some defiance. He cursed God and howled at the heavens. *What have I done but try to defend my country? Why did You take her? Why did You take my boy? What have You left me to do? How much do You think I can take? How do You call Yourself a God of love?* Blaze knew in his heart the answers to his cries. He knew God's nature was pure love, but he could not see it or believe it in his agony.

Memories of Diem and Shane stung in his mind and provided both strange comfort and cruel reminders of the loss that had plagued him. His body temperature rose and he became overheated. The emotional tumult drove his bio-chemistry. He thought of the joy that Shane had when he would play guitar and make music. He was getting really good at it and was even writing some impressive originals. The day Shane shot his first rifle stuck out in Blaze's mind as well. He had been so proud of him. He had already become a good shot. The simple things he did with his young son continued to come to mind. Playing a round of horseshoes in the back yard. Grabbing a slice of pizza for lunch. Praying at the dinner table. Lighting fireworks in the back yard.

He remembered the sweet support of Diem. Her loving embrace, even when she was scared. Her understanding nod, even when she had no clue as to why things were happening. Her faith in Blaze's instincts and nature. The way she managed the house and took care of the kids without complaining. She was an amazing mother and made it all seem so effortless. The images flooded his mind. He wasn't sure whether to indulge in them or attempt to push them away. Either way, he couldn't stop his mind and he had no will or energy to move. He lay staring at the ceiling for hours, occasionally leaning over to urinate in a bucket by his bed.

He was proud of Dennis already. Dennis was staying at his aunt Melissa's, Blaze's sister-in-law. Blaze was too distraught to even keep the company of his only living son. He knew Dennis needed him. Blaze needed Dennis too. They would come together and support each other in time, but not now. Blaze needed to heal alone and Dennis would find more tangible support in his aunt. Blaze saw him briefly before retreating to his dark bedroom. He wept profusely and gave Dennis a long, strong bear hug. Dennis was notably unemotional and displayed a strength and maturity way beyond his years.

"You're still here for a reason, Son. You're alive for a reason." Blaze proclaimed to Dennis.

"I know Dad. Don't worry about me. I'm all right. You'll be too, just wait. Mom and Shane are safe in heaven now. We're still here for a purpose. You'll see. God doesn't make mistakes."

Blaze pondered the words his son had uttered and tried to let them soak in. He wanted to believe what Dennis had said. He knew in time he would. But right now they were an empty comfort at best.

He thought of what Gallagher had told him. It had finally happened. Everyone had feared that these types of horrors would ultimately emerge. It had been known for some time now that Iran, via Hezbollah, had made real alliances and partnerships with the Mexican drug cartels, but until now, America had not felt any harm from this nefarious marriage. *Hezbollah even had the balls to take responsibility and leave their card.* The enemy was getting brazen and their reach was getting longer. He thought of the other victims. Other CIA families effected. He knew this couldn't go unanswered. This couldn't be permitted to escalate.

Blaze forced himself to think about what happened. He imagined all the details that led to these hits that Iran commissioned, Hezbollah facilitated, and the cartel fulfilled. He tried to focus his thoughts. He tried to arouse his anger in search of some motivation or purpose. He lay in bed struggling through his thoughts, darkness all around him and deep inside him.

He had not eaten in over ten hours and his stomach was beginning to growl. His cell phone had been turned off for weeks. Blaze, in a single motion, swung his body up out of his bed and grabbed his cell phone off the nightstand. He determined to go fix himself something to eat. He turned his cell phone on as he made his way into the kitchen. He couldn't go on hiding like this. He felt his anger and purpose. His phone rang.

"It's about time you picked up your phone."

"Really? You're gonna talk to me like that after what just happened to me Chuck? Really?"

"Sorry, Blaze. I didn't mean it like that. I'm just…well, we're all just really worried about you. You can understand that, right?"

"Yeah, I understand. And you should be worried. I'm not fine. Not sure I'll ever be."

"There's someone you should talk to. An old spook who went through something similar. A bit eccentric, but I know he can help. Will you see him Blaze?"

"Who exactly is 'him'?"

"Yoda."

CHAPTER FIFTY-SIX

Tehran, Iran

Zack Batt felt as if he had slipped through a wormhole. The whole scenario seemed surreal. His cover persona as a Nazi skinhead. The rhetoric flying around at the *World Without Zion Conference*. Just being in Iran on a consequential op a week after he was holed up in prison. Zack adapted well to the scenario but still marveled at the oddity of it. He took it all in. Pamphlets everywhere. Anti-Semitic slogans spoken as if they were profound. Zack avoided shaking his head in disgust and kept his thoughts deep inside. *My grandmother would be rolling in her Jewish grave. Here I am hob knobbing with those who seek to destroy the heritage she upheld and annihilate all Jewish remnants the world over.*

Zack ferried around the conference floor at the *World Without Zionism Conference* searching for his digital Persian pen pal, Hamid. He struggled to be in the moment because he still harbored an extremely heavy heart. After completing a very successful mission at Evin Prison side by side with his old warrior pal Blaze McIntyre, Zack couldn't help but feel an intense sorrowful drag on his spirit because of what happened to Blaze's dear wife and oldest son. This empathetic grief swirled nonstop in the core of his heart and the back of his mind. It took everything within him to try to block it out so he could focus on the undercover task at hand. If he knew Blaze, and he was pretty damn sure he did after all they had been through together, then Blaze had already purged himself of the initial shock and was hastily planning strategic revenge for whoever was involved with the hit on his family. Zack had already vowed to assist in any way possible. His bond with Blaze was deep, and it was his desire to continue to fight side by side with him no matter the mission and no matter the arena. For a matter of national security or for a personal vendetta—which in this case would likely be both.

Zack had dressed the part with blue jeans, Doc Marten boots, and suspenders. *Boots and braces in full effect.* He wore a white power tee shirt that he had ordered off the Internet that had made him cringe when he had slipped it on. He was indeed *Doug Schmidt,* an American White Power Skinhead from head to toe.

As he walked the conference floor, he engaged in a good amount of people watching and was trying to take in the bizarre scene the best he could. For the most part, it was Iranian Muslim extremists and Twelvers yucking it up as they readied themselves to hear about a future Islamic utopian world order that had 86'd America and Israel. But there were some slightly unusual suspects present that had caught Zack's eye. He noticed good ol' David Duke making his now expected annual appearance at the event. Nothing like whack-a-doo American KKK members linking arms with Iranian hate mongers for the world to see. It was amazing to Zack that such a person even existed in modern America, let alone one who was so brazenly open and evangelistic about his twisted views of hate.

He also noticed several other self-identified members of other fringe white supremacist groups from the US. There were several high-ranking members of the Aryan Brotherhood floating around the conference doing their best to make strange allies in a strange land. Zack had encountered many Brotherhood members in prison. Sometimes he won those fights, and sometime he lost, but he never backed down, and he was often the one who started them.

Also in attendance was a leading member of the White Order of

Thule. This was a strange elitist white supremacist clique that embraced pre-Christian European paganism. The group had disappeared and reappeared at various times since its original inception in the mid-1990's. The latest incarnation that had proved to have some nominal staying power was headquartered in the U.K. The fellow Zack had spotted was clearly a Brit and from that contingency. This strand of hate got its fuel from a belief and focus on Wotanism. Wotanism is a religious affiliation with the indigenous faiths of the Pre-Christian European world that is centered in an affinity and association with the ancient European warrior culture. They rallied around a rejection of what they saw as a Jewish-influenced Christian culture and instead they embraced folklore and mysticism passed down by their Nordic ancestors. When all was said and done, it was yet another Nazi focal point that was positioned to worship all things Aryan and reject all else. As far as Zack was concerned, it was yet another fear-driven, hate-laden sub group of white fascists who would latch onto any ideology that seemed to justify their hate. On top of that, like most white power groups, the White Order of Thule co-opted the skinhead aesthetic and further defiled what was originally a wholly non-racist sensibility. How the skinhead lifestyle had somehow been birthed from black Jamaican immigrants to Britain only to be somehow claimed by these boneheads was beyond Zack's comprehension. As far as Zack could remember, he never saw any images of ancient Nordic warriors with shaved heads; they looked more like Fabio.

Zack also observed the contingency of attendants who were members of the Golden Dawn party. This was a Greek nationalist group shrouded in fascism, Nazi praise, and blatant racism. They held up Greek dictator Loannis Metaxas as an iconic figure. Metaxas reigned during World War II. Since their advancements in Greek parliament, which resulted in them gaining twenty-one seats in the 2012 national elections, the Golden Dawn party had consistently achieved membership growth within Greece and extending globally. They even had a burgeoning office in New York. Now, they were linking arms with the Islamo fascists of Iran.

Trying to weed through all the Persian natives in attendance and locate Hamid was a challenging task. It was going to be much easier of course for Hamid to seek out the very few white people in attendance and locate Zack, whose nametag deceptively read *Douglas Schmidt.*

Zack stopped to graze a bit at one of the spreads that was laid out for the event. He had a few servings of dukkah with some pita bread choosing not to sit at a table but to stand out in the open and be as visible as possible. He washed the spicy dukkah down with some doogh, a refreshing drink that contained yogurt and carbonated water and had a nice salty, minty flavor to it. It was a strange and somewhat exotic drink that made him think of the 'fizzly bubbly' drink from Adam Sandler's movie *Don't Mess With the Zohan.* Zack may be half Jewish, and whole spy, but he wasn't about to live out the *Zohan* movie and start hairdressing and copulating with old ladies anytime soon.

Finally, after loitering around the table for a few minutes after his snack, a slender man with a close-cropped beard, caramel skin, and jet black hair began pointing at him excitedly and walking fast towards him.

"Douglas Schmidt? From Twitter in America? Is that you?" The moment was here.

"Hamid! I finally meet you in person! I'm so excited to be here and to see you face to face. This is such an amazing and important event. I can't believe I'm actually here." Zack was on.

"Brother Douglas, you have no idea. This conference is a window into the future. A bright future without America and the Zionist. Just wait until you hear President Samani's speech!" Hamid's eyes were aflame.

"I'm eager to hear them. Aryans from all around the world need to unite to help make this vision a reality. I'm so glad to be here with you. Should we go find our seats for the presentation?" Hamid agreed they should. So far, *Doug Schmidt* was a hit with Hamid.

They took their seats and watched some ceremonial shenanigans for a while before Samani's speech began. There were some messages from some well-known Imam's and some skits and such that resembled variety show acts of sorts. Eventually the headliner took stage.

Samani was his usual self, but with more pointed words than normal. He was in his element and was there to cement his vision of the world in the minds of those that most faithfully upheld his worldview. The backdrop was an upgraded version of the same visual they had displayed since the conference's inception. It displayed a ball wrapped in the American flag having dropped through an hourglass. The ball was shattered as it hit the bottom. Falling right behind the American-flag draped ball was a ball adorned in the Star of David. The image was spruced up with some modern graphic design trimmings, but the main thrust was still clear: a world without America and Israel was coming, and possible. Not only was it coming, but the sequence of this expulsion was also clear. America had to be destroyed first, *then* Israel would naturally follow. After all, America was the 'big Satan' and Israel only the 'little Satan'.

The rhetoric that Samani spewed was more of the same. He delivered the same message as his predecessor Ahmadinejad had but with a lot more flair and charisma. He drew upon the struggle of the Palestinians, the arrogance and decadence of the west, the apostate nature of Christianity and Judiasm, and Iran's strategic plan to bring the West to it knees. He reiterated that they had well-drawn plans on how to attack over thirty sensitive sites in the US and at least a dozen in Israel. He scoffed at the impotence of the economic sanctions that had been imposed upon them. He repeatedly heralded the glory of the Mahdi and insisted He was already here and had made himself known to Samani. It was not just America and Israel that found themselves liquidated in Samani's new world Islamic vision. It was also Britain, Australia, New Zealand, Canada, France, and Germany. They would also naturally be destroyed in short order according to Samani's apocalyptic plan. Zack had heard it all before. *Arrogant*

Anglo-Saxons bad, righteous Islamic faithful good. Blah, blah, blah. If only Samani's words truly didn't have any real effect on anything or anyone. Zack knew better. He sat there listening to every word with the English sub titles supplied by the video monitor to the left of the stage. Hamid would glance over to Zack every few minutes or so looking for excitement in the eyes of his newfound Aryan brother. Zack made sure Hamid was not disappointed.

When the intermission presented itself, Zack followed Hamid into the lobby for some tea. The two men shared each other's stories as to how they grew so passionate about their Aryan heritage and how they had developed deep convictions that it was something to preserve and fight for. Zack stuck closely to his pre-fab story and Hamid told his honest one. At one point, Hamid asked Zack why he was not affiliated with any Aryan groups in the states.

"Most of the Aryan groups in the states think small. They don't think internationally. They digress into detestable activities of organized crime to survive. They're an embarrassment to any real ambition to dignify and elevate the Aryan cause. That's why they're powerless and get nothing done but running prostitutes and selling drugs and leading half their members into prison. If we're to really achieve goals such as the ones laid out today by your President Samani, we need big thinking from smart, globally minded people."

Hamid was mesmerized by Zack's ability to posit a broad brush, big picture perspective on a path to global Aryan dominance. He was finding himself enamored with this *Doug Schmidt.*

"Your words are spoken with much thought and wisdom. You should attend our NINP meeting this week while you are here in Iran. We have one two days from now. Will you be able to attend?"

Now we are cooking with gas. This was what Zack was hoping for. "Absolutely, it would be an honor and a great privilege! I'll be there."

CHAPTER FIFTY-SEVEN

Chincoteague, Virginia

Gallagher wasn't kidding when he said this fella lived out in the middle of nowhere. His address did not show up on any GPS system that Blaze had tried to access. Blaze regrettably resorted to the directions he had written down from Gallagher's dictation. He followed them meticulously and found himself finally getting to what he imagined was close to this old man's dwelling place.

He traveled rough dirt roads bordered by wild brush growing in thick mud beneath. The passages leading to the house were narrow and limiting. They discouraged unwanted or unexpected visitors. Swamp-like land peppered the areas leading up to the house. Gallagher said he was a strange old dude. The 'Yoda' moniker was making more and more sense to Blaze at each turn he took through the swampy island woods.

Finally, he made his way to the small dirt driveway in front of Yoda's modest house. There were random auto parts, antique junk, and motorcycle parts littered all around the property. Yoda's joint looked like a picker's dream. An old gas station pump stood proudly out front of the small shack that sat adjacent to his home. One old pick up truck sat in the driveway on cinder blocks. Bumper stickers on the truck read 'Rapture Ready', 'Keep Your Friends Close and Your Guns Closer', and one had the American Flag on it with the word 'Redneck' on the red stripe, 'White Trash' on the white stripe, and 'Blue Collar' on the blue stripe. Yoda must have heard Blaze's vehicle pulling up because he immediately emerged from his front door and stood out on his porch peering at his arriving visitor.

Hunter 'Yoda' Davis was one weird dude. He stood out on his porch wearing blue jeans, suspenders, and a wild life tee shirt with a raccoon on it. He wore a baseball cap with an American flag patch. The hat contained a hell of a lot of flair as well, with all kinds of military buttons. Hunter Davis earned the name Yoda because his mere existence, the aura of his residence and its surroundings, and even his white hair and grizzly aged skin, brought to mind an earthly redneck version of the olive green, intergalactic patriarch of sci-fi cinema.

"You must be Mr. McIntyre." Yoda walked slowly down his front porch steps to greet Blaze as he got out of his truck.

"That's right. Pleased to meet you Mr. Davis. I've heard a lot about you."

"I'm sure it's all exaggerated and the stuff of false legends and trumped up folklore. As far as you know."

"As far as I know." The two men both chuckled and strangely Yoda waived Blaze on to follow him into the shack besides the house. Blaze wasn't sure what to think, but followed him all the same.

"Step inside here Mr. McIntyre. This is my workshop. I built this after I lost my family, a story I may tell you about some other time." Blaze nodded his head and began looking around the inside of the shack. His eyes widened with the beauty of what he saw. The shack was stuffed to the gills with the most beautiful and diverse wooden bird and duck carvings he had ever seen. This was no ordinary decoy maker.

Yoda continued, "After I lost my precious wife and young children, I retreated into solitude, as one would expect. As you have, Blaze. In that solitude, I went through terrible pain and unspeakable misery. I let it linger much longer than I should have, but I hadn't had anyone in my life really reach out and attempt to pull me back into the world. There was no Chuck Gallagher in my life lobbying for some sort of help for me." Yoda paused and turned his head staring at some of his favorite decoys.

Blaze asked, "So what did you do?"

"Well, the only positive thing I had to hold onto to purge my pain, occupy my time, and help me rediscover some beauty in life was what took place in this shack. Birds and ducks Mr. McIntyre. Birds and ducks. I spent mostly evenings in here enjoying the peacefulness of the night. The stillness of the night. Nothing but the sound of the crickets and the swamp critters to fill my ears. No sunlight to taunt me with hope that I hadn't yet been able to welcome. But I had these blocks of wood, these carving tools, and an indescribable attraction to the beauty of birds and ducks. I carved and painted like mad. Sometimes spending the entire night in this shack and returning to my bed at dawn to sleep all day."

"And that did the trick?" asked Blaze.

"For me, yes. It was beyond therapeutic. It was a spiritual endeavor. I was like a redneck monk cast away in the swampy woods creating the only thing that made me feel like a human being again. Every time I completed a bird or a duck and put the finishing touches of paint on them, a piece of me healed and a part of my soul re-united with God."

"How long did this go on for?" Blaze asked—now fully immersed in Yoda's life story.

"To tell the truth, I don't know exactly how long, but it was well over a year and half. I didn't talk to a single soul outside of a few 'pleases' and 'thank yous' to the good folks at the market. I had pulled the plug on interacting with other people. I wasn't ready, or I chose not to be ready. Either way, my healing process took a lot of time. Time I now regret I took. You see, as imperative and necessary as that process was, I enjoyed it too much and I made excuses for myself constantly so I could continue to justify delaying getting back into life. This is a mistake you mustn't make."

"And now?"

"Now? Well, now I still do live as a recluse. I know that. And to a large degree, I still am, and I struggle with that instinct. But I force myself to regularly get together with friends, I continue to consult with the CIA and do anything they ask of me, within reason, for which my experience can be of value. I write all the time and am on the verge of releasing my first memoir about my years in the field—all of course, to be thoroughly cleared and rubber-stamped by Langley. And I meet all kinds of people all over this great country who come here to buy my carvings. That internet is one hell of a sales tool." Yoda turned his eyes away from his hanging wooden birds now to look Blaze square in the eyes. He then continued, "My point is, Blaze, you gotta push through the pain. You gotta get back in life's game before the opium of seclusion sucks you away and makes it harder for you to ever get back on life's wagon. You were left to live for a reason. Even though with your loss it doesn't seem your life is worth much to you. Know that those feelings are lies, Blaze. The good Lord has got a plan for you, and from what I hear of your abilities, He likely has a lot of plans for you."

Blaze had heard his words and was internalizing them as quickly and as deeply as he could. He waited for a pause in Yoda's story and asked, "Mr. Davis, if you don't mind me asking, could you tell me exactly what happened to your family? Mr. Gallagher never did tell me exactly, only that it was similar to what happened to mine."

Yoda looked at Blaze and then slowly put his head down. He then looked Blaze in the eye, and nodded his head. He began to respond, "Well, it was a long time ago, so I'm not going to go into much detail Mr. McIntyre, I hope you understand. Let's just say that it was during the cold war and I was instrumental in helping America win that war. The KGB didn't like that. So much so, that they found their way stateside and picked off my wife and children one by one. That's all I care to recount on the matter at the present time."

"Understood. I'm not sure if I could say much about what happened to my family either. Thank you for sharing with me."

There was silence for about thirty seconds or so as both men stared off into the trees not knowing what to say, or if they should try to say anything more at all. The silence spoke volumes of the pain each man had endured, and continued to endure.

Eventually, Yoda broke the silence and asked Blaze if he cared to have a drink and a cigar with him on his porch. Blaze obliged and the two men fired up their stogies and drank a glass of bourbon as the sweet southern breeze mercifully began to pick up on the muggy, summer evening.

The conversation digressed into much less heavy subjects as the night proceeded. Both men were content to have hashed out the heavy stuff first. Now they were simply trading war stories, discussing past strategic approaches, and solving the world's problems one at a time.

After a while, Blaze had said his goodbyes, expressed his gratitude and vowed to keep in touch. Blaze was inspired by Yoda's past, the wisdom he had gained, and the responsibility he took to pass on his wisdom to a new generation of spies and warriors. Blaze thanked God that Gallagher had urged him to see Yoda. It had truly been an ordained meeting and had helped to lift the veil of darkness from Blaze's eyes. Hope was again tangible. His will to live was once again indomitable. His purpose became clear. His sorrow transformed into a motivation to stalk America's enemies—the enemies that killed his wife and son. He would avenge. Deep within him, a thirst for revenge had now taken root. And he was determined to quench it. He felt invigorated and emboldened.

It was almost as if the force was with him.

CHAPTER FIFTY-EIGHT

Bushehr, Iran

If one looked closely, the signs of long imprinted damage from wars gone by would be evident. The war with Iraq had left its stains on the city of Bushehr. Most living in the city and the surrounding fishing villages had cleared their minds of either their direct memories or the created impressions passed down by the stories of their elders, but physical signs still remained for those interested. Life in Bushehr and its surrounding villages did have its drudgery. The heat was tormenting and relentless. The brine hung in the air with an almost tangible quality as a constant reminder of the proximity to the ocean. Most spent their days minding their daily catch of fish and going about their business in Halileh, Bandargeh, and in and around Bushehr. Most also paid very little attention to the daily work that was being done at the Bushehr nuclear facility, the main focal point for the world outside of Iran when it came to their immediate geography.

Azad was feeling very important lately. His career had really reached its zenith and his work at Bushehr was exhilarating and wildly fulfilling. He was progressing by leaps and bounds towards his objectives, and more importantly, towards the goals of the regime. They actually were now calling him directly for status reports, to clarify technical issues, and to encourage him with his research. Azad's team had diligently been working overtime for the sake of the cause. They too were well aware of the historical and spiritual significance of their work, and the timely emphasis that was being placed on it by the mullahs. The Mahdi was here after all, and everyone was eagerly looking forward to the day that He was known to all and not just his main public conduit, President Samani.

Azad was only twenty-eight years old, but he knew he was living out his calling and serving Allah in the highest way possible. He was confident that the research he was spearheading would help to defeat the infidels. To demolish the cancer that was the west. To finally eliminate the Zionists and the Americans. His team felt the same way. They hated the Jews just as much as he did and were ready for not only a Caliphate, but one that was primarily guided by the superior Aryan blood of Persia.

Azad was still wearing his lab coat as he scanned his ID card and left the plant. It had been a long day, a twelve-hour race with very little time to eat or use the facilities. Azad was looking forward to retreating this evening to his cousin Hamid's house to meet with his brothers in the Neo Iranian Nazi Party.

He had joined the group, along with his cousin, when he was twenty-four years old after a period of intense study and introspection. It was around this time that Azad truly embraced his Aryan roots and the Aryan roots of his people. He also became more and more versed on the eschatology of Shia Islam, particularly those who embraced the anticipation of the great Twelfth Imam. The merging of his fully ignited religious fervor and his newfound deep commitment to preserving his racial heritage had proven to be a life force in Azad that was full of promise and ambition.

The meeting had already started but Azad had not missed too much. The group had begun with their ceremonial poetry readings about their ancestors and the power of their Aryan roots. They were now getting into the Quran readings before they began the evening's history lesson. Azad sat quietly smiling and drinking tea as he both learned new things and allowed known things to be reinforced. As the history lesson ended, the group broke out into a social hour of sorts and attendees broke into clusters of isolated conversations as they ate light finger food and drank tea.

Hamid walked over to talk with Azad and had a large smile on his face. Hamid was always extra happy at the weekly NINP meetings, and tonight was no exception. Azad barely noticed the white man walking arms length behind Hamid and acting as if he was there as Hamid's guest.

"Hamid! How are you my cousin! I'm so excited to tell you about the great work at Bushehr! We're almost there my friend, almost ready!" Azad could not contain his bubbling enthusiasm.

Hamid gave his cousin a firm hug and congratulated him on his work, "That's great news my cousin! I know you've worked so hard and so diligently and Allah has uniquely blessed you with talent! To think that it will be your research that leads the way to the ultimate annihilation of the Zionist and the Great Satan is beyond comprehension!"

"Hamid you have no idea the type of emotion that runs through me each day. I'm even speaking almost daily with members of the regime. They're proud of my work and encourage me daily. We're all excited for the coming of the Mahdi. The wait will be soon over. The time of the Caliphate is here, and Aryan dominance will be known throughout the new Islamic order." Azad's eyes widened and his smile extended with a hazy, visionary glare of imaginative fanaticism.

Doug Schmidt watched this exchange with particular interest and keen observation. Azad. The man he was looking for. This guy was the last step for the Bushehr plant to reach dangerous nuclear capacity. Azad confirmed that contrary to news reports, weapons-grade uranium was indeed being processed at Bushehr. This was the guy the regime was counting on.

"Azad, I almost forgot, this is my very good friend, Doug Schmidt, from America. He's strong in the Aryan cause and shares our goals. He attended the World Without Zionism conference with me and is our guest here tonight at the NINP meeting."

"It's a great pleasure to meet you Azad!" Zack extended his hand out and squeezed Azad's hand like a man.

"It's always a pleasure to meet a fellow soldier in the worldwide Aryan cause! It's nice to see some new blood around here!" Azad's enthusiasm was still driving him and he had forgotten all he had said prior to shaking Zack's hand.

The three men talked vigorously for about an hour about the history of Iran, the historic relationship of Persia with Nazi Germany, the plague of Zionism, the overreaching nature of America and the West, the glory of the coming Iranian bomb, and the messianic deliverance forthcoming courtesy of the Twelfth Imam. They drank tea the entire time and were quite at ease. Many others from the meeting came by and weaved naturally in and out of the conversation. Azad had left his cell phone and car keys unguarded on an end table near the bathroom surrounded by keys and phones left there by other members as they entered Hamid's humble domicile. Zack had studied each person as they left their items on this table upon their entrance.

It only took three minutes for Zack to grab Azad's phone on his way to the bathroom, copy his SIM card as he urinated, and return the phone to its position on the end table without a Persian soul in the room knowing any different.

He would now know all he would need to know about Azad. And this would suffice in determining exactly how and where he would decide to kill him.

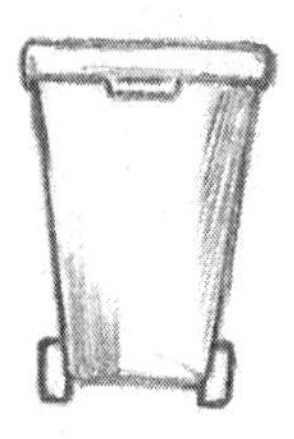

CHAPTER FIFTY-NINE

Sartal, Iran

There was not a whole hell of a lot happening in Sartal, Iran. Pretty much ever. Zack Batt had learned this grueling fact in the past four weeks. Long nights of tedious recon and forced interest into the life of his subject had taught him the immovable truth that one must never yearn to spend time in the town of Sartal in the country of Iran.

Zack had observed Azad's daily routine now for four weeks and had seen very little deviation to give him any pause about the execution of his plan. Azad was indeed a faithful servant of his employers at the Bushehr nuclear plant and an equally faithful husband and father. Like many people, he went to work and he came home. Not much else. Zack sat in the agency provided white Iranian Khodro Samand LX peering out the driver's side window with his binoculars. It was 6:30 PM. Another fifteen minutes. He once again read the plaque that hung in Azad's family room beneath the large painting of the ancient Persian King Darius. The plaque read:

I am Darius, the great king, the king of kings
The king of many countries and many people
The king of this expansive land,

The son of Wishtaspa of Achaemenid,
Persian, the son of a Persian,
'Aryan', from the Aryan race

This little ditty was all too familiar to Zack at this point. This was recited with glee in unison by all of the attendees of the NINP meeting where Zack met Azad. King Darius may have thrown Daniel in the lion's den in the days of old, but his chief psycho Aryan descendent was going to get his ass clipped.

Zack turned his binoculars and attention to watch Azad as he threw his young son up in the air and they both laughed as he caught him on the way down. It was the end of their dinnertime and it was pretty much the same every night. Zack had watched Azad's wife clean up after dinner as Azad played with his son on the living room floor for about fifteen minutes.

Then, he would see the bathroom light go on shortly after Azad's wife would take Azad's son in her arms and whisk him out of the room. Bath time.

Then, like clockwork, just as he had done every Thursday evening since Zack had been spying on him, at 6:45 PM, Azad walked out to the side of the house to take out the trash.

Zack quickly pondered the cold brutality of what he was about to do. He had done it many times before and the typical boundaries of normal human emotion and empathy had never hindered him. He knew his skills and he was at peace with the reasons for which he employed them. In typical circumstances, he did his best to isolate the target. This provided a very focused, narrow insight into the target's life and avoided the muddy waters of knowing the peripherals of the subject's life. He rarely considered the women or children of a subject, let alone watched them to the point of knowing the details of their daily lives. This made things easier.

Watching Azad with his family strangely penetrated Zack's now numb assassin's heart. His mind wasn't prone to second-guessing. But this time, his heart did temporarily bear a soft empathy. He felt a tug of pain for the pending loss that the mother and young child would soon experience to no fault of their own.

But Azad's wife and child would have to blame their father in the end, thought Zack. Azad was one of the crucial last steps to the acquisition of nuclear weapons by one of the most maniacal regimes in history. He was also a virulent anti-Semite and Aryan supremacist. Zack's emotions quickly began hardening once again as he reflected upon these realities.

Zack double-checked the silencer on his Glock 18 as he proceeded to roll up close to the target with a slow creep in the white Iranian made vehicle. He always insisted on eye contact if possible before the deed was to be done. It was Zack's way of owning the action.

Azad heard the slow, humming sound of the vehicle as it rolled up close to the curb. He casually lifted his head to view it with a disinterested glance as he lifted the lid off of the large rubber trash receptacle. His eyes met Zack's with no alarm, as it was too dark for Azad to distinguish his identity.

Azad placed the trash bag above the receptacle as he began to drop the garbage in. Before his hand could release the bag, a dime-size piece of brain matter left the back of his head and found its way to the fence that gated the entrance to his back yard. The trash bag managed to still fall perfectly into the trashcan. The only significant sound to be heard was the slight thud of Azad's body hitting the ground. Zack had completed his hit and Azad had still successfully completed his Thursday evening chore.

It was about twenty minutes later, with Azad's home about fifteen miles in Zack's rearview, that Zack picked up his sat phone and placed a call to Chuck Gallagher.

"The trinity is complete. I've had enough of this Islamic Aryan circus. Please get me the hell out of here, will ya?"

"You'll spend one night at the safe house and fly out in the morning. Stay out of trouble until then. Glad to hear you made out well on completing the trinity. Not that I ever had any doubts."

Zack noticed that Gallagher was calmer than usual—probably because he was awakened out of bed to take the call. During daylight hours, one does not receive a calm Gallagher on the phone in any circumstances. "Roger that spookmaster general. I've got some road ahead of me before I get to the safe house. Talk to you tomorrow."

"Roger…smartass."

CHAPTER SIXTY

Belfast, Ireland

The good Reverend Liam McCardle was plagued with pangs of lingering guilt as he sipped his steaming hot coffee while sitting on his mum's porch adoring the lush green landscapes of his beloved homeland. As his guilt merged with his ongoing sobriety efforts, the urge to pour a shot of Bushmills into his coffee grew strong. Liam decisively resisted that urge and instead prayed harder, asking the good Lord to forgive him—both for the urge to drink and for the wanton night of passion he spent with Erin. He had lost all control that evening and was swept away with the radiant beauty and glowing charisma of Ms. Erin McNeil. When the dancing was over and the night trotted on, there was no chance that his libido would tame. Liam fell short and succumbed to a blistering and passionate night of lovemaking, which he regretted deeply, yet cherished as an altogether enduring and fond memory.

Erin was a woman of faith, and she suffered from similar guilt as Liam did. They talked about the implications of their premature consecration and had both agreed to not let it happen again until they were married. They both knew it would be difficult, given how quickly and deeply they had fallen for each other, but they had managed to maintain their mutual promise thus far.

The wedding had already been set for the following fall, and the two had announced their engagement to a small gathering of Irish family and friends. Liam had yet to break the good news to his friend Blaze, mostly because of the bad news he knew plagued Blaze's life at the moment. It was this matter for which he began to pray as he read through his morning scripture discipline. He was expecting a call from Blaze shortly and he wanted to make sure that he was spiritually blessing the call in advance so that God could be demonstrably 'in on the call' and dispersing his spirit throughout the conversation.

He reflected on some passages in Isaiah, and then meandered into some verses in Romans, before finally revisiting the constant magnet that the 38th and 39th chapters of Ezekiel had become. It was after a deep scan of those chapters that the call came in from Blaze to Liam's mobile. He put down his Bible and cup of joe and took the call on his mobile while shifting back and forth on the front porch rocking chair.

"Blaze! I'm so glad we can finally talk. You've been very much on my heart and mind. I pray for you daily." Liam was truly happy to hear Blaze's voice, even though he did not expect such enthusiasm to be relayed in Blaze's tone, given the pain he was dealing with.

"Hey Liam. It's good to hear your voice too. Thanks for the emails and all your prayers. It's been brutal, and I'm not sure I will ever really recover, but I'm adapting and picking up the pieces quickly." Blaze's tone was calm and somewhat distant.

"I understand Blaze. You don't have to hide your true state from me. We've always been open with each other."

"I know, sorry it took a bit for me to call, I've had a lot to figure out. Every day I try to get back into as much of a normal routine as possible but I am constantly overwhelmed with memories of Diem and Shane. Nothing seems real or worthwhile. I keep thinking of how Diem was when I was away on missions, how she held fast at home and raised the kids so heroically. She rarely complained, and the kids always praised her. Even when Shane was at his most spoiled state, it was clear he loved and appreciated his Mom. I miss her,

Liam. I miss her bad. And I miss my boy."

Liam knew his friend was going through pain that had no foreseeable sunset. As a Pastor, it was his job to offer consoling words, but he found it hard to do. He struggled to come up with something fitting. "I know I can't relate Blaze. My son is all grown up and my wife passed in a much different manner and time in her life. But pain, anguish and grief are common to the human experience and I can hear the agony in your voice and I empathize."

"Thanks Liam. It means a lot."

"I also know who you are at the core of it all. We'll never understand the mind of God or why such horrific tragedies are permitted, but we can seek Him in these times and seek unseen ancillary purposes. In that spirit, I urge you to not abandon your recent reemergence into the field. You must find ways to utilize this pain to strengthen and motivate you to neutralize the enemies of freedom. I am convinced you're needed uniquely in these times. These times of Gog and Magog. These times of wars, rumors of wars, and pending all out wars. Harness God's calling for you in all of this. It will be your lifeblood." Liam worried he may be pushing too hard on this point, but somehow he sensed his words were Spirit-driven.

"I know. I've been feeling the healing lately and the visions I've been getting confirm my path. I had another visit from Harry's ghost the other day. I woke up in cold sweats and I saw him hovering above my bed. He was quoting Ezekiel 38 and 39. Talking about the hook and the jaw, the mountains of Israel, and enemies advancing like a storm. He was loud and dramatic and flailed his arms as he spouted on about it. He described in detail the hailstone and torrents that God would send. He painted a vivid picture of all the fire and burning sulfur and crumbling mountains. It was theatrical and terrifying and yet I laid there mesmerized with a peculiar sense of peace."

"What else did he say Blaze?"

"He told me Diem and Shane were safe and with the Lord. That they had immeasurable peace and that I shouldn't worry about them. He spoke of a strong future for Dennis. He told me that some people are watchman and some are warriors but that I need to be both. He said the Lord expects no less from me than to act as such. His appearance solidified what I already was feeling. The pain is still there and is strong, but my calling remains, and there is much more work for me to do."

"I'm glad to hear that you can see the signs and sense Providence through this trial. You'll overcome Blaze. You will adapt."

"Roger that, Liam. Zack has been a tremendous friend through all of this as well. I also met with an old spook named Hunter Davis that Gallagher sent me to. His story and his words to me also came as a much-needed comfort in this time. Well, enough about me and my dead friend showing up in the middle of the night—how are you and that Irish girlfriend of yours?" Blaze felt a quick need to lighten up the conversation and take the attention away from himself.

"Erin is magnificent. She's quite a lady, Blaze. She's beyond beautiful with her flowing red hair and glowing cheeks, not to mention the body God blessed her with. We've been inseparable since reuniting and I've come to quickly love her daughter McKinnis as well. It won't be long before she's my stepdaughter. Erin and I are engaged to be married next fall!"

Blaze's voice rose with excitement for the first time since tragedy had shattered his world. "Congrats! I'm so happy for you Liam! Make sure I get an invite. I'll bring Dennis to Ireland and we'll make a trip out of it. What are you going to do about the Church? I assume you're going to stay and live in Ireland?"

"Yes, we'll live here in Ireland. I'll finish out the year at the Church in Detroit and then begin a new job with a Baptist church here in Belfast that has graciously made me an offer. I'm very excited about what God is doing in my life."

"Well, give her my regards. I have to sign off now and get to my workout. If I miss a beat, I'll get soft. That can't happen."

"Godspeed, Blaze. Let's talk again soon."

"You got it."

A sparrow flew past Liam's field of vision as he hung up his mobile. *The birds have no worry for their needs.* It was beautiful and free and reminded Liam of the ever-present constancy of God's provision.

CHAPTER SIXTY-ONE

The office of President Hadi Samani, Tehran, Iran

It had finally come to a stop. No more days to count, no more waiting, no more yearning, no more hiding and no more occultation. The Twelfth Imam was here. He had taken the form of a man and made himself abundantly known to President Hadi Samani. There was no need any longer for the digital counter to track the days since His disappearance. The Mahdi had now fully and finally reappeared. The day had come.

Hadi Samani recognized Him instantly when he appeared to him and proclaimed His imminent arrival—a visit that would, this time, be permanent. He again felt paralyzed in the awe of His presence. The Mahdi emanated such strength of spirit that he literally enveloped Samani's entire being and enraptured him in a mystical spell. The Twelfth Imam dictated the nature of His power and the magnitude of His plans to Samani and ordered that the time had come for Samani to announce His arrival to the world.

Hadi was more than honored to be the conduit for the great message of the Mahdi. Hadi knew this was his destiny and he had been preparing for as long as he could remember. If only his mentor, Ahmadinejad, could be here to witness the glory.

The press conference was going to begin shortly and would be televised globally on every major news network around the world. It would also be live on the Internet on all conceivable news sites, large and small. The anticipation of the speech by the Muslim world was palpable. The reaction to the speech by Israel and the Western World was fearful. Word had spread quickly that Iran's president had claimed that the Islamic Messiah had arrived. The world was eager to hear just what, in fact, that meant in the eyes of President Hadi Samani.

Samani contemplated the recent developments that had led him to this moment. These developments confirmed for him the transformative inertia that had been ushered in along with the Promised One, the Twelfth Imam. The Zionists and the Americans did their best to cause destruction and chaos at Esfahan, but Allah miraculously limited the interruption and the Russians were able to have the plan back online and creating uranium fluoride in an astounding sixty days.

Thanks to some meticulous reverse engineering that Iran had employed after being hit with the first Stuxnet computer virus, the Natanz facility was prepared with a backup system that automatically deployed upon detection of any virus similar to the Stuxnet worm. This backup was designed to override and combat any new, oncoming virus while simultaneously repairing any damage such a virus might be able to accomplish in the time that the back up was still deploying. Unfortunately, it had not worked as hoped and a good amount of damage was still done. But, it did still work enough to truly mitigate the damage and downtime at Natanz. The backup served to sufficiently thwart the hopes held by the US and Israel that the Stuxnet 2.0 attack would purchase significant time, in the form of delay or destruction, on the Iranian nuclear countdown.

Bushehr was also prepared. Several ambitious apprentices were shadowing Azad's every move during his research and were fully up to speed with all of his progress and discoveries. They seamlessly took over once Azad was killed. The key research at Bushehr did not miss a beat when Azad was assassinated and not a single interruption in the fast tracked timelines was felt.

Feeling as if the wind was strongly at his back and all his faithfulness was being rewarded, Hadi Samani confidently began his address to the world:

"I come to you today as a committed servant of the global community and of all of those who value justice, equality, and fairness. The world is suffering as I speak despite the great wealth that exists in the hands of the few, and despite the sophisticated tools of technology that has so changed the way many around the world live their lives. Food shortages, wars, uprisings, massive unemployment, and lifestyle degradations of extraordinary measure plague our world like never before. Currencies are losing worth and national economies are faltering at an astonishing rate. Some of these problems are not unique to this period in history. I know this. But, the convergence of these problems, and the severity of their increasing nature, are unique to this time in history. The common factor that is also very unique to this time in history is the existence of both Israel and the United States of America.

Samani paused for effect, letting his words sink in. He then raised his arms and his voice as he asked, "Where was Israel one hundred years ago? Where was America three hundred years ago? What real contribution are they to our modern world? I will tell you. They are the problem. They contribute imperialism, war, pollution, greed, bigotry, and pain. This is the legacy of such nations. The world was far better off and full of balance prior to their existence. I am here to announce that the existence of both of these nations are near its sunset, and that the entire remnant of Judaeo-Christian civilization will, in short order, by overcome by the tenants and truths of Islamic civilization and thought.

Samani paused to take a quick drink of water and then continued. "I can say this today with absolute authority because the wait is over. The sweet scent of worldwide peace is upon us. I have told you before that I had received a temporary visit from Imam Al-Mahdi. But now, I am honored to proclaim that our beloved Messiah is now here. The Twelfth Imam, the Mahdi, is finally here and His presence and power on Earth will now be permanent. He will soon be visible to all and will make known His power through miracles unimaginable. He will have his hand over the control of the weather and spread his dominion over the crops of the earth. These are just a few of the astonishing works he will perform.

"His presence signifies a new era of tolerance, love, equality and equity for the oppressed of the world. No longer will the bully powers of the western world flaunt their wealth and overextend their military might. The Mahdi will save the world from such aggression. The downtrodden will be lifted, the poor will be fed, and the abused will be sheltered. Praise be to Allah.

"And what does the beloved Mahdi ask of the citizens of the world in return for his works? He simply requires natural submission to His majesty and His reign in the name of Allah, with his chief deputy Jesus of Nazareth by his side. This will be a reciprocal function that will extend out of the hearts of the entire world by a way of ease and love. Service for Mahdi and submission to Islam will be a worldwide state of normalcy and reality. There will be those who resist, but they will be seen for what they are: people who reject global justice, who block the fulfillment of long promised peace, and who stand in the way of equity for all. What does one who rejects such things deserve? One who rejects such virtues would indeed deserve death.

"But make no mistake, as the will of the Twelfth Imam is that none should suffer and that all would joyfully embrace the leader of the new age. The Caliphate is coming and submission to Islam will be the cornerstone of the new world order. Blessed be Allah."

Samani took no questions after his speech and wore a huge smile as he walked away from the podium and out of the light of the cameras and flashes. He knew the entire world was watching and that the global press would be talking about nothing else for days to come. He knew his words would be dissected, attacked, and also, by some, embraced with joy. His enemies were also watching, as he expected. They had been put on notice. Israel and America knew full well the implications of his claim of the arrival of the Twelfth Imam. Samani had been dreaming for this day for years and years, night after night of petitioning. *The sunset for the west is indeed near, and Iran finally now has the nuclear tools to complete the hastening of the setting of the West's sun. Praise be to Allah.*

CHAPTER SIXTY-TWO

The McIntyre residence, Romeo, Michigan

In his favorite leather chair, Blaze sat still in silence. Fresh off a call with Liam McCardle, his mind was reeling and his heart was alert. Resisting the urge to be overwhelmed, Blaze tried to assimilate recent events. The murders of his wife and son. The torture of Arash Jafari. Zack Batt's success in Bushehr. Samani's announcement of the arrival of the Twelfth Imam. He attempted to assemble all the pieces in his mind to ascertain what it all meant—geo-politically, spiritually, prophetically, and personally.

The pain from the loss of Diem and Shane was ever-present but Blaze had learned to deliberately push it away on most days. As a warrior, he knew that emotions could not be ignored and that sorrow must be revered and managed, but it was the managing that was key. He had to own it and not allow it to own him.

Operation Persian Trinity invaded his thoughts. On the surface, the mission appeared to be a great success. Esfahan worked out in the end, despite his Farsi foul up. Zack had a clean hit on the researcher in Bushehr. Jafari manned up and took care of business at Natanz and somehow lived to breathe another day after his interlude at Evin. But with Samani's recent announcement, it was clear the Iranian regime was more brazen than ever and exuded a frightening confidence that filled Blaze with trepidation.

McCardle had called him almost immediately after the live Samani speech. It was, of course, through a spiritual and prophetic lens that McCardle viewed Samani's speech.

He reminded Blaze of the warning of the scriptures that in the end of days there would be many false messiahs coming and performing miracles that would deceive many. Samani made clear that the Twelfth Imam was messianic in nature and was here to perform miracles and bring about worldwide peace, albeit via the sword of radical Islam and in the form of a caliphate. The timing of Samani's speech led Blaze to believe that Operation Persian Trinity did not stifle the Iranian nuclear program nearly as significantly as he, Gallagher, and POTUS had suspected. Samani would not announce the arrival of Mahdi without nuclear capabilities ready and at his fingertips.

McCardle also voiced his concerns that the Samani speech would be a tipping point. Israel would not sit still with such a message being sent. Both Israel and the United States knew full well the implications of the purported arrival of the Twelfth Imam. The hadiths made it very clear that He was only to be revealed when the world was in a state of chaos. Samani said that the Twelfth Imam "would soon be visible to all". If that was the case, global bloodshed and war would have to precede. When McCardle pointed this out, chills shot up Blaze's spine. The words hung in the air like a heavy mist.

The only question at this point was who would strike first.

McCardle posited that if the world was truly on the precipice of the war of Gog and Magog, it would be Iran, along with their Arab and North African neighbors, that would swarm Israel with the assistance of Maksim and Russia.

If the good Lord was delaying the fulfillment of Ezekiel 38 and 39, it could be Israel that pre-empts and attempts to mitigate worldwide catastrophe.

As if divinely rescued from the deep trajectory of frightening thoughts, Blaze was temporarily diverted from pondering doomsday to take a call from his old buddy Bernhard Miller.

"Hey old pal. I'm sorry I haven't been able to get in touch sooner."

Bernie and Blaze had not spoken since the loss of Diem and Shane.

"It's okay, I wasn't much for talking for quite some time, but I did get the check with the life insurance proceeds. Thanks for taking care of that so quickly. Not exactly how I envisioned becoming a multi-millionaire, but I'm thankful to not have to worry about money now for a long time." Blaze was at ease and his tone made clear to Bernie that he was doing okay.

"Well, I'm glad you can at least take the worry of finances off your plate so you can deal with everything else. Although, it sounds like your hanging in there okay, uh?"

"Yeah, just like Rocky said 'it's not how hard you hit, it's how hard you can get hit and keep moving forward'. Who'd a thunk it that it'd be Sly that would help me maintain through such hard times? Now all I need is Mickey to resurrect and coach me back into the war zone of life." Blaze laughed softly and Bernie reciprocated, glad to hear Blaze being light hearted.

"How's Dennis holding up?"

"That boy is tough. He's got McIntyre blood running through his young veins for sure. He's been mostly staying with his aunt so I can get my act together, but he has been like solid granite. Amazing. The Lord's blessed him with some serious maturity and coping capabilities for such a young kid. I'm so proud of him." Blaze's voice was full of emotion and joy as he praised his only surviving son.

"Great to hear Blaze. I've been worried about you but I knew you'd emerge with strength."

"I'll be fine, just gotta figure out my next move, or mission, as it usually ends up being. How are you holding up in the tumultuous world of finance?"

"Same old rollercoaster, but I'm managing. The gravy days are over and will probably never come back, but I find my optimism in hard to find places and hold onto it for dear life." Bernie's voice trailed off. It was clear to Blaze that business was tough.

Blaze's phone vibrated. Another call was coming in. It was Chuck.

"Bernie, I gotta pop smoke here buddy, got an important call coming through that I have to grab. Thanks for calling. Good lookin' out."

"No worries. Hang tough pal."

Blaze hung up with Bernie and quickly switched mental gears again.

"Chuck, what's up?"

"You got a few minutes? I got some intel I need to brief you on. It's important." Chuck's voice was urgent, serious and direct. No surprise there.

"Sure. I'm all ears."

"A sport bike was found ditched in a corn field off of I-75, somewhere near the Ohio / Michigan border. They found prints on the handlebars and a few on the frame. We think this is our guy."

Silence hung in the air and Chuck Gallagher was not about to break it. He was not happy to be the messenger for anything regarding the tragedy that Blaze was still enduring on so many levels.

"How do we know it's definitely him?" Blaze felt his heart beat with a vengeance. His mind raced—planning exactly that.

"We've got a full dossier on the guy. It will be sent to you shortly. He's a Mexican gangbanger from Laredo. A teenager. We believe he has connections to the cartel, but we don't have a smoking gun on that yet."

"So the cartel link to Hezbollah is looking to be a pretty strong working theory? First, the rape trees, and now this. Any leads on the attacks on the families of the other agents?" Blaze was struggling to repress his rage and ask logical questions.

"We're still working on that, but preliminary signs point right to cartel involvement, just like the prints on the bike." Gallagher knew that the investigation was still thin with results at the moment, but that momentum was going in the right direction.

"So it stands to reason, we really might have our man after all. Any links yet to a mole at Langley?" Blaze's fantasies of revenge extended not only to the killer of his family, but also to the traitor that set him up.

"Nothing yet, but we are vigorously mining data and we're pretty sure that we'll find something. Hopefully sooner rather than later." Gallagher was increasingly confident with the agencies ability to utilize their vast electronic reach to get the pieces of this puzzle they needed. The controversial data repository in Utah didn't hurt.

"What's his name Chuck?" Absolute rage boiled in Blaze's voice.

"You can't act on this Blaze. We have to handle this as an agency, the right way. But know that we *are* handling it."

"Chuck….what's his name?" Blaze was no longer asking. He was clearly and defiantly demanding.

"Juan Herrara."

CHAPTER SIXTY-THREE

The office of the Prime Minister, Jerusalem, Israel

He had been up all night. And this time it wasn't Abigayil that kept him from rest. It was of course, this time, the implications of Hadi Samani's announcement to the world. Chaim Simmons was not one to give in to anxiety. Typically, anxiety gave in to his relentless ambition and resolve. This time, however, in a time of unusual stress and trepidation, he felt as if he was about to collapse from the weight of the nuclear-laced anxiety that plagued him.

His breakfast sat there half eaten as he contemplated his situation. He did what he only knew to do in times of anxiety. He identified one action that he could focus on and complete that would mitigate the weight of his anxious feelings and hopefully give him a sense of positive forward movement. The last thing his nation could afford was a prime minister suffering from a bout with indecisive mental paralysis.

He picked up the phone and dialed the white house.

After several rings, he heard Jack Fitz's voice on the other end. "Chaim, how are you this morning?"

"Not good. And I think you already know that." Chaim was in no mood to dance around with preliminary niceties.

"You're obviously referring to Samani's announcement. I

suspected we'd be speaking today after that event." Jack said with sensitivity in his voice.

No attempt at sensitivity was going to soften Chaim Simmons' temper. "I think we're at the redline Mr. President." Chaim just came out and said it. If Fitz didn't understand the context by now, he never would.

"Now Chaim, I understand that Samani's announcement is great cause for alarm, but I don't think this is the redline. There are many positive developments that indicate this could be all a big bluff. They're wounded from Operation Persian Trinity and its successes. Their people are in great strife due to the economic sanctions. Their ability to get the bomb has been stifled. This is not the moment for Israel to act. I see this announcement as a sign of Iran's weakness. If anything, they're trying to send the West a false signal that they have the nuke so that they are not hit first." Jack wasn't even sure if he believed the theory he was positing to Chaim, but it rolled off his tongue as if it was a natural explanation of his position.

"Jack, I respect your optimism and your commitment to unfettered diplomacy, but what if you're wrong? What if you're *dead* wrong? What if Operation Persian Trinity, in reality, barely put a dent in their plans? What if Russia's assistance was so strong that any setbacks were immediately addressed and remedied? And as for the economic sanctions, what if the mullahs and Samani see the sanctions as nothing but a helpful tool to galvanize their nation against the west as a strong pretext for nuclear war? Israel can't risk its life on hoping your position is true with all these questions looming and unanswered." Chaim was more explanatory than he thought he would allow himself to be, but he had to do all he could to drive home his position to Fitz.

There was a dead silence that hung for a good forty seconds before Fitz managed to begin a response. "Chaim, there are still things we can do. Please, give me a little bit of time. I'll call Koslov and lean on him to mitigate the situation. I've been making great inroads with him lately and I believe I can have some influence. I think you're taking this Twelfth Imam stuff way too seriously. This is just window dressing to take the attention away from their real domestic issues. You can't allow them to provoke you on the basis of this Messianic claim. It's exactly what they want. Don't give it to them, Chaim."

Chaim's blood was boiling with indignation. Not only was Jack too blind to see the seriousness of the situation, but his tone was insulting. It was as if Jack was implying that Chaim was naïve because he took Samani's messianic obsession seriously. "You've made yourself very clear Mr. President and I've also made myself very clear. Samani believes with all his heart that the Mahdi has arrived. And I tell you with all sincerity that my redline has arrived. If Israel does not act soon, then Iran with the help of Russia and the Muslim nations of the Middle East and North Africa will act first. This can't happen. Not on my watch. I'm sorry you don't see this for what it is."

"I suppose it's clear I can't dissuade you. But know that I, and subsequently the United States of America, do not, and will not, support you in this. Not privately and not publicly. You're choosing to act and be alone. To my regret." Jack Fitz drew his line and his words struck hard and clear.

"We know how to act and be alone. If I was to follow your lead, the regret would be Israel's and not yours. I'd prefer, all things being equal, that the regret be yours Mr. President."

"Then I shall remain with regret."

And with that the two men hung up intending to go their separate ways. To Chaim, it was official—Israel no longer had the blessing of the United States of America.

CHAPTER SIXTY-FOUR

The McIntyre residence, Romeo, Michigan

Sweat dripped from Blaze's forehead as he pushed through his third set of pull-ups. He had to channel his anger or he knew he'd end up going postal. After the last set of pull-ups, he jumped onto the plyo boxes and continued his basement workout routine.

The speakers blasted the song "Hand Grenade" by the punk band The Welch Boys. The song was written as a tribute to the Irish American MMA fighter, Marcus 'The Irish Hand Grenade' Davis. Blaze was both a big fan of Davis' and, ironically, Davis' nemesis, the UK's Dan Hardy. The song set the mood for Blaze's heavy bag session.

It wasn't until he put on his training gloves and began pounding the heavy bag that his thoughts began to crystallize. The murders of the families of other CIA agents were heavy on his heart and mind. He pictured the rape tree in Utah and he felt like he was going to vomit. Female undergarments hanging from a tree—a grotesque symbol of sexual assault and torture. A calling card from hell. He hit the heavy bag harder. He wailed and grunted and screamed. In agony. He stared at the pipes above him, and the spider webs that had overtaken them, as his fists wailed. They taunted him as he thought of all the webs he needed to untangle within his cluttered mind.

He catalogued, in his mind, all those that he knew at Langley in quick succession. He had no idea who the mole was. But he was determined to find out. And when he did, things would get ugly.

He tried to steer his mind from it, because the rest was detective work slightly less close to home, but he couldn't control his mind. The name kept jumping to the forefront of his thoughts. *Juan Herrara.* Blaze wondered if maybe Chuck was wrong and this wasn't the guy at all. Their evidence wasn't yet fully conclusive, but it was damn close. He hit the heavy bag with a thunderous right. They had the prints on the bike. *The bike was clearly swiped, but he must've slipped up. Or did a weak job of wiping.* Blaze screamed with a thunderous howl, his fist impacting the bag with power. The rage was flowing back and he could not contain it. His mind kept racing. *Maybe this isn't the guy? They still don't have a smoking gun that links the bike to the crime scene. Yeah, they found it ditched on route 75—the most logical getaway path for someone heading back to his home state of Texas—but still no conclusive witness swearing it was the bike. The serial number was scratched, so no trace on the bike either. I gotta wait until they get through the questioning.* Blaze landed a sharp uppercut on the heavy bag.

Something deep within him was telling him that they had him. Juan Herrara was the guy. He kicked the heavy bag. *Its gotta be him. Its just gotta.* A wild, penetrating kick. Fully extended. *I will have my revenge.* He tried to fight the notion. He knew the danger of being led by revenge. He knew that vengeance was the Lord's, as the good book said. *Yeah, but there's no reason He can't use me as his instrument.* And so he resolved. He would find Herarra. And he would extract every bit of information he needed to track down those that commissioned the hit on his wife and son. He would hunt them to the ends of the Earth. Every last participant.

The heavy bag seemed to be begging for more punishment. Blaze visualized all his enemies each time he threw a hook to the bag. Herrara was clear. The others were fuzzy. He knew their stripes. The Cartel. Hezbollah. Ultimately, the mullahs. Samani. Big enemies. Strong enemies. Smart enemies. Organized enemies. He began to feel small, but strong. The Goliaths were his target. He knew he would need the God of David to defeat them. He prayed for strength. And a battle plan.

As he prayed, the magnitude of world events fell upon him with a debilitating weight. He hit the bag rapidly as if he was trying to wear out his anger. The vision of Ezekiel 38 and 39 raced through his mind. War of Gog and Magog. Like McCardle had pointed out, Russia and Persia had not been allies in the twenty five hundred years since Ezekiel wrote that prophecy.

And yet here we were and now they were. *Could it be? Who knows.* He kept punching. Sweat poured furiously from all his pores. He blinked to keep it out of his eyes. The mat beneath him was soaked. His endorphins were on high alert. He thought about Samani's speech. *Something wicked this way comes.* He knew it was significant. He knew the world was about to change. He wasn't going to sit idly by. The war may be pre-ordained, but that didn't mean the timing necessarily was. He was going to get in the game. Shivers traveled through his bones. He kept punching. With a sound, determined rhythm. The same sound, determined rhythm with which he would insert himself into the coming battle against the threatening caliphate. The same sound, determined rhythm that would methodically, and tirelessly, enable him to hunt down every evil bread crumb left by those that conspired to murder his wife and son. The same sound, determined rhythm that has preserved good in battles with evil since the beginning of time.

CHAPTER SIXTY-FIVE

Tehran, Iran

Koslov had been extraordinarily helpful in rising to the task of expediting all deliveries, technical and scientific support, and now tactical and military guidance and cooperation. Hadi Samani was pleasantly surprised that there had been no tension between them lately, at least in terms of recent days. There was synergy forming between them as they worked together towards their goal of destroying Israel. Hadi attributed that synergy to the divine workings of Allah in preparation for the mission of the Mahdi. Koslov attributed the synergy to the natural mutual interests of two ambitious world leaders.

All the alliances had been secured and all partner nations had been completing preparations, plans and contingencies. Lebanon, Libya, Sudan, Ethiopia, and many others. All of them, faithful soldiers who had submitted to Iran's leadership and the helpful assistance of Russia. Samani could feel victory in his bones. He could smell the sweet air of Allah's coming worldwide caliphate.

Samani knelt on his prayer rug and summoned the spirit of the Twelfth Imam with all of his might. He thanked Allah for the interesting times in which he lived and the blessed position that he had been given. He begged Allah for imminent success in Iran's plans to annihilate Israel with their recently acquired, and operational, nuclear weapon and delivery system. The time had indeed come.

The headache came on strong and the pain was piercing. Hadi Samani's eyes strained to open as the light penetrated them with overwhelming brightness. Imam Al-Mahdi, full of glory, stood before him, once again, in his office, with no other witnesses.

"You have called for me and I am here to answer. You are preparing and your plans are acceptable to me. The dogs of Zion will meet their final day and the day of Allah will be ushered in as I transform the world for Islam. You have been a faithful and honorable servant and you will be rewarded. I am here to affirm you plans. I am here to transmit strength to your heart. Be of cheer and do not be swayed from your mission. You have patiently cultivated the tools of destruction, against all earthly opposition, for years. It is now born and must be used. Do not delay. The time for the final annihilation and extermination is here. Move forward my faithful servant. Strike them now."

Mist remained. Darkness replaced the bright light. The power in the building went out with Imam Al-Mahdi's exit. And Samani lay prostrate with joy, purpose and solidified plans for historic catastrophe and death nestled deep in his dark, little heart.

—END—

AUTHOR'S NOTES

November 14th, 2012

BLAZE: Operation Persian Trinity is a fictional tale. The names, characters, scenarios, depictions, and anecdotes contained within the story are the result of the author's imagination, or they are a cornucopia of fictionalized, multi-layered composites. Any resemblance to actual people, real life occurrences, or functional entities is a coincidence, unless otherwise noted in the following text.

The firefight depicted between the ANA Green soldiers and the ISAF NATO forces in blue is based on real life fighting that has occurred at Afghan checkpoints.

The 'Pillar of Cloud' is currently being used to refer to Israel's organized defense campaign against Hamas' rocket attacks into Gaza as I type. It is a reference to the story in Exodus 13:21, in which God protected the Israelites when they were fleeing a horde of Egyptian marauders sent by the Pharaoh.

The Walther P99 MI6 pistol was indeed named as a tie in to the James Bond franchise.

The CTSA (Counter Terrorism Security Advisors) is, in fact, the real name for the counter terrorism unit within the Police Service in Northern Ireland.

Mark Loyd, the diversity officer for the FCC, has in actuality, called for actions that far outpace the punitive ideas of the Fairness Doctrine to censor the airwaves. In 2009, he praised Hugo Chavez' actions in Venezuela to take over the media for state control. He was quoted as follows: "In Venezuela, with Chavez, you really had an incredible revolution—democratic revolution—to begin to put in place things that were going to have impact on the people of Venezuela. The property owners and the folks who were then controlling the media in Venezuela rebelled—worked, frankly, with folks here in the US government—worked to oust him. He came back and had another revolution, and Chavez then started to take the media very seriously in his country." If such an effort were to take root in America, the setbacks for liberty and free speech would be devastating.

Cliff Bell's is a real restaurant in Detroit, Michigan. I've never eaten there, but if the menu posted online is any real indication, it sounds delicious.

The *World Towards Illumination* was a real series of radio broadcasts that aired on official Iranian radio back in 2006 and 2007 for the purpose of informing the Iranian people of the need to prepare for the imminent return of the Twelfth Imam. In the novel, I expand upon this concept of messianic indoctrination.

In Ezekiel 38 the term 'Magog' is mentioned. Biblically, Magog was a grandson of Noah. The descendants of Magog were known as Magogites and they lived geographically in the land we now know as Russia. Genetically, they were of an Aryan makeup. The Magogites were referred to by the Greeks as the Scythians. It is from this connection that I inserted the Scythian theme into the character of Maksim Koslov. The Scythian references described are based on true accounts of Scythian culture and history. Unlike Maksim Koslov, the Scythians historically did not drink the blood of their enemies out of a skull-shaped mug, but out of the actual skulls of their enemies.

The Solntsevskaya Brotherhood is a real organization. They are one of the most powerful organized crime groups hailing from Moscow, Russia.

The LDPR (Liberal Democratic Party of Russia) is a real political party that states one of its goals as being the conquering of land south of Russia ('the final thrust South") as part of an overall strategy of reestablishing the Byzantine Empire. Vladimir Zhirinovsky is one of the true-life leaders of the LDPR. Unlike I describe in the novel, it was not him, but the LDPR number two guy, Colonel Pavel Chernov, that was expelled from the LDPR for his drinking issues and loose use of machine guns.

There are all kinds of conspiracy theories about secret plans for a global currency. It is not these hushed fears that drove me to insert this idea into the novel, but instead, the actual words spoken in public by countries like Russia and China who have made very clear that they think the world would be best served by migrating to a global currency. The downgrading of the US credit rating and the perpetual quantitative easing taken by Ben Bernanke is not helping to restrain the global movement of pushing this idea.

GALOI, or the Gay And Lesbians Of Iran, is a completely fictional political action group. What is not made up is the fact that Iranian president Mahmoud Ahmadinejad has stated that the phenomenon of homosexuals does not exist in his country. Of course, in reality, Iran does have citizens who are homosexual, and their cruel persecution at the hands of the oppressive regime is barely noted by Western press.

The Hojjatieh Society is a real fraternity in Iran consisting of devotees of the Twelfth Imam who view themselves as the guardians of the Mahdi. It was founded in 1953 by Sheikh Mahmoud Halabi. They believe strongly in 'taajil', which is the notion that the actions of faithful followers of the Mahdi can effectuate the hastening of his return. It is believed that Mahmoud Ahmadinejad is a member.

'Dajjal' is the term used in the Qur'an and the Hadiths for the Anti-Christ as seen through the doctrine of Islam.

The character of 'Samere' in the novel, who serves as Hadi Samani's advisor on all things Messianic, is loosely based on the actual advisor on messianic issues to Iran's President Mahmoud

Ahmadinejad named Mojtada Samere Hashemi.

All descriptions, mentions, and outlines of the characteristics of the figure known as The Twelfth Imam, Imam Al-Mahdi, or simply the Mahdi are entirely based on thorough research over many years. I have consulted with way too many books, news articles, and commentary on this cultish sub-doctrine of Shia Islam to mention. I encourage you to research this thoroughly on your own and get a firm understanding of the seriousness of this belief, and the implications of this apocalyptic eschatological narrative in terms of being the main force behind current Iranian foreign policy. Regardless of how fantastical it may sound, those who believe it, believe it unequivocally, and we should take their belief as seriously as they do.

The mention of Kufa, Iraq in the novel was used as it is reported to have been the home of the Mahdi's birth, and the eventual location of his worldwide Islamic reign, according to the followers of the Twelfth Imam.

The mentioning of Jesus of Nazerath as the Chief Deputy of the Twelfth Imam was not included as a cute way to insert the main focal point of Christendom into an Islamic end times theology description. This is true to the narrative of the Mahdi's return according to the Hadiths.

There are many mentions of the 'Caliphate' throughout the novel. It is the word used to describe a worldwide Islamic order in which all non-Muslims convert or die. Again, it may sound like hocus pocus, but the achievement of a Caliphate is a real, stated goal of radical Islamists worldwide. Western civilization, and all free people, dismiss the threat of this goal at their own peril.

The prophecies outlined in the 38th and 39th chapters of the book of Ezekiel are a huge thrust within the novel. I am not a bible prophecy scholar. I am not a reader of crystal balls. I have no idea if the war described in this prophecy is on the horizon or not. There are a lot of different scholarly opinions as to the interpretation of this prophecy. Most believe it most definitely involves Russia, and undeniably involves the nation now known as Iran. Some scholars believe that the alliances described in this prophecy have, for the first time since it was written, now been formed. And not only do many believe that those alliances now exist, but that their overt hostility towards Israel is consistent with the scenario described by Ezekiel. The notion of the possibility of this prophecy coming soon in the near term is one I thought important to insert in the novel so readers can study, research and form their own thoughts on.

The Neo Iranian Nazi Party does not exist and is a fictional construct. However, the Iranian National Socialist Party did in fact exist and was formed in the 1930's. What is also not fictional is the reality that there are a growing number of Iranians embracing their Ayran heritage and co-opting the ideology of Nazi Germany, particularly the hatred of Jews. The history of the Persian Aryan sensibility, and its ties to Nazi Germany, as described in the novel is true.

The descriptions of the Stuxnet computer virus are a true depiction of the worm that infected Iran's nuclear facilities. The narrative of a 2.0 version is fictional. At least as I type this.

The relationship between Mexican drug cartels and jihadists is rarely exposed and as a result, rarely recognized. However, the relationship is a real one, and is a growing threat.

Also, rarely reported is the growing number of human heads left along the border as a result of Cartel beheadings.

The rape tree described in the novel is also a real hallmark of Cartel activity. Rape trees are places where cartel members and coyotes rape female border crossers and hang their clothes, specifically undergarments, to mark their conquest and territory.

The character of Juan Herrara was derived from real news accounts of the cartels hiring teenagers as foot soldiers. Various news accounts referenced that these teenagers literally sat in their homes playing XBOX as they awaited their orders.

DTE Energy did in fact repossess streetlights in the city of Detroit.

Crown David cigars are a real independent cigar brand made by an Israeli entrepreneur from Philadelphia. And they are a damn good smoke, even though they've now been re-branded as Cuban Stock cigars.

Anchor's Away cigar lounge is a fictional place. However, there are several great cigar lounges in Toledo, Ohio. I would recommend Port Royal and La Casa De La Havana. And if you find yourself in the Philadelphia area, stop into Old Havana Cigars in West Chester, PA—but don't stay too long as you may not be prepared for handling the mayhem of the regulars.

The Dodge Tomahawk motorcycle described in the novel is real, and although I've never ridden one, it sounds like a badass bike.

The World Without Zionism conference is a real event. And David Duke really did attend.

In regard to the idea of Israel experiencing a wealth explosion due to great discoveries of natural resources, many Bible scholars believe that this is prophesied in scripture to occur in the last days.

The history described within the novel of the skinhead movement is true. Most skinheads, now and historically, abhor racism. SHARP (Skin Heads Against Racial Prejudice) is a real organization.

The punk band Murphy's Law did indeed write a song entitled "Secret Agent S.K.I.N.".

I've never been to Charlestown, Massachusetts and have no real knowledge of the town's character. My only impressions come from the likely one-dimensional representations made in the film *The Town* and by the words sung on the album *Serenity* by the band Blood for Blood.

The street gang known as FSU is a real group, who is strongly identified with the straight edge lifestyle. A *Gangland* episode on the History Channel was dedicated to covering their history.

The mention of the character of Chuck Gallagher using a stand up desk was inspired by the real life fact that former Secretary of Defense Donald Rumsfeld still uses a stand up desk, even in his retirement.

Pussy Riot is a real all-female Russian punk rock band. They were arrested and imprisoned as a result of their outspoken protests against President Putin. Two of the members are currently imprisoned in Penal Colony 14, a camp that was formally part of Stalin's gulag system, as I type.

Reza Kahlili is the real life cover name for a defected Iranian Revolutionary Guard CIA spy who now lives in America hiding his real identity.

The story described of a Nazi being beaten with a chair by Zack Batt in the novel is a fictionalized account of a real life occurrence in which a racist was beaten to death at hardcore metal show in New Jersey. In real life, the victim was not simply paralyzed and no chair was involved. The man who committed the violence—a member of FSU—later was seen in a Rolling Stone magazine article wearing handcuffs and an orange jumpsuit in court.

Evin Prison is real. The torture scene of the character of Arash Jafari was inspired by written accounts of those who have endured stays at the facility. Some elements of the character of Arash Jafari were loosely inspired by the story of Iranian Christian Pastor Saeed Abedini. He was persecuted for his beliefs and served time in Evin Prison and wrote about the experience.

The Black Dog Group does not exist. It is an entirely fictional private mercenary firm.

SCG International is a real organization that contracts with the government and various private entities and individuals needing security. They assist many warriors in pre-deployment training.

I don't believe in ghosts in the traditional sense. The character of Harry Saylor as a ghost in the novel was inserted to illustrate the tormented mind of Blaze McIntyre and to hint at the possibility of spiritual visions and visitations in a world on the precipice of a nearing apocalypse. The character of Harry Saylor's ghost is loosely based on a very, dear friend of mine who has passed away after years of battling a heroin addiction.

Norman 'Sailor Jerry' Collins, the renowned father of traditional tattooing, and the namesake of some of the best spiced rum known to man, was indeed a conservative libertarian talk radio host.

The references to music are ubiquitous in the novel, as I am a huge fan of many genres of music. The references to punk and hardcore artists are more evident, as I am a particularly huge fan of those genres. I have always valued punk and hardcore music as a tremendous vehicle to express pain and personal struggle. To me, punk always meant independence of thought and action, and had nothing to do with being bound to one political or religious (or anti-religious) ideology. Punk has always showcased everything from the profane to the profound and all variances in-between. As such, in my view, libertarianism is the most approximate political ideology congruent with the free thought and DIY (do it yourself) attitude of the punk rock ethos.

I've never done time in prison, and don't intend to. However, I have many close friends who have, and the descriptions of Zack Batt's prison stay are fictionalized composites of many firsthand prison accounts that I have heard described by friends who have done time.

Until the next installment,
Andrew Thorp King

ABOUT THE AUTHOR

Andrew Thorp King holds a BA in English Literature from West Chester University and is a serial entrepreneur. He holds ownership in two independent record labels (Sailor's Grave Records and Thorp Records), is partner in a variety of consulting and marketing firms, and once owned a fitness center. He also works as an operations analyst for an online commercial bank and is the author of the forthcoming non-fiction title *Failure Rules!: The Hard Times Handbook for the Die-Hard Entrepreneur.* He has three children and lives in the Philadelphia suburbs.

Made in the USA
San Bernardino, CA
28 November 2014